Ifflepinn Island

A tale to read aloud for green-growing children
and evergreen adults

Written and Illustrated by
Muz Murray

evertype
2014

Published by Evertype, Cnoc Sceichín, Leac an Anfa, Cathair na Mart, Co. Mhaigh Eo, Éire. *www.evertype.com*.

Text and illustrations © 2014 Muz Murray.
This edition © 2014 Michael Everson.
First printing June 2014.

Edited by Michael Everson and Mathew Staunton.

ISBN-10 1-78201-052-1
ISBN-13 978-1-78201-052-4

Set in Coldstyle, Zwoelf, and Geistig by Michael Everson.

Cover by Michael Everson.

Printed by LightningSource.

Table of Contents

Illustrations

For my daughter Saffron,
who was Iffleplum's very first fan.

The Dwæmavâhl:
The language of the Half-Elvene
or Dwemmer-folk

he language of the Dwemmer-folk (the *Dwæmü* in plural) is an admixture of the Old Tongue of *Dævârkavâhl*—the language of the High Elvene) and *Vâhl-Ârkamän* (the speech of the 'Men of the High Refuges' who have descended from the *Ârkü* or Wise-Wizards of yore). Thus *Dwæmavâhl* is a hybrid working language, since the Dwemmers are half-Elven and half-Human.

In general, each vowel is pronounced on its own, as is every consonant. Where there is an 'h' as in *vâhl* 'speech, tongue' it is slightly aspirated before the 'l' is sounded.

The following key will help the reader to pronounce the words and names in this book.

A a   [ə] like the *a* in English *about*.
Â â   [ɑ:] like the *a* in English *father*.
Ä ä   [æ] like the *a* in English *cat*.
Aï aï   [aɪ] a diphthong like the *igh* in English *high*.
Æ æ   [ei] like the *ay-e* in English *way-eve*. Similar to *Ê ê*.
B b   [b] like the *b* in English *bin*.
Ch ch   [ʃ] like the *sh* in English *shin*.
D d   [d] like the *d* in English *din*.
Dh dh   [dʰ] like the *d* in English *din*, with a slight aspiration after it; can be pronounced like the *dh* in Sanskrit *dharma*.
E e   [ɛ] like the short *e* in English *den*.
Ê ê   [e:] like the long *ey* as in English *whey*.
F f   [f] like the *f* in English *fin*.

G g [g] like the *g* in English *gun*.

Gh gh [gʰ] like the *g* in English *gun*, with a slight aspiration after it; can be pronounced like the *gh* in Hindi *ghee*.

H h [h] like the *h* in English *hen*.

I i [ɪ] like the short *i* in English *pin*.

Î î [i:] like the long *ee* in English *free*.

K k [k] like the *k* in English *skin*.

Kh kh [kʰ] or [x] like the *k* in English *kin*, with a slight aspiration after it, or like the *ch* in Scottish *loch*.

L l [l] like the *l* in English *line*.

M m [m] like the *m* in English *men*.

Mh mh [mʰ] like the *m* in English *men*, with a slight aspiration after it.

N n [n] like the *n* in English *nun*.

Nh nh [nʰ] like the *n* in English *nun*, with a slight aspiration after it.

O o [ɔ] like the short *i* in English *cot*.

Ò ò [ɔ:] like the long *augh* in English *caught*.

Ô ô [o:] like the long *ow* in English *slow*.

P p [p] like the *p* in English *pin*.

R r [r] rolled like the *r* in Scottish English *grin*.

S s [s] like the *s* in English *sun*.

T t [t] like the *g* in English *tin*.

U u [ʌ] like the short *u* in English *cut* (similar to *ÿ*)

Û û [u:] like the long *oo* as in English *room*.

Ü ü [y] like the *u* in French *lune* or the *ü* in German *grün*.

V v [v] like the *v* in English *vine*.

W w [w] like the *w* in English *win*.

Y y [j] like the *y* in English *yen* or *hippy*.

Ÿ ÿ [ə] *uh* as in Ælfÿlon (or 'have a (*uh*) chair')

Z z [z] like the *z* in English *zen*.

An annotated glossary is given at the end of the book.

Part the First

Springshine

*In which the land awakens when a magical Horn is heard
to sing, and the madcap Scatterdance of Spring begins.*

nce upon a New Year's Day, over the hills and faraway, in a little village called Merry May, the villagers awoke to find their fields and gardens full of froaks.

All along the valley of Merryvale, where ifflepinns in roundy-houses dwell, doors and windows opened in excitement at the sight. Inside his ifflesnug, young Iffleplum awakened suddenly startled in his bed. The sound of froaksong echoed

in his head. And soon his sleepy soft-brown button eyes began to shine—*for now he realized what day it was!* And his fat face dimpled in a curling grin, around his pale mauve oval nose—peculiar to the ifflepinn.

At a glance it could be seen that Iffleplum was no ordinary ifflepinn: but then—no ifflepinn ever is.

"At last!" he cried. "It's Froaksday! And the First of Spring!" His little lilac nose grew rosy with delight. And with a whoop and a bound he cartwheeled out of bed. Throwing his bedroom window wide, he looked out upon the Merryvale. On every side, as far as the eye could see, like round green rubber bouncing balls, all over the lawn and across the fields beyond the stream, the froaks were all a-frolicking!

For miles around a quagmire choir of croaky voices resounded in the frosty air. *Ko-ak! Ko-ak! Ko-ak!* the froaks all sang. And the din they made was deafening! It echoed in the woody hills and dales as far as the Mauven Mountains in the west. And not an early bird was heard above the noise. But the country folk around all found the croaking sounds far sweeter than the song of birds that day: for now they knew that spring had come at last.

For when the water-froaks awakened from their winter sleep (beneath the ice and windy snows) and rose upon the surface of the rivers and the streams, then spring had truly come. And the First of Spring was New Year's Day[1] in the land of Ælfÿlon. In fact, they could not have a New Year's Day, until the froaks awoke.

But now, without a doubt the froaks were out! Here, there and everywhere—from ponds and pools and water-tubs, they peeped with cheeky grins, their skins all smooth and new: and

---

1 This is usually around 15 March in Ælfÿlon. See page ix for a table of pronunciation.

they hopped about and chortled with the joys of spring—you know, the way they do.

*

Ifflemother Mumkin, busy baking pastries in the oven, heard Iffleplum bouncing around his bedroom overhead. "Plumkin! It's brekker-time!" she called. "Come you down?"

No way! thought Iffleplum fancifully. *For I know full well the knavish cook has poisoned the porridge! Oh, thou scurvy rogue! Thou shalt not catch Sir Plumkin unawares!* "Coming, Mumkin!" he called out, as he and his fiery dream-horse came galloping down the stairs.

"Sunny New Spring!" said Mumkin, as he cantered into the kitchen.

"May Springshine make your heart sing!" said Iffleplum, correctly answering.

As always, Mumkin looked a treat. The tufty-topknot on her head and her long and floppy peachbloom ears, were washed and brushed and neat. A simple necklet made of fancy wooden beads was all the finery she cared to wear, except for a polka-dotted pink pinafore and a pair of woolly winter frostboots on her feet.

She pressed her warm and floury nose to Iffleplum's rosy one in greeting and wrapped him in a loving hug. "Oh, Mumkin!" said Iffleplum happily. "The froaks are out! They *only* are! Is Erf about?"

"Well, I've not yet heard his special croak. So I suppose he's still a-sleeping in the water butt. Let's you and I go out and look."

The family froak had wintered in a wooden water-barrel beneath the thatch, outside the snuggery of iffle-pinns. An *ifflesnug* is a kind of roundy-house, shaped somewhat like an old-fashioned kitchen pepper pot, with whitewashed walls and latticed windows and a roof of plaited straw. In the middle was a brightly orange-painted oval door, which opened at the top and bottom, for visitors both large and small. And here Old Ifflepaw (the father of the family) liked to lean upon the bottom half and smoke his pipe, and gaze across the orchard to the brook. Within the arch above the door, there hung a wooden sign on which the cottage name was carved in curly letters:

Ifflenook

The very last of winter's frost was steaming from the thatch. Dewdrops dankly dripped from the cottage eaves into the barrel of water below, which already was filled to its mildewed brim. Iffleplum tried peering in. But it was too dark and green to see a thing. And the water chilled his rosy nose to a paler shade of mauve.

"Can't see anything," he said. "But I'm sure he's still asleep." He kicked the barrel peevishly. "Erf! You soggy sink-sponge of a froak! Come out of there!"

"Oh, Plumkin!" said Ifflemother chidingly. "Let him be. You were late yourself today. So wait until he wakes up properly."

"Hur!" grizzled Iffleplum. "If I don't wake him, he'll miss the Froaksday Fair again! Erf can sleep until the summer comes and dries up every drop of water in his tub. He only can!"

"Why that's a mercy then!" said Granpaw, coming up behind. "That'll be one less daft doolally froak to muck up all the seed-beds I just made. I spent half the mornin a-fixing up froak-nets to keep 'em off. And the other half gettin out froaks and other froggy folk what got themselves trapped inside."

"G'morning, Gramps!" said Iffleplum. "A Sunny New Spring to you!" The old ifflepinn pressed his wrinkled snout to Plumkin's nose in greeting, as all the ummals[2] of Ælfÿlon do.

---

2 *Ummals* are the talking animals of Ælfÿlon; and *dummals* are those who can only bark, or whinny, or cackle or bleat, or gobble or grunt, or bubble and squeak.

4

Granpaw was a white-whiskered old gardener, who loved nothing more than "messing about in muck" as he called it. And since he lost his snuggle-mate, he chose to live alone in the potting shed among his beloved plants. "May your little heart sing," he replied. "But you best let sleeping froaks lie— deep in their barrel-beds, say I."

"No way!" said Iffleplum. "I want him out! You know last year, I waited by his barrel—for a wasting week I did. Until the frolic and the feasting was all done. And then he woke at last—espeshly *last!* He woke and cried: 'Surprise! Surprise! Am I too soon?' Some joke. My mauven nose had frosted blue by then, like the bloom of a new-picked plum."

"Arr! He were no more than a froakling then," said Granpaw. "Now he's growed. He'll know it's Froaksday soon enough, you'll see."

"Hur! He had better!" gruntled Iffleplum. "But where's Old Ifflepaw? He should be here when Erf wakes up."

Ifflemother Mumkin looked troubled suddenly. "Where do you think?" she said. She tipped her head towards the hill that rose beyond the garden gate. "I fear he's up there on The Rise again. While you were still abed, he's been out with his sailor's-eye spyglass since froakrise in the early morn. As anxious as a mother duck he is today."

"Oh gripes!" groaned Iffleplum. "Not on Froaksday too! He'll miss the Scatterdance and all the fun. He *only* will." His little lilac nose dimmed down to a pearly shade of pale.

All through the winter long he had watched his father growing gloomier every day. For every morning, noon and night, he went away alone upon the hill and scanned the roads and river with his spyglass: forever watching out for some strange and worrisome thing he thought was on the way. It was not very comforting. But what it was he would not say.

Ifflemother's nose had also grown a little grey. "Well, while we're waiting for our dozy froak to wake," she said, distracting him from gloomy thoughts, "why don't you nip up there and fetch your father down?"

"Oh! But I smell baking cakes!" said Iffleplum. "I've just got up! I haven't even had my Wakes."[3]

Ifflemother whisked back in and brought him out a bulgy little bag. Plumkin's nose went pink with pleasure at the smell.

---

3 *Wakes* is the first food of the day for ifflepinns; just a little bit of something and a hot cup as they rise (hardly counted). This is followed soon by *Breakfast*—called *Breakfirsts* if there is a chance of *Breakseconds* available. Then comes *Minch,* the mid-morning meal, and later *Muncheon* at midday. And just about mid-afternoon comes *Tiffin*-time, with muffins, toast, or cake. Then later on, the evening meal at sunset into twilight, is known as *Wyning* (from dining at the waning of the day.) And lastly there was *Snug*: a lightweight bedsnack round the fire (to stave off the grumbles of a hard night's hibernation). These are the *main* meals of the day.

"Gingerbread froaks!" he cried. "Still oven warm!" And he set off munching happily.

Meanwhile, Old Ifflepaw took the telescope from his eye and sighed. He pushed his Captain's cap to the back of his head and wrinkled his snout in perplexity. From where he stood, on top of The Rise, he had a clear view of the countryside for miles around. But there was nothing new to see. At first he had looked the right way, then the wrong way down his telescope: but it made no difference. Big or small, the view was still the same.

No sign of anything unusual.

The wide brown river Elventear wound slowly round the foot of The Rise below, and went on flowing like a swollen slow-worm down the vale. There was only a lonely umbelope in a rowing boat and a roister of river-pogs out for a sail.

The waiting was getting on his nerves.

He stared moodily down the river, absently sucking the ends of his floppy ears for comfort. But they were numb with cold. So he rolled them up and tucked them under his Captain's cap for warmth. He had never even seen the sea: but it was a cap he always wore when watching the boats sail to and fro.

He began to chunter to himself, in his rich slow-speaking country voice. "Now look you here Old Ifflepaw—just what do you think you're a-waiting for? You can't be *sure* that something dreadful's on the way. Well, that's what Ifflemother said."

He could hear her argufying in his head: "You might be right, me dear," he told himself. "Doddering old dimwit that I am. I don't even know if I got the message right. That there Soothsayer—who *warned* me with his words of woe—might well have been as witless as a wim-wom. Who's to know? I must be soft as muck to be taken up with such a tale." He frowned and thought again.

"But I dunno," he muttered, "somehow what he said seemed true at the time. Though Mumkin seems to take it with a pinch of salt. But then, she wasn't *there*. She never saw the strange look in his staring yellow eyes! Fair gave me the creeps it did. So better safe than sorry is what I say. I reckon it's wiser to keep on a-watching out awhile longer, till the danger's past. And something strange is in the air today."

He turned away from the river and raised the telescope again. His gaze swept over the cottage roof and the Ifflebrook, across the fields and up to the village of Bumble-on-the-Hill, where the Wossle Wood began. And higher still, to where a tall stone tower, overgrown with ivy, rose out of the ridge of wintry treetops, its conical cap of coloured tiles sparkling in the bright spring sun. There his friend Wood-Warden Cuppicks lived. He focussed on the windows of his den. Normally he could always see him scribing at his desk. But now the old umbelope himself was nowhere to be seen. Even at that distance, in the clear morning air, Ifflepaw could faintly hear the rooks from the rookery cawing round the tower.

He swivelled round and followed the river Elventear downstream again. All along the length of Merryvale he peered, until it disappeared around a bend. From there the river went beyond his ken. It slowly gathered speed and rushed and wound through many a rocky roaring gorge, before it burst from the mountains out into the wild and unknown lower lands beyond, on its way to the Silver Sea. But Ifflepaw knew no more of the Out-Lands than the tales that travellers told.

Above the snowy Mauven Mountain peaks he spied a golden eagle circling on the wind and watched it for a while. Then he swung his spyglass slowly down to where the mountains dwindled into woody hills, which came roundly rolling down in smaller mounds to the meadowlands below. With winter woods upon their backs, the huddled hills lay crouched like

8

giant hedgehogs steaming in the morning sun. Around their feet ran a ribbon of road from the riverside village of Merry May. All along it he could now see streams of excited ifflepinns and other oddling ummal-folk. Crowds were swarming out to the Festive Field from every whichaway.

What in Ælfÿlon was going on? He focussed clearly on the field. Brightly-coloured booths and tents were going up. Flags and pennants were wormling in the breeze. He could see jugglers, clowns and acrobats, all practising, preparing for the Froaksday Fair. "My hat!" he cried. "The fair's already on! I clean forgot! It's Froaksday! What will Plumkin say if I'm not there before the Scatterhorn is blown?"

He rummaged in his Hatbag and pulled one out. The villagers of Merry May had a whiskery joke that Old Ifflepaw had let hats go to his head. For he always wore a special hat for every different deed he did. This helped him on his dreamy-noddled way about. Whenever he was out and found his wits a-wandering, he simply tipped his hat to see which one he wore, then went upon his way once more, remembering the job in hand the hat was for. At home he kept a treasure trunk, crammed full to the brim with a jumble of curious hats collected down the years: a hat for every need. The old gold key he wore on a chain around his neck, was a fit for the lock of the lid to his trunk of delight.

Quickly doffing his Captain's cap, he swapped it for his Home-Going hat, to remind him which way he was bound. Folding up his telescope Ifflepaw set off briskly down the hill.

Iffleplum came up and met him halfway down. As he ran to press his father's nose in greeting, he saw its lilac colour had now grown grey with worry. A sudden sadness rose in Plumkin's breast, for there seemed to be no Springshine in the heart of Ifflepaw. "Cheer up Iffykins, my dear old Dad!" said he. "Don't look so sad. It's New Year's Day! And your Breakseconds is on the way. There's still a chance to eat again, before they start the Scatterdance! Come on!" He took his father by the waist and huggingly they ambled down.

Inside a clump of brittle bracken-fronds nearby, a wide-eyed something watched them closely as they passed. The fronds were stealthily pushed aside and a pair of staring yellow eyes peered out. They watched until the ifflepinns were out of sight. Then a hairy creature all wrapped around in ragged black, slipped silently out behind them. Creeping from rock to bush, and hedge to tree, it followed them unseen, right down as far the garden gate. As soon as the ifflepinns went inside, it wriggled its way under the border hedge and searched for a place to hide and spy.

*

While the ifflepinns were heartily tucking in to their mid-morning Minch, a frisky ring of froaks outside were making merry round the water-butt. In a ring-o-rosie circle dance, they sang a Froak-Arousing song and beat upon the barrel-boards with their tiny wet-webbed fists. Then they scampered away laughing in froggy-throated glee: *Oich! Oich! Oich!*

Inside the barrel, Erf slowly unwrinkled his mind from Wintersleep and wondered if he was awake. He yawned: a most unwise breath to take when sitting on the bottom of a brimful butt. But he did: and his cheeks chubbed out and smothered his shout with a mouthful of icy wet. He gave a hiccup, somersaulted, and rose feet first from the water, bobbing about the barrel like an apple.

"Stroofpt! I fink I've woken up!" he cried and tried a froaky *oich!* or two. Beyond the thatch above his head, the sky was blue and the sun shone warmly down. Erf splashed about and floated idly on his back, sunning his upturned apricot tum with newt-like limbs outspread. And all around was the *perfect* sound of froaks and frogs and warty toads, with melodiously odious voices, all belching from pond to pond. The birds were trilling in the trees and oh! but it was a glorious morning! He heard the creak of the kitchen window open wide and scrumptious pie-and-cakey baking smell came wafting warmly to his nose. Erf sniffed the air in ecstasy.

And suddenly a soggy slop of leafy sludge fell *splat!* across his snout.

"Hee hee hee!" A merry shout of glee was heard not far above his head. A cluster of coal-black eyes shone down a-twinkle in the shadow of the eaves. The fringe of muggy, moist and tunnelled thatch was thickly overrun with squirmy little things.

They had wings like bats and ears as large as cabbage leaves. These were the eavesdroppers who lived in cluttery holes in the riddled roof. Unluckily they had chosen today to set about playfully cleaning them out—and Erf was in the way.

Now when just waking up from a weary Wintersleep, such springtime silliness disgruntled him. (And he was never *very* gruntled at the best of times.)

He rolled around to rinse himself. And right away another shower of soggy sweepings fell *splat!* upon his head. He let out such a frightful yell that eavesdroppers came swiftly dropping from the eaves. Yittering like flittermice on flimsy wings, they zoomed about and snortled through their roomy noses, leaving little trails of frosty vapours in the air.

"Filfy fings!" cried Erf. "You filfy icky leaves-droppers!"

Inside the roundy-house, the ifflepinns heard the wroth of a woken froak in full croak, cursing the play of eaves-droppers. "He's woken up!" cried Iffleplum. "Hooray!" He jumped up quickly from the table. Grabbing a birch-broom by the door, he holloped to the rescue, waving it on high. *Fear not, good friend! Oh, faithful froak!* thought he. *Here comes Sir Plumkin of the Vale! His gallant heart shalt smite the foe! Have at ye, varlets!* And his make-believe

battle-axe swirled about his head as he hewed the fleeing foe. The air cleared as the eavesdroppers scrambled for their holes, deftly avoiding the sting of the birch-broom on their bottoms.

"Sunny New Spring!" said Plumkin in a cheery way (which is actually the correct thing to say to someone who has just woken from a Wintersleep).

"*Bu–ur–rp!*" said Erf (which is a very bad habit froaks have: frogs are just the same. You can't take them anywhere).

"Sunny New Spring!" cried three voices from behind, as the family gathered round to greet him.

"May Springshine fill all your hearts!" said Erf warmly. "And may it shrivel up certain fings wif beady-eyes, what flies and lives in eaves." He glared meaningfully towards the thatch. And the thatch snickered softly to itself.

"And how's my Sunny-New-Spring froak?" said Ifflepaw. "Okey-doke? How did the winter go with you?"

"How should I know?" said Erf. "I've been asleep. Apart from frozen nose and knees, and toes and tail and teef—I'm fine."

Ifflemother stood him on the barrel-rim and kissed the crown of his icy head. "Hoo! You *are* cold!" she said, rubbing him briskly down with her apron-front (which delightfully smelled of mother-warm, baking, and hot-buttered toast).

"Should fink I am!" retorted Erf. "You'd be too, if you slept frough vhe winter in a tub of fick ice! You might have fought to put it somewhere warm."

"Oh you poor little frozling," said Ifflemother, tweaking his tiny tail. "Well how's about a tiny tot of something hot, to keep away the chill? You are looking rather green about the gills."

"It's only slime," said Erf contentedly. "It grows on you in time. But fank you, Mumkin. It's hard to wait vhe Winter-long before your breakfast in the Spring. And my tum tells me it's time for Wakes."

"And Wakes it is!" said Iffleplum, as Mumkin bustled back indoors. He numbly fumbled in his pockets, which was odd, as ifflepinns have no clothes. But then, they *do* have what they call "pouch-pockets" in their skin: and slotted in the very trouser-pocket place they need to be. So anyone with frosty

12

paws had a handy ever warm and wetproof pocket-pouch to put them in.

"Here we are!" said Iffleplum. "A speshly freshly-baked sunflower seed and pondweed cake. Mumkin made it when she saw the froakrise on the Ifflebrook early on."

As Ifflemother brewed a bowl of hot toddy on the stove, Old Ifflepaw softly sidled by with his brassbound telescope beneath his arm. His eyes were glazed like someone walking in his sleep.

"Oh no! Not *again!*" said Mumkin, catching sight of the Captain's cap he wore. "It's too much!" But Ifflepaw seemed not to hear and dreamily opened the back kitchen door.

"Iffy!" cried Mumkin in alarm. She clapped her hands together with a smack. Startled, Ifflepaw awakened from his trance. He looked at her bewilderedly. She pointed to his head. Feeling with his fingers, he felt the peak of his Captain's cap. "Oh," he said sheepishly. Then, suddenly noticing the telescope, he tried to hide it behind his back.

"I didn't realize I was off again," said he. "That hairy old creature's warning is preying on my mind, I guess. I suppose I was on my way to have a last lookout. Just in case, eh?" He gave an unconvincing wink and grin.

"But you've already been up there half the morning!" scolded Mumkin. "Why not forget it for today? Come on— eh? Enjoy your silly self for once. And put that worrisome thing away. At least on Froaksday cast your cares aside."

"But Mumkin-mine! Don't you realize? By Froaksday it was due to come. That's what the Soothsayer said: '*Ere the fearful Day of Froak is done!*' And that's *today!* The *last* day of the prophecy." Ifflepaw frowned. "It might come upon us anytime. We have to be prepared. I've a mind to tell young Iffleplum at last. We don't know *where* he'll be today."

"Oh, *please!*" said Ifflemother. "Not just yet. He's been so looking forward to the fair. Let him have his fun and play awhile first. It would be a shame to scarify our Plumkin too, on such a larky day. And who's to say that crystal-gazing creature wasn't as crazy as a cuckoo in the spring? And

13

nothing's happened yet, for all your watching and your worriting."

"Not yet, maybe," said Ifflepaw darkly. "But I feel anxious in my bones. At least we ought to see that Iffleplum is on his guard today."

"But even if the tale was true," said Ifflemother, "I can't see what the likes of us could do against a thing like that—can you?"

"Look, I'm a-doing what I can!" retorted Ifflepaw. "Don't you understand? That's why I'm watching out. If we can see it from afar, we might have time to get away. But if we don't tell our Iffleplum—well you know what he's like—he'll run towards it when it comes, and not the other way!"

"All right," said Mumkin, "but let me break it to him gently then. I'll try to tell him in a way he won't be worrified. And if he stays among the crowds at Froaksday Fair, no harm can come to him among the ummals there. Now you just go and put your Sunny-New-Spring hat back on, and then we'll—"

But as she spoke, from faraway over the forested hills, came the sound of a Wondrous Horn. Its deep and mellow song was magical. And the swelling sound came rolling over the land like an unseen tide. It gambolled over hills and vales and thrilled the grasses in the fields below as if it was a breeze. And as it came the skies were of a sudden filled with startled birds. It boomed along the Merryvale and the villagers all paused, or scrambled out of doors with shining eyes. For it tingled in the hearts and toes of everyone who heard.

And every heart was gladdened as it came.

A thrumming hum of aftersound came running like a thundery river underground, arousing every growing thing around with a song of rising sap. Sleepy flower-eyes slowly opened in the greening meadows as the Hornsong rolled on by. It rippled upwards through the roots of trees towards their crowns. And with the sound their woody winter-sleeping hearts awoke. Beneath the bark of beech and birch and mighty oak, lay drowsy wood-fays dreaming of the spring: webwoven in the wooden dark. Now awakened in surprise,

14

the tree-deeves sprang up and dashed the dusty cobwebs from their eyes. Quickly then they crept from musty cracks and holes wide-eyed, to watch the giddy goings-on outside.

"Hark! Hark! The Scatterhorn resounds!" the folk all cried, and set aside their chores to dance. Then everywhere the ground began to sprout with pinky wrinkled snouts and the tiny hairy heads of the last of the weary winter lie-abeds. Up came dozy dormice, hedgehogs, meadow-pogs, and moles, peering bleary and bewilder-eyed about their holes at all the noise. Now other horns were sounding down the vale, for the mountain-folk had blown their own, like a herd of lost cows lowing in the hills. And all across the countryside, from every burrow, hamlet, hole and hill, the ummals and the dummals all took up the cry. "*Haroom!*" they sang in echo of the Mighty Horn of Spring, which awakens every living thing in the Ummal-land of Ælfÿlon.

It was impossible to feel down when the sound of the Horn thrilled through the land. Even Old Ifflepaw forgot his fears awhile. He slapped his Sunny-New-Spring hat back on his head and hurried out with a trayful of steaming toddy bowls. "You wrap your chilly chops round that, my froaky lad," he said. "It'll make your hairs curl."

Erf had only two hairs on his head. But they were long, for a froak, and he was proud of them.

Ifflepaw raised his toddy bowl: "All hail—"

"Wassail!" cried the others heartily, as they clunked their wooden cups together and tossed the hot stuff down their throats. And then they too began to caper round, as springtime silly as the froaks.

On the hillside over Bumble way, a sudden crash of cymbals rent the air. Somewhere a brass band had begun to play. They could hear it oomphing uncertainly into tune. The blare of wobbly music came drifting down from the Wossle Wood. And very soon, over the brow of Bumble Hill, the players on parade came proudly stepping into view. But now a bright and merry music filled the air as they all came marching down.

Boomp! Crash! Boomp! Crash!

The drums and clashing cymbals excited stragglers everywhere to hurry on their way. Crowds of ummal-kin were following on behind and other folk came rushing in to join them from the woods on either side.

"It's the Bumble Umbelope's Brass Band!" cried Iffleplum. "Come on! It's time! They're going to start the Scatterdance!"

They scrambled for their Scatterbags and baskets full of leaves, stacked ready waiting in the woodshed for the Dance. Dried leaves for scattering across the land, in memory of the autumn trees reborn again in spring. As the family dashed quickly in and out, a pair of owlish yellow eyes ducked down behind a stack of wood.

*

When the ifflepinns had gone, a hairy little creature warily crept out and stealthily followed them down the lane.

By now the band was at the bottom of the hill. The parade was passing by the old stone humpbacked bridge across the Ifflebrook, at the end of the little lane that led up to Ifflenook. A lively procession of bobbing heads came whirling and twirling on behind. The family hastily hurried down the lane to mingle with the merry throng.

But the ragged shadow was never far behind.

Sneaking along behind the hedgerows in the fields and hiding here and there, it secretly followed them all the way to the Froaksday Fair.

The Festive Field was already filled with ummal-kin when the Bumble Umbelope's Band came marching in. Then all the people raised a cheer: "The Daisy-Ringle Dance!" they cried. "Now let's begin!" All over the field the ummal-folk were forming circles everywhere. The band struck up the Oaky-Froaky song, inviting everyone to sing along and join the Scatterdance of Spring.[4]

---

4 The *Scatterdance of Spring* was as old as the hills. The ummal-folk had danced this rousing Rite of Awakening each and every year since time out of mind. After the Great Piper had blown his Horn and wholly woken all the land, then—and *only* then—the Scatterdance of Spring began.

Iffleplum joined hands in a dancing ring—and skipped and twirled without a care.
But little did he know what the day would bring!

Throughout the land the folk linked hands and did the Daisy-Ringle Circle Dance, now called the "Oaky-Froaky" by the country folk. Although the tune remains somewhat the same, the words of long ago have changed and lost themselves along with the meaning of this sacred celebration. Its ancient beauty gone, the way they dance it nowadays is raucous, rustic and lots of fun. Firstly, all the dancers ring around a mound of autumn leaves and sing:

> *Oh, we all do the Oaky-Froaky!*
> *Oh, we all do the Oaky-Froaky!*
> *You throw your fat froak in!*
> *And snuffle with your snout!*
> *Sniff-snout! In-out!*
> *Shakes the leaves about!*
> *Seek out your Oaky-Froaky,*
> *Twirl around and shout:*
> *Hooray! all the froaks are out—Heigh!*

And with the cry of *Heigh!* the nearest froak is *oops-a-daisied*, topsy-turvy head-over-heeled and hurled into the leaf pile. Then all the dancers shuffle inwards on their knees and thrust their snuffling snouts in and out of the leaves to the sway of the song. As soon as the froak is found again, they raise each other's finger-twined paws and rise, step-skipping outwards in a widening ring: a movement known as "Opening the eye of Spring" or "The Daisy Awakening". And then trolling like the cows come home, the clod-humpfing circle stumbles around, one way widdershins and then the other.

When the ringled froak escapes the whirling feet at last, the dancing daisy-ring unwinds. Then in a line the dancers peel away like a snake between the trees. And this they call a "Scatter-snake": for as they dance—like merry farmers sowing seeds—from baskets laden light with leaves, they cast the crispy old clothes of autumn trees into the air upon the breeze. They say this shows they way the Wheel of Seasons rolls around, for in the fall it strips the trees. And then all through the Winterlong the fallow land swallows up the lifeless leaf and in the New Year pouts it greenly from the ground again in a sudden sheen of spring.

Part the Second

The Storm-Pog's Warning

*In which Iffleplum hears of a phantom Fisher-Boat
and the tale of a horrid pog;
while hatstruck Ifflepaw plays the chump
and the family meets a mufflewump.*

The Froaksday Fair was in full swing in the field below. Many long lines of Scatterdancers had left the Festive Field behind, and were now wending their ways up the hillsides towards the Wossle Wood.

The Wossle Wood was really a vast and ancient forest, which stood on rising waves of woody humpbacked hills climbing higher and higher, until they reached the Mauven Mountains, three leagues away or more. None but the very bold ventured far inside its borders, for it was said to be enchanted in its Elder deeps. And also, there, amid the Sacred Groves, the Guardian of the Forest dwelled: Old Wossul, the Woodwose, wild Master Spirit of the Trees.

Every First of Spring, a pilgrimage of ummalfolk from miles around (and dummals too) all gathered round Wood-Warden Cuppicks' tower, to pay homage to the Master of the Wood and to see the New Year in. Hidden on a hilltop among the trees, in a long and grassy basin called the Flowing Bowl, they would spend the day a-wassailing—a festival of drinking to the health of Old Wossul and his woods. The Flowing Bowl had been a site of celebration since time out of mind. And there the ummal-kin would feast and dance, and sing Old Winter's frosty beard away.

*

Iffleplum, Erf, and Mumkin were halfway up the hillside before they realized that Old Ifflepaw was not with them any more.

"Oh, great greeny plum-tum gripes!" groaned Iffleplum, peering down the hill. "He's not in sight! Without us watching him, he might have wandered off back home again. Of course! He *only* did! We came so quickly to the fair—he forgot his bag of hats! *And* he left his ring of oak-leaves still hanging in the woodshed—the wreath he always wears to remind him to enjoy himself when a-wassailing in the wood—oh no, he *only* has!"

"Oh dear," sighed Mumkin, dumping down her basket on the ground. "That's most *unthoughtsome* of us all! Not noticing we have left Old Ifflepaw behind. I fear he's forgotten where he's at. If he's wandering in bewilderland again, he could choose *any* kind of hat."

"Don't fret," said Erf. "I'll hop off down again and seek him out. If he's not gone up wif Granpaw in a cart, I'll bring him back before you've caught your breaf!" And with a cheeky chortle, like the pockle of a tumbled bottle emptying, Erf bounced away back down to the Festive Field and home.

The two ifflepinns now stopped to rest beneath a twisted tree. Still breathing deeply from the climb, they sat and watched the clouds of frorebreath curling from their snouts. Although the sun was shining in the valley, they were sitting on the northern slopes of Bumble Hill and here the fading frost still held a tiny bite. Over the treetops further down, a rabble of raucous rooks was clamouring around their rookery. Iffleplum sat astride a tree-root and turned to watch them wheeling in the air.

Across the Festive Field below, he could see way down the Merryvale. Beyond the trees of Merrywood and the shiny roofs of Merry May, he spied the bobbing boats in Maypole Dock: a moment's glide away downstream from Ifflenook. Although his home was hidden by the trees, the rocky spear of land they called The Naze and the little hill behind the house could still be seen, where it rose between the Elventear and Ifflebrook.

20

"I bet Old Iffykins has gone up on The Rise again," said Iffleplum, "still watching for I don't know what. Can't see him though."

"Oh, deary me, I do hope not," murmured Ifflemother Mumkin turning round. "You know some strange ill-wind has blown your father's wits a-wandering, since last year's fall of leaf. He's getting more forgetful every day."

"Oh, but he always was a woolly-head," said Iffleplum.

"That may be so," said Ifflemother softly, "but it isn't *only* that." She gently took his hand in hers. And something in her tone and touch, made Iffleplum prick up his ears. "I know he's woolly-noddled anyway. But never was he glum and gloomy-wrinkled as he's been of late," she said. "He's even taken up with thinking things at *mealtimes* too! He's really not himself these days."

"That's true," said Iffleplum. "I noticed that. I wondered why he sometimes wore his Thinking Cap at meals, and not his Munching Hat. It doesn't suit an ifflepinn to carry on that way."

"I know," said Ifflemother squeezing his hand, "but ever since he saved that horrid pog from drowning, he's never been the same."

"What horrid pog is this?" said Iffleplum with widened eyes. "You never told me that!"

"Well now, little Plumkin—we didn't want to worry you. But now I have to share the secret with you too. And then perhaps togetherly, we'll find out what to do. Are you listening?"

"Uh? Oh yes!" said little Plumkin. "I just thought I saw something moving in that hollow tree just there: from the corner of my eye. It might be a *monster* watching us! With slobbery jaws! All yucky—*ugh!*" He clutched his mother's arm dramatically.

"Plumkin! Be serious!" chided Mumkin. "It's probably a squirrel, or a tree-deeve waking up. Don't stare: it's not polite. What I have to tell you is scary enough—if the tale is true, without making things up. Now listen carefully to what I say."

"All right, I'm listening," said Iffleplum. "Go on." He gave the tree another glance. But now there was nothing to be seen.

"Well," said Ifflemother, "this is how it came about. When I saw Iffy every day walk out with his sailor's-eye spyglass up The Rise, and then come back mumbling to himself in a broody-brown of reverie, I said: 'Great heavens, Ifflepaw! What has come over you? Your brow's as wrinkly as the ebbing sands. Why frown you so, old foggy-face?' I chafed him.

"But he turned to me with moony-mellow eyes as shiny as a grapefruit slice and said: 'Oh, Mumkin mine, I have a sorry secret I was keeping from you: but a trouble shared is half repaired, as they say. So here you have it. If I frighten you a little—please don't scream—just bite hard on your beads and be brave. 'Cause I've heard something strange and scarifying is on its way to Ælfÿlon!'

"'What kind of thing do you mean?' I asked him anxiously.

"'Well, I don't quite know for sure,' said he. 'But I've heard tell that there's some kind of wild and witchy ship—a ghostly galleon—that's sweeping on towards us, like an eerie bird of prey. And I fear it might be after me—or someone in my family! Our Iffleplum mostlike.'

"'Oh, Ifflepaw! You make me goosey-pimple cold!' I thrilled through a mouth half full of fancy beads. 'But why would phantom folk be after us? Just thinking such unwarmly things throw-twangles all my heartstrings in a tizz!'

"'Ah! There you have hit it on the head, m' dear,' says he. 'Heartstrings it is indeed! From what I understand, it seems that this here ship is sailed by a scary crew who fish for the hearts of unsuspecting folk somehow, in a fearsome faery way. And any day their ship may come to steal our hearts away!'"

As Ifflemother spoke, a delightsome creepiness crept over Iffleplum from head to toe. "Oh, Mumkin!" he cried excitedly. "You know, that's just like a story in my book! You know the one—*The Legends of the Isle of Ümmulon*. The one that Unka

Turnbuckle—that old sea-rat—gave to me, before he sailed away to sea. You remember? The one about the *Boat of Hearts*—and faery-folk, who fling out starry nets across the skies to snare the hearts of those who never use them any more. Do you think that that could be the *very boat* that Ifflepaw thinks is on the way?"

"Oh, Plumkin! So it could!" sighed Mumkin happily. "If so, you have set my heart at rest. I never thought about that tale. Maybe Iffy read your book of legends too: and then forgot about it all. And now he fancies that it's true! You know no ships can sail up through the Windy Way—that wildsome river-road between the mountains and the sea. Well, not this season anyway; especially with the melting mountain snows and the muddy winter water-flow, the way the river is right now."

"Oh—but it could come down the other way!" said Plumkin hopefully. "From upstream, rather than the sea. The way old Turnbuckle's boat came down."

"That maybe so; although they say the Elventear flows *underneath* the mountains in the south. It enters Ælfÿlon from caverns underground: so no big ships have ever passed that way."

"Oh! But anyway," objected Iffleplum, "the Heartboat in my story *flies!* It's a *magic* ship! A *Golden Galleon!* It sails among the stars at night. It's carried by the breeze and floats upon the clouds: not on the rivers or the seas. And it comes to rest on the snowy peak of Ümmûârkon—the mightiest mountain ever seen—on an island faraway in the Faeryworld of Ümmulon. And *that's* the island of my heart's delight! The *Legends* say that in the lands around the mountain's feet— there, every fabled creature ever known is still alive today!

"Oh, if only I could find the way to reach my isle of dreams. And see such legendary things as *Men!*—and Dragons, Knights, and Kings. And Elves! Or even half-elven folk like the Dwemmerlings. Oh, if I could sail on such a ship—if it should come—why, I'd *give* my heart! I *only* would!"

"Oh, would you now?" said Ifflemother archly. "You'd give your heart—for no more than a boat ride somewhere faraway? Be careful Plumkin, what you say! I told you: 'Think before you speak.' A heart's not something you should give away for a passing fancy, like a birthright for a turtledove. If you give your heart, it should *be* a gift: and not for any reason less than love."

"Oh Mumkin! You know I don't mean what I say. But why *does* Ifflepaw think the *Boat of Hearts* might come this way?"

"Ah, now," said Ifflemother, "when I asked him how he knew such grimsome things, he said some shaggy pog had told him so. Late last year he was walking by the Elventear on a windy day, when he spied this pog in trouble in his boat. It seems he had tried to come across in a leaky old coracle, when the river was a bit too rough. And the choppy water swamped his boat and whirled it round and round. The poor old pog was hanging on for dear life: but the boat was going down. He shouted out he couldn't swim, so Iffy jumped right in and pulled him out. And Iffy wouldn't make a story up like that. And I don't suppose this shaggy pog is written in your book?"

"No, he's *only* not," agreed Iffleplum. "Go on—then what?"

"Well, he says to Iffy he's a Sayer-of-Sooths—someone who reads the stars and tells of things to come. And Ifflepaw explained: 'As I was helping him to wring out his tatty cloak, the stranger said he must repay me for my deed, or be forever in my debt. I tried to disagree, but then he grabbed my arm and croaked: 'Old Owleyes Astronomo always pays his dues! And rightly, he expects his guerdon-gift for service done to others too!' Then he pulled out a ball of crystal from his soggy travel bag and set it on his knees. For a while he stared at it with his owlish yellow eyes, until I thought he had nodded off.

"But suddenly, 'Harr!' he cried. 'Beware! 'Tis in the stars for you, old fruit. Oh yea! 'Tis in the stars it's writ! Be thou ware I say: the scary snary Boat of Hearts! For it cometh on apace—and seeks a heart which resteth not in its right place. Beware I say, lest it should take thee unawares! For verily, for sooth I say! Eftsoons 'twill come—nigh ere the fearful Day of Froak is done! Thus doth I aid thee where I may! Forsooth! He-hey!' He cackled like a throttled crow, in funny olden words I didn't know.

"'I could tell he come in from the lands outside, by all that Out-Landish speech. He didn't talk quite normal, like what we do, in the Common Ummal-tongue. And so, before I understood the half of what he said, he flitted off.' And *that*—" said Ifflemother, "is what has made Old Iffy watch the waterways, for our sakes, ever since. I'm not sure now if I should let him see your legends book, in case it makes him worse. He might sit up on The Rise all night to watch the skies instead."

She fell silent and gazed down the rolling hillside, vaguely watching a line of happy Scatterdancers come revelling over a rise. The breezy strains of *"Oh, we all do the Oaky-Froaky!"* floated up to them. But Mumkin hardly heard them, for her mind was somewhere else.

However, Iffleplum was all aglow with what he had heard. He tingled with expectation: but not only from her words. Somehow he had a funny feeling that they were not alone. He peered around. There seemed to be no phantoms lurking anywhere. And the mouth-like jagged hole in the hollow tree looked dark and empty. But it made him feel uncomfortable and he turned his gaze away. Nothing he could see was out of place: except the look on Ifflemother's face.

He noticed that she still seemed slightly troubled and her eyes were very moist. "How bright your eyes become in spring," he said, to try and cheer her up, "as shiny as fresh conkers from their skins. And look! Much shinier than mine." He held up the last year's lucky conker[5] he kept hung on twine around his neck. "Don't worry now. I'm not afraid of flying fisher-folk."

He dropped to one knee and struck a knightly pose. "Sir Iffleplum of Merryvale, my lady, knows not fear. I *only* don't.

---

5 "Conkers" is a game children used to play with horse-chestnuts threaded on a string. One holds up his string while the opponent tries to "conk" his opponent's chestnut with one blow of his own. Each time the same conker smashes another it gains one point. Iffleplum's hardened conker was a one-hundred-and-eighter.

That's why I'd like to be a knight. I could wear my pirate patch and snaggle-teeth, and frighten every horrid creature out of sight. But in my *Legends* book it says 'the bravest knight is he who fights the foe afraid.' For if you don't know fear at all, you can't be truly brave. What can I do? I don't know what being really frightened is. So how can I be brave? What is afraidiness really like?"

"Oh, Iffleplum," said Mumkin. "Why think about such things? When you lose the spirit of a simple heart, that's when afraidiness begins. When something makes you start, and your heart jumps into your mouth. Or your throat goes dry and your little legs tremble like jelly. And your head pounds and your eyes grow wide with fright as if you've seen a ghost—why then you'll know you're scarified so much that you can't even move."

"Well, I've never felt like that," said Iffleplum.

"Because you have a simple heart," said Ifflemother lovingly. "And anyway, there are no horriferous things in Ælfÿlon to make you feel that way. Not since the ring of magic mountains rose up all around it, to protect us all—or so the storytellers say. No grimsome things can get in from the Out-Lands any more. Except for a few strange Out-Landish folk who wander in: not really horrid, but peculiar, like that crystal-gazing pog."

"Yes, what kind of pog was that?" asked Iffleplum. "He doesn't sound like any sort of pog I've met. Not a sand-pog, or a sea-pog, nor a meadow-pog or tree-pog."

"I think it was a shaggy storm-pog from the hills. They say they run around the mountains warning folk indoors before the rains. 'Glad bearers of Bad Tidings', that's what they like to be. They are always frightening folk with wild tales."

"But maybe something in the storm-pog's tale is true," said Iffleplum hopefully.

"Well, a Soothsayer means a Truthsayer, so he shouldn't tell a lie. But I take shaggy pog stories with a pinch of salt. And with storm-pogs you can never really know."

26

"Phner!" gruntled Iffleplum gloomily, "I thought as much. Nothing *ever* happens here in Ælfÿlon. It *only* doesn't."

"Oh, Plumkin! How can you say so? What about this Festival of Spring you've been a-waiting for all Winterlong?" Ifflemother waved her arm towards the wood. "Just hark at all that noise!"

"Oh, but Mumkin! That's just fun! Of course I'm glad today has come. But I mean no real adventure ever comes my way. Well, not the kind a King would cheer me for, and raise his sword and say: 'Oh, brave and noble Iffleplum! Since thou didst slay the foul and monstrous Ogre in fair fight, I honour thee in all my realm and dub thee—Knight! Arise, Sir Plum the Plucky!' Like they do in the *Legends of the Land of Ümmulon.*"

"Your heart is bolder than your head knows how to handle, little Plumkin," Ifflemother laughed. "It's far too full of wayward thoughts. And a restless heart, as the Soothsayer says, isn't in its proper place. Don't throw your heart away on wildsome things like these. For 'Those who seek the sword shall suffer by it'—so they say. And you may wish it now, while such things seem far away: but if that strange and shiversome ship should *really* sail between the mountains up to Ifflenook—you might just wish it *was* a legend in your book, and nothing else."

Suddenly three loud enormous sneezes exploded right behind the tree beside them. Startled, Iffleplum fell backwards off the root.

"Oh groo! What splendid fun!" said a dismal voice behind them. "That's all we need. How very jolly. It's not enough with freaking froaks and potty folks trolling through the woods all day—not to mention springtime floods as usual, I shouldn't wonder—now its phantom fisher-boats and chopping monsters into bits. It's fascinating what some folks will do for fun!"

The ifflepinns gaped in surprise as a tousled, beaky-snouted head with baggy eyes and great big ears peered wearily around the tree-trunk. It was otherwise a friendly face, but bunged with cold and filled with mournfulness and unhilarity.

"Why, it's a mufflewump!" exclaimed Ifflemother.

"Oh, very good," said the stranger, feebly patting his paws together. "You guessed. First Prize for Perspicacity." The mufflewump got up and came out droopily, dragging his tail behind him. He wore an oversize and hairy mushroom-coloured sweater to his knees and mud-red rubber boots, which matched his ripely reddish snout. He sat down gingerly in the end of Ifflemother's shallow basket.

"You see—I knew someone was there!" whispered Iffleplum.

"I wasn't trying to listen to your jolly little chat," said the mufflewump in a quavering voice. "I was already sitting there, hiding meself away in a hole, when you arrived. So I couldn't help overhearing you. I'm sorry, but me ears got in the way. *Stupid* things!" he said, slapping them irritably. "Just look at them! The *stupid* things! They make me look like an over-grown Eavesdropper. And when the rest of me feels all adroop and seedy, me great fat ears still stick up in the air! I feel such

a fool. And the people always say: 'Oooh! Look at his ears!' Wink-wink, nudge-nudge, snigger-snigger. I've seen 'em."

"Oh, you poor thing," murmured Ifflemother. (There's nothing a muffle-wump likes better than to be "poor-thinged".) "It must be difficult as you say, to live with ears like that."

"It *is!* It *is!*" moaned the mufflewump miser-ably, thoroughly enjoy-ing the sympathy. "It's all right for you with

dangle-flaps, but mine catch every bit of noise and draught. It's like living in a hallway all Winterlong. I wouldn't mind, but people seem to see the suffering of mufflewumps as something of a joke. So on such a crazy day, when everybody's everywhere—and people laugh at anything—I tries to hide meself away, don't I?"

"There, there," soothed Ifflemother, patting his shoulder and kutchy-cooing in his ear, in a way that's most endearing to a mufflewump. She touched her finger to her nose, then pressed it to his rosy snout, as ummals do whenever they are meeting someone new. "I'm Ifflemother, snuggle-mate of Ifflepaw. And this is Iffleplum, my son."

"I'm Plumkin to my friends. Pleased to meet you. And what's yours?"

"Pleased?" sniffed the sorry creature in surprise. "You must be trying to be kind. Nobody's ever *pleased* to meet a mufflewump."

Iffleplum and Mumkin smiled at each other helplessly.

"Oh, I see," said the mufflewump, "it's just some kind of secret joke. Ho-ho," he quavered dismally. Pressing his finger to Plumkin's nose he murmured, "Grubbin."

"I beg your pardon?"

"Thought you would. They always do. Granted. I hate this bit."

"I mean, what's your name?" asked Iffleplum.

"I just told you, didn't I?" groused the mufflewump. "It's *Grubbin*—Grubbin Hawkweed. And if that's not enough for anybody, I don't know what is. It's a sight more than enough for me I can tell you."

"Oh my!" said Ifflemother, trying to keep a straight face. "You mustn't feel that way on New Year's Day. You come along with us: we'll cheer you up. And look: tonight we're having a Froaksday Celebration Supper at Ifflenook-on-the-Naze. There's lots of folk invited, and more will come who aren't. Why don't you come along as well?"

"Eh? Who? Me?" said Grubbin disbelievingly. He looked around for someone else behind him. "I'm sorry: it's me ears again. For a moment I thought you invited *me*—"

"I did," smiled Mumkin. "Won't you come? We'll have stories round the fire, and crackers and food, and song and dance—"

"Oh," said the mufflewump weakly, half fearful and halfish eager for the treat. "Are you *sure*? I've never been to one before. I saw one through a window once. You mean it's to be a *proper* party? With—with *laughing* and things? And funny hats?"

"Why yes, of course."

"And—and all that—erm—fun and folly, hoo-ha and holly, and kiss-me-quick and jolly-jolly-there-we-go-ness type of thing?"

"That's right!" said Ifflemother warmly. "And we'd love to have you come."

"*Love* to have me?" Grubbin said, and a tear sprang in his eye. "But I'm a mulligrubbing mufflewump! I'd just get in the way. And everyone would tread on my tail and say: 'Why don't you get off out of it you great cloggy farmer-footed chump?' And so then jolly, jolly there I'd go. Oh no, I think I'd better stay away—"

But just then they heard a loud halloo. And looking round they saw Old Ifflepaw with a circlet of oak-leaves round his head, come huffing and puffing up the hill, with Erf not far behind.

"I say!" gasped Ifflepaw, staggering to a stop and panting heavily. "You'll never guess—what I was at—when froaky lad—came back—to find me."

"Chopping wood perhaps?" said Ifflemother knowingly.

30

"Well blow my hat! You're right!" cried Ifflepaw, pearly-huffing clouds of frorebreath round his snout. "Now how did you know that?"

"The axe is in your hand still!" said Ifflemother with a grin.

"Well soak me! So it is!" said Ifflepaw." He took off the oak-wreath he was wearing and held it up. "I went back home for this. But when I went into the woodshed, I forgot what I was at. I thought I'd toddled out to chop some firewood."

When the meeting with the mufflewump was done, and noses pressed, and Ifflepaw had had a rest, they all went on up together through the wood. As they left their resting place, a furtive figure in a ragged cloak crept out from a hole in the back of the hollow tree.

Stealthily it followed along behind them, all the way up to the Flowing Bowl.

Part the Third

A Shriek in the Woods

*In which Old Wossul of the Woods appears
and sings the Song of Spring for sap-rise in the trees,
and Iffleplum lets loose two precious things upon the breeze.*

hen they came into the glade, the Flowing Bowl was already filled to overflowing with the comings and goings of wagoners and festive folk. For Wagoner's Ride was a twisty road, which came winding up to it on the other side, and many wains and wagons and little carts were arriving from below. The end of the Ride ran all around the rim of the Bowl, in a long oval loop and back again behind the Wood-Warden's tower. There the horses were being unhitched and watered, while every kind of ummal-kin came tumbling excitedly from the carts.

Many of the merrymakers were milling about all over the Great Root Barrow: a huge, long rounded mound of grass-grown earth, running outwards from the tower-base towards the middle of the Bowl. The old ivy-covered watchtower rose up out of it beyond the treetops to the sky, its conical cap of coloured tiles glittering like a dragon's scaly belly in the sun.

The Root Barrow was hollowed out and dry inside, with thick oaken doors, which opened to the west. A causeway for delivery-and-collection carts came curling down towards them from the rim-road, for behind the doors were kept the winter stores for all the folk of Merryvale. As everyone in Ælfÿlon shared in the growing and gathering of crops together, they stored their spare food in the nearest Root Barrow, which was often built upon a hill in case of floods. And all the goods inside were left in the care of Barrow-Wards, or Keepers-of-the Stores.

The Barrow-Wards were chosen for their fairness in sharing out the food. This meant, of course, that most of them were umbelopes.

Umbelopes were very precise and ponderous beings, with a passion for counting things. Their snouts were long and pointed (and ideal for pinning papers to their desks on draughty days). They were grey and tall and umbelliferous antlers sprouted from their heads. Even when squatting on

33

their hare-like haunches and huge rabbit feet, they still stood twice as high as ifflepinns.[6] Although they could leap in the air like antelopes, they never did, preferring to slump their feet along the ground, considering it more dignified. Generally umbelopes were extremely staid and respectable creatures and always wore waistcoats, whatever the weather, to prove it.

Stag-umbelopes liked to live alone in their ivy-wreathed towers, among piles of paper and parchment scrolls. Their wives preferred to live their lives in bric-a-brac-filled burrows, or barrows down below. But for both of them an umbelope's delight was sticking labels on everything they owned, to tell them what it was—even on an apple or a chair. And they loved to write down long lists of everything they saw, three times or more, on separate sheets of paper, and saved them up to read in bed. So becoming a Barrow-Ward brought the happiest days of an umbelope's life. For many a Winterlong hour they would sit enthralled in their barrows, deliciously counting and listing and labelling stores, in a lamp-lit world of their own.

*

The ifflepinns stood on the edge of the Flowing Bowl looking down.

On the grassy basin's bottom before the Barrow-doors, an enormous and unlit bonfire had been built. But many smaller fires, with cooking-pots hanging over them, were already burning here and there. Around one of them a group was dancing to a fiddle, pipe, and concertina band. As soon as Grubbin Hawkweed saw the size of the crowd, his knees went wobbly-weak. Too many merry folk had made the muffle-wump feel giddy. So he climbed a tree at the clearing's side: "Well out of the tail-trampling way," he said, to wait for the Bonfire Ceremony to begin. But among the revellers the

---

6 That is to say, five or six "snout-lengths" up from the ground. An *umbel-snout* is a measurement used in Ælfÿlon, meaning about one foot long (or 30 centimetres if you are a metric-gnome.) To shorten the word to "snouts" is considered rather vulgar (by umbelopes at least).

family caught sight of Granpaw in his Gardening Hat (the only one he ever wore) carousing round a fireside. And they scrambled down to mingle among the merriment.

Wobbling unsteadily on a wooden keg, a wim-wom with a shaggy head was finishing a comic song and dance as they arrived. There was a burst of applause and calls for more.

But no more came.

For a strange sensation swept suddenly across the glade. The wim-wom went all glassy-eyed and his mouth fell open in surprise. With one leg still waving in the air (showing the white-and-red-ringed socks all wim-woms wear) he tumbled groggily off the keg.

But all the other revellers fell silent suddenly, standing still as stones.

A golden light blazed out between the trees, descending slowly from the higher hillside levels of the upper Wossle Wood. Then a twittering of twig-tips, like flocks of faery finches fluttering through the treetops, came rippling down before it from the forest deeps—though all the trees were bare.

An excited murmur whispered round the ummal-kin. "He's coming! He's coming!" And goose pimples prickled on their skin.

A flickering luminous cloud came floating through the trees. Drifting over the rim of the Flowing Bowl it smoothly flowed on down among the quickly parting crowd. And as it came, a rustling sigh was all around—as a wind in far off leaves—but no leaves were on the trees. Gliding up the Barrow-mound it paused and gently came to rest above the Barrow-doors. Now all the glade was bathed in a greeny-golden light, far brighter than the pale spring sun. Its shifting beams lit up the eyes of everyone, reflecting gold like cat's eyes in the dark. Children clutched their mothers in alarm. But their mothers simply stared amazed. And the faces of the ummals shone.

The cloud began to slowly fade. An extraordinary and bizarre being now appeared above the Barrow-doors. Many ummals fell upon their knees in awe. Some prostrated on the forest floor. Others bowed their heads and those that wore them doffed their hats in wonder and in reverence.

Old Wossul—ancient Spirit of the Trees—gazed down upon the gathering.

Like a figure carven from a tree he was: or like a tree itself, gnarled and twisted with the winds and weathers of endless ages gone. His unmoving face was seamed and furrowed like the bark of ancient oak, moss-grown and bearded with a mighty bush of roots, which fell in curling tendrils round his knees. Vines and creeping ivy twined about his wild and tangly hair, where blossoms bloomed and small birds chirruped in their nests. His eyes were the kindest ever seen: though ages old, they filled one with the feeling of freshly growing greenness in the spring. The mists of ancient mornings swirled about his feet.

The Woodwose raised his arms, festooned with robe-like russet-coloured creepers, and held his twiggy hands up in the air. Every ummal in the Flowing Bowl did the same, in salutation to the Spirit of the Forest and his trees. Even Grubbin Hawkweed, forgetting where he was, raised up his arms, entranced.

And promptly tumbled off his branch into a pile of leaves below.

He lay there muttering dismally, "Wouldn't you know? Didn't I say so? Jolly, jolly, there I go."

Then, with a sonorous, slow, resounding drone—like wind in wooden organ pipes, or a mighty horn blown faraway in fog—Old Wossul began to sing the *Song of Spring*. Once more a rustly whispering was heard in all the trees around and eerie harmonies from unseen singers filled the air. Looking up, the ummal-kin became aware of tree-deeves moving in and out among the twigs, transparently half-seen, like shimmering leaves lit up with sunlight shining through them, gold and green. Along with Old Wossul's woody drone, the forest fays now intoned their own strange song in the tree-deeve tongue, for awakening the winter trees from sleep.

And as they sang, all those who heard them seemed to understand the meaning of their song: for in a while they felt that their hearts too were growing green and flowing with the feelings of the trees. And so it was: for these companions of the trees were singing of their delight in all the seasons of the leaves. They sang of joyously unfolding them from wintry boughs—and of bursting open blossom buds in Spring—then shaping fruits and shining them, all through the long hot summer haze—until the mellowdays came round again—and then they would go from tree to tree, releasing all the autumn-coloured leaves and sailing with them wheresoever the windy breezes pleased to blow.

And they sang of sleeping seeds and roots and shoots, and rising things, of springing bulbs and bluebell woods, of dingles and of faery dells, and fresh-turned early morning earth and waking woody field and ferny smells. And as they sang the budding branches of the trees began to speckle with Spring-shine and a haze of twig-tip green was seen throughout the woods.

*

Iffleplum felt as if he was almost turning into a tree himself.

As the *Song* went on, he could feel a thrilling from the forest floor coming up between his toes. It rose up through his body to his treeing fingertips. He could sense the sap-rise climbing in the wood. And in his heart he understood joy of the trees in blossoming—of forming fruits and nuts and feeding all—and changing colours every fall... He looked up wonderingly, half expecting his fingers to burst out into leaf: and half-hoping that they might.

He could feel the majesty and patience of the trees. Trees that simply stand for centuries, forever watching other creatures freely come and go. But now—as the tree-deeves sang of the breezy season of falling leaves—he began to know how the trees themselves go travelling—when the thrill of the wild winds call—and the leaves let go! and the seeds blow scattering away on high, like flocks of birds across the sky...

And a sudden urge to fly like them arose inside his heart. He saw himself in his mind's eye, soaring wild and free—like a dragon-thing with flaming jaws and leaf-like wings spread wide. And *then!* He felt a fluttery feeling in his breast: like a butterfly awakening and flapping in a paper-bag. And suddenly it seemed as if two doors burst open in his chest and the wildsome spirit of his heart flew out.

There it was!

For a moment it was *there*, before his eyes! He could see it, like a ghostly wraith! A softly shining, heart-shaped thing it seemed. With smoky rainbow-coloured veils wisping from its sides like wings. Then slowly it began to fade away, floating way up in the air.

Oh! Oh! His heart cried out to see it go. *I didn't know the spirit of my heart could go away like that!* Then Mumkin's warning in the wood re-echoed in his head: "Don't throw your heart away on wildsome things," she had said. And suddenly he understood. He recalled the Heartboat in his storybook. It came and took away the hearts of those who never used them properly. *Oh, now I see! I understand. Oh! What if the Heartboat's flying overhead?*

Inside his heart he felt a sudden emptiness. And he heard these woody whisperings in his hollow-hearted breast: *Oh, why—oh, why—do all legged things have restless hearts, as if with wings—of course! They have no roots poor things, so naturally—they are always wandering and a-wondering where they ought to be*—or so the trees around him seemed to sing, all sighing like the sea—*Oh, yea—oh, yea—throw not your elfin-heart away*—the trees all sighed—*for life is empty when it's gone—they warned you well—they tried—they tried*—

Oh, please come back! he cried, in thought. *Come back! I need you still!* And to his joy, his wayward elfin-heart returned

38

again—like a songbird to its cage—and back into his body sped.

Then laughter burst like blossoms in his breast.

Once more he heard Old Wossul's tree-song sounding in his heart again. And soon he found himself singing something strongly without words, while tears ran down his face.

On glancing round he found that all the other ummals too, were moved to sing along: some singing high, some humming low, all weaving wordless wonder-tones in harmony with the deeves. A welling swell of rejoicing voices rose and fell. And the Springsong rolled over the rim of the Flowing Bowl, in waves of joy, down hill and dale and all along the Merryvale.

*

In a long and lingering wondrous while, the Wossle Wood fell silent once again. Slowly, the singers became aware that the *Song of Spring* had stilled at last. As everyone awakened from their treeish trance, they looked around and found Old Wossul Woodwose was no longer there. But everyone was all aglow. They stood awhile in silence, shiny-eyed, with warm feelings flowing through their hearts for everything that grows.

Then with a flourish and a sudden trumpet blare, the Barrow-doors were flung back wide. There stood Wood-Warden Cuppicks and his Barrow-mate Hennypeck, with flaming brands of fire held in the air.

"All hail!" cried Cuppicks to the crowd.

"*WASSAIL!*" the crowd cried back with a mighty roar. "Where's Old Winter? Bring him out!" they shouted. "The rascal's skulking in his lair! We know full well he's hiding there!"

The Barrow-Wards then stood aside, beside the doors. From beneath the Barrow-mound two streams of umbelopes came striding out, all dressed in robes of springshine green, and bearing blazing torches held on high. Between them they were dragging out a scarecrow figure fashioned out of whitewashed sticks and twisted straw. The white garments that it wore were all in rags, and dead leaves adorned its frosty beard and hoary glitter-dusted hair.

"Here he is!" the leaders cried, and marched Old Winter's effigy around the bonfire thrice. To the cheers and the jeers of the crowd, with a "One–two–three!" they hurled Old Winter upon the top of the woodpile. A tree-pog waiting there set him up straight and swiftly scrambled down. Now Wood-Warden Cuppicks called out with a ceremonial air:

> *"Begone Old Winter! For at last thy day is done!*
> *The Piper of the Spring his Horn hath blown,*
> *For spring hath come to banish thee!*
> *And thusly bringeth forth the sun!"*

And saying so, he thrust his fiery torch into the quickly kindling fire. Then all as one, the other umbelopes tossed their burning brands into the woodpile too. "Yaay!" cried all the ummal-kin as the bonfire blazed up with a roar. Old Winter vanished in a *whoof!* of flame and sparks and very soon was seen no more. His day indeed was done. The Sunny New Spring was under way.

And all day long they merrymade, over all of Ælfÿlon.

*

At first the day went wonderfully well for Iffleplum. But little by little things went awry. They made very merry Muncheon-meal at midday round a campfire. And then, when everyone was floppy full and lying in the sun, he asked to go down to the Festive Field again. By this time Old Ifflepaw, well fed, was in a sleepy and a mellow mood. The Barrow-Wards nearby were handing out the last of the winter stores, which the wagoners were carting off to deliver down to the valley villages and the Fair. So he suggested Iffleplum could hitch a ride with them.

After promising to keep among the crowds, to stay away from any strange ships that might be seen, and to be back at the Flowing Bowl by sunset, Erf and Iffleplum went down again on a laden cart.

But once they were there, Erf annoyingly went off with a madcap croak of froaks to the Spawnpool, and left him on his

40

own. And then, while mooching about alone, he found himself anxiously glancing back over his shoulder from time to time, although he saw no reason why. But the eerie feeling that he was being watched began to grow on him again. No matter what he did, he could not shake the feeling off.

Often he would quickly whirl about. But try as he may, he could never catch sight of anyone peculiar in the crowd. There were just the ordinary ifflepinns, oiks and umbelopes; some wim-woms, pigger-mice and lots of froaks; many meadow-pogs, a snooj or two; some rowdy river-pogs and here and there, a slurzy froad. Nothing special: no one new. But as the day drew on the feeling grew. He felt as if two burning eyes were boring holes in the back of his head.

And his heart began to beat a little faster than before.

He thought about the warning given to Old Ifflepaw. And the owl-eyed storm-pog and his story loomed large in his mind.

Perhaps the faery-folk have come! he thought. *And they are all around and watching me—invisibly! Maybe the GOLDEN GALLEON is already there in Maypole Dock!*

If it *was* there, he could be sure. But he knew he should not go. He tried to enjoy the fair for a while. But in the end he could not help himself: he *had* to know. So he left the fair and ran across the fields towards the river Elventear. He raced pell-mell along the riverbank to Merry May, then crept down to the quayside quietly. But no ghostly galleon was there: at least, none that he could see. Only a handful of bobbing boats. And the river Elventear was clear. With mixed feelings of disappointment and relief, he hastily hurried back to the busy road and the company of the fair.

*

There he was glad to find his friends fat Podge and Ifflepear. And for a while they wandered round the Froaksfair arm in arm. They rode upon the roundabouts and swings, and stuffed themselves with all kinds of yucky-sweet and sticky things. By the time they found a troupe of wim-wom clowns who were handing out balloons, Iffleplum's anxious mood had almost gone. He was given a balloon shaped like a heart and sunset red, with words upon it: *Love Me, 'Cause I'm Nice!* they said. It made him think of his elfin-heart and the balloon began to cheer him up.

Then suddenly disaster struck!

A smiley snooj with a trayful of cakes came by and offered them a choice. Plumkin was about to take a creamy apple tart. But greedy fat Podge grabbed it first and crammed it in his mouth. Then a push-and-pulling row flared up. Fat Podge fell down and Plumkin too, and in the fray, he lost his grasp and let go his balloon! Up and away it went upon the breeze.

And for the second time that day, he felt another heart of his had gone astray.

With a cry of rage, he thumped fat Podge on the head and set off quickly in pursuit.

From underneath the lifted canvas of a tent, a pair of owlish yellow eyes watched Iffleplum run off, and marked exactly where he went.

Up and up again and over the hillside trees, the balloon sailed on. Then in a sudden windy gust it tumbled round and seemed to come down in the Wossle Wood.

Iffleplum noted where it fell and stumbled up towards the spot. But when at last he got to where he thought it was, he could not find it anywhere. He looked up in the treetops and under the thickets to no avail. Plunging deeper into the wood he searched for ages all around. He got all sweaty hot and flustered. And now he really was upset.

He had liked that heart-shaped red balloon a lot.

Tired and scratched from scrambling though the undergrowth, he gave an angry shout. Ripping a whippy willow-wand from a nearby tree, he thrashed some toadstools in a fit of pique. "And that's for *you!* You great fat gobble-Podge!" he cried, slashing the fungi into bits. With every slicing swish and swipe, he cursed fat Podge with every unkind name he knew—and quite a few he made up by himself!

Then he yelled as loudly as he could and kicked forest floor about.

When his wild mood was over, he leaned against an ancient tree, gasping for breath. He could feel his heart pounding fit to burst. Then his eyes grew wide, remembering. "Oh no!" he cried. "What have I done?" He clasped his chest protectively, as if he could stop his elfin-heart from flying out that way. He feared the worst: for he realized he had wrongly used his heart again.

This time it might fly away for good! he thought. *I ought to have learned my lesson once today. If it's caught by the faery fisher-folk, I'll never get it back!*

He stood quite still and held his breath. His elfin-heart felt fluttery for a while and he waited anxiously. He tried to feel a little kinder in his heart. And soon the beating in his breast was growing less. But even so, he felt uncomfortable. The wood was strangely stuffy where he stood. There seemed to be a prickly, suffocating kind of feeling in the air. He peered about him carefully. Now the forest all around seemed to have grown a little closer and gloomier.

It was only then he realized where he was!

He was alone in the *Elder* Wossle Wood, where the trees were dense and dark and overgrown. More tales were told about that place than all the legends in his book. He tried to keep calm and look around. But a sudden thrill came over him. For he had never been so deeply in the woods before. And soon the sun was going down! He recalled the nursery rhyme the village oldwives tell:

> *"Oh, ne'er go near the Wossle Wood,*
> *My dear, I tell you true:*
> *For strange things happen there, they say,*
> *And you'll regret it if you do!"*

He stood in high hopes, expectantly, awaiting some strange thing to occur. But nothing seemed to change. And he heard and saw no more than the sights and sounds of deep woods—the hoot of an early owl, a falling twig, a streamlet trickling down the hill, the racket of the rooks at eventide, and the far off cries of revellers from the younger woods and fields below. And beneath it all—coming soft and slow—a sense of the silent sounds of the unheard inner music of the trees. Yet these things filled him with a quiet joy, like his feeling when Old Wossul sang the *Song of Spring*. And his eyes began to overflow. For now such simple things seemed to mean much more to him than all the frolicking and the feasting he had done that day.

*

By now his anger at fat Podge had melted clean away. He looked around at the wreckage he had made and felt ashamed. And he blamed himself for everything. "I was just as greedy as fat Podge," he said, "to make a stupid fight about a cake! And I'm more unkind, to treat the growing things this way." From his heart he said, "I'm sorry, sorry," to the toadstools he had thrashed, and now lay scattered all about. And also to the willow-tree whose branch he had ripped away so angrily. *The trees are all alive like me*, he thought. *I even felt their feelings in the Flowing Bowl today. How could I have forgotten it so easily?*

Now he could plainly see how he was not using his heart properly.

44

He knelt beside a rivulet running down between the trees. Scooping up some mud from its sides he went back to the willow-tree. Then with the clay he covered up the wound he had made where the willow-wand had torn away. As he tended to the willow lovingly, he felt his heart grow well again.

I how I love the woods! thought he.

And now there also came a change of feeling in the forest roundabout. For he sensed somehow the trees were growing warm towards him. And their silent sympathy was healing to his heart.

Slowly, as he stood entranced, the Wossle Wood began to hold him in its spell.

A dreamy feeling fell upon his mind, for here few people ever came and a timeless magic hung heavy in the air. He might still be standing there, were it not for the harsh croak of a passing crow flying overhead. It woke him from his reverie with a start. He looked around him in concern. By now the woods were deepening brown and he knew the sun he could not see for trees, was surely going down.

"Oh, gripes!" said he. "I mustn't stay! The Wossle Wood's enchanted after dark!"

Reluctantly he turned away towards the Flowing Bowl, torn between the twilight and the whispering magic of the trees. But now he felt no longer sad, for the trees seemed to have given him some strength. His heart swelled and laughter burst upon his lips.

Now he felt—invincible! And he whooped and sang as he as he ran and jumped the rivulets and fallen boughs, on the way down to the Younger Wossle Wood where the trees were thinning out.

The whippy willow-wand was still in his hand, and a thousand ogres fell before his valiant blade. *Swish-swash!* Who dared stand in the way of bold Sir Plumkin of the Vale? Another *swish!* and an overhanging oak-bough lost the last of its winter leaves, as Iffleplum lopped off the ears of an imaginary troll.

45

"And so perish all enemies of the King!" he cried, well satisfied.

The last rays of the sinking sun, now shining through the tops of trees below, lit up all the woodland in a golden glow. Sir Plumkin turned to spy the sunset in a fork between two mountains, redly glowing like a dragon's eye.

"Oh no! Not yet!" he cried. "Stay up! Stay up! Sir Plumkin's day is not yet done!" Never a truer word he spoke—for the adventure he had been waiting for had come!

The woody silence shattered, as a sudden shrill scream of terror rang out through the trees.

A cloud of cawing rooks arose in screaming echo from the treetops, complaining loudly over all the wood.

Iffleplum stood rooted to the ground in shock.

His ears sang. The wood rang. The cry had set the very trees aquiver! 'Twas the sound a tree itself might make when split by the wind or the woodchopper's axe.

The very voice of trees it was—the shriek of tree-sprite terrified!

"A tree-deeve in distress!" bold Plumkin cried. "Sir Iffleplum to the rescue!"

He firmly gripped his trusty twig, gulped, and swallowed hard—and with the sound still singing in his ears, he dashed boldly back into the ringing wood.

Owleyes Breaks the Spell

In which, from visions in a faery ring,
Iffleplum at last learns how to fear, and so—
makes a sorry bargain with Old Astronomo!

ursting through a bracken bank, Iffleplum fell stumbling into a little dell. At first it seemed no one was there. But as his eyes adjusted to the gloom, he saw a tree-deeve standing all alone, in the middle of a mushroom-ring. And there in the branches above her head, he suddenly spied his heart-shaped red balloon!

Then in a flash he understood. The tree-deeve must have caught its string for fun and floated with it through the wood. But when the breeze had dashed it in among the twigs, the sudden snagging of the string had flung her off. And in surprise she had tumbled like a falling leaf into a faery-ring below: and there was as surely caught as if entangled in a spider web.

Some say that where the wood-fays do their circle dance, next day a ring of mushrooms mysteriously springs up where they trod. And in such rings strange things occur. For the faery-folk are fond of dancing round those places where enchantment dwells: where energies well-up like unseen springs from underground. And tales tell that those who enter faery-rings may fall beneath their spell, into a deep and faery sleep: sometimes forever—never coming out again. Or if they do, they are greatly changed. So when the tree-deeve sprite had fallen in the ring, some force had held her fast and she was stricken where she stood.

She shrieked again. And Iffleplum without a thought flew arrowlike across the dell. Forgetting all he ever knew of faery-rings; forgetting everything, except the longing in his breast to save a damsel in distress, he foolishly leapt right in—from daylight into sudden dark!

In one bound the world he knew was left behind. *Thumpetty-bump!* his heart beat quick and strong. He thought he had fallen in a pit, for a darkness black as night was all about him. And the sunless wood was gone. But night it was. For in a moment more, from high above the chill light of a pale moon shone; though little use it was. Beyond the ring of mushrooms he could see no more than a misty world of shifting shadows and the shapes of ghostly trees.

His eyes grew heavy and he turned to stare at the tree-deeve as if in a dream. He had never been so close to one before. In the gloom she faintly glowed. As hazy as a dream she was herself, with wraith-like veils adrift about her delicate and fluent body. They glittered softly like the wings of dragonflies in the muted moonlight. Her large doe-eyes flickered greeny-golden with an inner light, like sunshine on the forest leaves. But now they stared about, alive with wonderment and fear.

"Are you all right?" he asked her hoarsely, unmindful that the forest-sprite lived half a world away from creature-kind and could not speak the Common Ummal-tongue. For nature-sprites speak only in a kind of flowing song-and-music speech, in rhythms followed by the growing plants and trees.

She made no answer. But suddenly she screamed again.

"*What is it?*" Iffleplum cried out in shock. But the tree-deeve clapped her hands across her mouth and made no other sound. She stared beyond him with a look of terror in her eyes. He tried to turn and look behind. But his body seemed to be of lead and the grasses held his feet. His armpits prickled with sweat and yet he shivered. A frightful feeling came into his heart, for he sensed that something horrible was creeping up behind. Now his teeth seemed glued together and he could not even shout. He could only make a fearful *ugging* sound. With an awful effort he slowly forced his head around. He glanced into the mist, where moving shadows caught the corner of his eye.

Two huge, dark shambling shapes came looming up in the fogging gloom. Then suddenly he could see them too! His heart jumped wildly to his throat. He gulped and swallowed it again. His mouth went dry. His little legs shook like jelly and his head began to pound. And his eyes grew wide a-fearing with a feeling he had never known before: he was afraid.

Two loathsome things dressed in twilight cloaks of shadows stood over them, groping and grunting at the edge of the ring. Their faces were as dark as nightly woods, with slimy snouts stuck out aglint in the soft moonshine, beyond the baggy brims of shapeless hats. They stood as high as umbelopes or more, but the shadows cloaking them around seemed to flitterbat about and fill the foggy wood. And their eyes! Their eyes were what terrified him the most. They were blind and bulbous as egg yolks. And they glistened in the gloom like the eyes of insects—like the orange-pink lustre of mothy-eyes in lantern light. A wave of malignant feeling poured from them like fumes.

The largest Creature of the Night smiled evilly and beckoned him. And Plumkin felt his heart contract. The other creature grinned and nodded slowly, showing rows of curved and broken teeth. A thin black hairy tongue came flickering through them, repulsively, in and out. Then the groping thing held out a sack towards him. Its awful baggy mouth was rippling as if it was alive. Somehow he felt it was eagerly awaiting a chance to swallow him.

Poor Plumkin reeled and his head swam with horror. He almost fell down in a faint. Unknowingly he clasped the tree-deeve's hands for comfort; although he could hardly feel that they were there. They were soft as baby mice's paws, or rather, more like smoke. But something surged from her to him as their fingers touched, like sap-rise freely flowing in his limbs. His tongue unleashed itself and cried, "Oh, Ühm! Oh, Ühm!" of its own accord; and Plumkin knew not why. "Oh, Wossul come! Oh, Ühm! Oh, Ühm!" his heart called out in despair.

Then from afar, a trilling sound of faery pipes, too sweet to bear, came floating through the misty air. The fine hair stood up everywhere upon his peachbloom skin, as its thrilling trill swept over him. The music magical was swiftly washing all his fearfulness away. Bright hope sprang back into his breast. And his heart leapt high as a lark in summer skies.

As his fear began to fade, the glitter of the creature's eyes grew dim. At once the fog billowed and broke and the glimmery-eyed creatures shrank back into the gloom. A moment more and the Shadow-folk vanished in the foggy fumes. For now the moving music made the mists curl up and roll and fade away. Once more the normal light of day returned. And the last rays of the setting sun shone redly through the reappearing trees.

Now Iffleplum turned towards the light. And there—to his delight and awe—he saw a shaft of red-gold dying sunlight strike the Piper's flowered head! A tall and flowing figure, dressed in all the colours of the spring, was wending down the hill between the trees and swaying as he played. The voice of his flute was a wondrous woody melody. And all of nature seemed to sway in harmony with his tune. It came drifting like the evening dew over each unfolding leaf on every forest tree.

But all too soon the piping softly died away. For the Piper's flowered head aflame with light, soon disappeared from sight among the trees below. It seemed as if he had gone down like the setting sun itself, for suddenly the landscape all around dimmed down to grey. And he had gone: leaving but an afterglow around the heart, behind the brightness of his being, and no more than a dullen rose-red light upon the sky.

Now Iffleplum awakened from his wonder with a start. He sensed a sudden movement somewhere way above his head, as a branch broke loudly with a *crack!* With a wailing cry a black and ragged batlike beast came crashing down in a shower of broken twigs. It hit the ground, rebounding like a rubber ball and tumbled roly-poly right through the mushrooms and into the ring.

Iffleplum jumped backwards in alarm. The spell was broken. And he found his feet were free! He hopped out quickly over the mushrooms gratefully. Then he turned to sweep the tree-deeve off her feet. But she had gone! At the moment of release she had swiftly slipped away into a crack of the nearest tree. But in the ring the dazed and tatty thing was still struggling to its feet. Now he could plainly see that it was not an iffplepinn-eating vampire bat, as the suddenness had made it seem. It was no more than a pog, in a black and ragged cloak. Like a shaggy ball of fur it was overgrown from head to foot with greying hair. His huge and yellow eyes were the only features of his face that could be seen.

But by these tokens Iffleplum realized who it was. *Oh, now I see!* he thought. *It's HIM who's been following me about all day! Without a doubt: it's got to be—what was his name?— 'Owleyes Astronomo', Iffy said: the storm-pog from the hills!*

51

The stranger stared wildly at him for a moment, then glanced down at the ground. When he saw the scattered mushrooms lying round, "Oh, for heaven's Sooth!" he cried in great dismay. He rolled his eyes and beat his fist upon his brow. "Hemlock and ratsbane! For fie! Our goodly self hath boobed again! The faery-ring! Get out of it, thou hairy fool!" he told himself. He hobbled quickly from the broken ring and scraped the fungus from his elbows and his knees. "Odds-bodikins! For shame! For *shame!* To think Old Owleyes Astronomo, the Sayer of Sooths, should stoop to such a dire deed!"

He talks like the knights do in my Legends book! thought Iffleplum, mighty pleased. "But what dire deed is that?" he asked, bewildered by the goings-on. "You broke the spell!"

52

"What dire deed, sayest thou?" cried the tatty pog. *"That!"* said he, pointing furiously at the broken faery-ring. "The spell we broke hath broken all our life as well!"

"I don't understand," said Iffleplum. "What happened there? What's going on?"

"Pestle and pound, thou baldy boy! Knowest thou not, thou stoodst there in an Elven-ring? 'Tis a sacred spot, where once the High Elvene and Wizards sat in days of old. Therein thy mind is mazed with faery-dreams. And many a mysterious thing is seen, that may *not* be gazed upon by uncouth lusty lads, the likes of thee. Egad, thou must be very couth indeed! For otherwise, thine unripe mind would only find the Wraithenworld: the abode of Shades and shivery Shadowfolk, whose visages might freeze the very marrow of thy bones! 'Tis rare that such a one entrapped, can flee the visions of the ring, unless some other creature sets them free. Ah, yes!—er—as like as how, at thy service, Old Astronomo Scragmire hath done for thee! For he who breaketh a faery-ring, doth also break the spell."

"Then all is well!" said Iffleplum. "When you broke the ring, you rescued me."

"'Tis well for thee, but not for us! Oh, woe!" the storm-pog cried theatrically. He rolled his froggy eyes and clutched his whiskery face on either side. "Oh, listen well, buffoonly boy! For he who dareth to touch the fungus of a faery-ring, doth feel the spellful curse of faery-folk! And that's no joke! For this poor cove hath squashed them flat! In saving thee—and risking life and limb, by jumping from the tree—Old Owleyes Astronomo hath brought the skies upon his head! Our goodly self is done for: good as dead!

"To think this Reader-of-the-Stars, who seeth ahead, should fall up to his hairy neck in fungus all the same. Were it not for half-baked brittle trees, and that foul Piper who did so unsettle us, things might have gone to plan—we mean, er— things might have worked out more reasonably."

53

"Oh, but I thought you just fell off the tree," said Iffleplum. "And it was the Piper who came to rescue me. His music seemed to break the spell."

"Nay! Nay!" the storm-pog cried out angrily. "'Twas *us*! Not he! Ourself it was! That was but enchanter's sorcery! A phantom piper from some other world, who curled our ears with faery sounds. Nay! Nay! Ourself it was, we say— Astronomo Scragmire, the Sayer of Sooths, who set thee free. Such gratitude we get from youth! For very Sooth! Oh, Rising Signs! Oh woe!" He thumped himself down upon the ground and rocked his body to and fro, alarmingly.

"Oh, well, I'm sorry then," said Iffleplum. "Can I do anything for you? If you it was—I owe you thanks, I *only* do." At this, the Soothsayer stopped his rocking and sharply cocked his head. "Harr! Well now, since thou so kindly askest," he said, and his eyes were sly beneath his overgrown eyebrows (which ended at his feet).

"In the books of Ancient Lore 'tis writ:

> *Should any creature-kin despoil*
> *The fungoids of a faery-ring perchance,*
> *Then Dame Misfortune shalt lead him*
> *In a doleful dance:*
> *Unless mayhap it should befall*
> *He sets another free,*
> *Who then doth render in return*
> *A service willingly, and—er—erm—*
> *And by this boon, thuswise relieves*
> *The Spellbound of his misery."*

"Oh," said Iffleplum. "What does it mean?"

"It means," said the storm-pog peevishly, obliged to lapse into the Common Ummal-tongue, "if you can likewise do a deed for *me* in kind return, the ring-breaking spell on Astronomo, will then get broken too.

"Oh! Then whatever I can do for you, I'll do!" said Plumkin dropping knight-like to his knee and bowing low. "Sir Iffleplum is at your service. Just name your need my liege."

"Harr! Sriffleplum is it?" said Astronomo. "Well now, Sriffleplum, that's what we like to hear! Now *there's* a promise from an honest lad. We ummals should stick together, eh? Well, as we say, there is a little something ourself is needful of, as is thine to give away." And as he spoke, a greedy glint was in his eyes. Then Plumkin felt an icy fist close round his heart again. He clutched his conker on its cord for comfort. He shivered suddenly and looked about, as if expecting two dark figures to be standing there.

"I—I did see shadow-folk, I think," he said. "Those hairy things—what are they? Did you see them there?"

"Oh ho! Hairy things is it?" the Soothsayer said, as sweet-voiced as a crow. "So—you've already seen them, eh? Egad! The visions of the ring! Signs and Portents! The time is ripe, forsooth! Those creatures are coming after you! Should we be not mistook, they want it too!"

"Want what?" said Iffleplum, alarmed again. "Who are they? Where are they from?"

The storm-pog drew uncomfortably close, breathing fumes of barleymead and onion and cheese all over him. Furtively he looked from side to side. He lifted up the floppy flap of Plumkin's ear and croaked in confidential glee. "Those are *Gropes!* That's what those slimy great black beasties are! For very Sooth, dear smoothly boy, those are *Dhârkäsü* from the Shadow-world!"

And then, for fine effect, he slowly looked about again. Then whispered loud and hoarsely in his ear, "'Tis thy very elfin-heart they're after!"

"What?" cried Iffleplum in alarm. "My heart? You mean they'll tear the heart out of my chest?"

"Odds-bods!" said Astronomo. "Thou surely jestest if thou thinkest that lump of flesh, which beateth in thy hairless breast, is of interest to Shadow-folk! Nay, nay. Thy heart is no more than a measly muscle, made to keep your body bit alive. 'Tis no better than the village pump, without the elfin-heart beside. *That's* what they want. 'Tis thine *elfin-heart* they're after!"

"My *elfin*-heart?" cried Iffleplum.

"Oh, yea! Knowest thou not, beside thy thumping body heart—there lieth, upon the right, thy very *heart of hearts*—a twin heart, belike a ghostly guardian-sprite, as one might say—the *Spirit* of thy heart. And forsooth, 'tis not unlike the deevish spirits of the trees. Just as every living flower or tree hath within itself its own true guardian deeve—in like fashion so do we. But then, the very deeves themselves have elfin-hearts, and even so the trees.

"Yea, everything that doth breathe is born with one, dear boy. Harr! Even Old Owleyes Astronomo, who hath lost his long ago. But no one knoweth it till it's gone. And then alackaday! 'tis far too late. And so thou seest, right kindly it would be if thou wouldst deliver *thine* up to *us*—Astronomo Scragmire—as promised us, for the service that we rendered thee."

"Give up my elfin-heart?" said Iffleplum. "How can it be? You said it's best to keep it, anyway. How can I give it up?"

"Harr! There's the rub!" said Astronomo, tipping him the kind of wink which is as good as a nod to a blind horse. "For very Sooth, 'tis said, as:

> *'He who doesn't rightly use it,*
> *Verily shall he rightly lose it.'*

"See thou, when someone's heart doth grow wild, or greedy, their faery elfin-heart doth find it hard to stay inside. Oh, yes indeed! And if a heart doth grow worse and if it curseth life, or causeth strife, then the elfin-heart shall surely flit away. And once 'tis gone, thy heart groweth sadder, colder, and more fearful by the day.

"That's why those Shadow-folk—which the Elves call *Dhârkäsü* and we call 'Gropes'—come flocking round. They feed on fears, thou seest. So they love to frighten anyone

56

whose elfin-heart is going, or has gone. And if they take thine elfin-heart into the Shadow-world for play, they can always feed upon thy fears from far away. And for very Sooth, we know thou art going to lose thine anyway. So gifting it to Old Astronomo should cause thee no dismay."

"But how? What have I done?" said Iffleplum. "What did I say? Why would my elfin-heart go away from me?"

"Cusps and Configurations! We heard thy words: we know thy ways. Woods have ears, dear lad, and so have hollow trees. Didst thou not wish for wild deeds? For killing monsters and the like? No need for finer feeling elfin-hearts for that! An empty body-heart doth well enough for dirty deeds."

"Oh, but I didn't really mean—!"

"'Tis too late now!" said Astronomo. "The words are said: thy thoughts have sped. Already thou hast wished thine elfin-heart away. So horrid pogs, or slobbery jaws, it may well be, dear boy—choose well!" Suddenly his scrawny arm shot out and pulled him close. He pressed his hairy ear on Plumkin's breast, whose heart was beating fearfully. "Aha!" said Astronomo. "Oh ho! 'Tis coming loose! 'Tis nearly time for it to go! Astrolabes and Alignments! 'Tis in the stars for us, Old Owleyes, thou hairy fruit! And very soon!

"Too long our elfin-heart's been gone. And old and gnarly now we grow. This very night we get another one. And now we know the spells to bestly use it for ourself—far better than those oafy Gropers can. A sprightly elfin-heart might waken up this aged ticker for another hundred years, as like as not." He tapped his hairy breast and a fire flickered in his greedy eyes. "So as we say, 'tis best to give it first to Astronomo—or *They* will come and take it anyway!"

"But—" Iffleplum began.

"No buts now!" said the Soothsayer, waving a warning finger. "Niggle not to one who saved thee from the feary faery ring! It looseneth in thy breast already. And soon it is to go. Break not thy word, oh glabrous lad. Eftsoons! Old Astronomo will come, when the time is nigh at hand. When the Shades of Night come creeping—so shall we as well! Be ready then! The storm-pog's sooth is said and done!" Then with a frightful wild and gladsome cry, he flitted off quickly through the woods, his ragged cloak rippling out behind him in the breeze.

Iffleplum stood looking numbly after him for a while. Then he realized that night was settling in among the trees. The sun had long gone down. And now the woods were deeply darkling as Iffleplum ran back all the way to the Flowing Bowl without a stop.

Part the Fifth

Horrid Pogs it is!

A party night and a merry feast are fun at first,
but end up with an angry storm-pog's curse!

"There he is! Good old Plumkin! Over here!" was the cheer of welcome that greeted him, as Iffleplum came over the rim of the Flowing Bowl. The grassy hollow was ablaze with lights and still full of feasting folk. Granpaw, Erf and Mumkin, and a crowd of friends were gathered round a horse and haywain, before the Barrow-doors. The party crowd were all awaiting Iffleplum, before they set off on the cart ride down to Ifflenook for the Froaksday Celebration Supper.

Lanterns were now hanging in the trees and the scene was bright and lively. The great bonfire was now a seething pile

of golden gledes, lighting up the faces of those still making merry round its edge. Many ummal-folk were roasting hot potatoes or wrinkled yellow apples in the embers. Other groups were singing round the campfires, or making music underneath the trees. Any other time, Iffleplum would have begged to stay longer, but now he was more than ready for the safety of his home.

He was well scolded for coming after dark. "But it's not my fault!" he said. "I was kept late by that Horrid Pog! 'Cause fat Podge made me lose my balloon up in the Wossle Wood and—oh! I forgot! It's still stuck up there! Oh, gripes! It *only* is! And then I got caught in a faery-ring! When I was rescuing a tree-deeve in distress! And then these big black monsters came, with awful sacks! And then I—"

"Oh, go on with you!" retorted Mumkin, in the way that mothers do. "Why, what a mess you look!" And he was hoisted up into the haywain before he could explain. Many other folk came scrambling over the sides. Iffleplum found himself quickly crammed in behind the driver's seat, squashed amid a motley crowd of very merry meadow-pogs, several tree and river pogs, some pigger-mice and ifflepinns, a couple of oiks, and a family of wim-woms too—and sitting knee-deep in countless froaks and mouselings.

Out came Wood-Warden Cuppicks from the Root Barrow, still fussing with his everlasting lists in triplicate. He was checking off the last few empty casks and barrels being rolled back into storage. Around the rim-road, one or two other carts and wagons were loading up with tired and happy revellers and setting off on the rocky road down the hillsides.

Old Ifflepaw emerged from the lantern-lit dimness of the Barrow, dragging Grubbin Hawkweed by the arm. "It's no use you hiding away in there," he said. "They're shutting up the doors. So up you get, and no more argufying. It'll do you good." And he bundled the still protesting mufflewump up and into the back of the wagon.

At last the old umbelope was rolling up his scrolls. His Barrow-mate Hennypeck came shlumpfing out of the Barrow, muttering, "Don't be tardy, Cuppicks, don't be tardy." She nuzzled his nose goodbye. "Mind how you go, Cuppicks," she quavered.

"And be careful on the bends," said Cuppicks quietly to himself, as he lit a lantern by the Barrow-door.

"And be careful on the bends," cautioned Hennypeck anxiously.

"Be back early," said Cuppicks, contentedly reciting their well-tried rigmarole under his breath: "And don't stay up too late."

"Be back early," called Hennypeck as he turned away. "And don't stay up too late tonight, reading your lists, with your head in the clouds, way up in your ivy-wreathed tower."

"You'll strain your eyes," murmured Cuppicks, well satisfied with all the old familiarities said and done. Everything was in perfect order.

"You'll strain your eyes!" continued Hennypeck. "Do it tomorrow, in the light!"

The talking ummal-horse stamping between the cart-shafts whinnied out: "Hey–ey–ey! Come on Cuppicks you old dodderer! I want to get back to my hay–ay bed and a bit of warm before the night is old. Hop along, old flatfoot, if you want to ri–i–ide!"

Cuppicks came along more quickly than he should for umbelopish dignity, in little leaps and bounds.

"Steady, Cuppicks!" called out Hennypeck from behind. He smartly closed up the back of the wagon, hung up a lantern at the front for the horse to see by and clambered up onto the driving seat. His good friends Ifflepaw and Mumkin sat beside him. Tucking his tail between his knees for safety he shook the reins.

"Gee-up, Dapplenose! And less of your horse's mouth!" he said jovially, slapping the horse's rump. The wagon started with a jolt, and everyone fell about with shouts of laughter and gleeful cries.

"Jolly, jolly, there we go," groaned Grubbin Hawkweed gloomily, extracting a young wim-wom's foot from his ear and setting himself upright again. The haywain rumbled off, with everyone calling and waving to the other wassailers left behind. As they jig-jogged down the hillsides, many a time they stopped to let off little passengers to pee, or pick up weary walkers on the winding road. Everyone was in high spirits.

But Iffleplum was uneasy in his mind.

After a while he climbed up onto the driving seat and squeezed himself between Ifflepaw and Mumkin. He was still feeling the strangeness of the things he had seen in the faery-ring. And the bargain struck with Astronomo, lay heavy on his heart. He took his parents paws in his and told them the story from the start. This time they listened well, especially when he spoke of Scragmire the Sayer of Sooths.

"Well, blow my hat!" said Ifflepaw. "That sounds like the very self-same storm-pog that I pulled out of the Elventear. He must be following us about!"

"He is!" said Iffleplum. "He *only* is!" He told them how the Soothsayer came tumbling from the tree and broke the faery mushroom ring. And then his asking for the elfin-heart to save him from the faery curse.

"Humph!" snorted Cuppicks, "I've never heard such stuff! Take no notice. He must have made the nonsense up!" But Plumkin saw him frown and he and Ifflepaw exchanged a troubled glance. They said no more, and for the rest of the journey jogged along in silence, while the wagonload behind them made merry all the way.

"Ah! But now I know what being frightened is," said Iffleplum. "I can learn how to be brave. And perhaps then I'll fight the foe afraid." Mumkin wagged her head resignedly. She smiled sadly, said nothing and simply patted his hand.

*

By the time they came down into the valley near Ifflebrook, the night sky was clear with stars. But the moon had not yet risen. Swinging lanterns twinkled on the roads and hillsides, as little throngs of local folk wended their ways homeward. Half the wagon party hopped off before the bridge, which humped across the Ifflebrook to join the Naze. With cheery goodnight shouts and calling out "A Sunny New Spring!" and a "Merry Froak's Night to all!" they disappeared in every direction.

The haywain rattled and groaned on over the old stone humpbacked bridge and up along the little lane that led to Ifflenook. The party throng was in full song by the time they reached the door. There they all tumbled out gladly, crowding in to the welcoming roundy-house. The tree-pogs brought in bundles of wood and in a trice they had the hearth and kitchen stove ablaze. Ifflemother and her helpers bustled busily in and out of the kitchen, for all were famished in spite of a day of fresh-air feasting.

Ifflepaw helped Cuppicks unhitch Dapplenose from the wagon. "Are you sure you won't come in?" asked Ifflepaw. "Neigh-neigh!" said Dapplenose. "It's far too stuffy for me indoors. And partying's not half so fun as rolling in the hay–ay–ay!" So they fed him with oats and hay and barley-mead bran, with a nosebag of apples for afters. Then making sure he was cosily bedded in blanket and straw, they left him well settled in the woodshed.

As he stooped to enter Ifflenook, Cuppicks caught his antlers up in the hanging sign above the door.

"Oops!" said Ifflepaw, untangling him. "I'm afraid an ifflesnug's not made for umbelopes, m'dear. Take care."

A cheery scene awaited them inside. Song and dance was already under way. A good log fire crackled up the chimney. Its flames reflected warmly on the brass and copperware warming pans and hanging mugs. It flickered on the fancy plates upon the walls and kitchen dresser tops. Lighted oil lamps hung overhead from low beams. And among bunches of dried herbs and strings of onions, three piebald pigger-mice were hanging upside down by their tails from hooks and chatting merrily.

Around the oval roundy-room were tall brown pots containing teasels, rushes, and pussy-willow wands, which stood beside the windows, now curtained for the night. On either side of the hearth were two old-fashioned fireside seats for two, with high backs. On one of these two meadow-pogs were sitting, with a tree-pog and a few froaks perched on top. A wim-wom with a mouth organ sat opposite, together with an ifflepinn playing on a jaw harp.

Some river-pogs sat on the hearthrug, playing flutes of reed and pogarinas (which were little balls of clay, with spouts to blow and finger-holes to let the flow of music out). It was a lively country tune and the mouselings and wim-woms were dancing on the wincing wooden floor. Other busy animals were bustling to and fro and the table in the ifflesnug was nearly laid. Most of the meal had been made at froakrise in the early morning, and the pies and pastries only need warming up.

Erf and other froaks were jumping in and out of water-buckets here and there, to stop their new-grown skins from drying out. Grubbin Hawkweed was sitting up out of the way on Ifflepaw's Hat Trunk by the door. He was shyly plaiting the end of his tail and trying not to be noticed. Above his head, a scurry of eavesdroppers twittered excitedly in and out of a hole in the ceiling, beneath the bedroom floor. There were even two on top of the longcase clock, peering all agog at the goings on through the holes in its carven crown

Some of the children were squabbling behind a chair. A young wim-wom and a noisy oik had picked up Plumkin's precious *Legends* book. They had unclicked the clasp-lock and were riffling through the pages. Unable to agree on what to see, a squalling tug-of-war tussle had started up. Ifflepilum came in from the kitchen with a trayful of drinks.

"Oi! Hey! Hands off! Stop that!" he cried. Swiftly setting down the tray he hurled himself angrily into the fray. "Give it to me! It's mine!" he shouted, lashing out on every side. He roughly snatched the book away. "You leave it alone! It's mine, I say!" Then all the wim-wom's children—Bibbetty, Bobbetty, Boo, and Hoo—began to howl.

"What the Merryvale is going on?" demanded Mumkin, poking her head around the door. "Oh, Plumkin! Can't you even share things with your friends? Now where's your heart in that? Let them see it if they want."

"No I won't! They'll only mess it up!" cried Iffleplum as he ran upstairs with it to his room. "It isn't fair! It's *my* book! I'll do with it what I want!"

"Iffleplum! I'm ashamed of you!" called Ifflemother up the stairs.

"Well, I don't care!" yelled Iffleplum as he stuffed his book beneath the pillow of his bed. But he did care, all the same. He sat there glowering sulkily. He cared a lot: for his eyes and nose in the mirror were much too red. And now he felt how badly his heart was beating in his breast.

"Oh no! Not again!" he groaned. "I try to be good: I *only* do! Oh, elfin-heart, please don't go away! It isn't fair! It's not easy to use you in the way I should." He cupped his hands across the fluttery feeling in his chest. His elfin-heart felt dithery. And for a while, he waited anxiously. But soon his breath grew calm again and his elfin-heart grew still. He wiped away a tiny tear that trembled on his eye, then tried to kindle a feeling of kindness in his elfin-heart, before he went downstairs again.

But even so, he left the *Legends* book where it was.

When his nose was still a shade too pink, he slipped back down to the kitchen with a surly, but a shameful face. "I'll read it to them later on," he said gruffly, "before they all go home to bed." Then mother Mumkin smiled again, and clipped his ear and scuffed his head. He followed her into the ifflesnug, where Cuppicks was warming his hands around a stewpot hanging over the fire. "Oho! And what's this nosesome farm-house brew I smell in the cooking-pot?" the umbelope said.

"It's a vegetabubbley stew, with mint and fresh spring onion greens," said Ifflemother. "And here's a favourite umbelopely dish of cabbage-pie, big Momma Wim-Wom made, especially for you!"

"And pondweed jelly tarts—hooray!—and munchy marsh-mallowgolds for froaks!" cried Erf to his friends, as they hopped about and burped in glee.

"And here be crusty cottage loaves and cheese," said a meadow-pog, setting down a trayful on the table. "And golden beet-and-onion pasty pies, all run upon with cheesy sauce and herbs. Fine fodder that be for field-folk!"

"And bottles of Old Blackberry Brew and Strawberry Wine!" said Cuppicks warmly, inspecting the labels. "By froaky, Ifflepaw; that's very fine." And he sat down happily to write a list of all the goodly things in his notebook for reading on a rainy day, as is the way with umbelopes.

Old Ifflepaw in a pink-paper party hat, proposed a toast to Wossul and the Piper of the Spring. Then everyone tucked in to the supper heartily, pulling crackers, playing the fool and cracking jokes. By the time the mince-pies and the hot buttered scones came round, dripping with honey, even Grubbin Hawkweed had begun to feel filled with the warm glow of ummal-animality.

By now the lanterns were growing dim and the fire was burning low, but everyone was too full to bother turning up the wicks or putting on another log. The mouselings lay all in a full-bellied heap on the hearthrug. Most of the froaks were floating lazily in their lukewarm water-buckets beside the table. Iffleplum was happily running his finger round the ruins of the trifle and rolling it in cake-crumbs. And all the others lay about upon the floor, or sprawled contentedly in their chairs, basking in the ember glow. The room was snugly warm and dim.

Outside, an evening breeze had sprung to life and scrabbled at the windows trying to get in. Poppa Wim-Wom idly drew back the curtain and peered out into the night. He caught his breath and jumped back with a sudden cry of fright. His stool went spinning over. Through the window came a ghastly light into the room.

"The moon!" the wim-wom cried. "The moon! It's blue!"

They all leapt to their feet in amazement. Above the trees the moon was full. It glittered with a baleful blue light through the diamond-lattice windowpanes. A shudder rippled through the room, and they clutched each other with a fearful awe.

A sudden *BAM! BAM! BAM!* beat boldly on the wooden door.

The mouselings shrieked and scattered in confusion. *BAM! BAM! BAM!* the doorboards shook. A lantern crashed and tinkled to the floor. The longcase clock broke into chime and wildly donged out thirteen times. A flurry of eavesdroppers eeked and yittered in the rafters. And beyond the door a gritty voice cried out, like a whetstone rasping on a blade: "A Sooth! A Sooth!" and Plumkin's heart went pitter-pat!

"By froaky! That sounds like a Soothsayer!" said Cuppicks. He strode to the door and flung it open. A breath of chilly air flowed in and a ragged shadow flitted to the doorstep, black against the blueness of the night. The ummals stood there stricken dumb. On the threshold in the eerie light, they could just make out a squat and shaggy creature clinging to a knaggy stick, its eyes no more than slits.

Owleyes Astronomo had come!

"That's him!" whispered Iffleplum hoarsely. "The storm-pog from the hills." He clutched at the conker round his neck, as was his habit when something troubled him.

"Here we go, then," muttered Grubbin glumly to himself. "Jolly, jolly. Fun and frolic. Had to happen of course."

The Soothsayer swung himself over the threshold on his staff and everyone stepped back. His large hypnotic yellow eyes broke open in the shaggy hump and glared about the room.

"The time is nearly nigh, forsooth" said he. "Astronomo Scragmire doth want his dues. Once in a Blue Moon we do get it right. And we get what we want—tonight!"

"And what is that?" said Cuppicks curtly, with a wrinkled brow.

"If it's fireside and food you want, old friend," said Ifflepaw, "then welcome in: no hungry stranger stands outside the door of the home of an ifflepinn."

"Ne'er fire nor food may feed the hunger of our bones!" said Astronomo. He pointed his staff at Iffleplum. "The youngling there hath promised us far finer fare. His elfin-heart is forfeit for ourself, see—young Sriffleplum hath promised us—since our goodly self hath saved him from the feary faery-ring."

"Stuff and faery nonsense!" snorted Cuppicks. "From what I understand, it was nothing but by accident that you fell in the ring! And I'll warrant, it was no-one but the Piper of Spring *himself* who released him from the spell."

"What? Lies! All lies!" screamed the storm-pog, thumping his staff on the floorboards in sudden rage. "'Twas us! 'Twas us! Ourself it was! Leaping to save the lad, we fell!" He shook his knaggy stick at Iffleplum, half hiding at his mother's side. "Hemlock and Ratsbane! Thine elfin-heart is forfeit anyway! Goest thou back against thy word, thou tricksome wretch?"

"You had no right to ask of such a thing," said Cuppicks sternly. "There's nonesuch written in the Elder Lore. Therefore you have no errand here, my lad—so now begone!"

"Ah, begone is it? So *that's* the way it is! What knoweth a scribing umbelope of Elder spells? For also in the Lore 'tis writ: Thou shalt not break a promise made!—especially to

68

Astronomo! Upon our goodly self you cry 'Begone'! Well, we shall see who doth bewend his way." He turned on Iffleplum again. "Thou'lt pay for this, poltroonly boy! For now the storm-pog's curse is on! Be ware, Oathbreaker! Be thou ware!" He turned sharply and fluttered through the door.

Outside, he whirled around once more to face them. Clutching his knaggy staff with one hand and a long-toed foot, three times he rapped upon the flagstones of the garden path.

"So! Horrid pogs it is!" he cried. His hand waved strangely in the air and he began to mumble some incantation of Out-Landish words beneath his breath. Then loud enough for all to hear he hissed:

> *"Beware! Beware! I say—be ware!*
> *For now the storm-pog's curse is on!*
> *A Blue Moon's blight be on you all*
> *Yet ere this fearful Day of Froak is done!*

> *Beware! Beware! I say—be ware!*
> *For little ifflepinns shalt rightly rue*
> *Their broken promise made—*
> *For hooving hoary Horses of the Night*
> *Astride with shadely Gropes*
> *Ride out at Nine!*
> *And there shalt be no place to hide,*
> *Should little folk be not abed*
> *And dreaming deep,*
> *Ere strikes the chime,*
> *When the nightly Nine-of-the-Clock Horses glide:*
> *For the Mares of Night come galloping,*
> *Come galloping, come galloping,*
> *When daemon Dhârkäsü ride.*

Upon the wings of wind they fly,
The Shadowfolk with gropely sacks;
Therefore thyself be gone, buffoonly boy!
For since thine elfin-heart is held
Within the spell of wanderlust,
There's nought can save thee now!
'Tis in the stars! And go it must!
To whom? To whom?
To Old Owleyes or to Shadely Gropes?
Or faery-fishers from the skies?

Beware! Beware! The time is nigh!
Beyond the clouds the Heartboat flies!
Beware the snary billowed Boat of Hearts,
Lest thou be taken by surprise
At starfall,
When the whirling winds arise.
For then, besides,
Thine eyes shalt see
The winding Worm of Waters rise—
And the Mares of Night come galloping,
Come galloping, come galloping,
When daemon Dhârkäsü ride!

Beware! Beware! You all inside!
And heed no howl in windy gloom—
But cloak and cowl, eye, ear and jowl
Fair warning foul
I give—be ware!

The storm-pog's Sooth is said and done!
Sooth said—Away!
Beware! Yeee–hey!"

—and with a fiendish glee, he cackled off through the bare and ghostly plum trees of the orchard, flapping wildly in the wind like a ragged bat.

Part the Sixth

The Mares of Night

Of Ümmûârkon and of umbelopes:
in which Iffleplum hears more of the Mares of Night
and meets two frightful uninvited guests—the Gropes!

uppicks slowly closed the door and sat down wonderingly. "Jolly, jolly, there he goes," said Grubbin Hawkweed gloomily, breaking the silence. "Told you so. Couldn't last. That's what comes of asking a Mufflewump to a party. *I* shan't get invited again."

Iffepaw moved over to a fireside chair, opposite the umbelope. "Well, my hat! What do you make of that, Cuppicks?" he asked.

"A bit too much barley-mead if you ask me!" quipped a meadow-pog with a grin.

"Or not enough!" said another and raised a laugh of relief. "Come you now, Old Iffepaw! Let's broach another keg! We need a spot o' merry-juice after that tomfoolery!" And everyone agreed.

"Stoke up the fire then," said Ifflemother, "and let's fill all the lamps. If others get the table cleared, I'll sweep away the bits. It's lucky that the oil

71

was gone before the lantern broke or it might have set the house alight."

She bustled in and out and set them all to homely tasks to soothe away their fright. "Get you up, you lazy lot! Put your paws together now! And when you've done, there are muffins for the toasting fork and butter's by the honeypot. And I've a crock of toddy-juice a-mulling on the stove: enough and more to set blue-moony eyes ashine again, as like as not."

They set to with a will and soon the pots were whisked away and washed. The mulled merryjuice was handed round as well as "Winter-Warm"—a fruity drink for all the tots.[7] After a bowl or two, an over-merry meadow-pog began a rollicking rustic song and before long the party was in full swing again. Old Owleyes' upset seemed forgotten: but not by Iffleplum.

*

When the music and the dancing started up again, Iffleplum crept quietly away upstairs to his room. He was feeling apprehensive and alone. The moon was shining with its aweful blueness through his bedroom window. He stood and stared at the ghostly underwater-looking world outside. The tree-boughs bobbed and scrabbled in the wind like clutching spindly fingers. He shuddered.

The wind was rising now and softly moaned about the house. It was a very lonely sound. And the moonshine made the landscape creepy. He began to feel as he did in the faery-ring, when the groping creatures came to him.

He dropped to his knees beside his bed. Hurriedly feeling under his pillow, he found his book of *Legends of the Isle of Ümmulon*. He pulled it out and clasped it to his breast for comfort. "Oh, Ümmûârkon—Magic Mountain—help me please!" he whispered to himself. "There's something coming for me—I can feel it! Oh, Ümmûârkon—please look after me!"

---

7 *Mumkin's Winter-Warm recipe:* Melt half an inch of brittle liquorice in a pint of hot water (or break up a stick of liquorice-wood); add two star-anise cloves, half an inch of grated ginger-root, half a cinnamon stick: let simmer for ten minutes. Add a squeeze of lemon and some clover honey. For a more fruity flavour, add dried prunes, apple or blackcurrant juice.

He held out the book in front of him. As usual, the picture on the cover gently glowed. It showed a pale, pastel-coloured painting of the mighty mountain—Ümmûârkon—shining softly in the dark.

"That's dwemmer-work, that is!" Turnbuckle had told him when he gifted him the book. Three years ago, or more, the kindly old river-rat had come sailing down the Elventear; from somewhere far away he called the "Back of Beyond". He had met Ifflepaw in Merry May, who invited him to stay awhile at Ifflenook.

It was he who taught Ifflepaw the astonishing art of snortling smoke down through his nose, by sucking on a hot pipe full of herbal-weed; and left him with a bag of seeds so he could grow his own. The villagers were all amazed to see the trick, for they thought that only dragons could make a chimney of their nose.

Then just before he sailed away, to seek the Silver Sea, old Turnbuckle had given his Captain's cap to Ifflepaw (for his collection); and a little chest of drawers filled with fragrant spices from hot lands faraway, for Ifflemother; and he left the ancient *Legends* book for Iffleplum.

"What's Dwemmers?" he had asked.

"Ah! Dwemmers are a magic race: a rare old breed," said Turnbuckle. "They're a silvery-skinned, fair-hearted folk with flaxen hair; halfway between the Ühmen-folk and Elves. For once upon a while, when the world was young, the Man-kin and the Elven-folk walked hand in hand. But nowadays all lands are bordered round, and kins estranged, and Elves and Men have gone their separate ways. Now Elven-kind has been forgotten in the mind of Man, or spoken of as little faery folk. A sorry shame it is: for the High Elvene are now rarely seen, and Men grow more in every land, while the Dwemmer-kin grow less and less. That's why they are known as 'dwemmers'—being but a fading folk. For to dwindle, or 'to dwem'—means 'to fade away' in the language of the Dwemmer-men.

"Anyway, 'tis them who made this book, with elvish arts and magicraft. You see these snow-capped peaks in the bottom of the picture there? That's where they live: way up in the faery-mountain land of Lün—the 'Mountains of the Moon' they're called. Yet even as they soar so high, they look less than a row of molehills—as you can see—beside the majesty of the mightiest mountain of the world—Ümmûârkon the Unbelievable!—rising up behind them forever to the sky!"

*

Iffleplum had been enchanted from the start. There was certainly some elvish magic in the making of the book. For sometimes when he looked upon the scene, it seemed so real he had a fear of falling in. At other times the mists around the Mountain seemed to shift and swirl and all the colours changed. And when the daylight dimmed and darkness came, then stars would slowly start to shine in the sky behind the painted Mountain's peak.

These faery stars would sparkle on all through the night, until they dwemmed away upon the dawn, when all the morning colours changed again; although strangely, others never seemed to see such things. Yet some days, or nights, he would lose himself for hours simply gazing at the scene. The

Mountain always gave him comfort when he looked at it, or even when it came into his mind.

But now the eerie moonlight made the colours stark and chill. It was if he had turned towards a friend and found a stranger there instead.

He shivered. The moaning of the wind outside made him feel uncomfortable as well. Taking the book under his arm, he hurried back down towards the ifflesnug. But halfway down his way was blocked by Ifflepaw and Cuppicks, sitting with their backs towards him on the stairs. They were deep in talk.

*

The room below was once more fire bright and merry and a Daisy-ringle dance was going on around the table. As Iffleplum came slowly down behind the grown-ups, he heard old Cuppicks say his name. He stopped and listened wonderingly. It was plain that the umbelope and Ifflepaw were sorting out the meaning of the storm-pog's curse. Iffleplum was half-ashamed to listen in, but he could not help himself. He stepped back up a stair or two, intending to come down thumping with his feet. But when he looked behind, it seemed too dark and disquieting to go upstairs again. So he sat down where he was.

They were speaking loudly above the party noise, so from where he sat he could not help but overhear. In fact, he rolled his ears up and wedged them tight against his head to make quite sure. But then he learned some things he really did not want to know.

Cuppicks was saying: "Well, I don't know so much of elfin-hearts, Iffy my friend; although they say it's the sort of spirit of your heart that keeps you young and merry. But I'm sure if umbelopes had elfin-hearts they'd caper like the froaks in spring. And yet, you know—you promise you won't tell?—I still have a little caper now and then: when no-one is about."

"Oh Cuppicks! You *are* an uncommon umbelope!" laughed Ifflepaw delightedly. "I never thought your kind of folk would even think about such things."

"I'm sure they do, my friend. But it's far too undignified to speak about them much. One doesn't stop playing because one grows old, you know; one gets old because one stops *playing!*

"And you may not believe this Ifflepaw—but it's said in umbelopish lore—that there's a hidden valley faraway somewhere, where all old umbelopes go to dance before they die. When their agèd hearts hear an inner call—the *Yearnaway* we call it—away they go, leaving home, their towers and all, behind them. I'm sure it's true, for I feel it in my bones. For the *Last Dance of the Umbelopes* allows us to leap and bound as high as we've sighed for all our silly lives—and have never done: for fear of what other umbelopes might say.

"So maybe if I really try to keep my umbelopish spirits high, my elfin-heart might just come back again—and lead me to that secret place someday."

"I doubt it ever woke enough, to up and go away," said Ifflepaw. "It seems that elfin-hearts—if they exist—are hardly used and half-asleep in umbelopes. So I'm sure you've still got yours, or you wouldn't even want to play."

"Oh, it's living in Old Wossul's Wood and mixing more with ifflepinns that makes me feel that way. But it's true; we umbelopes are just playing at being grown-up: as I believe all grown-ups do. But everyone foolishly thinks the others are *really* grown-up. So we play the game of being adult extra hard, to hide our childish ways, because we imagine that grown-uppishness is a serious state of affairs: even though we are *all* children at heart. It's just that we don't allow ourselves to enjoy it."

"Then I suppose *real* heavy-hearted grown-uppishness comes only *after* you lose your elfin-heart," said Ifflepaw.

"Why—I do believe you're right!" replied Cuppicks thoughtfully. "So perhaps there's still a chance for me. But what about poor Iffleplum? If only half of what the storm-pog says is true, it seems he has to lose his anyway, come what may."

76

"Ah, but *what* may come?" asked Ifflepaw. "That's what worries me. What about those 'Mares of Night' he prattled on about? Those 'Nine-o'clock-Horses' that come galloping, come galloping—"

"Oh, tosh! Really, Ifflepaw! 'Night Mares'! Children's dreams and faery fancy, I should say. I've heard some-such nonsense things before, from travellers in the Out-Lands. It's a tale they tell out there to get the little stay-up-lates to bed by nine o'clock—or they say the Shadow-folk come riding out to snatch them all away." He pulled a fob-watch from his waistcoat pocket, peered at it and said, half-smilingly, "Well, we shall see; it's nearly nine of the clock already: long past little folks's bedtime. The 'Night-Mares' should soon be on their way. Shall we barricade the doors?"

"Oh well, perhaps the party noise will put them off awhile?" said Ifflepaw with a grin. "But there's something else I didn't understand. What about this 'Winding Worm of Waters' that he warned us of? What's that? My hat! You don't think that could be a Loathly Gload? A monster serpent from the—?"

But then a burst of laughter, cheers and clapping from the dance drowned out his voice and Iffleplum missed the last thing that he said. A moment later Erf came bouncing up the stairs. He had played the part of the ringled froak and now had broken from the dance. Hopping between Ifflepaw and the umbelope, he bounded up the stairs past Iffleplum. Behind him came a singing "Scatter-snake" of ummal-kin, all hanging on to each other's waists or tails and loudly stamping up the stairs.

"Oh come on Cuppicks!" yelled Ifflepaw. "Let's take a walk and have a *quiet* talk!" He squeezed his way downstairs. "Righty-ho!" called Cuppicks, stepping sideways down on account of his oversize feet: a painful problem with a Scatterpillar-crowd still stomping up the stairs. Ifflepaw wove his way through the dancers to the Hat Trunk by the door. Lifting up the lid he started rummaging inside. "I won't be half a tick," he said, "I only have to find my Walking Hat and my Talking Hat and we're away."

His wine-red, winter Walking-hat was already hanging on a peg above the trunk. He slipped it on over his head like woolly helmet and slapped his broad-brimmed hat for Talking-of-Important-Things on top of it.

Now he would know, if he forgot, to walk and talk together: both at once. He grabbed his coat and hurried out, holding on to his hat as a great gust of wind came whiffling in. All the dancers gave a shout and quickly slammed the door and shut them out.

In the confusion, Iffleplum slipped down into the cosy kitchen, as the last of the dancers went prancing up the stairs. He closed the ifflesnug door behind him against the party noise. With a sigh, he sat down on a half-filled grain sack in the corner, between the woodstove and the backyard door. It was warm and full of homely smells in there. A globe lamp was burning low on the kitchen dresser beside his head. He turned up the wick and wriggled himself comfy on the sack.

Now he looked awhile at Ümmûârkon in a warmer light. Then, satisfied that all was well again, he opened up his book.

Suddenly the longcase clock in the Ifflesnug began to chime. *Oh, my!* His heartbeat quickened in his breast.

Dong! Dong! Dong! went the slow old chimes. The cogs whirled round and clicked. He could even hear them through the door. And Plumkin slowly counted up to—*Nine!* The chimes stopped: and his heart did too.

It's nine o'clock! And now's the time! he thought.

He looked about with wild eyes. Outside the wind was rising with a fearful whine. It almost drowned the cries of the Scatterpillar-snake of dancers singing loudly round the rooms upstairs.

But then—he heard a far off sound that filled his heart with dread.

On the wind came the sound of galloping! of galloping!— nor was he yet in bed. His book fell from his trembling fingers to the floor. He dare not even move to pick it up. His limbs grew hot and cold in turns. And louder came the howling wind: and louder still the sound of ghostly galloping!

78

Now it seemed horrid wailing laughter came carried on the wind. It whined and cackled like a flight of broomstick witches through the trees. Or were there goblins in the air? Or bogles, spooks, and gobbledy-gooks or other scary things?

The hoofbeats pounded loud and louder in his head. And his head began to roar. The cackling wind rose high into a shriek. And the Mares of Night came galloping, came galloping— along the lanes and over the old stone humpbacked bridge and thundering to the door.

Then suddenly—the hoofbeats stopped!

For just a moment too, the wind had dropped: and all was still. But that felt far worse even than before.

A menacing rumble of thunder came grumbling from the mountains in the north. A growing terror prickled over Iffleplum.

Just then he heard the reassuring sound of the Scatterpillar dance come stomping down the stairs again. He shot across the kitchen floor, flung back the door and leapt into the ifflesnug.

"Hey-hey! The galloping! The galloping! Oh, did you hear the galloping?" he cried.

"What?" shouted Poppa Wim-Wom leading the line, "Oh yes! I guess we do sound like a lot of horses galloping!"

"No-no!" cried Iffleplum. "I mean—" but the wim-wom was not listening and went on jogging by. Then Ifflemother Mumkin came dancing past in the middle of the line. He grabbed her arm: "Oh, Mumkin! I heard horses galloping! Come galloping—outside! But now they've stopped!"

"It's just the wind, my love!" she puffed, "A-rattling the shutters, like as not! Or perhaps it's Dapplenose gone off for a trot. Oops! Look out! The leader's off outside!" Poppa Wim-Wom had opened up the oval door and led the line of revellers out into the gusty night.

"Oh, greeny-gripes!" groaned Iffleplum. "What now? *DON'T GO!* There's *something* out there! Oh, my! No one listens! No one cares! Something awful's going to happen now! Oh, gripes! I'd better get my book before it does!"

He dashed back into the kitchen, followed by the wind. The lamp flame flickered, almost going out, then brightened once again. Iffleplum bent down to take his book—then caught his breath.

He stopped in awe. His skin began to crawl. Suddenly he could sense a horrid "Something" lurking just outside the door. Snatching up his book he bolted like a scalded cat. Too late!

For the backdoor burst open off the latch and the night came howling in. The kitchen lamp blew out and plunged him into darkness. The door to the ifflesnug slammed shut before him. And Iffleplum was trapped! He whirled about. A cry caught in his throat. For there they were. Two huge and hairy Creatures of the Night stood stooping at the door.

Yes—they were Gropes all right!

In the dim, blue kitchen-window light, he could see their awful eyes and slimy snouts. Plumkin's mauven nose turned white.

A fear fell on his heart like a wet toad in the dark.

The Gropes were wrapped around with flowing cloaks of blackness, showing blood-red linings as they rippled in the wind. Beneath their baggy shapeless hats their vacant eyes glowed greenly-yellow, with a ghastly inner light. One was holding out a sack, and both had terrifying grins.

The creatures stood and stared awhile in silence. And Iffleplum stared back. He swallowed hard, in awful fascination, as their long black furry tongues came slithering in and out between their teeth, like snake-worms in the air.

He wondered if they could see him in the dark, for they seemed to be *feeling* for him with their tongues. The taller Grope thrust its leering head beneath the doorframe. Its eyes glittered mothily.

"Well—we've come!" it hissed, in slowly whispering tones.

"And time is running out!" boomed the other one, whose voice was strangely hollow, like the echoes down a well.

"It didn't even give us chance to knock politely, though," the tall one said.

"No it didn't, did it?" smirked the squat and heavy one. "Now why do you suppose was that?"

"It shows it's being friends with us, Baggy: can't you tell?"

"How sweet of it. We like that, don't we, Nightshade, love? I'm sure we'll get on well." He grinned up at the taller Grope, showing rows of sharkish yellow teeth. As he moved, his many double chins wobbled horribly, like hairy bags of jelly hanging round his neck.

"Wh–what do you want?" stammered Iffleplum. "Wh–why have you come?"

Baggyneck grinned. Stepping cautiously into the kitchen, he held out his grabsack in reply.

Iffleplum backed away against the snuggery door. "I–I'm not afrope of you Graids!" he stuttered. "I–I mean—I'm not agraid of *you Fropes! No! I'M NOT AGROPE OF YOU FRAIDS!*"

The Gropes merely grinned the more and nudged each other. They came a little closer, their black tongues wormling in the air.

"No need to be frighty, my darling," said Baggyneck, "we're fellows after your own heart! Heh! Heh! Heh!" and they sniggered oafishly at their own secret joke.

Iffleplum felt his heart go numb. The peach-bloom hair all over his body stood on end. The eyes of the Gropes glowed brighter then and their bodies seemed to swell. Their tongues wiggled wormily towards him.

"Who's got a wibbley-wobbly heart then?" drooled Baggy-neck, breathing heavily. He bared his teeth and waved his glistening tongue about. "We *taste* it! Don't we, Nighty, love?"

"We does, Baggy! So we does!" breathed Nightshade, foully licking his slobbery chops. "We loves it! Ooh! The taste of frighty hearts! It makes us grow! Give him *Sack*, Baggy my dear. Give him Sack!"

The bloated Grope thrust out the open bagmouth towards him once again. Now Iffleplum was seized with a sickening terror.

In the square of moonlight through the window, he could clearly see the grabsack heaving, as if it was alive! Its loathsome mouth opened and closed by itself. It breathed and swelled, wheezing like a bellows in a forge. Iffleplum's elfin-heart fluttered in his breast like a frightened butterfly held captive in a jar.

"Aha!" cried the Gropes, deliriously licking at the air. "That's what we came for! Ooh! It's delumpscious! Uh! Uh! Uh!—Don't wait for the Hearty-fisherboat my sweet—the Wraithenheart's for us!"

"Bag him!" hissed Nightshade. Baggyneck hurled the grabsack in the air.

Or did he let it go?

It seemed to leap from the Grope's hands like a monstrous toad, its mouth about to swallow him. Its soggy weight wetly fell on Iffleplum. Ugh! He beat it off him madly with his book and whacked it to the ground.

Just then there came the joyous sound of the *Oaky-Froaky* song around the side of the house. The Scatterpillar-snake was singing loudly against the wind and making for the backyard door. Iffleplum cried out in relief. He had forgotten all about them!

The Gropes swung round, dismayed, and looked about them in alarm. Their mothy eyes glittered angrily and then went dim.

Nightshade snatched up the grabsack from the floor, then fell back gasping by the sink.

The merry songsters had almost reached the kitchen door. Their happy singing filled the air and seemed to suffocate the Gropes. They gagged and gurgled in their throats with horrifying sounds. As they choked and staggered about, it seemed they were shrinking down in size again. A moment more and the partyfolk were dancing through the door.

Yes! Now without a doubt!—the Gropes were dwindling down to the size of Iffleplum or more.

With a wail like the wind, they flung Iffleplum aside. Wrenching open the snuggery door they fled through the house, growing smaller still as they ran out and vanished in the gusty night.

A blustery wind roared right through Ifflenook and blew the dancers down like skittles tumbling everywhere. Iffleplum fell under a struggling heap.

Then everything seemed to happen at once.

Part the Seventh

Away on
the Winding Worm

Of whirling winds and waterspouts;
in which Iffleplum is whisked away
on a terrifying and unexpected trip!

here came an ear-splitting *kerrump-kerrack!* from the
sky way down the valley. So loud it shook the house
and set the eavesdroppers all a-screaming in the
thatch. Pots and pans tumbled off the kitchen shelves and
rained down around them. A fireside chair blew over in the
ifflesnug and fancy plates came crashing from the dresser-tops.
Smoke and ashes billowed out into the room as the wind came
whistling down the chimney. They heard Dapplenose
whinnying in fright, but before anyone could get outside, he
bolted off into the Blue.

As they scrambled to their feet, Cuppicks came bounding in
at the door.

"Shut the shutters! Bar the doors!" he yelled. "A frightful
storm is on the way!" Then Ifflepaw came stumbling in
screaming, "Sea-serpent! It's a Loathly Gload! Look out!"

Cuppicks quickly dashed outside again, with all the others
close behind. Way down the river at the end of Merryvale and
high above the treetops of the Naze, a shining neck of whirling
water reared into the skies. "Oh, my umbels!" cried Cuppicks.
"Gload be blowed! It's a waterspout!"

84

"Oh, what's *that?*" screamed Iffleplum.

"A whirling wind from way out on the sea!" bellowed
Cuppicks. "Sucking a weight of waters up into the sky! Some
seastorm must have sent it spinning way inland between the
mountains right to here! Now it's sucking up the Elventear!
If it falls on us then—my, oh my!"

Now they could hear its awful roaring down the vale. It was
even louder than the howling of the wind. It had come in
screaming spirals along the river-road they call the Windy
Way, while swirling up the waters as it came. Wildly spinning
like a top it had broken from the narrow gorge. Then burst
upon the valley like a thunderclap—*kerrump-kerack!* And
thundering like an upward whirling waterfall, it lashed the
clouds and hilltops with its spray.

Ifflepaw was staring, open-mouthed. "Well soak my hat! I
see it now!" he said. "The Winding Worm of Waters! So
that's what the pogging fool was on about! It's the waters of
the Windy Way all wound into a spout."

"And it's a-coming this way!" said Granpaw quietly. But they all stood hypnotized, as if in a dream.

The churning column of water was indeed following the course of the river Elventear upstream. It came steadily corkscrewing up the Valley, wobbling wildly as it came. Suddenly the streets of Merry May were awash with a muddy flood as the raging fury swept on by. They heard the cries of many ummal-kin surprised. Now its roaring deafened them as it howled along the vale, swelling like a monstrous slimy serpent, swaying to the skies. Winding high above the hills, its awesome watery-whirling head hurled flood and flotsam for miles on every side.

Heavy droplets of murk began to fall among them all; but the watchers still stood where they were, transfixed. The wonder of the waterspout seemed to hold them in its spell. But now the wind was growing wild and began to buffet them about. Another minute more and the whirl would hit the Naze—the neck of land on which they stood. A falling glob of sludge suddenly struck Ifflepaw's wide-brimmed hat and splattered everywhere.

"Thank heavens I got the washing in," said Ifflemother, as huge dollops of muck and water rained heavily all around them.

"'Soak my hat!' I said!" cried Ifflepaw. "And so it has! No wonder, when I've got the wrong one on! I'd better find my Dealing-with-Disasters hat!" He dashed back into the house, yelling as an afterthought: "Run for your lives!"

Mouselings, froaks and wim-woms, fled shrieking in all directions.

"Come back!" bawled Cuppicks, but they were too far-gone to pay him any heed. He turned and bounded for the house, crying, "Upstairs! Everyone! Quick!"

They all rushed back indoors: except Iffleplum.

He stayed where he was, watching the spout with widened eyes. Somehow he had the strangest feeling that it was coming especially for him. Its screaming, gleaming, twisting tower of darkness seemed to fill the sky and blotted out the baleful blue moon and the stars. Its roaring filled his mind with numbing dread.

And over all—again!—the sound of ghostly galloping, of galloping, of galloping, still echoed in his head. He stood stock-still and stared at the spout with dreamer's eyes, half-stunned at its immensity.

"Plumkin!" screamed Ifflemother, rushing out and yanking him off his feet. His book fell spinning to the ground. But she dragged him quickly to the house. Inside, Old Ifflepaw had pulled the Hat Trunk closer to the porch light. He was frantically rummaging in it for his Dealing-with-Disasters hat.

"No time for that!" cried Cuppicks, as he herded everyone upstairs.

"Oh come on Cuppicks! You know quite well that something worse than terrible will happen if I go without my hat!" objected Ifflepaw. "And since we haven't had anything like a disaster in a long while—well, not what you might call a *real* disaster—my Sou'wester's on the bottom, underneath all the other hats. And I've just got to get it out, or I won't feel right—" But Cuppicks grabbed him by the arm and hustled him swiftly up the stairs.

"But wait!" yelped Ifflepaw. "I'm lost without my hat! Like an umbelope without his lists—"

"Oh, my *lists!*" cried Cuppicks in horror, dashing down to retrieve them from the mantelpiece.

My book! thought Iffleplum. *It might get swept away! I'll never see the Magic Mountain any more!* His book was calling him. Quickly eeling out of Ifflemother's grasp he dashed back down the stairs. Jumping over the pile of hats he bolted out the door.

Oh, there it was!—faintly glowing in a flowerbed. He grabbed it up and turned to run. Too late again! A fearful roaring filled his head.

The waterspout was there!

With a tremendous *Thwack!* a wall of water crashed against the rocky Naze, where the Ifflebrook joined the Elventear. A great wave of foaming flood came rolling over the woody hill, smashing through the trees and sweeping all before it. Another roaring water-bore came storming up the Ifflebrook. Its swiftly rising tide was swallowing up the streamlet like a gorging monster swelling at its sides. Over-bursting its banks it swirled up through the plum trees of the orchard and raced towards the house.

Iffleplum ran for his life, with the waters frothing at his heels.

Full tilt he tripped over Ifflepaw's pile of scattered hats. His book shot from his hands wide open into the Hat Trunk. Too late to stop himself, Iffleplum went tumbling head-over-heels straight after it. He fell on his face among the hats.

Then the whole house shook as the floodwaters hit the walls and poured in through the door. Panicking eavesdroppers flew shrieking from the roof or tumbled squealing in among the rafters. The trunk was lifted off the floor and dashed against the chimney wall. The lid slammed down on Plumkin's head and knocked him back into the hats.

Old Ifflepaw—now hatless—flung himself boldly into the flood. He made a grab for the trunk, but it spun away from his grasp and the current carried him off into the kitchen. "I told you so!" he gurgled, as the water swept him under the sink.

With a deafening din the waterspout went thundering by behind the Rise. The madding waters swirling round its roots rose up and over the lower slopes and came rushing down to Ifflenook. A moment more and the roundy-house was the centre of a whirl itself.

"Oh, my poor garden!" groaned Granpaw as the potting shed was smashed to bits. Wild waters still swirled around the Naze and surged the wrong way up the Ifflebrook. It rose so fast that the deep-drowned humpbacked bridge was lost to sight in seconds. And on the current flowed, to where the land sloped dingling down between two birchy hills. And there the flooding waters poured away once more towards the Elventear and the wheeling waterspout.

As it went on by, the spout was strongly sucking up the waters left awash behind, and the sudden flood swept after it. As quickly as they came, the waters rushed back out of Ifflenook.

And with them went the Hat Trunk—with Iffleplum inside!

Before anyone could realize—he was off over the lawn and the hedgetops of the lower lane and speeding away on the crest of the running flood. Along the dwindling river-road the Hat Trunk flowed, beyond the reappearing bridge and through the birchy dinglewood. As the trunk was banged and buffeted against the trees, poor Iffleplum was stunned and battered in among the hats. But the softness of them all saved him from being really hurt: although he felt sick with fright and giddy in the dark. The trunk whirled round and round and sped out into the open Elventear.

Suddenly his stomach gave a sickening lurch. The trunk shot up and flung him down towards the other end. A louder roaring filled his ears.

Oh! Oh! I'm going down! he cried inside himself and clutched his open book for comfort, tight against his chest. It was only then he realized that he was sitting upright with his back against the *bottom* of the trunk. His eyes grew wide.

Oh no! I'm in the whirl! he cried inside himself again. *I'm going UP, not down!*

Without a doubt he was whirling up the outside of the waterspout!

Corkscrewing to the sky.

Oh my! he wept. *What happens when I reach the top? The spout will throw me off a mile high! And then I'll fall! I'll smash down on the rocky hills! Oh, Ümmûârkon, help me please! Oh, please don't let me die!*

His heart was pounding madly now, as if trying to get out. And the pounding water-roar thundered through his head. Like the sound of a hundred horses galloping, a-galloping, a-galloping—and he wished he was in bed!

Then the Hat Trunk spun into the air. His stomach turned a somersault. And his heart leapt up into his mouth. His head jerked up against the lid in shock. It flipped back wide and flung him out into the sky!

He gasped out loud in sudden freezing cold and fear. And with the gasp, his heart flew out between his lips. The book snapped shut! And his elfin-heart was trapped between its magic leaves.

Just then the Heartboat cast its nets.

A million pins and needles prickled in his breast. And a starry burst of blinding light exploded in his head.

His mind went blank with terror.

Then blackness came.

Part the Eighth

Breakfast in the Sky

*In which Iffleplum has a strange awakening,
with wonder in his head; and learns of the folk
who fish for hearts and feasts on faery-food in bed.*

Iffleplum slowly began to awaken, from a deep and refreshing dreamless sleep. He became aware of a gentle rocking of his body, as if he was a baby in a giant cradle. And all around, soft, slow, creaking sounds were in his ears, like the leaning of old trees in a windy wood, although no wind was on his skin. But the swaying and the soothing sounds were softly lulling him awake.

And slowly, as his mind arose again, his thoughts began to form somewhere inside himself, like figures looming from the mist. He tried to focus his remembering. Surely something strange had happened to him? And he wondered where he was. Was he under some enchanted spell—or had he fallen in a faint? Or was he dreaming in his bed?

Then suddenly it all came back to him.

With a rush of panic pounding in his blood, a nightmare mingling of memories came flooding through his mind. The tingle of the tree-deeve's scream re-echoed in his head—and his foolish jumping in the faery-ring! And then the coming of the Groping things—*Astronomo Scragmire!*—and the storm-pog's curse! And the sound of ghostly galloping—and the—the raging flood! And the Hat Trunk washed away—and its whirling up the waterspout!

The Waterspout! Oh my! he thought in sudden fear. *It flung me out! What happened? Am I dead?*

His eyes shot open wide. The brilliant brightness of the light of day made him screw them up again. But his brief and blurry glance had shown him sunshine flooding through familiar diamond-lattice window panes; although they had seemed so far away, like looking down the wrong end of a telescope.

I must be ill, he thought, *but I'm safe! I'm home again!* He sank back in his pillow, relaxing in relief. *I must be feverish, that's all—Oh, praise the Piper! I'm still alive! And it was all a nasty dream.*

But as he told himself these things, a sweeping sadness filled his breast. Something had gone from him it seemed. And now he felt the sorrow of its loss.

He could feel a huge, hollow hole in the deeps of his heart.

And then he knew!

It's gone! he thought. *My elfin-heart! I'll never be happy again.*

A sudden pang of grief bit into him. And he lay quite still as a silent tear crept slowly down his face.

Yet strangely, even so, he still felt snugly warm and safe. Although he ached deep down with an emptiness he had never known before, it was hard to feel unhappy or afraid.

At least—not here, he thought. And then the realization came; he was *not* in his own bed after all! His own bed didn't tilt and sway, nor did his bedroom beams creak all around him like a sea-sung lullaby. Of course! If he was lying in his own bed, the window should have been *behind* his head!

He slowly opened his eyes again and stared about in wonderment.

It was no longer as bright now as it first had seemed. Misty morning sunshine was falling rosily through *two* pairs of latticed windows on his right. Its light was casting dancing diamond dapplings across a warm and wine-red carpet-covered floor and over the silver-satin coverlet across his bed.

92

The bed was twice the size of his bunk at home and twice as soft and deep.

He was lying in a richly decorated chamber with curving walls, which arched above his head and narrowed at the end away from him, which made the room seem longer than it was. But what astonished him the most was a wondrous woven tapestry on the wall of the mighty Mountain Ümmûârkon—*exactly* like the picture on his book!

And there were lots of little latticed-windows on both sides of the room, divided in between by great gilded, curly-carven redwood beams, cleverly cut and fashioned in the form of rooted trees. They rose from the floor, arching over the ceiling with leafy branches intertwined and filled with all manner of curious carven creatures and birds. Many of them he recognized, but some he knew were legendary beasts. Down the middle of the room, two brightly gleaming brass lanterns hung from the bough-carved beams and swung gently to and fro.

Just like on Unka Turnbuckle's boat, mused Iffleplum sleepily. Suddenly his eyes grew wide and wonder gripped him once again. A boat! *Now* he understood the rocking and the creaking of the wood around.

"Where am I?" he murmured. "Am I awake or am I dreaming?"

"You are not dreaming," said a silvery voice as clear as the tinkle of a fountain in his ear. "And if you were? What of it? What is a dream but another way of seeing things without your eyes? That's when you see with the only part of you that's still awake, when your body-thing is fast asleep. But 'tis just as real as when thou art awake. Is it not so?"

"*What?*" Iffleplum sat up and turned his head. He looked over the top of the huge lilac pillow he had been lying on. Sitting on a stool beside his bed was a beautiful young elfin-like creature, with graceful pointed ears and shining eyes. She reminded him right away of a tree-sprite, but she was pearly-pale as moonlight and almost twice as tall as Iffleplum. And her eyes were not woody-deep and dark, but light as sky-bright-blue forget-me-nots in the morning mists of spring. He felt suddenly very shy and looked at her askance.

Her hair was white as winter, braided neatly from her brows and bound around her head. And two long, beribboned plaits with ends like snowy horse's manes, hung almost to her waist. She wore a long, soft, summery gown, all over white and gathered at the waist, with a silver thread and a locket-clasp in the shape of a tiny silver heart. Its wide and flowing wraithlike sleeves rippled mistily as she moved. She leaned towards him and laid a rose-pink pearly hand on his.

"Good morrow, Iffleplum," she softly said. "The name I'm known by is Çhelône. I bid thee welcome, Heart, upon the fair ship *Âhn-Ühm Òrôniæ*—as we call it in the Elven Speech. But in the Common Tongue 'tis better known as the 'Good Ship *Golden Heart*'—although many other meanings are woven in the Elven name."

"The *Golden Heart?*" cried Iffleplum excitedly. "Is this a ship? The *Golden Galleon* that's in my book? Where are you from?"

She waved her arm towards the tapestry. As her delicate hand moved in the air, the sunlight shone pinkly golden through her fingers, fragile as a seashell. "We sailed out from yon misty mountain faraway in the middle of..."

"From Ümmûârkon?" exclaimed Iffleplum, sitting bolt upright. "Then this is *really*—oh, can it be?—the *Boat of Hearts* of Ümmulon?"

Çhelône nodded warmly.

"Then it's *true!*" He clasped his knees and hugged himself for joy.

"Of course," the elfin maiden smiled, "you always knew it, didn't you?"

"Oh, I did! I did! I *only* did!" said Iffleplum. "But I never knew it was an Elvish ship! I thought it had a crew of spiteful snary-faery sprites, who stole folk's hearts away."

"Ah, that's only what the ugly-hearted say, who have lost the love-light from their own," replied Çhelône. "But it isn't true. We only catch the elfin-hearts of those who have left their body-things behind—or 'died'—as some folks like to say. Or, we save the ones let loose from dying trees. Or perhaps, the elfin-hearts that eased away from folk who never feel them any more. Or sometimes, simply those that go astray. We only harvest with our elven-nets the ones that come our way."

"But why are you collecting them?" asked Iffleplum. "What for?"

"Why—it is our work: 'tis what we are here to do. For the High Elvene—that is, the Wisest Elves they call the *Dævârkü*—have charged us with the task of tending them, until their time has come anew. So we are somewhat like your Barrow-wards, who take care of your food and drink the winter through, then give them out again in spring. And likewise you might call us 'Heart-wards', as we are only looking after the *ælfÿnühm*—that's 'elfin-hearts' to you—until it's time for them once more to go their way."

95

"Oh! But mine's gone too!" said Iffleplum, remembering. "I feel all empty now inside. It's gone astray. Do you think I'll ever get it back?" He bit his lip tearfully.

"That's not for the likes of me to say," the maiden said.

"Oh, but aren't you of the High Elvene? Aren't you an elf? I thought the elves knew *everything!*"

"Not everything," she said, "though wise and wonderful they are. But I can't really say that I'm an elf—"

"Then you must be an angel-deeve—to help me now I'm dead?"

The young girl clapped her hands to her mouth and laughed enchantingly.

Iffleplum blushed at her beauty and his nose grew lilac-pink.

"Nay—nay, little heart," she smiled. "You're far from dead. And anyway, how could you die? You would but drop your body off and take another shape. Just as a caterpillar seems to die inside a chrysalis, then next year wakes up as a butterfly.

"Why, we even have some few aboard this ship who have already so-called 'died' to those left living in the world below. But they have simply 'slipped their moorings'—as the Ârkühm says—which only means that they have gone from their old earthbound bodies into new ones, light as dreams. They eased away from flesh and bone as easily as sun-warmed solid sheets of ice dissolve in steam. And now they have left their earthly homes, we serve to ferry them to other worlds— the Worlds Within: to faery-worlds, or Lands of Light, like Ælvenhôlm and Dwêmòriæ, or other realms; where they may learn awhile new ways to be. Until of course, it's time again for them to change their shape and travel on: like it is for everyone—like you and me."

"Have you gone on?" asked Iffleplum, his mouth agape, "and dropped your real body off? Are you a lady ghost?"

Çhelône snortled merrily down her nose: "Nay—but seem I so? I still live lightly in the flesh. Pray, touch my hand and see. Not yet the other worlds for me. I may be pearly-pale in skin, but that is because the form I'm wearing for this life, is shapen as the Dwæma-kin. For we are silvery folk, unlike the

96

golden *Dævârkü*. But it means that this time round I'm *half* an elf at least. And half of Ühmen-kind. For in *Vâhl-Ümmulon*—the Common Tongue that is—I'm just a dwemmer-maid: if that means anything to you?"

"A dwemmer-maid!" said Iffleplum eagerly, "Oh it does! It *only* does! So you're half-human too! So they *do* exist! I only half-believed that human folk were true! Oh, I love the Dwemmerlings! Unka Turnbuckle said they made my book— Oh *no!* My book's gone too! I lost it in the waterspout! And with my elfin-heart as well." He grasped his conker and ruefully rubbed it on his downy chest for comfort.

The dwemmer-maiden squeezed his forearm tenderly, "Fear not for that," she said, "at least something has been saved." She turned aside and took a soft brown bag from a table by the bed. Opening up its flap, to his delight, she shook the book of *Legends* out onto his lap. "You can keep it safe in this shoulder-bag," said she, "and carry it about like that. Please young master Iffleplum, do take it as a gift from me."

Tears of gratitude started in his eyes. He hugged his treasure happily to his breast. "It's all I have left," he whispered. "And you can call me Plumkin—*you're* a friend." Suddenly a thought struck him. He riffled quickly through the pages, half in hopes: but deep down he knew the elfin-heart would not be there. But where the book had snapped shut upon it, he found the pages softly stained with rainbow-coloured watermarks and some parts of the print had gone. He shook his head. "Look what it's done," he said.

He stared at the stains awhile and then slowly closed the book. As his eyes roamed sadly over the cover, he felt a sudden awe. Looking up he saw the shining tapestry upon the wall.

"But it's the very same!" he said. He held up the book before him to compare. Both pictures brightly glowed with their own inner light. The only difference he could see was that the woven tapestry seemed as real as a window in the wall. He gazed between them for a while, which quickly cheered him up.

And very soon the wonder of where he was once more came over him.

"Oh, am I really on the *Golden Heart*?" He said excitedly. "Oh, let me see!" he jumped out of bed and ran quickly to the window. But a breath-taking glimpse of green and brown way down below was all he saw before the world went blinding white.

"Oh, oh! What's happened now?" he cried, as the room around was plunged in gloom. Golden sunspots danced before his eyes.

Çhelône laughed gaily at his surprise. "'Tis no more than a bank of cloud we are sailing through. The sudden burst of sunshine on its edge bedazzled you, that's all. We often sail inside the clouds in daytime, when we would rather not be seen."

"Who by?" asked Iffleplum.

"By those who shouldn't see!" replied Çhelône, wagging a warning finger not to ask. "Come on with you. 'Twill be some time before we are out the other side. 'Tis rather bumpy in the clouds. So back to bed this instant! Or I'll be scolded for a sorry nurse."

There was no more to be seen outside but a foggy whitish glare. And the lurching ship made him wobble on his legs. So reluctantly he allowed Çhelône to shoo him back to bed. By now the cabin had grown quite dim. So with a burning taper the dwemmer-maiden went around lighting all the lamps softly swinging on the beams. She then sat down beside him once again.

"Now, is there aught else you would like to know before I go?" she asked.

"Oh, Çhelône! There *only* is! There's lot's of things I want to know! Like are we *really* flying in the sky? I can't believe it's true. And how did I get here anyway? Where are we now? And where are we going to? And if you have my *Legends* book, what happened to my elfin-heart? And what about my folks and friends and things? And can I get up now and see the ship? And—"

98

"Oh, Ühm! Slow down my little skyrocket! Not so fast! You've had a busy night and need your rest. It seems your mind is already mending from the Mares of Night and terror of the whirl. You can thank the Ârkühm's Healing Heart for that: but your body still needs aftercare from shock. Just wait awhile and take your ease. I may tell you some of it, but you must ask the Ârkühm for the rest."

"The Arkoom? Who is this 'Arkoom' you keep on about?"

"Well might you ask," replied Çhelône. "The Ârkühm is the—the—" She waved her delicate hand vaguely in the air. "He's the Master of the *Ârkü*—the Wise Wizards of the land. Therefore he is the Ârk of Ühm—that is—what can I say? He is the Kingly-Servant-Sage of Ühm of Ümmûârkon—the spirit of the Land of Ümmulon. He's the *Âhn-Ühm Òrôniæ*'s Ârkühm-Mage: he is the Master of the ship. And he's *the* Ârkühm of the Age.

"He is—who he is: there's no one else quite like him. You will have to see him for yourself. I cannot speak of him." Then she grinned impishly. "He already says I talk too much: for 'tis why he left me here with you. But he will explain everything you want to know—and more. When he is ready, that is. Although he is often half in other worlds and mostly on a wordfast until wyning, so you may not see him until then."

"What's a wordfast?" queried Iffleplum.

"Oh, dost thou not do it then?" replied Çhelône, slipping back into her normal formal speech. "For all we dwemmers do. A 'wordfast' is when we take a rest from words. 'Tis our quiet time: when we curb our tongues from waggling, and try to still the thoughts forever turning in our heads. For then we listen for a while to what our hearts might say instead."

"But how can you do that?" said Iffleplum. "Hearts can't speak."

"Oh, can they not?" She looked at him with an eyebrow raised. "Sometimes a silent heart and smiling eyes, speak far more than words can *ever* say. As well you know: when you look into your mother's eyes—is it not so? Otherwise, without

99

a doubt, too many words and worries make our minds go round like whirling waterspouts! But when we listen to ourselves within, we can get to know that healing-feeling that a quiet heart can bring."

"Ah yes," said Iffleplum. "I understand. I can feel it when my Mumkin looks at me. And I felt it in the Wossle Wood, when the elfin-hearts of all the trees were growing warm to me."

"There! You see? When elfin-hearts can feel another's love, they sing heart-songs to one another, in happy harmony. For the elfin-hearts of everyone were Sung into life by the Song of Ühmkyn the Awakener—when all the worlds first came to be. And if we listen carefully, we can hear the Ühm-Song still singing on inside our hearts, to guide us on our way.

"We try listen to the Song like *this*—" Çhelône put her thumbs into her ears. She then covered her eyes, her nostrils and her mouth with her fingertips.

Iffleplum tried to do the same. "I can't reach my snout," he sniffed. "My fingers are too short."

"Not to worry," Çhelône chuckled. "Just thumb your ears and cover your eyes then. And listen for a high fine ringing sound."

"I can only hear thunder in my ears," said Iffleplum, disappointedly.

"Never mind, that's how it is at first. It will come to you in time. Listen long. Then underneath the thunder, you will hear that high fine ringing sound: first in one ear, then the other. And in the end you'll hear it in your heart. *That* is the *Song of Ühm* inside of us. It will keep you calm when troubles come.

"But if we listen not to the Ühm-Song—without words awhile each day—that's when our hearts and minds begin to go astray.

"So—as often as we can, we fast from words—the way you fast from food when you are ill. And now I had better go and do just that! Methinks I have said too much already for today. But perhaps you are ready now to break your fast since yesterday? Your breakfast's on the way." She rose and turned aside and pulled a silver-tasselled cord beside the bed. The far off tinkle of a bell could just be heard.

"Oh, but Çhelône—" persisted Iffleplum. "Please stay! What is Ühmkyn the Awakener? When you say that Ühmkyn is the Spirit of the Land—is Ühmkyn a giant ghost then? Does Ühmkyn live on Ümmûârkon Mountain in a grave?"

Çhelône laughed gaily in her lovely way. "Don't be such a dottykins!" she chuckled. "I said Ühmkyn was *the* Spirit of the Land—not *a* spirit! The 'Spirit' is the energy—the force—the life in everything! Like when we say a lively horse has spirit. It doesn't mean it has a *ghost* inside. 'Tis more true to say its elfin-heart is dancing to the Song of Ancient Ühmkyn the Awakener."

"So what *is* Ühmkyn then, if not a ghost?" frowned Iffleplum.

Çhelône smiled and shrugged. "What can I say? You'll have to ask the Ârkühm to explain—Oh, but wait! Oh, yes! I know a little story that the Ârkühm told, to help me understand. Listen:

"There was once a curious fish that swam around the seabed, asking everyone, 'Have you seen the Ôçhî-an? I've heard of a wonderful world called Ôçhî-an, but I don't know where to go to look.' The other fish thought he was crazy. 'What Ôçhî-an?' they laughed. 'There's no such thing. It's just faery-fish tale. Wherever did you get such a ridiculous idea?'

"The little sprat replied, 'But the wise old hermit-crab told me about the great God Wôh-Tah, who is everywhere. All creatures live inside him, in a world called Ôçhî-an.'

"'Oh, the hermit-crab!' they smirked contemptuously. 'His shell's cracked! Nobody's ever seen this Wôh-Tah he's always on about. We don't believe such silly stuff.' And they swam off mockingly, saying, 'Don't waste your time looking for it.'"

Çhelône cocked her head and looked at him enquiringly. "So?"

"But... but the fish are *living* in water," said Iffleplum.

"Exactly," said Çhelône. "They are born in the ocean, they're *made* from ocean and they *breathe* the ocean; they swim in it all their lives and then they disappear in it. So how is it they don't know that it's there?

"Likewise, 'tis the same for you and me and everyone. We live in the invisible ocean of Ühmkyn—the Sea of Ühm—but know it not. Of this, most folks are unaware. But 'tis little wonder, for no one really knows just *what* Old Ühmkyn is— we only know that Ühmkyn's there."

"Not even grown-ups?" asked Iffleplum.

"No—not even grown-ups," said Çhelône, "except perhaps, the Ârkühm. There are mysteries in the worlds that even grown-ups have no answer for. But dive deep into your heart and you can *feel* Old Ühmkyn there. You might say that Ühmkyn is the elfin-heart of everyone, as well as Ümmulon— and *all the worlds*—for the Song is everywhere!

"Although, some say The Mountain—Ümmûârkon—is Ühmkyn's Elfin-heart made visible—for all Ühmkyn's power seems to come from there. In spring Ühmkyn makes the Mountain *Sing!* When the wondrous Hornsong-sound resounds from caverns deep inside the unseen misty Mountain's peak—then, all over Ümmulon, all growing things awaken to the Song. The woods grow buds and fresh new grasses green the land. Its music thrills us from our toes and fills our elfin-hearts with joy.

"So the more we let the Ühmsong sing inside ourselves, the more we feel that we *belong*—in Old Ühmkyn's family. And— my goodness!—Plumkin! With such a name, you must surely be the kin of Ühm! For if you say it slowly—'tis *Plühmkin*— is it not?"

"Hoo!" hooted Iffleplum in wonder. And his heart began to beat with gentle joy. Then his brow wrinkled in perplexity. *But*, he thought, *we can hear the Hornsong too, in Ælfÿlon. How can it be?*

Before he could pose a question to Çhelône, he was interrupted by a soft *rat-a-tat* on the wooden wall beside the bed.

Çhelône arose to answer it.

A panelled door swung open in the
wall. A merry whistling followed it.

In hopped a silvery, longhaired
tree-pog, carrying a tray. Its eyes
were hazel-brown and beady bright.
It beamed broadly as it set the silver
tray of goodies on his lap.

"Meet Master Tryllyon, the tree-
pog," said Çhelône.

"Good morrow, Tryllyon," bowed
Iffleplum, remembering Çhelône's courtesy. "I'm Plumkin—
and my tum tells me it's time for Wakes—as Erf my froaky-
friend would say."

The tree-pog pressed his long-muzzled mousy snout to
Iffleplum's nose, in the ummals of Ælfÿlon way. "Mmm—well
met, young Master Plumkin sire," he answered in a singsong
humming voice. "I've brought you then, your heart's desire.
Sweetbreads and mountain-berry tea, fresh curds and fruit—
as you can see! Walnuts, buttered toast, and cheese—so help
yourself and take your ease." He hopped up onto a bedpost at
the bottom of the bed and perched there, cocking his head in
a comical way and humming softly to himself.

Iffleplum felt his heart grow warmer as he watched in
fascination.

"Eat up!" Çhelône encouraged him. He took his eyes away
from the swaying tree-pog and tucked in eagerly. The food
was strange and beautiful to see. The curious fruits with
delightful smells he had never seen before: but they tasted
heavenly. The iffflepinn thought he could never have enough.

"Fare thee well: I'll leave you now," said the dwemmer-maid
and rose to go. "And when you have finished, take another
nap. You have not had an easy night and need your rest. I'll
come and see you later in the day."

"No, no!" cried Plumkin, with his mouth half-full. "Oh,
please don't go! Not yet! I really amn't sleepy now! I want to
know how I got upon the ship. And I couldn't rest until I
know! I *only* couldn't!"

Çhelône hesitated at the door. The ifflepinn looked bright and chirpy now.

"Oh, very well," she said and sat beside the bed again. "But as I told you how we harvest elfin-hearts, I thought you might have guessed. Knowest thou—I mean, do you know—when elfin-hearts are freed from people's body-things, they rise up to the skies, attracted by the stars?

"For 'tis said that when the world began, the Voice of Ühm broke into stars and filled the heavens with their light. And in the Making, many million particles of living light—we call the *lûmenü*—came tumbling to the worlds below. And there the stardust drifted into people's hearts like snow; and so it was that elfin-hearts began to grow. So now, when anyone ever lets them go again, they float away towards the stars from whence they came.

"And if we weren't there to catch them first, forever there they'd stay: filling all the hearts below with longing and with starry wonder. But, alas—from far too far away. As it is, there are hardly enough hearts still shining warmly in the world today. So we must catch as many as we can, before they drift away."

"Oh, I feel strange stirrings in my heart as you speak of it!" said Iffleplum. "It makes magic pictures in my mind. But if elfin-hearts so often go astray, how is it no one ever sees them go?"

"Ah, but they *do!* It's just that most folks refuse to see the things that they don't know. Without their elfin-hearts within, their hearts and body-eyes are blind. And they become so shrinkle-eyed, they'll tell you what you have seen yourself was nothing of the kind: until even *you* believe it wasn't so. And if they really see an elfin-heart, to them it seems to be a butterfly by day, or a shining moth by night; or perhaps a swirling leaf, or a paper bag, or wisp of smoke. And if at night the *Golden Heart* itself is seen, like a dreamy light that drifts across the sky, it is usually explained away as 'burning marsh gas' or 'balloons' by staid and stuffy umbelopish folk."

"Oh! but I saw *my* elfin-heart went it went out in the Wossle Wood."

"Ah! Then you were seeing with your elven-eyes! Your inner eyes, and not your normal ones. There are many things seen with elven-eyes that no one else perceives: and no one else believes. But all the company on board the ship has learned to see the elfin-hearts when they are coming in. Although the Ârkühm usually lets us know when elfin-hearts are ready to be released from beings in the worlds below, for he feels it in his own.

"And when elfin-hearts rise up in the air, we snare them all with starry nets of light and gossamer, spun specially by the *Dævârkü*—the High Elvene, I mean, for lesser elves are known as *Ælvenü*. Oh, Plumkin! You should see them go! When we throw out the elven-nets across the skies! Like starry rockets in a stream! Then folks below cry out: 'Look! Look! A shooting star! Another! And another one!' But little do they know that things are not always what they seem.

"Now last night, when the storm was wild across the valley of your home and the river rose in savage flood, then many trees were swept away in it. They loosed their roots and lost their elfin-hearts in shock. The sky was full of fluttering hearts when you lost yours and caught it in your book. We cast our nets the very moment you were flung way off the waterspout. And you were struck by an elven-cord and blinded by its light. But luckily, the star-nets caught you up: your book, your elfin-heart and all! So here you are. Now are you satisfied?"

"Oh! So you have my elfin-heart as well?" said Iffleplum. "Where is it then? I want it back!"

Çhelône clapped her hands across her mouth. "Oh, Ühm! I talk too much!" she said. "'Tis not so easy, Iffleplum. You will have to see the Ârkühm first: then ask the Umbelope of Hearts for that."

The ifflepinn sensed the sorrow in her voice and felt his empty-hearted pain come on again. But sulkily he replied, "Who's *he* anyway—the Umbelope of Hearts?"

"The Magister Umbelliferous is the Inspector of Hearts: the Warden of the heart-shoals. He inspects them when they are caught. And he tests them all to see what kind of hearts they are and where they are from, and what they are suited to. He catalogues them all and pops them into labelled jars, until they are needed once again. I help him sometimes when I can."

"Then what do you do with them?" asked Iffleplum.

"Do? We don't do anything. As I said to you, we simply keep them safe, in case the bodies they are from have a change of heart and call them back again."

"And how can one do that? I called mine back when it was close. But now I feel it's gone too far. How can I call it back?"

"Ah, Plumkin: that I cannot say. It is different for everyone. Each one must discover for themselves what is wrong with the way they think and do—and put it right—before an elfin-heart can come back home to stay."

"But—if they don't come back before you die?—I mean, before you drop your body off and travel on—what happens to them then?"

"Ah, then! That is a secret of the *Dævârkü*—but—*perhaps*—" she paused considering "—methinks, that maybe I can speak of it to you. They become a part of Ühmkyn's Magic Mountain Heart!

"There is a cavern hidden deep in the heart of Ümmûârkon's mountain peak, in which there lies a Lake of Light, illumined by the elfin-hearts who swim therein. We let them loose in there for the shining waters hold them in. And there they stay for just one lifetime to the day: unless their owners truly call them home again: for then they fade away, returning to the hearts from whence they came.

"But if the hearts that they are from, forget to call them back and 'travel on'—then by Ühmkyn's secret arts of Shepherding—they dwem away and vanish from the Lake of Light. Then once again they awaken in the hearts of newborn babes, or in those still waiting nine-months-and-a-day. And well 'tis so; for as I say, there is hardly heart enough to go around these days."

"And now, dear Heart, I really *must* get on." Çhelône said, rising. "You will meet the Magister, the Umbelope of Hearts, a little later in the day. I'll take you round the ship—I promise you—and show you his Alchemery, where I often work with him."

"I'll get up now!" decided Iffleplum. "I've nearly done. And I can easily cram my mouth and pockets full of figs."

"You stay just—where—you—are!" Çhelône said firmly. "It's very rare the *Golden Heart* picks up passengers from out of the air. Especially one whose elfin-heart hurls him high into the sky to visit us. So let's be sure you are well enough to enjoy the trip, before you rise. The Ârkühm has been singing healing songs by your bedside half the night. He firstly freed your heart from fearfulness and dark disturbing dreams, before you passed into an easeful sleep. And he says you should rest awhile more—at least until midday—"

"But—" said Plumkin, sitting up.

"And rest awhile you *shall*, I say!" Çhelône insisted, pushing him back down.

"But what about my friends and folks back home?"

"Hush now! He also says your friends and family are all quite safe. The Ârkühm's heart, you know, is like a crystal ball—he sees things in it far and wide with his inner eye: in many worlds at once. So no more need for worry now. Just snuggle down again and sleep again. Tryllyon will watch over you. And if you need to wash, or go, you will find a squattery and a bathtub, just through that other door beyond your bed.

"So finish up your food and rest until Tryllyon awakens you. You still have very sleepy eyes."

"I don't feel tired at all," yawned Iffleplum. "I feel a kind of secret thrill for where I am. Yet all the same, I'm sort of happy-sad." He drained his bowl of red-brown mountainberry tea, and then lay back yawning hugely once again.

Were it not for gnawing emptiness in his heart and the sadness settling in his bones, he would have felt contented now, as never ever, with his belly full of faery food. But even eating such delightsome things, gave him only half the pleasure now that he would have had before.

His lower lip trembled: "I've got all I ever wished for now," he sniffed," and I can't enjoy it any more."

"Alas! Poor Heart," said sweet Çhelône, "We say:

> *What use are vittles, health, and wealth,*
> *When your heart's an empty one?*
> *To own the world won't fill the hole,*
> *When your elfin-heart has gone."*

She hugged him close and kissed his cheek. His eyes misted and he blinked back tears. "Oh, jolly, jolly, there I go. I pity poor old Grubbin Hawkweed, if he always feels this way."

Suddenly the room sun-brightened once again.

The tree-pog started humming louder then and swayed around in circles on his post. Iffleplum began to smile again at his amusing face. Then the shimmering threads of the tapestry beyond the tree-pog caught his gaze. As the sunlight shone upon them they seemed to come alive. Tiny points of light like jewelled beetles went shuttling slowly over the surface, back and forth, and changing colours as they went. He watched awhile in captivated wonderment, as waves of sorrow, then delight, swept over him in waves.

In a while he came to realize the dwemmer-maid was singing some sweet lullaby to sooth away his tears, in tune with the tree-pog's hum. He yawned and wriggled deeper in the bed. Still watching the moving magical tapestry his eyes began to droop. The singing softly stilled to the sea-song play of the wind outside and the wincing wooden timbers of the ship. With a nod to the tree-pog, Çhelône stepped backwards to the door and slipped silently away.

And soon Iffleplum was fast asleep.

Part the Ninth

Off the Deep End

*In which Iffleplum explores the GOLDEN HEART
and visits the Alchemery, espies his elfin-heart once more
and jumps into a faery sea.*

t was past midday when Iffleplum awoke again. Once more the sun was shining, slanting sharply down through the cabin window lattices. The tree-pog was still sitting on the bedpost, as if he had never moved. He was humming a gentle lullawake[8]—awaiting signs of life from Iffleplum. As the ifflepinn yawned and stretched himself, Tryllyon hopped off into the anteroom to prepare a bath, trilling like a treeful of birds.

As soon as he had gone, Iffleplum threw back the covers and ran to the window to gaze his fill. With a thrill he realized that they must be miles up in the sky, for he could not even see the ground. Way below was a sunlit sea of clouds, like a giant fluffy bed. And all around the ship was a shimmering, like warm air rising from a summer road. It seemed as if the *Golden Heart* was floating on an airy and invisible ocean, which billowed and broke beneath its bows like the waves of a real sea. Light reflections rippled on the cabin ceiling as they might from waters rocking in the sun.

Now the tree-pog poked his snout around the door and called him to his bath. Half an oversize barrel made of yellowy wood was set deeply in the bathroom floor. Iffleplum stepped down

---

8 A *lullawake* is a loving song of awakening, for rousing sleepers softly: the opposite of a lullaby.

into it and the tub filled nearly to the brim. Tryllyon tipped a flask of aromatic essence-oil into the steaming water and soon the room was filled with all the fragrant flower smells of spring. As the ifflepinn luxuriously lay half-floating in the tub, all his trunk-battered bruises, aches, and pains, were slowly soaked away.

He rose from the water feeling much refreshed. Even the longing in his heart was much fainter now; but he knew that yearning emptiness would never fully go away.

Tryllyon laid out a mustard-coloured robe for him, humming the while: "*Mmm*—wear this well, young Master sire, for the air grows chill as we fly higher—*mmm—mmm*—" The dwemmer-coat was slightly too large for Iffleplum, having a hood which fell across his eyes when he raised it over his head. He stood and chuckled at the sight of himself in clothes, reflected in an oval mirror on the wall. The cloth was light upon his limbs, yet warm as heavy wool.

The tree-pog showed him how to clean his teeth with a chewing-twig that tasted half of mint and liquorice. Then he was more than ready to explore.

Tryllyon led him out along a short passageway onto the upper deck. As he came into the sunlight, Iffleplum gasped and caught his breath. As the tree-pog had said, the air was sharp enough to sting one's nose with freshness at the first. But it was not unpleasant out of the wind, and they were sheltered by the cabin bulkheads in the stern from which they had emerged.

However, it was not the sharpness of the air that made him gasp.

It was the ship!

It seemed larger than the Flowing Bowl in Wossle Wood from stem to stern. And the sky was thrillingly filled with a maze of ropes and riggings, flags, and full-bellied sails whumping wildly in the wind. Three pale-yellow pine masts seemed to rise higher than the tallest trees that Iffleplum had ever seen. Streaming forth from their tips were long pennants proudly wormling in the breeze. Great golden sails whacked and billowed above him, with many a tree-pog and pigger-mouse swarming over the rigging, happily hooting and trilling to each other across the spars.

The air was rife with the sweet-smelling timbers of the ship. It made him feel light-headed with their fragrance and his nose grew rosy pink. They crossed the poop deck, passing over ornately balustraded terraces and down two flights of steps they called "companionways", before they reached the main deck. Everywhere the wood was carved and polished, shining in the sun. Even the smallest scrap of metalwork was gleaming goldenly and worked with loving care.

All the gangways and passages were carpeted in the dark red-orange colour of the saffron herb and were silken underfoot. All kinds of oddling unknown ummal-kin were wandering here and there. Many dwemmer-folk with pearly skins and flaxen hair were passing to and fro about their tasks. And some, as Iffleplum was quick to note, were carrying trays of food. Following them with his eyes, he suddenly saw Çhelône in the middle of a crowd of curious characters.

She was sitting in a sunny sheltered spot, on a slightly raised dais between the companionways on either side of the ship. Beside her was a small circle of dwemmer-folk and assorted ummal-kin. They sat on cushions on the ground, gathered around a low picnic table on which Muncheon was being served. Enwrapped in a fuzzy-fine cloak of tangerine, Çhelône seemed as radiant as the sun. She waved and called him to her side.

Iffleplum fancied he could see a golden glow about her, reflected in the moonsilver faces of her friends. Or were they all glowing with an inner light? For even the ummals of the kinds he knew seemed strangely beautiful somehow: bright-eyed, but almost wispy as the deeves. He wondered if some of those who seemed to glow, were those who had left their other bodies in the world below. The very next breeze, he thought, might blow them all away.

Çhelône took him by the hand: "Come, welcome, Heart! How now? Well rested? How feelest thou?" But the warmth in her voice only echoed in his emptiness and made him feel it all the more. "Oh, wonderful!" he exclaimed. "But weepy too! I could burst with happiness if my heartache would only go away! How can I feel so plummy-tum pleased and greeny-gripe glumsome both at once? I can't believe its me."

"We understand," Çhelône said soothingly. "There are many among our Company who lost their wayward hearts when young and found them once again. Pray talk with them and take courage and good counsel from their tales. For fair companionship may mend what wildsome ways have cast upon the winds. Therefore, take heart dear Plumkin, and meet thou now our gathering."

The dwemmer-men and dwemmer-maids pressed their hands upon their breasts and inclined their heads in greeting. He felt as if their elven eyes were bathing him with love. He bowed shyly and touched his finger to his nose and then towards them all, as one might blow a kiss, which amused and charmed the dwemmer-folk no end.

Çhelône sang out the names of everyone: but names so odd and beautiful like their owners, he found it hard to remember them. Most of them were strange to Iffleplum's ears, like Òrafîn, Ümenel, Aurelîon, and Hysselîn; but among them were a few simpler ummal-names like Ruffkin, Snout, and Flairtail, belonging to some furry, white beaver-looking ummals of a kind he had never seen before

Among them were a couple of wrinkled gnomes in pointed hats, some woolly-whiskered sea-pogs, a beardless brownie, and a dwarf with rosy cheeks, his large red-ginger beard overflowing on his knees. Alongside Çhelône sat an elderly umbelope, in a russet-red waistcoat and a full-length fawn-coloured smock. His name was Fogdish: an ordinary umbe-lopish name and easy to recall.

*

Before they began the meal, they bowed their heads in blessing and hummed a drone, like a hive of happy bees. Now the midday Muncheon meal more than made up for missing his mid-morning Minch, and Iffleplum tucked in eagerly. A fair-faced dwemmer-man beside him asked him news of Ælfÿlon; for his land was well-known to the dwemmer-folk it seemed. It was once a land beloved of the High Elvene, they told him, from whence their kindred came in times of yore.

But Iffleplum told them that no elves were seen there any more. "Although," he said," the mountain folk do sometimes talk of shining strangers who go singing through the high woods of a moonlit night. But we think it's just a tale they tell to twit the valley-yokels down below. Ah no, nowadays nothing happens there any more. No kings or knights, nor

elves or dwemmer-folk. There's only tree-deeves now. And old
Wossul of the Woods, of course. But mostly life in Ælfÿlon is
just a bore."

The dwemmers smiled among themselves at this.

"Oh well—" said Iffleplum, "at least, it *was*—until yesterday."

"Well, 'tis certain something's happened now!" they said
laughingly and for the moment asked no more. Respecting
the appetite of an obviously underfed ifflepinn, they spoke
among themselves instead. Soon Iffleplum was lost in the
mysteries of "blocks and tackles over the mizzen mast or the
jib" and better ways to "pawl the capstans" and suchlike
sailor-talk. Happily this left him free to sample all the dainty
dishes set before him, with all kinds of amazing tastes he had
never tried before. A variety of many-coloured pastel shades
crept across his nose like shot-silk as he sampled every dish.

Little silver serving bowls surrounded every plate, in which
were salads, sweet creams, soft flower petals (which melted
like marshmallows on the tongue), all kinds of unknown
things and mountain fruits preserved in nectar wine. Beside
each bowl was a silver lid, with which to cover it, as a signal
to the servers that one had had enough; or else they would fill
them endlessly. Luckily for Iffleplum, he never noticed this,
until almost everyone had covered theirs.

At the end a golden jug was passed around and every goblet
filled with a drink like liquid sunlight sparkling. Its taste
brought tears to Plumkin's eyes for the beauty of everything.
Then a number of dwemmers began to sing. As the sunwine
went to his head, the rest of the meal, the talk, the jests, and
the soothing songs in the Dwemmer-tongue, all passed like in
a dream.

*

A sudden thunder of the sails awakened him, as the ship
turned slightly in the wind. A wonderful thrummelling sound
filled the air, along with the clack of blocks and screeling of
the pulleys overhead, as ropes ran slithering through them.
He raised his eyes and watched the canvas billowing.

114

Magnificent! The thunderous drumming of the sails and creaking masts were thrilling music to his ears. He gazed around contentedly and found himself alone. The picnic plates and table had been cleared away and the company had gone. A few odd folk were still moving about the decks.

He rose to his feet and stumbled unsteadily this way and that. The deck was forever tilting one way or the other and walking was not an easy affair. At times the great vessel bucked and plunged, riding the blustery oceans of the air as it might have done upon the sea. But soon Iffleplum gained the mastery of his wobbly sea-legs, or "sky-legs" as he thought to call them. And he tottered up and down, exploring all the different decks, the fascinating fittings of the ship and poking his ever-changing multi-coloured nose in all the corners.

*

In the middle of the main deck, his curiosity was aroused by a row of mysterious wooden machines all covered in canvas. Some were wrapped around with yellowing ancient sails. The only parts still visible were their thick wooden wheels and the platforms on which they stood. But peeking underneath the coverings, he found enormous crossbow-like contraptions mounted on the heavy trucks. Their mighty bowstrings were drawn back in readiness, behind long-handled throwing arms thrust tightly through pivots of twisted rope. Powerful weapons of war they seemed: except they were highly decorative. For all the wooden parts he could see, were finely worked with scrolls and curlicues, or sculpted in the shapes of fish and shells and other strange creatures of the sea and air.

He could not imagine the *Golden Heart* could be a ship-of-war, or need such strange things to defend itself. What danger could there be so far up in the air? He clambered up the bulwarks and peered gingerly over the side. It seemed a frighteningly long way down. His knees went trembly with the wonder of it. They were sailing high above a raggedy blanket of boiling clouds; but right below small baby clouds were floating by themselves like little puffs of smoke. At times, through the swirling sea of faery-air around the bows, he caught a dizzying glimpse of a landscape far below: the mottled green and browns of fields and forests and hoary-headed mountains looking from above like wrinkled prunes in cream.

Suddenly he gave a gasp. His heart leapt in his breast. For a moment he saw strange beings swimming in the hazy air about the ship! Wraithlike fishy-folk they were, with flowing hair and shining tails. They were surging and plunging like a shoal of fish, half-seen in the sea of dreams. But the shimmery airy-ocean broke and curled into puffs of mist—like frore-breath from a frosty mouth—and they were gone as if they had never been.

He gave a disappointed cry, uncertain now if he had seen them after all. He rubbed his eyes and stared on down.

"Nay, 'tis not the Sunwine you've been drinking, that makes you see your dreams," said a voice beside him. "It seems your elven-eyes are opening, just being in our company."

"Çhelône!" he cried. "I saw flying fishy-folk swimming in the sky beneath the boat! Mer-men and mer-maids too! At least I think I did. Can it be true? I read about them in my book." His nose now shining with a tinge of gold.

"Not quite—but almost so," Çhelône said smilingly. She winked and pressed a finger to his nose (which now was pink with pleasure). "There are, of course, the mer-folk living in the ocean deeps below: but those you see around the ship are called the *Khämmârkü*—the Shepherds of the Inner Airs—or maybe 'sky-deeves' to you. Sometimes they let themselves be seen, sometimes they fade and dwem away."

"To where?" cried Iffleplum, peering overboard excitedly. "Where can they go to in the air? Can you touch them? Are they real?"

"Oh, Plumkin! Have a care!" Çhelône restrained him. "Do not lean out so far! They are as real as you or me, in their own way. Or perhaps I had better say as real as dreams—for that's the stuff of which they are made. So of course you cannot touch them: although they might touch you. But you would only feel them like the wind or wave upon your skin.

"But seen or unseen, they are always there—inside the *Khämmârkäçh*—the Inner Airs. There are many other worlds in there you know; much finer ones, invisible to our normal eyes, though strange it seems. And the *Khämmârkü*—the sky deeves—live and work mostimes in a realm we call *Dwêmòriæ*—the Land of Dreams."

"The Land of Dreams?" queried Iffleplum. "Is that a place? A really one? I thought that was just a name for sleep, and we just dreamed in our heads."

"Then your head must be but wondrous large," Çhelône replied. "For when you dream of mountains, meadows, monsters, rivers and of seas—it needs a world to hold all these. Just think! When your flesh-and-bone body is lying in bed and fast asleep and dreaming deep: where are *you* when you find yourself awake and running around in another one? In what world do you suppose it is going on—if not *Dwêmòriæ*—the Land of Dreams?

"Our thoughts are not caught up inside our heads, like fishes in a net; they spread out everywhere. Not only thoughts and dreams, but all our *feelings* too! They float out upon the *Khämmârkäçh* and drift across the Inner Airs: no matter be they foul or fair. They rise inside our elfin-hearts and ripple out like rings of water widening everywhere. And every little thing we think or feel, goes rolling on, and touches every other elfin-heart it comes upon: no matter where. And each one reached, rings out again—like raindrop ripples on a pond— and sends our feelings flowing on, from heart to heart, through *every* world—including Ümmulon! And then they all flow back again, rebounding through Dwêmòriæ—bringing either joy or pain, back to the hearts from which they came.

"And that is the work of the *Khämmârkü*—they gather all the dreams and fancies we let loose upon the Inner Airs, and bring them back to me and you. That's why *Khämmârkü* in the Dwemmer-tongue means 'Shepherds of Dreams.' But they are also 'Heart-herds' too. They help us greatly harvesting the elfin-hearts, for they can catch them easily: even with their

117

hands! And then before they haul the nets aboard, they breathe upon the catch and all the elfin-hearts fall fast asleep."

"Oh! Where do you keep them all?" asked Iffleplum. "That must be a sight to see! Am I allowed?"

"Why certainly! I came to take you there. I promised you you'd see the Magister's Alchemery. Down in the hold we keep them floating in a huge glass tank. It's filled with a haze called *dævakhäm*—that's the name for 'elven-breath' or the faery-air you see that swirls about the ship down there. Although the Hearties—that's the sailor-folk—simply call the stuff the 'Sea of Dreams'. But anyway, it somehow holds-in the elfin-hearts, or otherwise they would float away. And there they swim, until the Hearties haul them out for the Inspector of Hearts—and sometimes me!—to try and find out what kind of creature hearts that they may be.

"Come on! If you can drag yourself away from trying to see more *Khämmârkü*, I'll take you down and show you round."

She took him by the hand and led him down deep into the belly of the ship. They passed many cabins full of fascinating things; ship's stores, the galley (oh, the cooking smells!), the chart-rooms full of maps and scrolls; the workshops with a glowing forge and full of busy dwarves and dwemmers hammering; and dormitories where curious members of the crew lay lolling in their hammock-beds. At length, down a deeper corridor, she paused before a richly ornamental door marked:

INSPECTOR OF HEARTS
ALCHEMERY
Pray Silence as you pass

Çhelône laughed mysteriously and a light was in her eyes. She put a finger to her lips and ushered Iffleplum inside.

The sight he gazed upon quite staggered him.

At first it seemed as if he had stepped down into an underwater cave. But then he realized it was a chamber of tremendous size. At its centre was a vast aquarium filled with

light, reflecting rainbow-coloured ripples everywhere. It rose
from floor to ceiling and higher still, for it passed right
through it to the deck above. Around the walls, and in many
bays, were row upon row of labelled jars, in which gently
glowing elfin-hearts could now and then be seen. For each one,
in its sleep, would flush with colour of a different hue, then
slowly fade and dwem away, and in a while again return to
view, like strings of softly pulsing lights.

But the greatest glow was coming from the tank, for the
misty *dævakhäm*—the elven-breath—seemed luminous. Beyond
the wall of glass, the shimmering shapes of elfin-hearts were
flowing through the sea of dreams like pale prismatic jellyfish
with fluid tails.

Globes of lantern-light also stood about the room, on tables
thrung from end to end with bowls and pestles, potions, phials
and bulbous jars, brass instruments, and strangely spouted
balls of glass. Higgledy-piggledy piles of ancient books lay
everywhere. From one of the carved beams hung a fancy
thurible of gleaming brass, swinging gently two and fro.
Wisps of smoke came curling out of it, scenting all the air with
a sweet and heavy perfume.

After a while they noticed Fogdish working at a table over
by the tank. As always, he was making lists and labels, half-
hidden by decanters, jars and demi-johns atop the table and
aclutter round his feet.

They were about to go and greet him when a creaky voice
nearby cried out: "Oh, fiddle-faddle! Not *again!*"

Behind a mound of bric-a-brac they found the Inspector of
Hearts himself. The Magister Umbelliferous was immersed in
viewing an elfin-heart through a large magnifying glass.
Without a doubt, he was the most moth-eaten and venerable
old Umbelope that Iffleplum had ever seen. Lace ruffles graced
his wrists and throat, and over his silken smock-like shirt he
wore a weathered waistcoat with a fob-watch on a golden
chain. His long lank, silvery hair hung straggling over the
velvet collar of his aged claret-coloured coat, in a very un-
Umbelopish way.

"Oh dear, dear," he was muttering to himself in a quavering voice. "This heart has paint in its ears! Another wretched artist. How very tiresome. Fogdish! Make another 'Arty-Heart' label: *'Bold and brash; but warm-hearted with it.'* I never know what to do with these tricky ones."

"Ahem! Ahem!" prompted Çhelône, clearing her throat noisily.

"Cough quietly, can't you?" said the Inspector of Hearts, not looking round. "Can't you see I'm concentrating?"

"I just thought you might like to meet our passenger: an ifflepinn from Ælfÿlon," Çhelône said brightly.

"What? What? An ifflepinn?" The Inspector of Hearts raised his eyebrows and turned towards them. "A real *ælfÿnpinn*? From Ælfÿlon? Upon my Heart: it *is* one! Bless me: what's it doing here? We didn't start with one. How did you get here my lad?"

"I—I came up on a waterspout and got entangled in your nets," stuttered Iffleplum.

"Good gracious!" mumbled the Inspector of Hearts. "Whatever next? Most extraordinary! Very confusing. Highly irregular. What if every one started—"

"And I lost my elfin-heart!" Iffleplum burst out.

"You lost your elfin-heart? Already? And you've not transmogrified? You've not gone on?" He turned in puzzlement to Çhelône. "He's not in the *Khämmârkäçh*, is he? Not dead? He seems like solid flesh and bone to me."

"No he's not! You daft old thing!" Çhelône said with a grin. "It's just that his heart and his head are in a different place."

"Oh, one of those again," sighed the umbelope. "Hmm! One of those. The jars are full of them these days. So young too. What a pity. What have you been playing at to do a thing like that then, eh? Hmm?"

"Don't know," shrugged Iffleplum. "But if you've got it; can I have it back?"

The umbelope looked up in surprise. "Bless your Heart, my boy: it's not as simple as all that. Perhaps the Ârkühm will know the way to—"

120

Just then a voice cried out above: "Hearts away!" And a hatchway in the ceiling opened up. A wide-brimmed crystal bowl of saucer-shape came swiftly down on cords. It was filled with threshing elfin-hearts.

Fogdish rose and grasped it with outstretched arms. He and Çhelône then tilted it and a cascade of heavy essence-fume and elfin-hearts went slithering over the rim and spilled into a shell-shaped pool below. The pool was made from one enormous scallop shell, all pink inside and set before the centre of the tank. The empty bowl was quickly drawn away.

Iffleplum looked up to see some dwemmer-Hearties looking down. They stood upon a walkway round the top edge of the tank, holding specially woven elven-nets for fishing out the hearts. Wondering how to get up there, he spied a spiral stairway he had missed before, which wound up from the shadows in a corner.

"New delivery," muttered the Inspector of Hearts, as he always did, slowly slomphing to the poolside on his great plodding feet: *slomph–slomph–slomph!* He scooped a heart-wraith from the pool with a circle of gold on a pearly stick. It spread across it like a film of soap on a bubble-ring. The umbelope trudged back to his bench and held it up to the light. "Aah, now look at this!" he cooed. "Now *here's* a heart! All frilly-edged like lace. Oh isn't it a pretty one? Who's a little sweet-heart then?"

They were startled by a small rude baby sound, like a raspberry being blown. Iffleplum looked quickly round for Erf. Then he realized the sound had come from the elfin-heart the umbelope had put aside. "Oh, deary me, Fogdish," said the Inspector of Hearts, "you'd better add another label to that Arty-Heart: put 'Warm-hearted' but 'With Complications' too. And bring another flagon of Elven-breath: not the green carboy, but the blue. It's high time we bottled this one off to sleep. Now where's my magnifying glass got to?" He rummaged on his desk, wrapt up in his work again, forgetting anyone else was there.

"I have to work a little now," whispered Çhelône. "But you can look around." She stayed beside the umbelope, preparing potions and putting things into his hands whenever he had forgotten what he was looking for.

Now left alone, Iffleplum soon turned away towards the glimmering wonder of the tank. But as he ambled past the shelves, the pulsing multi-coloured magic of the jars caused him to pause. Perhaps what he was looking for was there? He tried to read the labels and inscriptions. Some were in the elvish script, or *Dwæmavâhl,* and some were in the Common Ummal-tongue. As far as he could understand, the bottom rows were all of "stony hearts" and "hard-hearted" ones, their colours dark and dim. But just above were those of natural things; the elfin-hearts of vanished hills and megaliths, or of broken standing stones. And after these it seemed to be all those who worked with stone: such as the hearts of dwarves, and delvers of the earth, like kobolds, or trolls and gnomes, and even ghòrs.

The next row up (to his delight) was obviously the elfin-hearts of tree-sprites and of fallen trees, with labels he could read, like: "Oakenhearted", "Elmwraith", "Sycamore Sylphs (Assorted)", "Willow-wraith", "Beechensprite", "Apple Dæva (Blossom Sprite)" and so on, all glowing like a wood in spring. And these felt very good to touch. There were several shelves for animals and also ummal-kin, and even more for human-folk (marked "Ühmenü"). And higher up and out of reach, were others only written in the Elvish and the Dwemmer speech, or other tongues he did not know.

Not one of them said "Elfin-heart of Iffleplum".

But he wandered up and down the rows entranced. As he gazed upon the elfin-hearts; their coming and going, their dwemming and glowing, a dreamy feeling crept over him and slowly mazed his mind. His eyes went glazed. And like a sleeper, raised his arms and turned about, drawn irresistibly towards the tank. When his fingers and his rosy nose came up against the glass, he stopped, his arms spread wide. He stood there staring, hypnotized, watching the undulating shapes of elfin-hearts flow by.

Suddenly he caught his breath and realized why!

Before his eyes an elfin-heart loomed up against the glass. For a moment it was clear to him. It shimmered with a rainbow hue, but its heart was softly red, with wraithing veils on either side. The ifflepinn shook from head to toe. He knew it instantly! For the surface of the heart was flecked with dots, quotation marks, and little bits of print! By this he surely knew it for his own: besides the maddened thumping in his breast! Those marks! They must have come off when the dwemmer-book snapped shut! A strangled cry choked in his throat. The elfin-heart had swum away.

An overwhelming longing for it filled his aching heart.

He dashed back to the workbench. "It's there!" he cried. "It *only* is! My elfin-heart! My very own! I saw it in the tank!"

But the Magister was deeply absorbed in studying the frilly elfin-heart through different coloured sheets of glass. "Oh well, that *is* exciting isn't it," he said absently, patting Plumkin on the head. "What a bit of luck; we have it then. Well, we do get all kinds of them you know. Now look at this one for example; see how it glitters and glows through the violet glass? It's not very often—"

"Oh, please!" cried Iffleplum, yanking the tail of the umbelope's long frock coat. "Oh aren't you going to get it out?"

"What? Get it out?" the Inspector said. "Oh, don't you worry about that, little Heart: we'll get to it in time. We can't expect to find it in among the rest. And even if we did, there's no way we can give it back to you. We can't just—"

"I knew it! So it's true!" cried Iffleplum, no longer listening. He was madly desperate now. "You snitchy heart-snatchers! You want it for yourselves! Like Owl-eyes and the galloping Gropes! Well you can't have it, cause it's mine! It's *mine!* I'll get it back myself!" He shot across the room, dodging Fogdish who jumped up quickly from his chair, and in a moment ran madly up the spiral stair.

"Stop him!" shouted Fogdish, standing on a pair of steps, with bottled hearts in his arms. "Hoy there! Hearties, up above!" A dwemmer with an elven-net came running up and lunged too late, as Iffleplum burst out onto the walkway round the tank.

In one bound he leapt across the rim and hurled himself headfirst into the hazy *dævakhäm*.

Part the Tenth

The Master
of the Golden Heart

*In which Plumkin meets the Ârkühm-Mage
and learns the ways of Wayward Hearts.*

ffleplum was laughing long and loudly in his sleep as the others tried to wake him up. "They told me to bring you out on deck to freshen you," said Çhelône, when Iffleplum came round at last. He laughed uproariously at that, as if she had made a hearty joke.

He was lying in the bows, between the companionways, with a blanket over him and Tryllyon and Fogdish were kneeling at his side. The sight of their solemn faces set him off again. He thrashed about in merriment and hugged his sides. "*Ow-ouch!*" he groaned. "I ache so much from laughing. It was wonderful in there. Why did you pull me out? I felt as light as thistledown; like floating in the sun. And Oh, Çhelône! *They* were there! The Mer-folk!—the *Khämmârkü* I mean— the sky-deeves! All filled with light they were. And I was too! It made me laugh and laugh—I don't know why; it felt so good."

"The elven-breath, I guess," Çhelône replied. "They must have breathed upon you. That's the stuff we use to keep the elfin-hearts contentedly asleep when bottled up. It sooths the hearts all right, but seems to make all other creatures laugh."

125

"It *only* does!" said Iffleplum. "I'd love to take a bottle back to let old Grubbin Hawkweed have a sniff; just so he knows what loving-laughter's like."

"Oh, my greying umbels no!" said Fogdish gravely. "It isn't done. We mustn't waste it on frivolity." The ifflepinn gave another hoot at that and fell back helplessly, shaking with mirth. The thought of seeing Grubbin Hawkweed have a belly laugh brought tears to Plumkin's eyes. And he laughed again until he cried. And then he wept. His tears kept flowing down his face. For after being with the *Khämmârkü*, he realized even more the light inside his heart he had lost. "And I didn't even get it back," he sniffed.

"You cannot catch it with your hands in any case," said Çhelône. "You need an elven-net for that. And if you did— what then? What would you do? How can you put it back inside your breast again? You must ask the Ârkühm how it's done."

"Oh, I hadn't thought of that," frowned Iffleplum, "I thought it might just slip back in." He fell silent for a while. Seeing the ifflepinn was calm again, Fogdish asked to be excused. He bowed, hands over heart, and hurried back to his beloved labels and his lists. Tryllyon then took them up a flight of steps into the lookout post beneath the prow.

They entered into a cave-like chamber, like the inside of a mighty mask, behind the face of the gracefully fashioned figurehead, fancifully carved as a Mer-deeve maiden of the sky. The eyeholes in the great head served as open windows to the view. Her wooden body, pressed back upon the bows below, had a fish's tail of silver scales and her arms had rainbow-feathered wings, spread out on either side.

Iffleplum looked out from an eye and gasped.

For the first time he beheld the miracle of the moving sea! The clouds had gone and an endless ocean rolled below. He gazed in amazement. For it seemed that all the world had changed into a truly "flowing bowl" with its margins lost in mist. As the figurehead overhung the bows, it was scary looking down, down, down into the foaming blue and silver sea. Iffleplum clutched the wooden window-ledge dizzily: and for a while his mauven nose went slowly green.

He stared on in silent wonder; filled with strange forebodings in his breast. The world was wider than he had dreamed. It was awesome and magnificent: but terrifying too! And he began to think more fondly of his home and the land that he had left. He stood there, unseeing, deep in thought, for a long time.

*

At sunset Iffleplum descended to a lower deck. Çhelône and Tryllyon came to sit beside him on the stairway steps. There they watched the last rays of a glorious setting sun gild all the masts and sails with mellow yellow light. The sun went down and slowly vanished in a misty sea. But a golden glow still lingered on about the ship, which only deepened as the twilight grew.

Silence fell. And stillness settled over all the ship. Although a few Hearties moved about the decks, attending to their tasks unhurriedly, they spoke no word. Many simply came to rest, just standing silently, or sitting here and there. A waiting, breathless hush was in the air. Mizzen-gnomes moved restlessly upon the masts and yardarms and tree-pogs hung quietly on the shrouds.

Iffleplum felt his fingertips and toes begin to tingle with expectancy. He raised an eyebrow at his friends, but they just smiled and nodded in return.

Then, way back in the stern, the storm-doors opened suddenly by themselves. Iffleplum sat up with a start. A wave of energy washed over him, which seemed to emanate from someone coming up the stairs. A tall, cloaked figure of great power emerged and strode across the deck. Around him seemed a radiance and his flowing robes of uncertain hue changed colour softly as he came. His mane of wild white hair was bound about the brows with a silver circlet, but its freely flowing ends were wafting on the air like gossamer. His curling beard was half as long, cascading only to his waist.

"The *Ârkühm!*" said Çhelône in an undertone—as if he could not tell.

The Ârkühm-Mage stayed his pace before them and stood there looking down. Like a towering giant he seemed to Iffleplum, who until then, had only half-believed such fabled creatures lived!

128

So this was Man! He seemed far more than the legends in his book had led him to expect. The Ârkühm beheld him with a piercing gaze from deeply disconcerting eyes. The ifflepinn hunched himself into as small a ball as possible and tried to look as good as gold. But there was nothing he could hide from such a stare.

This strange great being could see into his very heart he knew. Yet to Iffleplum it seemed quite difficult to keep the Ârkühm-Mage himself in view. Unless he concentrated on the Ârkühm's word, he found the Master seemed to fade and flicker like a frail and aged ghost. He could not tell if this was so, or just the glowing of the ship, his aching eyes, or the shimmering of the Ârkühm's robe. But it was hard to hold him in his sight: like trying to recall to mind the snatches of a dream.

"Well met, once more," said the Ârkühm gently. "But you knew it not before: when first we shared our company. And though now your body is healed of hurts you have a troubled mind it seems." He looked awhile lovingly in Iffleplum's eyes, which quickly filled with tears.

"I see: you mourn your elfin-heart and feel we've stolen it away," he said, with softness and with sorrow in his voice. "Nay, say not so, for we steal nothing my young friend: especially hearts. And *that* you know. You gave yours up— the time had come—and we were there to gather it, that's all."

"Oh, I know! I know!" said Iffleplum in tearful awe. "I'm sorry to be so. But it isn't fair! Why did it go?"

"Why, within your waking dream you wished it so. Did you not say you would *give your heart* to sail on such a ship as this? To fight with monsters and suchlike and slay them merely for the sake of honour from a king?"

"Oh! Oh, yes I did!" said Iffleplum remembering. "But I didn't really mean it all and—anyway, how did you know that?"

"Wherever elfin-hearts are coming loose in people's breasts, I come to know, and attune my thoughts to them. My spirit wanders freely in the world of the *Khämmârkü*—we call

Dwêmòriæ—where dreams and fancies, thoughts and day-dreams can all be seen—I see them now: yet even as I speak to you." His pupils glazed and softened as he espied things with his inner eye.

"I see..." said Iffleplum slowly. "I think I understand. But now it's gone—I'd rather have my elfin-heart, than see *all* the kings of Ümmulon. I only would. Oh, Ârkühm-Lord, please won't you let me have it back?

The Ârkühm raised his hand. "No titles please—just Ürû-ühm will do. That means 'Old Heart' in the Dwæmavâhl—the language of the half-Elvene. But as for giving back your elfin-heart, it's not as easy as it seems. 'Tis not for me to do. To have it back is up to you. The Laws of Life are not ours to make or mend: we simply see them through. I could not do it if I would; 'tis far beyond my means.

"Let me explain: for I fear the ways of wishes cannot be changed. You see, young Iffleplum, when once you set a wish free on the Inner Airs—the deed is done! You cannot take it back to make amends. 'Sow a thought and reap a deed', we say. Our thoughts and wishes flow away from us like little fishes fleeing outwards on the tide. There's nought can stop them when they go! And as they glide across the *Khämmâr-käçh*—the Inner Airs—the Dreamherds of Dwêmòriæ can see them coming into view: emerging from the mists of *dævakhäm* between our world and theirs. For every thought becomes a living thing—appearing as strange creatures seen—when passing through Dwêmòriæ.

"And when they do, the *Khämmârkü* spread out across the Lands of Dream to try and herd them in. And then with voices magical, the Dreamherds all begin to sing! Their songs so wondrous strange and beckoning, they sing our dream-thoughts to their sides and thereby try to wisely guide them on their way. For by their songs our lighter thoughts grow brighter still: and then return to us another day.

"But often many monstrous, dark and thorny thoughts come roaring in. And even so, they try to lead them all towards the light. But some escape! And those are the sneaky,

130

slithery ones that slip away and hide in darksome holes deep underground; and by the time they are found again, they have grown more gross and loathsome than before.

"But either way, one thing is sure! On passing through Dwêmòriæ our Thoughts are changed—for better, or for worse! But then the *Khämmârkü* can do no more than send them home again. For once they have tried their work is done. The tide must turn—and back they come—to each of us from whom they came.

"And *then?* What happens *then?*" said the Ârkühm in a louder voice, suddenly stooping down on Iffleplum. The Mage's voice had enfolded him like a warm blanket and had begun to maze his mind with dreams. He jumped awake again as the Ârkühm's amazing face came close to him. His eyes were alive like whirling stars in space. Iffleplum's head begin to spin. He shook it dumbly; mouth agape, in answer to the Ârkühm's words. As the Master stood upright again, the dizzy feeling passed away. Nervously he twiddled with his conker on its string. Once more his mind was clear and listening.

"When all your wayward wishes, thoughts and dreams come back to you—what happens then?" the Ârkühm asked. "If you have any hope to earn your elfin-heart's return, you *must* know this. The most important thing to realize is that each time your thoughts return to you they come back *in disguise!* And who but the wise can recognize them when they come? Strange as it seems, they take the shapes of all the things you see before your eyes! You look surprised: but all the same, 'tis true. They are hidden away in the everyday things that happen to you.

"They are there in the knife when you cut yourself: and in the pain you feel. They are there when you stumble and fall, or stub a toe, or when your wounds won't heal. Or when you break a pot and mother scolds, or when others laugh at you— know then, that nothing comes to you by chance. These things are only your own unworthy thoughts, coming home again to you. And often you'll find them secretly clothed in the good

131

and the bad things other folks do. So remember then! Your good thoughts will later bring you back much better times and happy surprises too!

"But in truth, there really is no 'good' or 'bad'—for all the happenings are only hidden messages from Ühm—to wake you up and make you understand the way that is right for you. So watch whatever happens to you, carefully!

"And realize, you only *ever* get what you deserve: no matter be it good or seeming ill—otherwise, there is no way it could come to you. So you see, there is no one else to blame. To swear and curse, just makes it worse. For if you find the things you wished for first, are not the things for you: it's you alone who brought upon yourself, the deeds you have to do."

"But—what if my heart's not in them any more?" objected Iffleplum.

"Yea or nay, you wished your heart away," the Ârkühm said. "And now you needs must do your deeds and see what comes of that. But just be sure you take everything as kindly as you can. Just know whatever hardship comes your way, 'tis only your own thoughts rebounding through Dwêmòriæ. Such debts each one of us is bound to pay. How can your own thoughts rebounding be unfair? 'Tis you who let them loose upon the inner air. And screaming and sulking, or carrying on, will never begin to right your wrongs. So remember— whenever your 'reboundings' return again to rankle you—a humble heart, accepting all, may even call your elfin-heart back home where it belongs."

"Oh, really? Is that the way? If my heart stays kind and open—it might come back to me and stay? There's still a chance?"

"Indeed! There's still a chance: there's always that! Accept whatever comes—but keep your heart and head in Ühm. For a heart that's closed lets nothing in or out. And now we've saved your elfin-heart from its journey to the stars, at least it won't go on. But it's not our place to give or take: that's in the hands of Ühm. And Âhn-Ühm's heart is with you still:

Ôâh dwa-Ühma, kha-Ühma dhûm.
Oh, Ühm! Oh, Ühm! Ôâh dhanüm!
Vîl-ôhma kwa-nevâhl iyl-ühm—
Êyâ iyl-Ühm iyl-Ôhm êyl Ühm."

"What's that poetry you say?" asked Iffleplum.

"I'm quoting from an Elvish chantrelay,"[9] the Ârkühm said, "which roughly rendered in the Common Ummal-tongue, might be:

From Ühm I come, with Ühm I stay.
Oh, Ühm! Oh, Ühm! I come! I come!
For home is where the heart is—
And the Heart of Home is Ühm.

"'Tis a play on words, belovèd of the Dævârkü. For *Ühm* is the word which means the Unseen Heart of all the worlds and also *ühm* is heart inside each and every one of us. So it simply means that each one of us is sailing on the *Song of Life*, as Sung by Ühm—the One Great Elfin-heart of All. And if we can feel that Song inside ourselves, forever going on, what does it matter where we are—or how far we have to go? When Ühmkyn Sings, the world appears! Why, that very Song we are! If we exist, we know that the Song's still *Singing* us! And so, in truth, there's nowhere we can ever go away from Ühmkyn. For *anywhere* we are, we are always *there*—inside the Song—our real home—'tis comforting to know."

"Oh, Ælfÿlon!" said Iffleplum. "I don't know if I follow you! I'm all confuzled when you talk like that. And yet, perhaps there's something getting through? You say that when Ühmkyn Sings, what's Sung is the world that we can see? So then—in the Song Ühmkyn is Singing *me*?"

"Ah now! You understand it well!" the Ârkühm smiled. "Indeed, without his Song you would not *Be*. We live in Ühmkyn, like fish live in the sea. They breathe water and we breathe Ühmkyn and the Song. When things go wrong, each

---

9 A semi-chanted song or minstrel lay.

one of us, deep down inside can hear Ūhmkyn's Song, and know the true reality. So whenever you feel yourself all alone and full of fear: just listen well. For rising from your heart you'll hear a singing-sound, like something ringing in your ears—the *Song of Ūhm*—'twill be! And then you'll know, you're not alone, for Ūhm is there. Ūhm is the Singer and the Song and all that's Sung as well.

"Ūhm is Singing now this very boat on which you stand—a Ship of Light—which floats upon his breath alone. When he Breathes out our sails are filled and off we go! And then return again when he Breathes in. And the same could be said of these—our body-boats—these steerless ships of skin, that lead us every whichaway the wind doth blow. But if ever there should come a day when Ūhm falls silent and no longer Sings his Song, then you and I, and all the worlds we know, will on the instant, dwem away—"

The Ârkühm's eyes had grown more lustrous as he spoke and seemed to glow with inner light. His gaze grew far away. Then suddenly he was back again. He turned towards the waiting crew and raised his arms.

"*Haroom!*" he cried and the Hearties sprang up quickly to their posts.

Iffleplum blinked stupidly. While lost in listening to the magical melodies of the Ârkühm's voice, and hypnotized by his starry eyes, he had forgotten where he was. Now all about him was activity, as Hearties bustled to their posts. Once more the sails were thundering overhead. The night was darkling fast, but the ship was slowly growing brighter with a golden light.

"Stand-by!" the dwemmer-captain cried.

"'Tis time!" the Ârkühm boomed. He raised his arms. "And now to Middleworld we must go! *Breathe deep!*" And he cried out in such a voice as made the timbers of the ship crackle white with light.

"*Ôâh dwa-Ūhma kha-Ūhma dhûm!*
Dwa-nära dwârn Ämidhakhüm!"[10]

The force of it shook Iffleplum. It seemed as if lightning had struck the ship. The woodwork everywhere now sparkled brilliant white. And particles of light fizzled and hissed like hot fat in a frying pan. An electric thrill ran over him. He clung against Çhelône with frightened eyes as the ship began to disappear. They reeled and their heads swam.

A moment more and they were through the *Khämmârkäçh* and out the other side.

---

10 "From Ühm I come, with Ühm I stay.
   Now hence we go to Ämidhakhüm!"

Part the Eleventh

Thunderfleet

Of screaming Sky-ships and a Dwem,
in which the elfin-hearts of Men are gathered in a Wild Catch
and oh! so magically tumbled down the hatch.

ffleplum felt very strange. "Oh! The air!" he gasped. "The world has changed! What happened then?" Gusts of vapour came sweeping over the decks and a tangy smell of salt was on the breeze. The clamour of strange birds filled the air. He scrambled up the companionway steps and leaned out over the side. After the brightness of the sudden light, the dusk now seemed much darker than before. And looking down through shifting mists he saw the Silver Sea no more! Now below him he beheld a rolling dark green and different sea!

His nose became a pearly bluish-grey.

"Oh, great greeny gripes!" he cried out in alarm. "Oh, where are we? The ocean's not the same! And the sky has changed! Are we in another world?"

His companions hastened to his side.

From the poop, Captain Alberon was busy booming out instructions to the crew. Topsail tree-pogs, mizzen-gnomes, and pigger-mice were swarming up the masts and riggings. There was much activity overhead as they deftly made adjustments to the sails. White screaming seabirds wheeled about the shrouds, with lonesome cries like pulleys screeling under ropes.

136

"What's happened?" asked Iffleplum anxiously. "I can smell a different air! Where are we now?"

"*Ämidhakhüm*," replied Çhelône. "We are in the Middle-world, where mostly Manlings dwell. I am sorry, Plumkin, but I forgot to warn you we might go through a demi-dwem."

"A demi-dwem? What's that?"

"'Tis what just happened then—when the Ârkühm takes us through the *Khämmârkäçh*. We slightly fade away when shipping-out from one world to the next. It does feel funny for a while: but 'tis not unpleasant like a proper *Dwem*. A real *Dwem* is way far worse than that. For then we disappear into the Lonely Realm where nothing is at all! And we never know if we are ever coming back! But let's not speak of that. *For what we think of, we attract.*

"Look! See the birds that cry so curiously? They call them seagulls in this world. And that is the Great Salt Sea down there. It smells not sweetly as the Silver Sea of Ümmulon. But yet it has a flavour rare all of its own."

"Hoo!" hooted Iffleplum. "But how did the Ârkühm get us here? And can he get us back?"

Adventures were all right, as long as there was still a way back home.

"Ho! Fear not for that!" Çhelône said cheerfully. "Well does the Ârkühm know the way to say the words of power, to bring us through and back again. We have only one more night aloft before our work on this voyage is all done. With another catch or two, we'll be away back home to the Mountain and the Land of Lün!"

But as she spoke, a loud hail from above distracted Iffleplum.

"Land ho!" cried out a sea-pog way up in the crow's nest.

Iffleplum stared excitedly down through the swirling sea of *dævakhäm* around the ship. It was faintly shining now like the milky sheen of stars he had sometimes seen in a stream across the sky. But in the gathering gloom faraway below he caught the flash of foam and twinkling lights. "Oh, plummy-tums!" he cried. "Are we going down to visit them?"

"Oh, Heavens, no!" replied Çhelône. "We never go down where they can see what we are about. 'Tis dangerous enough avoiding all their skyships in the air! Not that they can do us any real harm; for we are not solid in their world. We are but like a faery-phantom ship to them: at least, for those who see us well. But mostly we are seen as a strange light in the sky. Although as they fly, their skyships make a fearful noise, which half destroys the workings of the Inner Airs as they go by. Sometimes they shudder us and make us dwem."

"Oh! Then why have we come?" asked Iffleplum anxiously.

"Why, because the Middleworld is where most of our fishing's done. For folk are always giving up their elfin-hearts down there. They seem to live in such a warring way, that their hearts are often in their mouths. In such a world, it is not easy for a loving elfin-heart to stay. So we try to save whichever ones we can. And that way, secretly, we also serve the world of Man."

138

"But why?" said Iffleplum. "Why not leave them be? If it's dangerous and they never know: why try to help them secretly?"

"Why, Plumkin! No world is a world alone!" Çhelône said in surprise. "Each world needs the other one: just like we need each other. We are all the music of the *Song of Ühm*, you see? Only all together can we sing along in harmony. Leave out some notes in any song—it all goes wrong! Then it is not music any more. And each and every elfin-heart—in *every* world—is like one note in the score. So we are all here to help each other's hearts to sing, just as every tiny flower needs bees and butterflies in order to survive. Without either one—then neither one could thrive."

"But what has the world of Man to do with you and me?"

"Oh, Iffleplum—do you still not understand? Now listen carefully; you know that everything we *feel* and *think* flows outwards, everywhere. That means no barriers are there between the worlds all through the Inner Airs. Therefore we must be careful with the thoughts that we send out. And wary of the ones that come our way: especially those from wild worlds—like the Middleworld of Man. For the world down there is wild indeed! It seems forever filled with hearts at war with one another, needlessly. Be they mean and wordy wars by quarrelling, or mighty ones by force of arms and battling. But either way—their ill-feelings foul the Inner Airs, and darken *all* the Worlds Within.

"As you heard the Ârkühm say—when savage thoughts arise from *anywhere*—it fills the land and skies with *monsters* in Dwêmòriæ! And in faeryworlds like ours, when wild and stormy feelings come our way, it fills our elfin-hearts with pain—as I thought the Ârkühm had explained? That's why we sing the healing *Song of Ühm* to every elfin-heart we catch; to make them feel again the wondrous Faery-Heart from whence they came."

"You see, the world of Faery needs to be remembered in the weary hearts of Man. Should they forget us in their hearts, the faeryworlds are doomed to fall, in savagery and fearful dark. And such forgetfulness can cause the faeryworlds to dwem—*forever*—never to return."

"Oh," said Iffleplum pensively. "Now I think I begin to see why my elfin-heart went out of me. I was angry often: and half in love with wild ways. But if the Manling world is like you say, it must be worse for them!"

"Indeed it is! For once Mankind was also of the Faery world: a noble folk and magical. Is it not magical to grow from seed? And then sprout arms and legs, and talk, and walk about? But they have lost the wonder of what they are. Yet the Elves and Dwemmer-folk still call them *Ühmenü*—the Sons of Ühm. And *hümans* is the name they give themselves—although few ever seem to think of Ühm. They walk about and talk like folk asleep: for they have long forgotten whence they came.

"And without the world of Faery in their hearts, they grow all twisted up inside: unhappy people, cold and grey. And since they live themselves so crabbily, they try to stop all other folks from living happily. No need to wonder why their children's elfin-hearts so often slip away.

"I will tell a rhyme I made about it, if I may?

> *"On nights when fleeting shadows pass*
> *Across the starry sky,*
> *Or strange and unknown lights are seen*
> *Should you look up and wonder why;*
> *Then know my friend, the Sea of Dreams,*
> *The only sea that flies,*
> *The only sea, the lonely sea,*
> *O'er which the Heartboat glides*
> *Is surging through the heavens then,*
> *So keep a weather-eye.*
>
> *In the Middleworld where Manlings dwell,*
> *The worried mothers cry:*
> *'The Sea of Dreams is out tonight!*
> *And the Heartboat's sailing by!*
> *Hush, children! Out of sight!' they say,*

For fear we will snatch their hearts away
In the twinkling of an eye.

But should they burst into a room
Where happy children play,
And hasten them and chasten them
To whisk their things away:
Their elfin-hearts may jump right out!
At mother's shout—
And they will lose them anyway.

When thoughtless parents turn their heads
And look the other way,
When those who need their smiles and touch
Have just come in from play;
If caught up in adult affairs,
Unlistening, no time for theirs; and they
Just pooh-pooh fears, and scold their tears,
Then in a while their deaf ears may
Soon dwem young elfin-hearts away.

And when they grow with empty hearts
Their angry parents caterwaul:
'Oh, how we tried! We yelled and lied!
To make an adult of the brat.
We smothered it with sweets and toys
To shut its noise,
Still all it ever does is squall.
It's simply bad! It makes us mad!
And drives us up the wall!'
For they have forgotten how it feels
To be so very small.
'Grow up, my lad! Grow up, my girl!
And leave your faery-books behind.
There's no such thing!' the many say,
From empty hearts, already blind.
With shrinkle-eyes they cannot see

That all their logic only leaves
A lack of magic in the mind,
A deadly dullness of the kind
They like to call—
'Reality'.

"I am not so well in rhyming in the Common Tongue," excused Çhelône. "It sounds much better in the Dwæmavâhl. But it says the things I want to say."

"And fairly spoken too!" said a deeply mellow voice behind them.

Çhelône spun round to find the Ârkühm standing there. "Oh! Ürû-Ühm!" said she, softly blushing, beautifully. "I knew not that thou wert listening there."

"I fear my ears are everywhere," the Ârkühm smiled, his eyes twinkling. "But since they are oftimes tuned to faraway, I mostimes miss the things said near to me. So forgive me if I listened in: for your rhyme well pleases me. Nay, be not abashed: for you spoke well and wisely too. Although there are also those among the *Ühmenü* with hearts like fountains flowing-over, filled with love and wonder of the Worlds Within. But as you say, alas—too few, too few! 'Tis true: Mankind is a wondrous strange breed of folk indeed."

"Oh! But—but I thought that you were one of them?" said Plumkin disappointedly; for the Ârkühm's face was very like the Kings of Old as pictured in his Dwemmer-book. "You are not a Man? Are you a Wizard then? Or are you of the High Elvene?"

The Ârkühm looked at him bemusedly awhile and paused, as if the question needed thought. His long white hair was billowing about his head, and floating on the misty airs. So long it was that its ends were lost in the streaming vapours curling and tumbling over the decks. Wizardly indeed he looked: for it truly seemed as if the mist was flowing from the roots of his hair.

At length he mused: "Am I of the High Elvene? If my far memory serves me well, an Elf I never was: in any life I can

142

recall. Nay, I cannot claim distinction in that way. A Wizard now—a 'worker with the Inner Airs'—or *Khäm-Ârkü* as they are called: there is some of that in me. Although—now let me see—a *Man*, you say? A Man? That strikes me strange." He paused awhile and gazed within, as one who sees things far away and long ago. And a loving smile began to play upon his lips.

When he spoke again a laughing light was in his eyes.

"A Man!" he laughed. "You know, 'tis true! I think that's what this body was an age or two ago. I was once born of the *Ühmenü*. I wonder does the Man-shape show upon me even now?" He held up his translucent hand, and with wondering eyes he studied it anew.

"Yes, fair father," said Çhelône, her eyes aglow. "Thou lightly hold to Man-shape still."

"By Âhn-Ühm's light, that's good!" he smiled in deep amusement. "'Tis truly so: a Man! Of course! I had long forgotten." He wagged his beard and chuckled at the humour of his discovery. "A *Man!*" he said and laughed aloud. And then threw back his head and roared both long and merrily.

All those around him found themselves laughing helplessly along with him. The Hearties on the decks, and even those below, without knowing why, began to chuckle as they worked, infected by the Ârkühm's sudden strange hilarity.

Still shaking his snowy head in disbelief, the Ârkühm turned and paced across the deck. He stopped in thought before the stairs, and then stepped slowly down. They could hear him laughing loudly once again as the storm-doors closed and he descended deep into the ship.

*

"All hands on deck!" The cry rang out above. Many voices echoed it on different levels of the ship. Iffleplum and Çhelône had been dining on delicious pancakes in the messroom with the crew. They had hardly finished supper when the summons came.

"All Hearties to their posts!" said Findor the Dwemmer bo'sun, rising quickly from his seat. The crew members hastily left their plates and hurried out. There were many shouts and the sound of running feet on passageways and stairs.

Çhelône jumped up excitedly, pulling Iffleplum by the arm. "What is it?" he asked her in alarm.

"A Wild Catch coming up!" she cried. "No time to explain! Come and see!" And she hustled him out and up the companionway.

*

As they came on deck, the thundery thrummel of the sails sounded loudly in their ears, like a line of giant's washing *whapping!* in the wind. Iffleplum looked up. The night was dark and gusty. Black clouds tumbled all around.

Way overhead, spread out across the spars, the tree-pogs and pixie-folk were wrestling with the topsails as a stiff breeze whacked them to and fro. Some pigger-mice were clinging, precariously, by their tails and toes to the yardarms. All were heartily hullabalooing to each other as they lashed and loosened ropes. Luminous lines slithered up and down around them, over screeling pulleys on the yards. On the starboard side, the crew were lowering overboard great glittering ghostly nets.

Everywhere Hearties were busy about the decks. Some were hauling out huge armfuls of glimmering elven-ropes and tackle from chest-like lockers here and there. Fore and aft, a score of chanters churned the capstans: winching the great wooden-wheeled hurling machines to either side of the deck. The canvas coverings came off quickly, as many hands humped the hurlers into place and began to bolt them to the bulwarks.

Now Iffleplum could see how beautifully every part of them was worked with patterns and sculpted scrolls. Even the hurling-cups were carved in the graceful form of scallop shells. And into these the Dwemmers, bearing glowing globes upon their shoulders, gently laid their burdens down.

Not only were the globes aglow, but Iffleplum became aware of the eerie radiance of the ship itself. The hint of luminosity he had seen at twilight was now much deeper in the dark of night. The masts and woodwork all around shone softly with a golden glow. Their inner light was like a sunken flame as seen agleam through honey-yellow walls of candle wax. He stood astounded at the scene, entranced.

*

A sudden piercing cry close by awakened him.

Iffleplum whirled around. The weird sound had made his heart jump in alarm. Not far away the Ârkühm stood amidships, strangely poised. His arms were held outstretched, like some great bird about to fly: his hair and clothing rippling in the wind. His eyes were closed. But his face was winced as if in pain. And the ifflepinn knew somehow that the wild cry had come from him.

It might have been some sort of signal: for suddenly the decks were deathly still. The Hearties all had paused amid their tasks. They stood attentively; tense and breathless, as if awaiting new commands. No one moved. All eyes were on the Master of the ship.

The Mage turned slowly in a circle, as if feeling with his graceful fingers in the air.

The watchers stood transfixed, following the mysterious movement of his hands. The Ârkühm turned this way and that. The atmosphere grew tense. Only the wind and drumming canvas of the sails made any sound. Suddenly the Ârkühm wheeled about. And his voice roared out above the windy thunder of the sails: "Hold fast! *Iyl-lämnü iyl-Ühmenü hâe!*[11] Manships! Astern and starboard ho! Stand *firrrm!*"

Many Hearties on the decks clutched heavily at ropes and rails. All eyes looked apprehensively astern. Çhelône was nowhere to be seen.

Iffleplum stumbled to the side. Hauling himself up on a hawser line, he peered out anxiously through a square port in the bulwark. He scanned the dark sky for whatever was coming on behind. But nothing could be seen but black and boiling clouds. Now and then a fitful lightning flickered in the distance, and lit them from behind. He could smell the

11 "The ships of the Humans are upon us!"

moisture of the distant rain upon the wind. More misty vapours began to sweep across the decks.

Then from somewhere way out there in the darkness, Iffleplum became aware of a far off keening whine. At first it seemed like a ringing in his ears. *Is this the Song of Ühm?* he thought. But as the noise grew louder, it became frightening, and he knew it was outside himself. Slowly there arose a deep and dreadful growling sound like a growing grumble of thunder without end, which steadily filled the air. The sound was eerie and unnatural.

And swiftly growing ominous.

The ifflepinn began to grow more frightened by the second. His eyes grew big and round. He somehow sensed that the source of the dreadful sound was hurtling on towards them at an awesome speed. And now it drowned the rumble of the coming storm. He found that he was trembling. His left hand clutched hard his comforting conker, while his right grasped hold of the hawser line. The fine hairs prickled on his skin. He could feel some enormous thing was rushing through the sky behind them with the fury of an avalanche! The pace at which it came was frightening.

But not knowing what it was, was even worse!

And in his mind he heard the sound of galloping! Of galloping! Now even the roiling mists of darkness created frightening shapes before his eyes. And he fancied he could see a horde of *Dhârkäsü* coming riding through the clouds.

His heart grew tight and panicky. The whole ship was trembling now, as the thundery sound rose into a devastating roar. And beneath it all a high-pitched whine now pierced him like a skewer through his head. He threw himself this way and that in agitation. A fearful moan escaped his lips. Hanging grimly to the hawser, he stared about him wildly in the gloom.

Then all at once he saw them!

And Iffleplum was seized with numbing dread. He choked back a cry; for they were worse even than his wildest dreams.

A sudden swarm of things like monstrous metal beetles of horrendous size, with redly flashing eyes, came screaming from the clouds. The dwemmer-sailors cried aloud. For a dreadful menace flew before them like the wind. It clutched at every heart. But their cries were drowned in a sound more deafening than a thousand waterspouts at once! The dinning deadened every thought. And throbbing tremors beat upon their brows. Then a nightmare noise of roaring tore the night apart.

Vast shrieking shapes screamed by on every side, like showers of fiery spears with eyes. As a goldfish overtaken by a school of killer-sharks, so was the *Golden Heart* lost among these screeching monsters of the skies. The whole ship was shuddering at the sound as they hurtled overhead and under, all around.

There came a staggering *crump!* that shook the decks. And swiftly following, a barrage of thunderous *whumps!* which broke behind the skyships as they passed. Several sailors, stunned by the sonic blast fell senseless to the deck. The galleon rocked wildly in their wake. It shimmered for a moment, trembling in a blaze of light. Then briefly bursting into brilliant stars, the *Golden Heart* began to dwem.

Iffleplum's teeth rattled in his skull. He clasped his hands about his ears and stumbled to his knees in terror. It seemed as if his eyes had turned to prisms. The whole ship was shattering into sparkly points of light, like red hot metal hammered in a forge. His body felt as if made of sand, being shaken through a sieve. And his eyes were filled with stars.

Suddenly the ship tilted violently and pitched him forwards on his face. And he tumbled endlessly into a sea of golden *lûmenü*.

*

On coming round, he found himself swimming in a sparkly sky. His head was spinning. Then all of a sudden: nothing. The lights went out. The spinning in his head slowed down and stopped. And he was gone! All was dark. He was lost in the Lonely Realm. *Oh, this is it!*—he thought. *This time I'm dead for sure!*

Then somewhere it seemed his name was being called. A distant voice cried out, "Call Iffleplum of Ælfÿlon!" A nearer voice called out the same. Then one voice after another repeated the command, coming closer all the time.

"Located," said another voice close by.

"Bring him through then," said another.

Iffleplum heard footsteps echoing in his mind. Then the feeling came as of many presences around him.

"Ahem! Ahem!" said a throat-clearing, attention-gaining-kind-of-voice. "Item: One Being, temporarily embodied as an Ælfÿnpyn of Ælfÿlon. Caught him lurking out in the Lonely Realm, your Honour."

"Aberrances?" said a Commanding Voice.

"According to the *Khämmârkäçh's Book of Records* here, the Entity stands accused of—and I quote: 'Constant and Wilful release of Wild Thoughts into the *Khämmârkäçh*; Neglect of Finer Feelings in his Elfin Heart: Misuse and Premature loss of same; Desire for Fights and Fearful Feelings'—thereby Dreaming up of *Dhârkäsü*—or Shadow-folk. And last but not least, 'Criminal Persistence in the Belief of Death'. A sad case, your Honour."

"I see," said a stern but Understanding Voice. "Iffleplum of Ælfÿlon: what have you to say for yourself? Are you still convinced of being dead?"

Erm—well, yes, I suppose so, replied Iffleplum to the Voice. Or rather, he *thought* his answer and the speaker heard.

"Even now? As you mind-speak to the Assembly?"

Well, I don't know. Everything is so strange. I don't know where I am. It's not like anything I knew before.

"See the twisted convolutions of its thinking, milord," said an Inquisitorial Voice. "It would appear that whenever it finds itself in another space, unfamiliar to it, it concludes that it has died."

"Hmm," said the Understanding Voice. "I suppose if he wakes up in another mother, he will conclude that he's due to be born again. Do you imagine that you have been born already, Entity?"

What? said Iffleplum. *Born? But of course I have!*

"Culpability confirmed!" exclaimed the Interrogator. "Iffleplum of Ælfÿlon stands accused of being born and dying, being born and dying, being born and dying without end. A truly hopeless case."

"A pity, that. It seems a shame," said the Understanding Voice. "He might as well have a froak's body next time round—or a wim-wom's. He's certainly not thinking well in this one."

"Quite so, milord. And speaking of *bodies*—" rasped the Inquisitorial Voice, "Iffleplum of Ælfÿlon—do you believe you are the body you were wearing last time you saw it?"

Well, of course I am! retorted Iffleplum. He looked down at where his chest and little round belly ought to be, but there was nothing there. No *body* at all. Yet somehow it was no surprise to him. *Well, I mean—that is—I THOUGHT I was—*

"He *thought!*" said the Sarcastic Voice nearby. Iffleplum turned towards the sound of the speaker.

He became aware of a large auditorium full of shadowy beings. Row upon row of strange and bizarre creatures of all shapes and sizes, seemed to be seated tier on tier all around him. A soft light as through a mist was slowly growing behind them. He felt he would rather not see them any clearer.

"If you have no body—" enquired the Inquisitorial Voice, "—and therefore no *eyes* to see with—just *what* is now looking out of *where* and seeing us? And *what*—may I ask—is it that is *hearing*, if you have no ears? Do you *still* think you are the body? When you see your body is no more—and you still think you *are*—what are you then?"

The question made Iffleplum dizzy. *I—I—I don't know any more*, he stuttered. *I thought I was an ifflepinn.*

"Obviously," said the Inquisitorial Voice. "*Bodies* may *appear* to be born, entity! But whatever *you* are, is never *born*. If you are the body—how is it that you are here and the body is not? Is what you are *now*—actually *wearing* an iffIepinn form at this very moment?"

Erm— well, no— said IffIeplum, looking down. There was still nothing there. He tried hard to recall what he had been before. It was difficult to remember now. He stretched out his imaginary arms and concentrated hard. Slowly, his old iffIepinn body began to mistily appear again around the place where he felt himself to be.

"Ha!" said the Inquisitorial Voice. "*Projection*—your honour!"

"Yes, but naturally," said the Kindly Voice. "*How else?* All *is* projection. Does not Ühmkyn project all worlds—and then look at them through all our eyes? Now the Entity is learning how all worlds come to be. And in so doing, he may solve the age-old puzzle—which came first—the chicken or the egg? *Projection*—of course, they both came simultaneously. Just as everything appears already-made whenever one finds oneself inside a dream. Projection it is, indeed."

"Ah, yes—er—quite so, milord. I stand corrected. However, *entity*—now you have thought yourself back into a body, do you think it has just been born?"

Er—well, no, of course not. I just thought—

"Precisely! You just *thought*. And then—the body just appeared did it not? And each time you dream up another body—or another life—you still think you have been born? What a dreamer!"

But I didn't know—

"Ignorance is no excuse, milord."

"And yet—" said the Understanding Voice, "he *is* aware that he lives inside the *Song of Ühm*..."

And as he spoke, something went *ping!* in Plumkin's ear. A musical ringing tone sounded somewhere deep inside himself. Then warmly he remembered Ühm. *Oh Ühm! Oh, Ümmû-ârkon! I can hear your Song in me! And while you Sing, then I still am! Wherever I may be!*

"Hmm. It seems he *has* understood something, after all." said the Sympathetic Voice. "Perhaps his heart is willing to mend its ways. I feel he deserves another chance. What shall we do with him?"

"We should send him back," said a faraway echoing Voice. "Yes, send him back..." said another. And many voices echoed "Send him back... back... back... back..."

*

The ifflepinn thought he was whirling slowly round in space. But the dwemmer-maid found him rolling in the scuppers, moaning and whimpering to himself. She was gently shaking him awake.

"Come back, Iffleplum. Come back! Come back!" He felt as if his head was in a bin, with people banging on the outside of it with sticks. A prickly pins-and-needles feeling came over him as he found his body coming back around him once again. His eyes were blurred. But the deck of the ship came back in view and he saw Hearties stumbling here and there. The *Golden Heart* was reforming itself with *lûmenü*. Then for a while, once more it dwemmed away and slowly came and went again in waves.

Çhelône helped him slowly to his feet. "Easy now, easy," she soothed. "They have gone. We are out of it. But we are in the way. Come on."

"Mind your heads!" warned a Hearty, as a hurling arm came swiftly down beside them. They ducked and Çhelône dragged Iffleplum unsteadily to a sheltered corner. He collapsed on a pile of canvas coverings the Hearties had bundled aside. He looked about him in a daze. "Oh, Çhelône, Çhelône!" he groaned. "I feel so strange. What happened? Did we dwem?"

"Oh, aye!" Çhelône said loudly over the Hearties cries and the windy whumping of the canvas overhead. "A proper one, that was! We dwemmed awhile until they passed! 'Tis hard to ride a dwem at first. Are you all right?"

"I—I think so," said Iffleplum shakily. "I'm still alive, at least. I heard strange voices in my head. I thought I was dead. But I feel like a jigsaw puzzle all broken up! With all the bits bodged back together badly—back to front and upside down.

"Yeurk!" He shuddered. "Those big screaming *things!* What were they?"

"War-ships of the sky!" yelled back Çhelône.

"I don't like them! I don't want them to be!" wailed Iffleplum.

"Aye, no more do we!" Çhelône replied.

"Stand by the chocks!" cried Captain Alberon. The Hearties were hastily clearing the decks for action. "What's going on?" bawled Iffleplum. "Are we attacked? Is there going to be a fight?"

"Nay! Not for us!" Çhelône replied. "We have no need for that. But others might. I fear there is Manstrife in the world below! Those skyships in their bellies bore destruction—Oh!" She stopped suddenly, as a muffled roar of explosions sounded in the air ahead. Fiery flashes flickered on the boiling clouds.

"Work of the Warlock!" cried Çhelône. "I felt it so! Hark! Hark! They War! *They War!* Oh, Ühm! There'll be a *really* Wild Catch now! A heavy one, I'm sure!"

"What is it?" screamed Iffleplum, clutching her arm. "What *is* a Wild Catch?"

"'Tis when many elfin-hearts arise of a sudden—unforeseen! A battle has begun down there! The skyships drop doom upon the land. Wild hearts will rise aplenty now! But the Ârkühm has brought us here in time. He must have *seen!* There's senseless slaughter happening! And that lets loose the elfin-hearts upon the Inner Airs—"

Suddenly her voice was blotted out. A zigzag fork of lightning crackled down the sky close by. A colossal thunderclap followed after it. Huge drops of rain began to fall. They huddled back under the companion overhang.

The commanding voice of Alberon the Dwemmer Captain roared out loudly over all, "Hard aport!" And the two helmsmen swung hard on the wheel. Hearties leapt to the pulley ropes. The golden sails rippled and thundered as the great ship heeled sharply round, creaking and groaning. The ummals up aloft had struck the topsails against the coming of the storm.

152

Now others just below were swarming over the spars. Squeaking pigger-mice were taking in the gallants too.

On the main deck, the Hearties manned the hurling machines: snap-locking silken cords onto rings on the shining floats. And the luminous lines ran snaking over the sides to the harvest-nets blowing freely in the wind.

"Broadside ready; larboard floats!" sang out the Dwemmer Captain.

"Aye, ready! Holding firm!" the bo'sun cried.

The Ârkühm's eyes flashed the go-ahead.

"Chocks out! And fire away!" commanded Captain Alberon.

In perfect time, each Hearty whacked away the catches of the catapults. With a wondrous *whoosh!* like rockets, the throwing arms flung out the floats across the sky.

A great *Oh!* swelled in Plumkin's breast as the harvest-nets soared out behind them in an arc of light, like starry spider webs bedecked with dewy diamonds, flashing in the night. Then plunging down the shining floats fell streaming through the clouds.

Oh, glorious! Now the ifflepinn's heart was quickened at the sight. And his fear fell away in wondrous awe.

"Come! Quickly! to the other side!" cried out Çhelône. "'Tis worth a wetting to watch the catch come in!" They skeetered down the tilting deck and slid up against the bulwark with a smack. Clambering up and clinging to the shrouds, they hung breathlessly over the side. The tumbling sea of *dævakhäm* swelled and swirled below them, phosphorescent now, like a mist around the moon.

The falling nets of light and gossamer went speeding round full circle far below the *Golden Heart*. As the arc of light came swinging up again the floats came homing-in.

"Here they come!" Çhelône said excitedly, her eyes shining with delight. The line of glowing globes came streaking up towards them through the shimmering *dævakhäm*.

Then thrillingly, along the whole length of the ship the faery-airs burst upwards into sparkling foam. A shoal of shining *Khämmârkü* came surging from the starry sea, each one holding high a glowing float. Curly-bearded skyfish-men and mer-maidens bare of breast soared over them, like dolphins in the air. They hurled the globes onboard towards the Hearties ready waiting on the deck who caught them as they fell. Moving all as one in graceful harmony, the *Khämmârkü* turned themselves tails over heads right over the topmost masts, and plunged back down into the *dævakhäm* below.

In the dark, even they seemed luminous. Transparent too: as Iffleplum could see right through them as they swam. "Sky-deeves!" he chortled in delight.

"Indeed!" replied Çhelône. "See how they guide the nets and herd the elfin-hearts within. And now they have gone to breathe upon the catch."

"Stamp and go, lads!" the bo'sun cried, thumping his foot down on the deck. And right away a fiddler and a piper, sheltering beneath the bulkhead overhang, struck up a sprightly tune. The Hearties began to beat time with their boots, and sang a sky-shanty as they worked. They pushed the windlass so heartily it fairly whirled around. Capstans creaked as the harvest-nets came winching up beneath the belly of the ship. It was a heavy haul and elfin-hearts were threshing wildly like a shoal of netted fish. Their softly coloured inner light lit up the keel in rippling waves and shimmered up the planking of the sides.

Rain was bouncing off the polished bulwarks. Lightning flashed and thunder rumbled all around. But Iffleplum hung on doggedly to the forechain shrouds, determined not to miss a thing. His dwemmer-cape was warm and kept away the worst of the wind and rain.

Now with a cry the Hearties loosed the net-lines on the starboard side. The sky-deeves dived down with them and sped beneath the shining keel and up the other side. Again the *dævakhäm* exploded into sparkling light as the *Khämmärkü* came bursting through with the bulging harvest-nets. They rose above the spars and shook the nets like sheets to cast the catch aboard. A rainbow rain of elfin-hearts came cascading to the decks.

At once the Hearties went wading in amongst them with their elven-nets, swiftly swooshing them down the open hatches to the hold. Glowing shapes of every softly coloured hue went slithering through the scuttle-holes, drifting down into the immense aquarium below. Their light-filled ripples reflected in the dwemmer's eyes and danced upon the wood-work everywhere.

It was a sight to bring delight to any heart.

But the work was swiftly done. And all too soon for Iffleplum, the Hearties cleared the decks. The last few elfin-hearts here and there were scooped up in the elven-nets and tossed down into the hold. The hatches closed. And the crew began to tidy up.

"Oh,!" breathed Iffleplum, his eyes aglow. "Oh, Çhelône!" I've never seen anything so wonderful!"

"Nor I," Çhelône agreed. "No matter how many times I have seen a Wild Catch, it still gives me a thrill. Although 'tis saddening know that many in the world below have lost their lives in violent deeds. But now they have flown from fight and fury, I hope they find themselves in peace and pleasant dreams. I know not to which of the Inner Worlds they have gone. But at least their elfin-hearts live on—with us!"

"Do you think there'll be another one? A Wild Catch, I mean?" asked Iffleplum eagerly.

"Alas! I fear we can save no more for now. The tank is full to overflowing, I am sure. We have already harvested in every world we can. And now, methinks, our fishing work is done. On the morrow morn, we will awaken over Ümmulon, ere the rising of the sun."

"Ümmulon!" cried Iffleplum delightedly, as another of his dreams came true.

Part the Twelfth

Dawn Flight

In which Iffleplum does a bit of burglary, makes a bad mistake and lets his elfin-heart go flying free

here am I? Iffleplum asked himself. *What am I doing here?* He found himself wandering down an endless and gloomy corridor, anxiously opening door after door, and peering in. But whatever he wanted was never there. Each door strangely opened into a forest under fog.

What is a forest doing on a ship? he wondered. In every room he could see no more than the shadowy shapes of ghostly trees. He was searching for something important he knew, but he could not remember what. Even the corridor now seemed full of fume and curls of mist came creeping down the hall.

Way ahead of him two large figures were looming up in the fogging gloom. He caught his breath and flattened himself against the wall. He had seen those shambling shapes before! But the moth-eyed Creatures of the Night seemed unaware of him. They were prowling on ahead and he was coming up from behind. Now they stopped and paused beside another door. With a brief and stealthy glance around they swiftly entered in.

Cautiously the ifflepinn crept up. They had left the door ajar. On it was a sign that said: INSPECTOR OF HEARTS— ALCHEMERY. Suddenly his heart was filled with dread.

Now he knew what it was he was looking for! And what *they* were after too! Afraid, but angrily, he pushed the door aside. It was just as he thought! Nightshade and Baggyneck both were there! The taller Grope was reaching up to the shelves where the elfin-hearts of Ummals stood! With a cry of anger and despair, Iffleplum hurled himself across the room. Night-shade hastily humped down a labelled jar marked "*Elfin-heart of Iffleplum*" and Baggyneck quickly stuffed it in his sack. Clutching their booty, the Gropes whirled away and clattered up the spiral stair.

With a final desperate leap and bound, bold Sir Plumkin grabbed hold of Nightshade's flowing cloak and tried to drag him down. But the cloak came away in the ifflepinn's hands and he tumbled backwards down the stairs, enravelled in its folds. As he hit the deck he banged his head and woke up from his frightful dream in shock.

At that moment, faraway somewhere a strong commanding voice boomed out:

"Ôâh dwa-Ûhma kha-Ûhma dhûm
Dwa-nära nâhl dwârn Ümmulon!"[12]

Once more the ship dissolved in crackling light. Sparkling pinpricks of light danced before his eyes. The peach-bloom hairs all over his body deliciously stood up on end with the thrill of going through a dwem. Tiny golden *lûmenü* were fizzling in the cabin walls. But in seconds the sparkle faded into the woodwork and the room grew quickly dim.

A grey light before the dawn came softly through the latticed windows. The ifflepinn groaned and shook his head.

Dazedly he looked around and found he had fallen out of bed. He was lying on the cabin floor, rolled up entangled in his bed sheet, not a cloak. But his heart was beating fast and fearfully.

We must have gone between again, he thought: then sat up suddenly, his head pounding. *But oh! That means we must be over Ümmulon!*

He thrust open the nearest lattice and looked out. The air was cold and blustery. Way down between the clouds, a grey and misty morning twilight lay like a blanket on the dark and chilly-looking lands below. The starless sky, above a band of grey, was deeply coloured indigo. Only a thin and rosy glow flushed the far horizon on the edge of sight. And down below a yellow light twinkled in the darkness of an early morning farm. Although dawn was growing in the sky, he could see little of the landscape steeped in gloom.

But the very thought of it was cheering to the ifflepinn.

Ümmulon for sure! he thought with glee. *It ONLY is! I might even see the real Ümmûârkon when the sun comes up!* But the gusty air out there was chilling to his snout: it stung his eyes and flapped his floppy ears about. Soon he closed the window against the wind. Yet even as he thrilled, his joy was softened by a gentle pain within. And the fearful feeling of his dream returned again to trouble him.

---

12 "From Ûhm I come, with Ûhm I stay.
Now hasten we to Ümmulon!"

What if the Gropes—or other folks—should *really* come and steal his heart away? *If they take it to the Shadow-world*, he thought, *how could I get it back?* His nightmare had made him feel his elfin-heart was no longer safe in the Magister's Alchemery. He had to get it back. The need of it was preying on his mind. *I ought to have it with me all the time*, thought Iffleplum. *But how?*

He fumbled for the flintlight by his bed and found his fingers trembling as he lit an oil lamp. He pulled out his book of *Legends* from its bag. The colours on the cover warmly glowed, as they always did at night. Stars were slowly winking out, as dawn arose behind Ümmûârkon's pearly rose-tinted mountain peak. And the magic of the picture was once more soothing to his heart. As he stared at the scene, a startling idea suddenly came into his head. Flipping open the book to the place where the elfin-heart had stained the pages: he gazed upon it wonderstruck.

This was made with elf and dwemmer enchantery! he thought. *If it caught and kept my elfin-heart before—perhaps it could again? And I could keep it with me in my book! Oh, yes!* Now he was sure: he *only* could!

In a moment or two, his mind was made up. At last he knew what he had to do. Quickly, he dressed in his dwarvish-looking dwemmer-coat. He replaced his book in the shoulderbag and slipped the strap over his shoulder. Then quietly opening his cabin door, he crept out along the passageway unseen. Few folk were about so early and none were curious as he passed them. With his head held down, his face and excited scarlet snout were hidden inside his hooded robe. He wobbled his way down five flights of stairs to the hold, as the *Golden Heart* dipped and rolled in the windy weather of the dawn. A sudden lurch of the great ship dashed him against the wall and he stumbled down the last step into the corridor.

Now he was shaking. His hand trembled on the handle as he furtively opened the Alchemery door. *Am I doing right?* he wondered, for his heart was beating fearfully. *No, it can't be wrong*, he told himself. *I'm only taking what belongs to me.* But still somehow he felt ashamed. Although he had never heard of burglary, he felt perhaps he should have asked permission first. But now it was too late: he had come too far. And his elfin-heart was calling him.

Inside, the great chamber was much dimmer than before, for all the lamps were but one were out. The only other light came from the tank of *dævakhäm* and the softly glowing jars, which gently slid and clinked together on the shelves with the movement of the ship.

Anxiously Iffleplum looked around. Dark shadows were shifting scarily as the ship swayed slowly from side to side. But there was no bad feeling in the air: so at least he knew there were no Gropes about. There came a sudden loud snore close by his ear and the ifflepinn jumped aside with fright. Behind a pile of books and scrolls he found Fogdish fast asleep across his desk. After the heavy Wild Catch, he had been working on his lists and labels half the night.

Iffleplum chuckled at himself, after his scare. He teetered down towards the tank, as the floor tilted slightly to one side. But coming up against the glass, he knew instantly it wasn't there.

Of course! It was where he had seen it in his dream. It was bottled-up and sitting on the ummal-shelves; seven rows up beyond his reach. But in the semi-dark the folding-steps were nowhere to be seen. Besides, their clatter might just wake Fogdish up.

The stub of one last candle still burned feebly on the umbelope's desk. He unstuck it from the pooled wax on the table-top and picked it up. Holding his breath, gingerly he began to climb the shelves themselves. It was tricky and precarious with the ship still swaying to and fro and the candle in one hand. But slowly hauling himself up by the safety-rails (which stopped the bottled elfin-hearts from sliding off in storms) he clambered on. At last he reached the shelf on which the Ummal-hearts were stored.

Panting heavily, on the tips of his toes and hanging with one hand to the rail above, he sidled slowly along the row, reading the labels by the candle's tiny flickering flame. It was sweaty work and Iffleplum's arms began to badly ache. He was getting hot and flustered and he felt could not hold on for very much longer. Just then, a little further along the row, a certain jar began to glow.

Oh, plummy-tums! There it was! He sidled along the shelf to read a label written in the Elven-tongue: "*Ælfÿnpynn ÿ Ælfÿlon*". His nose grew bright and rosy-gold. And just below it, written in *Vâhl-Ümmulon*—the Common Ummal-tongue— he read wide-eyed: "Owner known as *Iffleplum*"—and underneath again, in brackets and red ink, the strange word— "*(Untransmogrified)*".

He grabbed the elven-jar hurriedly with his candle-hand and heaved it over the safety-rail. It was only then he realized his mistake. He needed both his hands to climb back down again!

"Oh, gripes!" groaned Iffleplum. But he had no time to think, as the *Golden Heart* suddenly heeled over sharply on the starboard side. His foot slipped off the jar below. Making a wild grab for the safety rail, hot wax spilled over on his wrist. The jar slid swiftly from his grasp. He yelled in pain as the shelves leaned over him and he swung out into the air. Books and decanters slithered across the floor. The bottled heart crashed to the deck and burst with a bang into smithereens.

And Iffleplum went tumbling down as well.

Oh, help! The elfin-heart was flying free!

It shot up from its little cloud of elven-breath and drifted like a smoky wraith across the Alchemery. Briskly Iffleplum brushed bits of bottle-glass from his bump-bruised knees. Then looking up, he cried out in dismay. He spied the elfin-heart twisting away up the spiral stair. Dashing through the elven-breath, he was after it without delay.

Fogdish sleepily raised his head. "What in Ümmulon—or whatever-other-World-we-are-in—is going on?" he murmured groggily. He turned to see Iffleplum clattering madly up the stairs. Then he saw the broken jar and scattered glass upon the floor. In a moment he was wide-awake!

"Oh, my giddy Heart's-Ache!" he gasped. As he crouched down to read the label on the broken glass, a wisp of elven-breath went up his snout. He drew his head back with a start. "Oh dear, oh dear, oh, deary me! I've really done it now!" moaned he. "I've snuffled up some *dævakhäm*! Hee-hee!" he tittered merrily: "My goose is cooked! Its eggs are fried! Oh, Ühm! I've lost Iffleplumkin's elfin-heart!" he cried, collapsing in his chair. "I had it there! And bottled it! I wrote it down in triplicate! It's been already catalogued! And now it's gone! It's out the door! Such a thing has never happened to me before! I'm a disgrace to the umbelopish family!"

And he threw his head down in his arms and sobbed: "Alas! Alack! Oh, woe is me!" then slid down slowly on the floor and laughed and laughed hysterically.

*

Up on the walkway round the tank, Iffleplum snatched down an elven-net that hung upon the wall. His elfin-heart was floating slowly over the aquarium towards a scuttle-door. As he ran around the other side and up a tiny stair. *Hooray!* he thought. *The hatchway to the deck is shut! It's trapped! It's nearly caught!* But the wraithen-heart passed straight on through the wood—as if it wasn't there! And his elven-net swished down too late, on nothing but the empty air.

Thrusting aside the sloping-doors he jumped out quickly on the deck. The sky was fresh and sparkling in the brilliance of the rising sun. The golden sails were tipped with shining light, and drumming loudly in the wind. He could see some pigger-mice unfurling canvas up aloft, which thrummelled wildly as it filled. Only a Hearty or two were working quietly on the decks below. But his elfin-heart was nowhere to be seen!

Iffleplum looked about him in alarm. It surely hadn't been blown overboard? Oh no! Impossible! There wasn't time. But the wind was very blustery. Just in case, he ran rapidly from side to side. But all he could see were only huge great gleaming clouds down there, like a dreamy landscape of misty valleys and feathery mountain crags. All were moving in slow-motion and brilliantly lit-up by the sun. He tottered away from the bulwark down the deck.

Then out it came! Oh, joy! He saw his elfin-heart again!

Like a startled bird, it fluttered from below a canvas-covered catapult and alighted on a mast. But as fast as his little legs would go, he could not catch it yet. It quickly wafted up and away towards the bows. He leapt and bound all over the deck, as he swished and swiped with his elven-net. Up and over the fo'c'sle steps it flew, like a buffeted butterfly in the breeze. Then twirling round it came whirling down inside the mask-like chamber in the prow, just behind the face of the figure-head. As he scrambled up the companionway, Iffleplum gave a sudden anguished cry of dread. For as if taken by a gust of wind, the drifting elfin-heart sped suddenly out into the sky! Out through the sky-deeve maiden's open eye!

He rushed to the ledge and looked fearfully up and down and all around. It was nowhere to be seen through the faery air! Only an ocean of gambolling sungold clouds rolled by below. He could not see it floating anywhere. He rolled his eyes upwards to the shrouds and—

Oh, Great Greeny-Gripes! he thought, for it was there! It *only* was! Lightly perched up on the bowsprit sticking outwards from the prow—a long vibrating spar projecting forwards from the sky-deeve maiden's crown. The elfin-heart lay upon it trembling. And any moment now, it might just tumble down.

Iffleplum glanced up in desperation. Just above his head, there were stay-lines running out to the bowsprit from an iron gem set in the sky-deeve maiden's brow. The rigid ropes were there to hold the bowsprit firm—along with many more which ran out from the forechains[13] hidden in her hair. It was only then he noticed that beside her nose, was a ring-ladder set into the wood. Without a thought, he slipped out swiftly over the eyehole with his net.

Tightly grasping the rungs—as the wild wind flapped his ears about—he clambered grimly up the sky-deeve's face! Just below the metal gem, he paused for breath, panting heavily. Then, heart-stoppingly, he let go the ladder rungs. With bursting lungs, he flung up his arms to grasp a rope and swung himself up astride the stay. From the corner of his eye he glimpsed the land of Ümmulon way down between the clouds, a frightening mile or two below. "Don't look down! Oh, don't look down!" he told himself, his eyes closed tight. He lay there for a moment, breathing hard, hoping his dizziness would pass away.

Slowly he lifted up his head. *Yes! The elfin-heart was still there!* It was quivering on the spar. He thought he was near enough now for the net to reach.

"Don't move! Don't move!" breathed Iffleplum. "Stay just where you are." Shakily, he raised himself to his feet. With one hand on a sparline just above, he held his breath and stealthily lifted up his elven-net.

---

13 *Forechains* are metal plates bolted to the outside of a sailing ship, to which all riggings, shrouds and stay-lines are attached.

It was then the *Golden Heart* rose and burst over an ocean of snowy-white breakers, billowing and thundering overhead.

And it rolled on down again cleaving the clouds apart like foamy seas. His heart thumped thrillingly with fear and wonderment—but his nose grew pearly pale! And his stomach heaved and fell as the great ship rose and plunged again; surfing slowly down through the clouds like a playful whale.

He was suddenly chilled to the bone: in the midst of a dark and dazzling fog atwinkle everywhere with *lûmenü*. Swirling grey mists went streaming by as the ship went surging down. His skin and mustard-coloured robe were soon bedewed with misty pearls. His hands grew cold and numb. *Oh, Ühm!* He could not hang on any more. Just then the *Golden Heart* burst out below the clouds into brilliant sunshine once again. There came a sudden *whack* of windy sails and the ship heeled over crazily.

"Oh, no!" cried Iffleplum as the elfin-heart went swirling off the spar. He lunged out wildly with the net. But the spar-line gave a sudden *twang!*—and with a stinging snap it flung his holding hand away. The shock of it sent him spinning. And he tumbled sideways as his foot skidded off the dewy rope. His stomach turned a somersault. A cry caught in his throat *Oh-oh!* as the ifflepinn, with outstretched arms, fell headlong into space.

And no one saw him go.

Part the Thirteenth

Dwêmòriæ

In which Iffleplum passes through the Land of Dreams,
where nothing is ever what it seems

lowly Iffleplum became aware that he was not alone. He had the feeling of someone close on either side of him; and his arms were tingling to a thrilling touch. Fearfully, he opened his eyes. Hardly daring to turn his head, he glanced askance from side to side. With a sudden burst of joy he recognized the broad bare shoulders and curly beards of two mighty mer-men of the sky—the *Khämmârkü*—gliding along beside him; their huge hands beneath his arms supporting him like a buoyant wave.

Oh, plummy-tums! He was no longer upside down, or falling anywhere. As far as he could see—through the misty air— they were carrying him over the luminous waves of a ghostly soundless sea. And looking down, he saw his feet were dangling in the unwet waters of a strangely silent surf.

In a moment more, the *Khämmârkü* gently set him down on a sparkling sandy shore. And with a cheery wave they turned and swiftly whirled away back from whence they came. A cry choked in his throat to see them go. And wretchedly he watched their fishy-tails undulating through the foggy air as they vanished in the *Khämmârkäçh*. For now the loving tingle of their touch was gone, the sudden parting pained his heart. But he had no time to mourn their loss.

With a sudden start, he realized that all around him, strange and phantasmagorical creatures were emerging endlessly from the misty vapours of the sea. He gazed about him in astonishment. Bizarre beings of every unbelievable shape and size were streaming over the strand on either side. Ignoring Iffleplum, they passed him by: their staring eyes all steadily fixed ahead, as they followed the sea mists rolling in and flowing far across the land.

He turned towards the sea again, and then staggered back in fright! A band of scary-looking trees came stalking swiftly from the foggy deeps, walking from the waters on their knaggy roots. Like giant, long-legged, seaweed-covered crabs, they scuttled over the beach and up and over the sparkling dunes, leaving clouds of powdery stardust in the air. A moment more and they were gone: swallowed in the mist.

Now looking up, he saw a shining stream of phosphorescent light come snaking in across the sky. It brightened all the air about it with a sheen of softly sparkling stars. His heart leapt up towards it, for its beauty and its grace. And as if responding to his call, the stream of light came briefly dipping down towards him and then went shooting up again. As it skimmed over him, not far above his head, a burst of happy bouncing things, like tumbleweed or fuzzy balls of light, came falling from it in the gloom. They bounced clear over him and all around. And the feeling of them made him laugh again and soothed away his fear. The fuzzy balls then bounced back up into the stream of light and disappeared.

But as he looked around again, some beastly things came by that felt too dark and dangerous to be near.

Oh, where have the Khämmârkü brought me to? thought Iffleplum. *I don't think this is Ümmulon! And where's my elfin-heart got to now? How can I catch it if it's gone on?* It was only then, to his surprise that he found the elven-net was still clutched in his hand. But alas! his elfin-heart was not inside.

At least the comforting weight of his *Legends* book was still there in the shoulder bag. He glanced about him hopefully. But seawards it was nowhere to be seen. There was only an endless flow of the weird and wonderful creatures coming in.

169

A huge white-winged silvery horse came flying in over the waves and landed some way down from him along the shore. Its forelegs kneeled on the sand and a large man-like being slid down from its back. A broad-brimmed tall and shapeless hat shrouded his face and a night-sky cloak of black floated about him, glimmering with tiny stars like elven-nets. Placing a large hourglass on the beach, he quickly filled the top with sparkly sand and mounted the horse again. Flapping its great wings, it took off gracefully into the air. A fine trail of sandy sparkles twinkled behind them as the rider waved his hourglass like a sprinkler everywhere.

So that was the *Sandman* stories told about! And that's where he collected his supplies!

As the horse and rider vanished in the mists, a shoal of elfin-hearts came swimming slowly overhead. Iffleplum's heart jumped momentarily—but no, it wasn't there. And he strained his eyes in vain. Open-mouthed in wonder and disappointment, he watched them pulsing off, like phosphorescent faery jellyfish rolling on the surface of an unseen sea.

As there seemed no other way to go, he turned about to follow them. Scooping up a handful of the glittering stardust sand, he stuffed it in the pocket of his dwarvish dwemmer-coat and stumbled up the dunes.

Beyond them, he could see the teeming hordes of creatures spreading out across the mist-enshrouded land. Scattered

DWÊMÒRIÆ

shafts of soft sunlight were shining downwards through the
mist, picking out patches of the landscape faraway: the dim
rays revealing distant dreamlike hills and mountains bare, in
hazy shades, as woolly as the mould on long-forgotten cheese.
And as the sunbeams slowly came and went, there—wondrous
valleys, huddled houses, castles, woods and waterfalls emerged
awhile, and then mysteriously disappeared again from view.
And here and there flashed many golden-gleaming
waterholes, where the wandering creatures stopped to drink.

"Oh, where am I?" he cried. "And why did the *Khämmârkü*
leave me here and go away?"

Then he heard a deep voice in his head that said *"You are
passing through Dwêmòriæ—and the Khämmârkü who carried
you—belong with me, in the Only Sea—around the Âhn-Ühm
Ôrôniæ. For the Sandman's Shore to which you came, is the end
of the Heartboat-Khämmârkü's domain."*

"Hoo!" cooed Iffleplum, looking up, as an image of the
Ârkühm-Mage appeared before him, hanging in the air. "Oh!
Ürû-Ühm! Save me Master!" he called out in despair.

"Fear not, young Iffleplum!" the Mage replied. 'For you are
Seen! And there are helpers on the way! Just listen for their
song! For the Shepherds of Dreams will guide you through
the Whirl in the middle of Dwêmòriæ."

"What Whirl? Oh! Dwêmòriæ? I'm in the Land of Dreams?
You mean I'm—then am I—am I dreaming this? Am I
asleep?"

"*All* are asleep—except the Awakened. For what others call
the 'waking world'—is no more than another form of walking
in their sleep."

"I don't understand—I *only* don't!" moaned Iffleplum.
"Çhelône said something of the same. But now I don't know
now if I'm dreaming or awake! I don't know what's *real* or
unreal anymore!"

"Ah then! That is well," the Ârkühm smiled kindly.
"Uncertainty is the first step towards becoming wise. Only
fools are absolutely *sure* of anything. Does your dream world
still exist when you wake up? If not—then ask yourself—does

171

the world you dream up when you are awake still abide there—when you have left it and gone on? *Ühm knows.*

"Whatever world you are in—although as real as a rainbow it may seem—like a rainbow it will be; for a moment only it is there: and then it's gone! For a moment—or a day—or maybe three score years and ten. But every dream will pass away and every world will dwem. And I too must leave you now: for my time with you is done."

"Oh Ürû-Ühm! Don't go away!" groaned Iffleplum. "I need your help. I *only* do!"

"Nay, dear Heart, I may no longer stay," the Ârkühm said. "For I am not here where I seem to be: I rest upon the Heartboat still. 'Tis but a 'Sending' of my form—a 'glamour' that you see. And even now I feel it starts to fade away. I fear we cannot aid you more, for you are passing way beyond my care. We are on a course we cannot alter: as you are bound on yours. And alas! My duty lies elsewhere. Fare thee well, young master Iffleplum. May the *Song of Ühm* guide you on your way. Farewell—"

"Oh! But—but Ürû-Ühm!" cried Iffleplum, as the image of the Ârkühm began to dwem. "I don't know what to do—or which way I should go!"

"Do as always—*follow your heart.* Without your heart, your mind is blind. Only your heart will find the way."

The fading Ârkühm held up his hands; his wrists together and his fingers curled inwards in the form of a heart. A growing light began to shine between his palms, softly pulsing from white to rosy red. The Ârkühm slowly faded away, until only his hands remained. Parting his palms, an elfin-heart came swirling from them like a bird released into the air.

Then Iffleplum's heartbeat quickened in his breast. Oh, yes! It was! It *only* was! He did not need to see it's peppering of little bits of print, to know it for his own!

He was after it in a flash. Waving his elven-net on high, he flung himself down the dune in hot pursuit. Across a spongy grass and flower-speckled land he ran. But no matter how he jumped and swiped, his elfin-heart was always just beyond his reach. The more he tried, the more he found himself slowing down.

He seemed to be running and jumping in slow motion, or a like swimmer forcing his way through a sea of thick molasses. And all the while the heart-wraith went on drifting further and further away. Then he saw it twirling round and floating down towards a luminous golden pool some forty strides ahead. Descending on its smoky veils, it settled like a butterfly in the heart of a huge water lily on the surface of the pond.

Iffleplum staggered on towards it step by step, as if struggling through a bog. His mind grew cloudy and his nose shone redly with a growing anger. But deep inside he felt anxious rather than angry, so he could not work out why. And looking down, he saw that he was walking in the edge of a stream of creeping darkness that slithered on the ground.

It was flowing on before him over the rolling land, like a sluggish, smoky worm. And he could feel its clamminess crawling up his legs. Now he realized the fume was darkening his heart and mind. Hastily he jumped up out of it in fright. Scrambling up a grassy mound he tore the grass and rubbed the bad feelings from his legs. And just in time! For suddenly a dreadful thundering sound came roaring from the smoky stream behind.

He turned and stared aghast as a monstrous, black and bristly slug-like thing came storming by, wafting waves of fear before it like ripples in the air. The ghastly grub was even higher than his house back home! The ground-mist fanned out all around it as it came. For its thousand slithery millipede legs were drumming horribly up and down. And stabs of flame and lightning crackled on its back in the darkness that surrounded it.

Poor Plumkin gasped and clasped his hands across his breast. For now he realized the monster's pulsing sides were covered with a mass of clinging Gropes! They hung upon it like a swarm of parasitic ticks blood-sucking on a beast: though they were bloated not from feeding on its blood, but from the fear the flaming creature created as it passed. It crackled by with a stifling smell of burning flesh! And the greedy Gropes all yelled and screamed delightedly, their redlined cloaks flashing out behind them with its speed.

The ifflepinn fell to his knees. He cowered down, groaning in horror. Covering his head with his elven-net he buried his face in the sweet-smelling grass. His ears were filled with the thunder of the beast and the fiendishly raucous glee of the Gropes. But as he lay there all atremble, he became aware of an eerie singing from strange unearthly voices all around him everywhere. He raised his head cautiously, peering out and wondering what new terror might be about.

The monster maggot-thing was now four furlongs far from him: still slithering on, along the darksome smoky river-road inland. Forks of lightning were flickering on its back, either leaping up from it, or drawn down from the skies. But hovering all around it, he espied a flock of what seemed reddish man-like things with dragon's wings; like giant fireflies swooping in the air. And from where he lay, he could hear the weird enchanted singing came from them.

He stuffed his ears and plunged his face back down in the grass again.

Suddenly he screamed as a pair of hands clutched him from behind and lifted him. The ifflepinn lashed out with his elven-net and leapt away. He spun around and found himself face to face with one of the flying creatures standing there.

A strange, benign, bronze-bodied being, with glowing golden eyes and flowing golden hair looked down on him. It observed him with a friendly, but a cautious stare. Its huge wings were folded high behind its head. The being's face was softly scaled, as was its breast, bared between the open "V" of its wispy white tunic, which was belted at the waist with a golden clasp, and skirted to its knees; from there its legs were bound with criss-crossed thongs, down to sandals on its feet.

"Well, bless my wings! I pray you, do not jump about like that!" it said, ruefully rubbing its arm where the cane of the eleven-net had slashed across it. "I was but helping you up to your feet! I had bethought that you were fallen in a faint. I would not wonder it, with such phantasmagoria passing by."

As curious as the creature seemed, its face was kind, and Iffleplum felt no harm in it. In fact, he now felt reassured and bathed in love, as he did when carried by the *Khämmârkü*.

"I'm sorry, but you startled me," said he. "I was a bit upset. I *only* was! What was that awful thing?"

"That would be what they call a Mhoggoth down in Ümmulon—a 'Living Nightmare'—we find them coming through our country now and then. That one was the 'Spirit of a War' dreamed up by many Men—full of fear and fury— we could feel it coming from afar. When collective dreams like that come in, we try to Sing them off the Darkstream in hopes that we can shepherd them onto wiser ways."

"Then—then you must be the Dreamherds of Dwêmòriæ that the Ârkühm told me I should meet?"

"Aye, so it is: from him it was the message came to search for you. I am Kaïdar *Khämmârkaï*, Second Singer Wing of Flock Two of the Flying Force. We are the *Khämmârkü* of

Dreams and also guardians of the two opposing Streams—the Lightstream and the Dark."

"Oh! Was that slithery stuff the Darkstream I was walking in?" asked Iffleplum. "What is it? It made me feel quite bad."

"Oh aye, it would," the Dreamherd said. "The Dark-stream—or the *Dhârkästir* as we call it—is a force that flows through all the worlds: a channelling of all the lowest heavy thoughts of people everywhere. It is made up of Greed and Anger, Misery and Despair, Self-pity, Hate and Jealousy; Hopelessness, Unkindliness and wilful Negativity. And those who forget their elfin-hearts and go astray, get sucked along in such a stream—becoming even worse—and try to drag in others with them all along the way.

"But bless my wings! I am glad to say we also have the Lightstream—that we name the *Lûmentir*—you see it way up there?" He pointed to the sky where the snake of starry light he had seen before, was flowing ghostlike through the air. "That be the stream that flows through all the elfin-hearts where love and kindness dwell. And when it does, it makes each heart swell even more—so all those around them feel their joy as well."

"Then why's it up there, so far away?" groused Iffleplum.

"Why—it must avoid the downward pull of the dense Dark-stream, when passing through Dwêmòriæ," Khämmârkaï Kaïdar said. "But you can bring it to you anytime! Whenever you recall good feelings in your heart, then the Lightstream is flowing through. You may not *see* the *Lûmentir* down in your world, but when it is flowing through your heart, for sure you will know it's there!

"To call it in is easy. But to stay in it, is quite an art. But come! We may not tarry here. I must take you on towards the Whirl and then be on my way."

"Oh, yes! What *is* the Whirl?" asked Iffleplum. "It's something that I heard the Ârkühm say."

"Ah! Of course, you know it not! In the very middle of our realm, there is a vast and spiral cloud, ever turning—like a whirlpool—in a wide round valley shapen like a bowl. It is somewhat like a funnel-hole, where all the disappearing Dreams flow down. There lies the Doorway back from our world into yours. Every creature you can see around—here, there and everywhere—is someone's thought or Dream. And every Dream or fancy coming through, takes all kinds of shapes upon itself as it wanders through our world. We call them 'Dreamlings'. And when a Dream is nearly done, these Dreamlings swirl away back down the Whirl, returning to the sleepers who are dreaming them.

"And if we succeed to firstly Shepherd them along the Lightstream Way, then the Dreamers will awaken feeling happy and refreshed, after passing through Dwêmòriæ. Not all of them, alas! I have to say. For some escape our Songs and slip away to darker dreams. And they go back down to folks enshrouded in the Darker Stream. Then those unlucky dreamers will awaken feeling troubled for the day. We cannot help them all. But what to do? There are far too few of us, for all the bad dreams coming through. But come now, we must be moving on."

"Oh, but wait! My elfin-heart's over on that pond! Oh no! It's gone again! That Mhoggoth thing must have frightened it away!"

"Well, flap my wings!" said Kaïdar in surprise. "Your elfin-heart is flowing free? Then certainly it has gone on towards the Whirl. All Dreaming things must pass that way. I doubt that you will catch it now. But it landed on *that* pond there, you say? Good! Good! A good sign, that! 'Tis well. My counsel is to take the water there before we go."

"But—but what about my elfin-heart?"

"All elfin-hearts that pass through here are attracted to the *Lûmentir*. No doubt it will have floated up into the stream by now and have been swept upon its way. I have seen it happen many times before. The Lightstream draws all elfin-hearts and takes them through the Whirl. You will find yours again; back in your waking world somewhere, I am sure. But will help you find it, if you sip the water where it lay."

"Ah yes, well, actually—I was rather wondering more where I might get just a little snack?" After all the excitement, the ifflepinn now realized he was very hungry. He had not even had his Wakes, let alone breakfast. And what was there to eat in this curious country? Everything seemed to come and go and nowhere seemed to stay.

The Khämmârkaï looked at him awhile and laughed. "Nay—in the Land of Dreams we have no need of food and drink. We *Khämmârkü* need nothing but the Lightstream in our veins. When we bathe in it, the joyous feeling fills us to the brim. Can you not see it glowing from our eyes? Just as the Shadowfolk—the *Dhârkäsü*—feed on fear, so do the *Khämmârkü* feed upon the love-light flowing from the hearts of Men, along the *Lûmentir*. And without it, we would surely dwem.

"What more could you wish for in Dwêmòriæ? This dream-body you are wearing now has no need of normal food or drink." Then as he saw Iffleplum's face fall and his nose grow pale and grey, he laughed again. "But all the Dreamlings passing through—and others having *Daymares*—such as you, must drink at dream-pools on their way. For each pool fills a different need."

"I'll be surprised if it fills mine!" gruntled Iffleplum. "I won't get fat on that!"

"Ah! But these are *feeling*-pools! Your dreams but show you what you really *feel*. And each pool makes the feeling of your heart grow clearer still—for better or for worse. The fizzier pools are full of light-filled feelings: and when folk drink of them, they feel much lighter too. Some feel after drinking that they can fly—and so they do! Some pools are steadying, some give you strength, and others bring you down. So with our Songs we try to guide the darker dreams towards the lighter pools. But it does not always work. We may Sing a *Dreamling* to a finer feeling-pool, but we cannot make it drink.[14] We only guide, we cannot choose for them, or you."

---

14 This later became a proverb about horses that were not particularly thirsty.

Just then a country voice cried out, "*Âyô* there! Flyer Kaïdar-kin!" They looked around to see a wingless khämmâr-kaï come bounding over the land like a gazelle, in long swift bouncy strides. He came to rest before them, not even slightly out of breath. "*Âyô*, Kaïdar-kin! What are you about?" said he. "Why are you not in the Mhoggoth hunt along with all the rest? They haven't Sung it off the Darkstream yet—and it's halfway through Dwêmòriæ! It is a mighty terror, that! And they need all the Flyers they can get!"

"*Âyô*, Good Bounder Tômukh-Ar!" replied Kaïdar Khäm-mârkaï. "I was upon my way to do so. But I had an errand to this *Dreamling* here—this faery Ælfÿnpynn. I espied him on the ground, forlorn and prostrate as the Mhoggoth passed. Therefore I wingèd down. And now I am duty bound to see him through the Whirl."

"Oh, don't you fret for that! I'll see him through. I can't handle Nightmares, you know that. That's more your line. Daymares and Fantasies are my speciality, as well you know! Anyways, the word is out that Wing Command wants all the Singers as are flying free. Hark now! There it goes! The call is out!"

And indeed, there came a deepening vibration through the air—*Vwuum! Vwuum! Vwuum!*—like the sound a child's bull-roarer toy might make, when something heavy on a cord is whirling round and round. But it was growing deeper as it came, resounding with an urgent sound.

"The Spirit-Catcher calls!" said Kaïdar. "Forgive me, I am summoned! I'm sorry, Dreamling, I must go. We must Sing this Mhoggoth off its track! If it does not drink at lighter pools—there will be far more chaos in the worlds below. And the Lightstream will then no longer flow in many people's hearts. Farewell!" So saying, Kaïdar swiftly launched himself into the air. His scarlet webbed wings spread wide as he flapped away with strong slow steady beats. Yet soon he vanished in the mist.

"Do you drink now at this pool?" said Tômukh-Ar, pointing down.

"So Kaïdar said," sighed Iffleplum, thinking a nice bowl of
Wakes-flakes would suit him more. A white stone statue of
what seemed to be a dragon, stood beside the pool and water
poured from its mouth. The ifflepinn cupped the water in his
palms and drank. And soon a warming feeling stole steadily
through his limbs. His eyes began to sparkle like the stars.
"Oh! Oh! It's good!" he chortled, "It's better than I thought!"
And he quickly guzzled up three handfuls more.

"*Âyô!* Steady now!" said the Daydream-herder. "Three sips
is quite enough to start!"

But Plumkin hiccupped and he laughed. Then turned and
gazed about him, open-mouthed. For as he drank, the dreary
mists had on the instant drawn away. It seemed as if many
veils were now lifted from his eyes. The sky was clear and blue
and sparkling bright with *lûmenü*. And the sun was shining
down. All around them flowers and trees were busily blooming
everywhere, bedecked with butterflies and buzzing bees. And
every growing thing seemed to radiate with a softly bluish
light. "Why! I can see a shiny haze around everything! And
round me too!" cried Iffleplum delightedly, seeing a sparkling
aura round his arm. "And I can see inside the trees! Oh, look!
There are tree-deeves swimming up inside the sap and feeding
all the leaves!"

He looked around him in a daze. Now many more ponds and
pools were slowly coming into view. And he realized that all
the feeling-pools reflected different colours—rose and green,
and gold and lilac too. Some pools there were of darker hue,
of olive green, or purple, black, or blue.

"*Âyô!* It be like that all over—all the time—my friend," said
Tômukh with a wink. "The veils betweens the worlds are thin.
There's light and dark worlds everywhere, right here and
now. It just depends on how you look! If you look out from
your heart, the world doesn't seem so dull and grey. Most
folks don't look out from their elfin-hearts. They're only lookin
from their heads—mostimes through minds chock-full of
thinking-mist! They're so busy with their thoughts, they don't

even realize—it's who they *really* are—who's standing back inside and a-watchin what they think!"

"I'm so amazed, I can't think anything!" said Iffleplum. "It feels so strange! I don't even know who's looking anymore! I don't even feel I'm me!"

"Ah! Well glory be! That's cause now your elven-eyes have learned to *see!* When you've forgot yourself—you'll find it's Old Ühmkyn looking from your eyes—instead of who you *think* you are!

"Old Ühmkyn's looking *out* of me?" burbled Plumkin, laughing merrily. "How can it be?" His chest was full of chuckles at the thought. His nose grew golden and shiny with joy. With outstretched arms he started spinning round and round.

"Old Ühmkyn's looking out of everyone," said Tômukh-Ar earnestly. "Just as soon as who *we* think we are has 'gone.' It's like the water spouting from that stone-dragon's mouth there. We don't think it's coming from the dragon, do we now? We know it's coming from the Source. Likewise, Old Ühmkyn is the SOURCE of *us!* What words come out of all our mouths, or what shines from all our eyes, is just Old Ühmkyn's Dream of *being us*. It's just Ühmkyn's play—you see?"

The ifflepinn laughed dizzily. Still twirling round he now went whirling off the ground and shot up in the air.

"*Âyô!* Mind that tree!" cried Tômukh-Ar as Plumkin banged his head upon a branch, sending blue electric sparkles everywhere. He then came floating slowly down, still giggling helplessly.

"Oops!" said Tômukh-Ar. "I reckon you've drunk overmuch at the Pool of Levity. You'd best come along and bound aside of me. The exercise might work it off!"

And to his amaze, the next moment, the ifflepinn found himself bounding along beside the *Khämmârkaï*, as fleet and graceful as a deer, as if springs were on his feet. As they loped across the land, he saw little knots of other Bounder *Khämmârkü*, harrying droves of Dreamlings, here and there,

181

like sheepdogs tracking sheep. By striking up strange harmonies with their eerie sounding songs, the Dreamherds helped them huddle away from darksome pools and flock to brighter ponds.

*

At length, on passing through a cleft between two craggy cliffs, they came down into a dreary vale. Here the light was dull and grey. Scrubby bushes without blooms were dotted here and there. A murky-looking pool lay in a hollow someway below them to their right, beneath a frowning rock-face full of holes.

"I don't much like this place," said Tômukh-Ar, "Too many darker Dreamlings get attracted here. Look you! There's a few we've missed!" Several creepy-looking creatures were slithering around the pool and slavering at the water's edge. A giant copper-crested lizard bared its fangs at a smaller crocodile-like creature coming down to drink. The reptile sprang at it angrily and bit the lizard on the neck. Immediately they rolled over and over, snarling and scratching like a pair of scaly cats.

"See those two there? I know who they are. Those Dreamlings are the 'thought-forms' of two brothers who hate each other," Tômukh-Ar sighed. "Poor lads! One thinks he lost his mother's love when the little one came along. But it isn't true. She was just busy with the new babe, that's all. But now he tries to get everything for himself. He's spiteful to his little brother, kicks the dog, and stays angry all the time. So he gets a ton of anger in return. But bit by bit, when he gets back double what he gives out, it might teach him. If it doesn't, he'll get it in the neck twice as bad next time. Getting clobbered oneself, is powerful good medicine—if you stop and wonder why, that is."

"Can't you sing them to another pool?" asked Iffleplum.

"Not by myself. Anyway, I don't really need to," answered Tômukh-Ar. "They'll sort it by themselves, sooner or later. I've seen the dreams that lie ahead. Some futures throw a shadow in the Now. One day the little lad will fall out of a tree and nearly die. Then the older boy'll get to feel sad and sorry by himself. So he'll start to care for his little brother as he's getting well. And in the end they'll grow up to be good friends. He'll learn. Ah look! With all their scrapping they've rolled over near a brighter pool just there! Ha! It's the Pool of Tolerance just come up! Better make sure. Hang about!"

The bounder *Khämmârkaï* swiftly looked around in case anyone was watching him. Inhaling deeply, he slowly filled his chest. Then with a long and mighty breath like a steady wind he let it go. The fighting creatures went bowling over like the leaves from the bushes and tumbled straight into the pool.

"Ha! See! They've both swallowed up some mouthfuls of 'Good Humour' now—with a little help. Hmm! Don't say anything. I'm not supposed to do it like that. Against the rules. Anyway, the fight's over now." The lizard and the crocosaurus now clambered out of the pale green waterhole. And amiably they waddled off together down the vale.

"They're not so bad," said the Dreamherder. "But the big ones, they can hide away from us in the maze of caves up there. As you can see, the cliff is honeycombed with tunnels in the rock. But they all run down to the Deepest, Darkest, and most Deadly-Feeling pool of all—the Pool of Doom, Despair, and Dreadful Death. All the foulest Dreamlings gather there. They drink the dark and stagnant waters until they've gorged themselves on all the hate and horrid feelings they can hold. Then they sit there seething in the gloom, devising darker deeds, before returning to wreak havoc in the world again. And then—*Âyô!* Look you! There's one coming out! Oh, no! Not Old Slobberchops again! I've seen that one too many times before!"

A huge, fat, slimy creature like a giant eel came suddenly pouring out of the cliff-face, like a maggot from a rotting dog. Its body, half a furlong long, was scarred and pitted all along its length with the festering wounds of many battles past. And here and there, from red-raw gaping holes, fresh flapping gobbets of its flesh hung down. It plunged into the darksome pool and reared up right away, roaring like a serpent from the sea. Its blind and eyeless head thrashed savagely from side to side. And its rows of curvy fangs snapped senselessly at unseen creatures in the air. The drinking Dreamlings fled scattering before it as it came.

"Just watch that great dumb dim-witted beast!" said Tômukh-Ar. "It's always seeking enemies. It thinks that if it can savage others first, then it will save *itself* from hurt. But look! See how it thrashes all about? It wriggles like fish-bait on a hook! And being blind, when it feels its own coils flip-flopping all around it, it thinks it's some other creature looking for a fight! So it pounces on itself and bites great chunks out of its own flesh! See, there it goes! Watch the way it does!"

The Blindworm jerked back as it sensed its own hind-quarters slapping down before its nose. It then lunged forward and savagely sunk its teeth into its own tail. "Just what I said!" said Tômukh-Ar. "By the time the message of its pain arrives back to its tiny brain, the daft thing will think it's been attacked!" And so it seemed. The Blindworm now bellowed out in anguish and in rage, having bitten itself to the bone. It wildly lashed its tail about then bit itself again—and then again—to try and save itself from further pain.

"Oh, gripes! What is that horrid, stupid thing?" asked Iffleplum.

"Mankind," said the Khämmârkaï. "That's what it is. At least—it's all the unthinking, mindless mass of *ühmenü*, who live like sheep. The kind that follow blind their leaders into war! When the poor things haven't got a clue! Knowing nothing of what's behind the lies they're told, and the dreadful things they are led to do. *Âyô!* Many a time we've tried, but we've never budged the Blindworm from its track. The blessèd thing is *always* coming through! Best keep away from things like that. We waste our time with those whose minds are blind. Let's go."

And with that, Tômukh-Ar bounded off once more. Iffleplum set off after him, still bouncing like a Khämmârkaï.

184

Leaving the dreary vale behind, they loped out upon a grassy plain. But now the sky had darkened once again.

Not far away, a range of hills and misty-looking mountains rose up before them. Their snowy sides were softly looming in the sun-rays shooting down from the storm-clouds rolling past their peaks. Flying *Khämmârkü* were turning in the air, their red-wings storm-lit, stark against the darker clouds. And the plains below were filled with herds of drifting Dreamlings and their shepherds herding them.

"We now be coming closer to the Whirl," said Tômukh-Ar. "It be just through a vale beyond the foothills there. The Dreamlings here are being driven on towards what you Day-Dreamers call the Waking World."

As the mountains neared, a brilliant beam of sun blazed down. Before their eyes, a wondrous city on a mountain-top appeared. It seemed lit up in luminescence magical.

"*Âyô-ah!*" cried all the *Khämmârkü*. They gazed upon the white-walled city, golden-domed with temples, towers, and minarets, which climbed upon a craggy mist-enshrouded cliff, rising up and up into the sky. The voices of the Dreamherders everywhere rose in exultation, in a paean of great joy. And even all the Dreamlings scattered on the plains, stopped still awhile in awe. A blissful happiness and delight came wafting down in waves from the City shining like the moon.

"*Âyô!*" cried Tômukh-Ar in great joy, his golden eyes shining in the stormlight. "There's the City Celestial!"

"Oh, what is it?" breathed Iffleplum in happy wonder.

"There be an hour in Middleworld when many Ühmen-folk in every land, stop awhile, and let the love of Ühm flow through their hearts. Some there be who build the Celestial City in their minds. And their loving thoughts create it in our world. Oftimes we see it—and it grows! Oh, glory be! It *grows!* And the feeling which comes down from it, oh!, can help us break the Mhoggoth in our midst. Yes! Look now! The Flyers are all away! They're filled with it! Charged up with such a feeling, they can Sing that there Mhoggoth into bits!"

185

"Oh!" cried Iffleplum. "Oh! It's too wonderful!" His heart felt near to burst with joy. "Oh, it's too much! I feel too full of love and featherlight!" And saying so, he found himself bathed in a golden glow and rising from the ground.

"*Âyô!* The Lightstream's taken you!" cried Tômukh-Ar happily. "Go with it!" he called out. "Stay in the Stream! It'll take you where you need!"

And indeed, the *Lûmentir* had dipped down from the sky and lifted the ifflepinn off his feet. He went tumbling over in the air awhile, until he learned the way to ride the Stream. By holding his breath, with his arms out wide, he found he could easily glide along and let it carry him over the plains. His heart swelled as the feeling of the Lightstream filled him with its joy.

Beside him in the Stream were many other creatures flowing by—some glowing sprites of light—like golden tree-deeves; and there were fish-tailed *Khämmârkü* he could see right through—and shoals of humming elfin-hearts with suns inside them—all went flashing by before his eyes. Just then a shimmering rainbow came arcing down the sky ahead. As the *Lûmentir* went streaming through its dazzling light, the air grew bright with colours all around. Then it was out the other side.

And now suddenly it was soaring high above the City Celestial, whose towers, turrets and dreaming domes, were blushing in its passing glow, with a gleaming, soft-hued mother-of-pearl-like sheen. But to Iffleplum's dismay, it carried him up and far away beyond the shining Citadel. A yearning cry escaped him as he far too swiftly passed it by: for the call of the moonlike City had touched something in his heart.

Now the Lightstream went snaking down through a vale between the hills, and there!—the Darkstream, rippling like its shadow, went running all along the land below. But soon the vale came to an end. And both Streams sped out into a wide and open space, where a ring of mountains formed a vast and cloud-filled bowl.

And there below at last, he saw the Whirl!

A swirling funnel of cloud it was, slowly disappearing down an unseen hole, like foamy water down a sink. The Lightstream went swooping over it like a swallow skimming the surface of a lake.

Oh what a delight! thought Iffleplum. *I could fly forever doing this!* His closed his eyes and sighed in bliss: *I only wonder how long it will last?*

Of course, the moment he thought this, the *Lûmentir* went sharply shooting down and plunged into the Whirl. And the ifflepinn cried out again as he tumbled topsy-turvy through the air. His stomach churned and came down plunging after him.

A blast of rushing air now buffeted his face and body. And his dwemmer-robe flapped wildly round him, rattling like a ship's sails in a storm. His eyes opened of themselves in wonder and in shock. Then terror came again! For he found himself once more upside down and cartwheeling through the sky!

And lo and behold! There on high, the keel of the *Heartboat* could still be seen sailing blithely overhead. And it was swiftly shrinking smaller as he fell. Below him mountains, valleys, woods and lakes were dizzily whirling round and round. "Oh, Mumkin!" he wailed as the ground came rushing up to meet him. The flash of a river snaking across the land below, like the glittering trail of a slurmy snail, was the last thing that he saw. For suddenly his head went woozy and the next moment he was gone!

He lost his mind again—and fell into the limbo of the dark unknown!

Part the Fourteenth

The Hunters
of the Ifflepig

*From the Whirl of Dwêmòriæ Iffleplum fell through,
to a land where he is hunted by the Ühmenü*

Iffleplum felt a coldness slowly creeping to his bones. He tried to snuggle down deeper in his bed, rolling over to pull the blankets closer round him. But—ugh!—they were all wet. And he heard them splash as he turned over! Suddenly he was wide-awake! With a start he found himself floating in shallow water, at the edge of an icy mountain lake.

Oh! Oh! Am I dead again? he thought. And then began to laugh in shock, lolling among the reeds and wheezing helplessly in silent mirth. He shook his head in disbelief. *Dead again?* he thought. *How can I be? If I'm awake—then Old Ühmkyn is still Singing me! But I fell off the GOLDEN HEART! And tumbled through the Whirl! How could I have fallen so far without a broken neck?*

He tried to remember. Surely the *Khämmârkü* had been beside him as he fell? Or had that been a dream? But no! Even out in the Lonely Realm he had felt somehow that they were there. They must have slowed him down before he landed in the lake! He sat up and splashed the water with his hands. This time it really *was* wet water! And very chilly too. He clawed away a wad of slimy green weed draped across his snout and stared about him in amazement.

The lake he lay in was a shimmering brilliant blue and glittered in the morning sun. Shining dragonflies skimmed over the surface still as a pond, which scarcely rippled unless he moved. And there! What luck! He saw his elven-net floating nearby in the reeds. He grabbed it up and floundered to the shore.

Peeling off his dripping dwemmer-coat, he draped it on a flowering bush to dry. Feeling in the pocket, he found the powdery stardust from the shores of Dwêmòriæ was slightly damp. So he stuffed some in the pouch-pocket of his skin, to dry it with his body heat. But to his delight, his shoulder-bag from Çhelône seemed waterproof. Inside, he found his *Legends* book was fairly dry. But even so, he spread the pages to the sun that was warmly shining down. Then he cast himself in weary wonderment upon the grass.

What *had* befallen him? He remembered blacking out as he tumbled from the *Golden Heart*. And somehow he had awakened in Dwêmòriæ. And then he had journeyed with the *Khämmârkü* all through the Land of Dreams. Could that have really been a dream? It seemed so real. But all that time there it seems, had been no time at all! How could it be? When he awoke and found himself falling through the air, he had seen

189

the Heartboat still flying there above him in the sky! How was
it possible? It seemed that sometimes and in some places, no
time was. And then there was the Lonely Realm too! A
Nowhere Place where nothing was.

And come to that—where am I now? thought Iffleplum.

He gazed about him wonderingly. The scenery was
beautiful all around. Bushes bloomed along the shore and
wooded mountains rose on every side. Even here the shrubs
and grasses sparkled with a bluish glow, as he had seen them
in Dwêmòriæ. He wondered if his eyes were playing tricks.
But then they opened wide in wonderment. For suddenly he
realized that the leaves on all the trees were bright with
autumn colouring, in russet reds or yellowing. And many
were now gently falling to the ground! *How could it be—in
Spring?*

Had time gone crazy? How long had be been in Dwêmòriæ?
His head grew dizzy with puzzling. But a rustling sound
behind distracted him. He whirled around.

The bush beneath his dwemmer-coat was trembling
violently, for no reason he could see. He looked closer,
blinking in bewilderment. A swarm of half-seen tiny figures
were scrambling all around his robe. He rubbed his eyes and
looked again. Dozens of greeny-golden flower-deeves, were
shaking the branches and tugging at his coat. To Iffleplum's
astonishment, he heard one of them cry out, "All together
now—shiver it, lads!"

"Oh!" he gasped. "You talk! I can understand your speech!"
The tiny flower-elementals froze and stared at him.

"*Ay up!*" cried one. "We're spotted!" The imp looked up at
Iffleplum, quite unafraid, but curious. "Are you seeing us?"
he asked.

"Why, yes I can! I *only* can! But I don't understand. How
come you speak the Common Ummal-tongue?"

"We don't. We're speakin Sylvan, matey—what we always
speak! *Sylvanavâhl*—you know—the Tree-Talk. Seems as
how you're pickin up what we say. We can hear you in Sylvan
too, like what we can with Elves. You don't look much like

190

an elf to me. But I reckon you've been a-mixin with 'em—or was it Dwemmer-folk? There's a powerful scent o dwemmers on y'coat!"

"Oh, yes! I was travelling with the Dwemmer-folk—up in their boat! But I fell off—"

"Arr! Well that explains it then!" said the sprite. "If you've been along with them, you'll be seein with your elven-eyes awhile—and hearin with your elven-ears. But it won't last long. It fades off in a bit. You'll soon get shrinkle-eyed again, like all the rest. Then you'll think we're talkin gibberish. Or you'll think it's just the rustle of the leaves. Anyways; no time to chat. We're busy folk. We've still got lots of flower buds to burst out into bloom, before the season's over..."

"Oh, yes! But please—fair dævas all! What season is it here? How come so many leaves are falling in the spring?"

"*Dævas* is it?" cackled one. "You're a caution and no mistake! We ain't dævas—we are *barksprites*, matey! Dævas be a bit beyond the likes of us!"

"And it ain't spring, it's autumn, matey!" piped up another. "Where've you been all summer long?"

Iffleplum was too stunned to answer him. *Autumn! How long HAD be been in Dwêmòriæ? Half a minute—or half a year?*

"In any case," said the leader, "we'd be mighty obliged if you can get your jacket off of our flower-tops, so as how we can get back inside our own front doors?"

"Oh, sorry!" said Iffleplum lifting it down, "I didn't realize—"

"Aye, they never do," said the barksprite. "Drying their pants and towels and what not... Anyways, nice chattin to you. But we've got work to do—"

"Oh, but can you just tell me where I am, because—?"

But just then the cries of children's voices laughing and squealing came down the hillside from the nearby wood.

"Ay-up, lads!" cried the barksprite, "There's kids a-comin! Scarce yourselves! Cheerio, playmate!" And in a twinkling they were gone. The barksprites plunged into the open flowers and vanished down inside the bark and branches of the bush.

Two scruffy girls and a ragged barefoot boy came running and laughing down the slope towards the lake. They burst upon him from the bushes, stopping in surprise to see him there. Iffleplum's eyes grew big and round. Surely these were children of the *Ühmenü*? Had he fallen in the Middleworld of Man?

"Ooh! What's that?" the youngest girl exclaimed in fright, hiding behind her sister.

"I dunno," said the boy warily, backing away. "Never seen one of *them* before." He bent down to pick up a heavy stick, looking ready for a fight.

Alarmed at the turn of events, Iffleplum tried to soothe their fears. "It's all right, I'm just an ifflepinn," he said.

The effect on them astonished him. The boy yelped in fright and dropped the stick. "Aah! Aah! It's a talkin animal!" he cried. "Mama!" He turned and fled back into the forest. And the girls went running after him, screaming for their mothers.

This upset the ifflepinn mightily. He quickly gathered up his things and slipped into his dwemmer-coat, which now was nearly dry. If the grown-ups were more aggressive than the children, it was dangerous to stay around. And if they had never seen ummals before, he had best stay in disguise. He pulled the dwemmer-hood down to his snout and set off along the shore. In a while he came onto a track-like road that ran along the lakeside. At first he hesitated to walk on it. But it had been difficult picking his way over the rocks along the shoreline. His stomach was reminding him how hungry he was. And a road might lead him on to food!

Shortly on the track ahead, he saw a shepherd boy coming towards him herding a flock of goats. There was nowhere nearby to hide, so Iffleplum stayed where he was. Besides, whatever the risk, he had to find out where he was and where to go.

A rank smell drifted to his nostrils as the goats approached. His nose twitched and yellowed with disgust. As the boy neared, the ifflepinn saw that it was another Manling child. But this one was a youth, much older than the children he had

192

seen. The young man touched his forelock as he neared: "Good day to you, my good gnorf!" he smiled, obviously mistaking him for something else.

Norf? What in Ælfÿlon was a Norf?

"Catch anything, have you?" asked the goatherd, nodding at his elven-net.

"What? Oh! Erm—no. N–n–not yet," stammered Iffleplum.

"Pity," said the boy. "Just fancied a fish dinner. I got a spare thrupenny bit."

Iffleplum had no idea what he was talking about, but the word 'dinner' warmed his heart and emboldened him.

"Erm—is there somewhere I might get something to eat around here?" he asked tentatively.

"Oh, arr!" replied the goatherd. "There's an Eatery up at the village, yonder." He pointed back the way he had come. "It's down at lakeside, by the jetty. 'Tain't far."

Iffleplum beamed with pleasure. Now that sounded a lot more hopeful. Perhaps the Ühmen-folk were not so bad after all. "Please, could you tell me where I am?" he asked.

"Why—you're at Pikesmere in the Lakenland," the boy said in surprise. "You travelled far?"

"Quite a bit," said Iffleplum. "But I got lost. So—in what world is Lakenland—I mean, what country is that in?"

The goatherd looked at him strangely. "Why—*Ümmulon* of course!" he said. "What did you expect? There ain't anywhere else, is there? Good day to you!"

Clicking his teeth at the goats he moved them on. "*Rum cove*," he muttered under his breath, as he went on down the track. "These gnorfs've got their heads in the clouds. And he's got *mustard* all over his nose."

But Iffleplum was overjoyed. *Ümmulon!* he thought in glee. *I'm here! At last!* Now anything was possible! The very thought gave him courage. He could even manage a village full of *Ühmenü*, if he had found himself at last in Ümmulon!

He stepped out boldly and soon the village came in sight. At the roadside, a rotting sign fallen in the grass bore the mouldering word, "PIKESMERE". The dwellings at the edge were rather ramshackle and ragged children hugged the doors. Some shouted taunts at him as he passed:

> *"Gnorf-Gnorf! Half a Dwarf!*
> *Half a Dwarf and half a Gnome!*
> *Got shacked up in the hills alone!*
> *When both of 'em was far from home!*
> *Tinker-peddlar, stinky-poo!*
> *We don't want no more of you!"*

A large lady in a grubby smock appeared in a doorway and smacked their heads, shouting at them in a high-pitched voice. "Stop your cheeking the gnorfs, you little brats! How can we get anything we want, if there ain't no peddlers?"

Iffleplum lowered his head and hurried on. *So that's a Gnorf,* he thought. *Half a Gnome and half a Dwarf. That's what the goat-boy thought I was. But what's a peddlar?*

Peering under his hood, he saw there was no need to ask the way. The main track went on uphill through the rambling village. The only other one branched off down towards the lake. Iffleplum shrank inside his hood and set off cautiously. He soon found himself in a busy, narrow street of higgledy-piggledy black and white half-timbered houses. Their upper storeys leaned in from either side, so close that people could shake hands across the street from opposite windows. Crows squawked on the chimneys, beating fish-heads on the roofs of slate, or circling noisily in the air. Donkey-carts full of wood, or barrels of fish and lumpy sacks, were trundling up and down. Chickens, clucking excitedly, scattered before them with a flurry of feathers.

Some men were cursing when their cart got stuck in a rut, where the cobblestones had come away. They took no notice of the ifflepinn as they sweated and struggled to get the wheel out. Only the occasional mangy dog grizzled at him half-heartedly as he passed.

At the bottom of the street he found the Eatery, as the boy had said, beside the lake.

Facing the jetty, where a few small boats were tied, stood a scruffy-looking, once-whitewashed, wattle-and-daubed building with low thatch. Above its door, was a hanging sign, which bore the words: *The Brindled Pike*, with a picture of a savagely grinning fish below. In front of the inn, behind a section cordoned off by ropes on posts, a few long tables and benches were set out under awnings, shaded from the sun.

Around them, several large men (frighteningly large for Iffleplum) were tucking into huge platters of food. They seemed to be mostly farmers and fishermen, all talking at each other and no one really listening. Most were laughing loudly and drinking noisily out of huge tankards. Strange aromas filled the air. Iffleplum's stomach rumbled. But it was too daunting to join the loud-mouthed throng. He fingered his conker in uncertainty, his nose growing slowly grey in his dismay.

Then suddenly he noticed a smaller and lower table to one side. Three silent gloomy-looking dwarves were sitting at one end, wafting away the flies on the table as they ate. Iffleplum timidly entered the enclosure and approached their table.

"May I sit here?" he asked. The hooded dwarves looked at him without expression. With a jut of his chin, one dwarf thrust his greybeard in the air, as if suggesting him to sit. Iffleplum nodded his thanks, courteously placing his hand upon his heart, as he had done among the Dwemmer-folk. He sat gingerly at the other end of a bench, sniffing the heady smell of spilled ale on the tabletop.

Now he was beginning to feel uneasy. The rough voices were growing louder all around. It came to him then, what the wispy smoke was he could see snaking faintly through the air. *The Darkstream must be flowing through the hearts of the all people here*, he thought. It was no place for an ifflepinn. He had to leave, immediately. He rose and picked up his elven-net again. But a beefy barman with sideburns down his face came out just then, and spotted him from behind.

"Sit yourself down, me old dwarf!" he cried, quickly dishing out more mugs of ale and plates and coming round the table. "What'll be yours?"

"He's not a dwarf—he's got no beard!" cackled a yokel. "I expect he's come down from the mountains in the *gnorf!* Ha-ha!" he chortled squiffly, obviously under the impression he had made a hearty joke. The others banged their metal mugs and slapped the table, laughing fit to choke.

"I don't care what he is," grinned the Barman, "so long as he pays his whack! Ain't that right, Squire?" he boomed at Iffleplum. "Here's the menu. What's it to be?"

"Oh! You mean I can have *anything* on this list?" asked Iffleplum eagerly.

"All you can eat, me old gnorf! So long as you pay for it. Hur! Hur!" the Barman laughed oafily, nudging one of the locals with his elbow, to appreciate his wit.

"Er—pay?" asked Iffleplum, uncertainly.

"Just a minute! Hold your horses, Squire," said the Barman suspiciously. "Before you choose, let's feel the weight of your moneybag first."

"Moneybag?" said Iffleplum. "Wh–what's money? Oh, yes! I remember! I read about it in a book!"

The Barman's brow darkened. "Read about it in a—? You fall out the sky, squire?"

"Why, yes!" said Iffleplum amazed. "Yes, I have. How did you know that? Do a lot of people fall out of the sky round here then?"

"All right, toss-pot! Out you go!" The Barman grabbed him by the scruff of his neck and seat of his coat and hurled him over the rope into the road. Iffleplum fell sprawling in the dust and his hood fell back off his face. As he quickly bent to snatch up his elven-net, his long ears flopped around his head. The men jumped up from the tables with a shout. "Look at it! What is it?" cried one. "Strewth! It's a dog! A dog that talks!" squawked another.

"A dog?" retorted Iffleplum. "Since when does a dog have a lilac nose? I'm an ummal! I'm an *ifflepinn!*" In fact, his nose had gone from white with fright, to red with rage.

At this the yokels burst out in guffaws of laughter. "An *ifflepinn* he says! From the faery-world of Ælfÿlon, I suppose? Ha! Ha! Get off with you—you squiffy little ratbag! Lilac! That's a right red boozer's nose, if ever I saw one. Don't you give us faerytales!"

The Barman rushed at him brandishing a beer-mug, as if to throw at him. "And don't you come back here again!" he yelled. "We don't take to tramps like you, trying to take us for a ride! We don't give free meals here!"

Calling roughly to his hounds: "Hey, Gnasher! Spot! Here boys!" Two scabby curs came dashing from the smoky kitchen. "See him off, lads!" he cried.

Iffleplum took to his heels and ran as fast as he could. The snarly dogs barked after him and chased him off along the shore.

A couple of hunters at another table looked at each other meaningfully. "Well, well, well," said the huge black-bearded one quietly. "That there creature ain't a gnorf."

"Right you are," said the other in a floppy hat. "It *is* a animal that talks though, isn't it? An ifflepig, it said it was— or something of the sort. Do you reckon we ought to—"

The other nodded knowingly. They rose in haste and called the barman for their bill.

*

As twilight settled in among the trees, Iffleplum lay groaning in a birch wood on a bed of leaves. Almost without a stop he had run and run from the lakeside village and clambered up the hills. After several hours, he had struggled up into the high-forested mountains, as far from people as he could get.

And there his trembly legs gave out. The long climb and thinner air had made his heart thump like a hammer beat. He sat down, exhausted, weak and ravenous. To the ifflepinn it seemed like weeks since he last ate. So when he had spied a clump of fresh young reddish fungi on the forest floor, he was too hungry to resist.

But eating unknown mushrooms is a dangerous thing, as everybody knows. So at first he tried a morsel in his mouth. As it didn't taste too bitter in while, he gladly scoffed the others down. But before too long, he felt his head and stomach turning round and round. Then in a while, he had fallen in a laughing fit and rolled upon the ground.

And soon he slipped away into a weird and woozy dream. It seemed to him that all the trees around were glimmering, and glowing with a growing inner light. He was seeing with his elven-eyes again, he knew for sure. For looking down, somehow he saw the *Lightstream* gliding far beneath the forest floor!

It rippled like a golden river underground, its runnels rising upwards through the roots of trees and shimmering from their crowns. And in a flash, he understood why those who sat beneath them in a wood were often eased of all their worries and their cares. For now he knew that inside every living tree, there the Lightstream was forever flowing free—although unseen by anyone!

And slowly he became aware of tall, transparent, tree-ish *dævas* of the forest, standing dreaming here and there. No wonder that the silent singing of the trees was all around him in the air. His heart swelled with the joy of it. And he felt himself once more in wondrous *oneness* with all woodlands everywhere.

But suddenly his stomach sickened with a lurch. His head went woozy once again.

Now he was not feeling well at all.

And instantly, the feeling of the forest changed! The luminosity and the shining dreamers now dimmed and swiftly dwemmed away. A dizzy darkness fell.

Spots danced before his eyes. He blinked and peered about uneasily. Dimly, he could sense a seeping pool of deeper darkness creeping all around him on the forest floor.

Gooseflesh prickled on his skin.

Although could not see a thing, he knew the frightful feeling that the *Darkstream* brings! A misty shadow swirled around his feet and toes. It quickly rose about his ankles like a swamp and seemed to suck him down, as if his feet were sinking deep in boggy ground! A clammy feeling slithered up his legs. He felt it rising up his body to his breast. He tried to struggle free, but then—he stopped! His heart went cold. On every side, he saw pale slimy things were bursting up like fungi sprouting from the mould.

But fungi with fiery eyes!

They glittered all around him in the gloom. With a start, he realized that a ring of furious fungus-faeries now surrounded him! Glaring angrily from under shaggy mushroom caps, of every grotesque fungal form and size, they shuffled in towards him. And as they came, a suffocating stench of squashed and rotting fungi riffled up his nose. His senses reeled. His legs gave way and he stumbled to his knees.

"Hah! We have him now!" he heard them cry. "We have him, Kingy! See! He's grovelling down with guilt and awe, before your wondrous majesty!"

A great fat fungling in a crown leaned down and frowned on him, peering over his protruding puffball belly, bulging out above the ifflepinn.

"Oh," said the fungling King disdainfully. "So that's the fungus-flogger is it? What shall we do with the prisoner, now the culprit's come our way?"

"Prisoner? Why am I a prisoner?" asked Iffleplum plaintively. "I've not done *anything!* And—and I'm not feeling very well."

"Really?" replied the fungling King loftily, looking down his nose. "Done *nothing?*" His chest and bloated belly began to swell up even more with indignation. "How *dare* you say you've done nothing—Eh? Who was it thrashed the toadstools in the Wossle Wood with a whippy willow-wand—upon a Newyear's Day? You thought you could get away with that, did you? Hah!"

He turned away towards the crowd. "What say you, good funglings all?"

"Smash him! Thrash him! Sit on him and squash him flat! Just like he did to us!" the funglings cried. "Tie the fungus thrasher up and feed him to the pigs!"

Then all as one they rushed on him from every side. And in the scrum, the great fat fungling King fell down on top of Iffleplum. In haste he threw his elbow up. And with a mighty *POUF!* the King's balloon-like, puffball belly burst and filled the air with dusty spores. A wailing cry went up. Confusion reigned.

Poor Plumkin's stomach churned again. And his head began spin around. He felt heavy hands roughly rolling him and thought the wood was turning upside down. His nose was bumped and dragged along the ground. The smell of leaf mould strongly struck his snout. He vaguely sensed something hurting him, but what it was he could not tell. Unknowingly, he groaned aloud.

200

At that, a rough voice grated in his head, "Hang on a bit! Hang on! I think the creature's coming round!"

"No, he's not!" boomed another voice. "It's just a twitch! He's still deep in foggy fungal dreams! I reckon he'll be out of it for quite a bit."

But coming round he was. And waking up was far worse even than his dream. His head swam and he was feeling very sick. Worse still, he couldn't move at all. He found his hands and feet were bound.

And he was tied on to a stick!

Two dark figures swam before his blurry eyes. His heart jumped, for at first he thought that they were Gropes. But his head began to slowly clear. Squinting carefully, so as not to appear awake, he saw that they were Ühmenü.

Two men were sitting there, close by. One was a big burly fellow with a great black beard and a bandolier across his chest. A fat-barrelled shotgun was strapped across his back. On his head he wore a woolly pom-pom hat. The other one was more thin and wiry looking, with an unshaven, wind-burned face and a floppy feathered hat.

He had seen them both before somewhere. Ah, yes! At a table, back down at *The Brindled Pike*. Definitely they were Darkstream types: and not much better than the Gropes. He tried to stop himself groaning and listen to their talk. They seemed to be arguing over the bother of carrying him.

"Nah—come on then!" growled the black-bearded one. "We can easily sling it in between us like a pig. And this here pig-dog—or whatever it is—isn't half as heavy as a deer."

"No, I won't!" retorted the shifty-eyed one in the floppy-hat. "Carry it yourself if you want. I've been tracking it all afternoon—grubbing about on the ground for spoor. And all over them rocks and shrubbage! 'Twern't easy. Fair done my back in, it has! I done my part. I'm knackered now."

"Well, we could've found it a lot quicker, if you hadn't been following them there badger-droppings for half the afternoon!"

"Well, how the hell was I to know the difference? I haven't ever seen one of these things before. Nah—you can just wait till it wakes up. We can get it to walk by itself."

"Stuff it! We can't wait for that!" snarled Blackbeard. "Looks like he's eaten enough fly-spot fungus for week! We don't know how long that might last! Anyroad, we can't hang about any longer. It's getting dark and there's wolves about, for one thing! This is dodgy country, mate. And we're right on the edge of the Lands Where the Mountains Walk. And that's a sight too close for my liking."

"Get off with you!" said Floppy-Hat. "You don't believe in that stuff, do you? The mountains walking and all that?"

"Well, I don't know. I've heard tell of it for years," said Blackbeard. "I'm not so sure. And I met this bloke in the Grog Shop—a woodcutter he was—and he swears blind he was about to climb this hill one night and cut some brushwood, when up it got and walked away!"

"Well, you won't want for moonshine in the Grog Shop!" retorted the other. "No doubt he *was* blind—blind drunk, I reckon—if that's what he thinks he saw!"

"Anyroad, there's talk of trolls and whatnot that's been seen in these here parts! So we can't stay here," said Blackbeard. "It's six hours back the way we came. And there's no trade there in Pikesmere, for this kind of merchandise. Let's get on! I want to get somewhere safer, before we set up camp. Now, if I remember right, there's an old road they call 'the Ledge-way' somewhere round this mountain. It goes on up a ways, hugging the side of the cliff for a mile or two. Then round the other side, it drops down through several valleys into Angarsland. And our little pet might fetch a pretty penny in the market there."

"Yes—especially an animal that reads a book, by the look of it!" said Floppy-Hat. He pulled the *Legends of the Isle of Ümmulon* from the dwemmer-bag. But the feel of dwemmer-magic from the book, upset the tracker mightily. He grimaced with distaste and quickly stuffed it back. He couldn't read a

202

word of it himself in any case. "But nah!" he groused. "That Ledgeway's not used any more. I heard it fell away."

"No, not all of it. The track's not wide enough now for baggage-mules, they say. But gnorfs and porter dwarves still use it, so I've heard. They still come down it now and then at times, to trade. Anyroad, we've got no choice. The nearest town to us now is Gauhngarth—and that's a good week of walking if we go round by the proper road. But by the Ledgeway, straight up and over the mountains and down into Angarsland, shouldn't take more than couple of days in all. And as I recall, there's a bit of a hamlet halfway there, where we might shack up, instead of sleeping wild. I want to be some-ways down the other side before the night is old. So if you—"

As he spoke, a sudden chilling howl came echoing eerily from a mountain faraway. Another answering howl went up from a hillside near at hand. That decided them. They leapt to their feet. Snatching up their packs, the hunters hurriedly strapped them on. Without more ado, they grabbed up each end of the sapling Iffleplum was tied onto. Humping it onto their shoulders they set off swiftly through the darkling woods. The ifflepinn swung bouncily on the pole between them. His long ears hung down and snagged on bushes, as they went crashing through the undergrowth. And his dangling conker cord sometimes caught on twigs and tightly choked his throat.

*

In half an hour they had left the birch woods far behind. Breathing hard, they gradually climbed up through a pitch-dark forest of fir trees. The fresh sweet smell of pine cleared Iffleplum's head and helped him to revive. Despite the pain in his wrists and ankles, he let them carry him until his fuzzy feeling finally went away. After much stumbling and cursing in the dark, the two men found the ancient track at last. They struggled up a last steep slope, dislodging earth and stones and finally fell over onto a rock-strewn, rutted road. Iffleplum was banged about and bruised, but now he was not feeling quite so sick. As the hunters picked themselves up, he murmured, "Erm—excuse me, but I think I could walk a bit myself now."

"Strike a light! The animal's woken up at last!" said Floppy-Hat in relief. He was getting a sore shoulder. Happily set his end of the sapling down.

"Well, well, well," boomed the barrel-chested Blackbeard. "We won't have to carry the creature any more."

"I'm not a creature, or an animal," said Iffleplum, "I'm an *ummal*. And an ifflepinn."

"Whatever," grinned Floppy-Hat. "As long as you can walk yourself, I don't mind."

"All right then," growled Blackbeard reluctantly, loosening his bonds. "But let's keep it on a leash." As soon as Iffleplum's hands and legs were free, they tied a noose around his neck and held him on a length of rope. Rubbing his raw chafed wrists and ankles, he tried to get the blood-flow back again. He sat dangling his feet over the edge of the road, staring up at the stars that began to speckle the inky sky. Night mist was creeping over the fir trees on the slopes below.

Meanwhile the two men sprawled on their packs against a large boulder, their legs stuck out in the road. Both were wheezing with their efforts in the rarefied air. A mist of frore-breath began to gather round their mouths. It was getting too cold to sit about. They struggled up, stamping their feet and soon set off again. "And you can carry your own baggage, and all," said Floppy-Hat, thrusting the dwemmer-bag and net at Iffleplum. "I don't like the feel of 'em." The ifflepinn took them back gratefully. There was something comforting in their touch. And they brought back memories of the kindly Dwemmer-folk.

Now Blackbeard strode on before them, looking anxiously from side to side, his gun clutched ever ready in his hands. Iffleplum followed in the middle, with Floppy-Hat holding him on the rope behind. Laboriously they picked their way up the twisty track. It was slow going. The trail was overgrown with bushes in many places and cluttered with fallen rocks and

204

stones. But steadily they climbed on, way above the level of the trees. A full moon, shining with a softly orange hue, was rising over the forest now disappearing in a misty haze far below. Their shadows loomed large on the rough rock wall that rose up on their right.

They kept close to the cliff face, for on their left, the track was now no more than a broken edge of crumbling cliff. But on it went, winding up and up, precariously hugging the mountainside round many a hidden bend. Blackbeard crept round every corner cautiously. But so far the road was clear. No wolf or bear, or other dangerous beast appeared. Sometimes rock-falls and slides of scree, completely barred their way, having slipped down from the stony slopes above. It was perilous climbing over these, for often loose stones began to slip away. Then they had to scramble hastily to the other side, before the whole thing began to slide and sweep them over the edge. And what slender way there was often fell away in parts to nothing more than a thin goat path or narrow ledge. Then they had to sidle by on tiptoe, clinging with their fingers to the cliff, with a slithery slope or a dreadful drop beneath their feet.

In one such place, Blackbeard stopped, cursing bitterly. A splashing rivulet falling from an overhang somewhere high above had caused a chunk of the track to fall away. A gap as wide as a wagon now lay across their path, with a foaming pool ten feet below. Here the Ledgeway had slipped down a ways and bulged out onto a spur of the mountainside. Tumbled scree and soil had piled up like an earthen bowl, collecting falling water into a darksome pool. The hunters could not hope to jump the gap with their captive on a rope. Angrily, they dumped their packs down on the ground and stood awhile in thought.

Blackbeard-of-the-bigger-belly, sourly eyed the rind of a rabbit-path against the cliff wall, wondering if it would bear his weight. In places it was splashed and damp and looked as if it might give way. "Perhaps you and the ifflepig better try it first," he said. Floppy-Hat looked at him darkly, knowing what was on his mind. "No, I don't think so, matey," he replied. "I don't much fancy that. You try it out yourself."

"Oh, arr?" said Blackbeard. "Well, well, well. So that's how it is, is it?" He swiftly swooped down and grabbed up the tracker's pack. With a swing of his burly arm he hurled it across to the other side. His own pack quickly followed it. He smiled grimly. "Now we're obliged to get across, ain't we?"

Floppy-Hat muttered curses behind his teeth. Holding his breath, he set his back to the sloping cliff. Slowly, he inched his way around the gap, paying out the rope to Iffleplum as he went. He was almost at the other side, when a clod of earth slipped away beneath his feet. With a cry he jumped smartly to the road. The rope jerked tight round Iffleplum's neck and dragged him stumbling to the brink. But it was just long enough to bridge the gap. He scrambled to his feet again. "Come on!" shouted Floppy-Hat, his voice echoing off the rock. "Get a move on, ifflepig! Don't hang about!"

Iffleplum sidled along the narrow strip. It was solid enough for his weight, so long as the rabbit droppings didn't make him slip. At the wet patch in the middle, the falling water finely splashed his face. But the earth held firm and he safely gained the other side.

Blackbeard gingerly stepped onto the tiny ledge. It was little wider than his boot. But before his other foot was off the road, a sudden shower of rocks and stones came hurtling down. He yelled as a large stone hit him on the knee. At that, a burst of raucous laughter echoed overhead. "Trolls!" cried Floppy-Hat, looking up in alarm.

"You stupid dungling!" snarled Blackbeard, "You've brought 'em on us with all your flodding noise! I told you— keep your trap shut in these here parts! But half a moment— hang on a bit! Hark to 'em! They're not grown trolls. They're only toss-pot *trollings*, by the sound of it!" The cat-calls and drunken jeering of young trolls filled the air. Over a cliff-edge high above, a bunch of shaggy, horned and spiky heads peered down at them, sniggering to themselves.

206

Blackbeard swiftly raised his gun and fired up at them. The blast echoed across the mountains. The trollings responded with an angry roar. Another load of rocks came bouncing down the sloping cliff. One struck Blackbeard a hard blow on the side of his head. With a yell of fury he lost his balance and tumbled heavily into the pool below. The young trolls guffawed with glee at his discomfiture.

"Sling me the rope!" yelled Blackbeard as he surfaced, thrashing about in the water. Floppy-Hat unthinkingly threw down the end he was holding. When Blackbeard grabbed hold of it, poor Iffleplum fell flat on his face and slid along the ground. The heavy weight of the hunter nearly yanked him over the edge. Floppy-Hat suddenly realized his mistake. In the nick of time he grasped the rope again before Iffleplum was dragged in too. It was a huge struggle for him to pull the big man back up the bank, without them all falling into the pool. The ifflepinn was half strangled before Blackbeard managed to clamber back up.

The hunters hastily grabbed up their packs and fled, dragging Iffleplum stumbling along behind them. There came a parting hail of rocks and hoots of laughter. The young trollings were having a ball. They were too high up to get down and do them further harm. But the two men ran on up the Ledgeway at a wheezing trot, until winded, they could run no more.

But still they tottered on. Low cloud had come down upon the heights and soon they climbed into a mist. Blackbeard was now limping with his damaged leg. And his wet clothes were freezing on his back. Finally, he sank down with a groan. He had lost his woolly hat and blood was clotting on his face. Floppy-Hat collapsed on the ground, arched over on his pack. Lying there, the hot sweat from running went cold and clammy on their skin. Iffleplum was faint from hunger. His little legs ached from keeping up. But at least the lightweight dwemmer-coat kept him warm, bedewed with moisture as it was. After a while the hunters found their breath. But now their teeth were chattering. As the mist began to shift, they realized that they were over the pass and the track was going down.

Blackbeard dragged himself to his feet. He had to haul up Floppy-Hat, who could hardly stand up by himself, being strapped into his heavy pack. They yanked up Iffleplum with the rope and started off again. After staggering on miserably for another mile or more downhill, they left the mist behind. Coming down into a more secluded valley of thickly wooded hills, they stopped to set up camp. It was a few hours earlier than they had wanted. But Blackbeard was getting blisters from squelching in his boots. Besides, he needed dry clothes from his pack.

In the moonlit dark, Floppy-Hat's quick-eyes espied a couple of caves close together, higher up on a bushy hill. They left the track and climbed up to investigate. But the "caves" turned out to be two smallish holes in the hillside, with a spike of jagged rock rising up between them. They were too small for the men, being no higher than an ifflepinn. And they were not even deep enough for a bear to curl up in. Now and then, from crevices at the back, a breath of warm air softly wafted out of them, as if rising up from hot springs or lava down below. "Well, at least we might sleep with our feet inside of 'em and toast our toes a bit," said Floppy-Hat.

A streamlet trickled down the hill nearby. So as Blackbeard changed his clothes, Floppy-Hat lit a fire and began to cook a pot of porridge. 'Since you never shot anything all day, it's all we've got," he grumbled. "I could eat a whole leg of bear tonight, after all that effort." Iffleplum's eyes went wide. He cringed back in alarm.

These men were eaters of flesh! *How could they eat dead bodies?* he wondered, aghast at the thought. What if they fancied a bite of *ifflepig*? They had tied him up by his ankle to a tree stump, so he could not run away. But for the moment, Floppy-Hat seemed satisfied with dishing out the porridge into a couple of wooden bowls from his pack. Suddenly he dropped the spoon and leapt to his feet in fright. A chain of wolf howls broke out in the hills around. Another much closer call answered them, welling up from the woods nearby.

"Curse those flodding trolls!" cried Blackbeard, jumping up. "My gun's all soaking wet and the powder's useless! We've got nothing to protect ourselves, except a knife!"

"I'm not stopping to fight a pack of wolves with that!" retorted Floppy-Hat. "Let's scarper, quick!"

As they scrambled for their packs, a dark slinking shape suddenly loomed at the edge of the firelight. A huge grey wolf stood there, its teeth bared in a ghastly grin. Red fire blazed in its eyes and a furry ruff bristled about its neck. Floppy-Hat yelped in fright. "Here they come!" he yelled. "Run for it! Let 'em have the ifflepig!"

The two men turned tail and fled into the dark, leaving Iffleplum to the wolf.

Part the Fifteenth

In the Lands where the Mountains Walk

*In which Iffleplum re-finds his heart
and with a wolf, wakes up a walking mountain,
whereby all tumble down a gulf.*

Iffleplum stared at the wolf, its amber eyes flickering red in the firelight. Stealthily it crept forward, its teeth gleaming. There was nowhere to run. The rope was still tied around Iffleplum's ankle. And the wolf was less than a leap away. Swiftly, he snatched up a burning brand from the fire. With a scream he thrust the flames at the wolf's

face and staggered back as far as the rope would allow, to the edge of the cave. The beast jumped in the air and scrabbled at the sparks around its snout.

"Oh, rats!" snorted the wolf peevishly, with a sweet-sounding a lisp. "That's nice, that is! That's *very* nice!" It squatted down on its haunches by the fire, ruefully rubbing the singed hairs on its muzzle. "It's *always* the same! I'm sick of it! *Sick! Sick! Sick! Rotten rats!* I'll sit here all by myself then—*as usual.*"

Iffleplum lowered his blazing branch. He gaped in astonishment. "But—you're an *ummal?*" he gasped.

"Of *course* I'm an ummal! I'm speaking, aren't I?" retorted the wolf. He pointed a paw at his face. "Look closely! Can't you see *intelligence* in my eyes? *Intelligence!*"

"Oh! Oh, oh, yes!" stammered Iffleplum. "Then—if you're an ummal—you won't—you won't *eat* me then—will you?"

The wolf's jaw dropped in amazement. "Eat *you?* Good heavens, chubby-chops! I wouldn't think of such a thing! Not in my wildest wolfy dreams!"

Iffleplum stepped cautiously forwards. "But—I thought wild wolves savaged sheep and things—"

"What? You can't be serious? Savage *sheep?* Have you seen the *size* of them? They're *enormous!* Most of 'em are bigger than us! And rams with big horns! Savage sheep—I should think so!"

"But—but in all the stories I've heard, wolves are always wild and vicious," said Iffleplum hesitantly.

"Yes, I know—it's scandalous! They *all* say that. Us wolves always get bad press."

"Oh, well—perhaps you should try cleaning your teeth more often then," suggested Iffleplum.

The wolf's eyes grew big in surprise. "Clean my teeth? Don't be ridiculous! I said 'bad *press*', not 'bad *breath*'! I mean, we always get bad things written about us in the books and journals and newspapers—in the press!"

"Oh, sorry," said Iffleplum. "But don't wolves go raiding farmer's fowl pens in the winter?"

"Oh, yes, there is that!" admitted the wolf. "We're not averse to chickens. Or ducks—or geese! If we can surprise them, that is! Otherwise they peck us to pieces! And the feathers get up our noses and stick in our teeth and throats. Not nice. Birds are a last resort."

"So—what—erm—what do you normally eat?" asked Iffleplum carefully.

"Mice," said the wolf. "Mostly mice."

"*Mice?*" said Iffleplum in amazement. "Wolves eat *mice?*" He began to shake with nervous laughter after his fright. His branch was smouldering and his eyes were smarting from the smoke. He thrust the brushwood into the fire and a rush of sparks crackled in the air.

"Yes," lisped the wolf. "Nice mice. Very tasty, mice."

"Some of my friends are mice," frowned Iffleplum.

"Oh, my!" winced the wolf. "Only *small* ones, though. Less dangerous. And just in the winter—when there's nothing else to eat. Seriously, I much prefer nuts and vegetables—and berries. The other wolves think I'm silly. They sent me away—because I'm not fierce enough. So now I haven't any friends."

"Oh! Well—" Suddenly remembering his ummal-manners, Iffleplum touched his finger to his nose and cautiously touched the wolf's wet snout.

"My name's Iffleplum. What's yours?"

The wolf wriggled with embarrassment. "Aw—I don't like to say."

"Oh, come on—don't be shy," encouraged Iffleplum. "*My* friends call me Plumkin. What do they call you?"

"Well—all right then—you promise not to laugh? *They* call me—Fluffykins."

"Fluffykins?" snortled Plumkin in his nose.

"Yes. That's what they heard my mother call me. Because the ruff around my neck is fluffier than most. My proper name is 'Fluff-Ruff'. Are you sniggering?"

212

"N–no—I was just stopping a sneeze," said Iffleplum quickly, as his nose began to pinkly blush. "Perhaps I'm catching a cold. It's bit chilly here in the mountains."

"Chilly! It's freezing! That's why I was hoping to sit by the fireside."

"So why did you snarl your teeth at me, when you came creeping up?"

"Snarl my—oh, for heaven's sake! I was *smiling*—not snarling! Don't you know the difference? I was only trying to be friends. Nobody understands us wolves. When other folks are all warm and cosy, sitting round their campfires, we creep up softly, smiling—and what happens? They go berserk! Screaming and shouting! And thrusting burning brands up our noses! No wonder some of us wolves get wild. Nobody wants us. Everybody hates us—I think I'll go and eat worms—"

"You don't need to do that," said Iffleplum. "Just look! The hunters have left us their porridge! If you can help me untie this knot, I'll dish it out." So with a little nibbling from the wolf's teeth, they worried the rope undone and loosed it from around his ankle. Then to their delight, they found the cookpot full enough for three bowls each! It was wonderfully warming and they ate until they were fit to burst.

Afterwards, Iffleplum recounted his adventures to the wolf. Then Fluff-Ruff told him wolf-tales of his lonely life. In a melancholy mood, the ifflepinn sat stoking the fire, idly watching the sparks rise in the air. He stared up beyond them to the stars, wondering if his elfin-heart had gone that way and was lost to him forever. Growing sleepy, his eyes began to droop. Smooring the fire, he banked it up with moist leaf-mould to keep it burning slowly through the night. He took off his shoulder-bag to use as a pillow and hung up his elven-net on a jag of the craggy spire of rock between the caves. But he kept his dwemmer-coat on for warmth. Then they both curled up to sleep, each in their own cosy little cave.

They were just dropping off, when somewhere over the valley another wolf howled eerily at the moon.

"Why do they howl so mournfully?" yawned Iffleplum. "It freezes the blood."

"Isn't it obvious?" said Fluff-Ruff, opening an eye. "It freezes our blood as well! *We* don't have any fires. So on icy cold nights, we sit and howl our lonesome little hearts out."

"Oh, that's very sad," soothed Iffleplum. "If only I had known—but when you came, you gave me such a scare!"

"I did?" exclaimed the wolf, sitting up excitedly. "I scared you? Really? Well, wet my whiskers! That's very nice of you to say so! Nobody's ever scared of me. That's the nicest thing anyone's said to me for ages."

Fluff-Ruff settled down again happily, draping his paw across his snout to keep the cold air out and softly chuntering to himself, "Well, well, wet my whiskers! *Scared* of *me!* That makes me feel most courageous. Fancy that, silly me, scaring folks—well, well—"

Iffleplum could still hear him snortling happily to himself as he slowly fell into a fitful sleep. And exhaustingly, for half the night he dreamed of a pack of howling wolves chasing his elfin-heart all over the hills and dales of Ümmulon, as he ran behind them forever waving his elven-net wildly in the air.

*

The ifflepinn awoke surprisingly refreshed. Warm air was still wafting now and again from the crevice at the back of the cave, so the cold night had little troubled him. He had awakened to the smell of wood smoke softly drifting to his nose. It was hardly dawn and the light was dim. But the wolf was already up and about. He was busily trotting to and fro and tending to the fire. He came huffing up with a mouthful of leaves and bits of wood and dumped them onto the feebly smouldering logs of yesternight. "Phoo! Not very tasty, mouldy leaves!" he snorted, spitting out the bits.

Crouching down, the wolf began to blow on the dying embers. But the leaves were damp and billows of pungent smoke blew up into his face.

214

A sudden shift of air sent a cloud of it wafting all over Iffleplum. It stung his eyes and made them water. Picking up his shoulderbag, reluctantly, he crawled out of his cosy cave.

Outside the air was chill. A morning mist still lay draped upon the deep-dark valley far below. The lower Ledgeway track was empty. He could just see it winding down between the forested hillsides until it vanished in the valley glooms. On the left side of the hill, a precipice fell away to unknown depths. Iffleplum hadn't noticed it in the dark the night before. He was glad he hadn't walked that way.

Now cautiously, he tiptoed towards the edge. The clifftop overhung the brink, then slanted sharply down for thousands of feet, its bottom hidden somewhere in the misty vale. Harsh cries of swirling birds in the air across the valley faintly echoed off the distant crags. Meanwhile, a dawn chorus of sweeter-voiced songbirds began to tootle in the trees nearby.

The day was slowly waking up. But gazing giddily into space, Iffleplum fell into reverie, wondering what he was doing there. In his mind's eye, adventureless Ælfÿlon now seemed more comforting than anywhere.

And he wondered if he would ever find his way back home.

A sudden excited clamour of piggy squeals distracted him. Up on the hillside, he espied dozens of fat little stripy creatures, happily bustling about and snuffling under the bushes with their snouts. Impulsively, Fluff-Ruff scampered up a huge boulder towards them. He stopped on top of it, bristling like a guard dog at a gate. "Woof!" barked the wolf. Startled, the squeaking piglings ran scattering all over the hillside. Fluff-Ruff was overjoyed.

"Did you see that?" he called out in surprise, as Iffleplum came back to the fire. "I *frightened* them! *I* frightened them! Oh, at *last!* I'm a *wolf!* Yes! Oh, yes! I'm a *real* wolf!" Raising his foreleg he struck a noble pose, his muzzle proudly nosing in the air. "Fluff-Ruff the Ferocious! Scarer of piglings!"

At that moment, the boulder he was standing on began to quiver. Strangely, its surface began to slowly wrinkle up towards his hind-legs like a ruffled skin. As it rolled back, it revealed a huge eye glaring out of the ground! An eye as big as a cartwheel! It stared quizzically at Iffleplum. The ifflepinn gaped in astonishment. But the wolf was still proudly watching the piglings run helter-skelter all over the hill.

"Erm—Fluff-Ruff?" said Iffleplum timidly.

"Yes?" said the wolf brightly, turning round, unaware that he was attempting to yank his hind-leg out of the folds of the wrinkled eyelid. Iffleplum frantically pointed down. As Fluff-Ruff dropped his gaze, the pupil of the great eye rolled up to peer at him. With a yelp like a trodden dog, the wolf leapt wildly in the air. He somersaulted and came down head over heels. Bowling right over the muggy fire, he crushed it flat. Sparks scattered everywhere and black smoke billowed in the air.

At that, a boulder on the opposite side of the hill rolled up and another eye appeared. There came a sudden snort from the twin caves and jets of smoke shot out of them. The elven-net spun off the spike of rock and went flying over their heads. With a terrible tearing sound like an earthquake in eruption, the ground before them slowly ripped apart. Both the caves and the spike of mottled rock rose steadily in the air. A huge red cavern opened up beneath.

But a cavern bordered round with *teeth!*

Great flat grinding teeth, like standing stones. And a huge red tongue came lolling out! The ummals stood rooted to the spot. They looked on aghast and trembled in shock. Now they realized where they had slept. Not in "cosy caves" at all, but in the nostrils of some great enormous beast!

A deafening roar issued from its mouth. Like a blast of wind it bowled them over. The remains of the fire went skittering all over the rocks. The hillside behind it rippled and shook itself and birds flew off it screaming. The tiny piglings ran squealing in all directions. Slowly, the hill stood up, on legs as thick as ancient oak-tree trunks. More ripping sounds were heard as it detached itself from its long contact with the ground.

The great creature was all overgrown with grass and bushes and had a knobbly skin that that looked like lumpy boulders here and there. The spike of mottled rock between the "caves" they now saw was a huge horn protruding from its massive snout.

Sleepily, it gazed down on the stunned and fallen ummals.

"OH, MY GOODNESS!" it boomed in a great dozy voice, "I'M SORRY. DID I STARTLE YOU? I WAS ONLY YAWNING." And so saying, it opened its cavernous mouth and yawned again. They both grabbed hold of bushes to avoid being blown away. The wolf hung on by his teeth, until the gale of the creature's warm breath dwemmed away.

"OH, DEAR—I CAN'T SEEM TO GET A DECENT DECADE'S SLEEP THESE DAYS," the hillside groaned. "IT'S THE LICE, YOU SEE. I'M TOO MUCH TROUBLED WITH ALL THE LICE."

"L–lice?" stammered Iffleplum, amazed and all atremble. *How could tiny lice trouble a mountain that could walk?* he wondered.

"YES. PIG-LICE," the creature said. "I'M COVERED WITH LITTLE PIG-LICE. THEY JUST WON'T LET ME HAVE A PROPER SLEEP. THEY'RE FOREVER TROTTING ABOUT ALL OVER ME, NUZZLING IN MY SKIN, DIGGING FOR TRUFFLES AND WHAT-NOT, THE PESKY LITTLE EEJITS."

A bright idea suddenly struck Iffleplum. "I know someone who could keep them off for you," he said. "This ferocious wolf here, could scare them all away for you and keep you trouble free."

"YOU COULD? YOU REALLY COULD?" the creature rumbled.

"Aw—" responded Fluff-Ruff, wriggling his shoulders modestly. "Well—yes—I suppose I could—they seem to run away from me, at least."

"OH! IF THAT IS TRULY SO—IF YOU WOULD STAY BY ME—I'D BE FOREVER IN YOUR DEBT," the creature said. "YOU'D BE MY FRIEND FOR LIFE! WHENEVER I'M AWAKE, THAT IS."

"A friend?" said Fluff-Ruff brightening. "I've never had a proper friend."

"OH, HAVEN'T YOU NOW?" the creature boomed. "HOW VERY SAD—OH—WAIT A BIT THOUGH—" it pondered for a while; "COME TO THINK OF IT—*I* HAVEN'T EVER HAD ONE EITHER. WHICH REMINDS ME—YOU HAVEN'T SEEN A *YAKKABOO* ON YOUR WAY AROUND, BY ANY CHANCE, HAVE YOU?"

"A Yakkaboo?" said Fluff-Ruff, wrinkling his brow. "I can't say that I have. And to be honest, I don't really know what it is."

"OH, THAT'S A SHAME," the creature said. "THAT'S THE TROUBLE. NO ONE EVER DOES. WHAT A PITY. THEY MAKE WONDERFUL MATES FOR MY KIND, THEY SAY."

"Well, what does it look like?" asked Iffleplum.

"AW—IT'S TOO BEAUTIFUL TO DESCRIBE—" the creature shrugged bashfully, swaying the hillside and treading on its own claw-tipped toes in embarrassment.

"Well, can you just give us a little hint," said Iffleplum. "Then if we see one, we could let you know."

"AH, WELL, YOU SEE... I HAVEN'T *ACTUALLY* SEEN ONE; OR— WELL, I MIGHT HAVE DONE, BUT I'M NOT QUITE SURE. I *THOUGHT* I SAW A YAKKABOO ONE FINE SPRING NIGHT—OR WAS IT MORNING? SHE WAS SO LOVELY; I CLOSED MY EYES AND WROTE A LOVE-SONG FOR HER IN MY HEAD. I DON'T KNOW HOW MANY WEEKS IT TOOK, BUT TO MY SURPRISE, WHEN I LOOKED UP AGAIN, SHE WAS *GONE!* SO NOW I'M NOT SURE WHAT I SAW. BUT MY POEM GOES LIKE THIS:

> *I THOUGHT I SAW A YAKKABOO*
> *ONE DARK AND DAWNISH NIGHT*
> *ITS HEIGHT WAS TALL*
> *AND ITS FEET WERE SMALL*
> *AND ALMOST THE COLOUR OF WHITE.*
>
> *I'M SURE I SAW A YAKKABOO*
> *AS PLAIN AS IT COULD BE,*
> *IT GRUBBED ABOUT*
> *WITH ITS MASSIVE SNOUT*
> *AND ITS FACE WAS LIKE A TREE.*

AND THERE IT STOOD, THE YAKKABOO
AS FAR AS THE EYE COULD SEE,
WITH LIME GREEN EYES
AND SHUDDERING SIZE,
OR WAS IT ONLY ME?

OH! IT MUST HAVE BEEN A YAKKABOO!
THERE WAS CHOCOLATE ON ITS KNEE.
IN THE LIGHT OF DAWN,
ITS SHIRT WAS TORN
AND ITS EARS ALL SMILED AT ME.

OF COURSE IT WAS A YAKKABOO!
WITH AN APRIL IN THE MONTH;[15]
WITH ODDS LIKE THAT, IT MUST BE TRUE.
OH! YES, IT WAS A YAKKABOO!
AS SURE AS I'M A GNUMPF."

Iffleplum and the wolf looked at each other blankly and shook their heads in unison. "No, we haven't seen one of those," said Iffleplum. "But then, we've never seen a Gnumpf before either."

"YES, WELL—HMM—WE DON'T LIKE BEING SEEN TOO MUCH—BECAUSE WHENEVER WE WAKE UP, PEOPLE ONLY SHOUT AND SCREAM AND THROW THINGS AT US—AND THEN THEY RUN AWAY. THEY'RE NOT VERY SOCIABLE."

"That's just what I say!" said Fluff-Ruff eagerly. "Huh! Humans! They do just the same to me! It gets on my nerves! It must be worse for you. How can you stand it?"

"OH, BUT *PEOPLE* PARASITES DON'T REALLY BOTHER ME. IF I DON'T *THINK* ABOUT THEM—OR BOTHER WHAT THEY DO, OR SAY—THEN THEY CAN'T TROUBLE ME, ANYWAY. *HEAD FREE: HEART FREE*—THAT'S THE SECRET OF CONTENTMENT, *SEE?* I FEEL QUITE SORRY FOR THEM, ACTUALLY. THE HUMAN-FOLK DON'T SEEM TO KNOW ABOUT REBOUNDAGE MUCH."

---

15 April is the mating season for Gnumpfs; every fifty years or so, if they manage to wake up in time.

"*Reboundage?* What's reboundage?" asked the wolf.

"OH, SURELY YOU KNOW THE *REBOUNDAGE LAW?* I LEARNED IT AS LITTLE GNUMPFLING, AT MY MOTHER'S HAIRY KNEE. HOW DOES IT GO? OH, YES: *WHATEVER YOU DO TO SOMEONE ELSE— ONE DAY, SOME WAY, ANOTHER WILL DO THE SAME TO YOU.* THAT'S NATURE'S WAY OF BRINGING BALANCE TO THE WORLD—WHAT GOES UP, MUST THEN COME DOWN. *WHAT YOU GIVE OUT WILL COME BACK ROUND.* IF YOU THUMP SOMEONE ON THE HEAD... SOME OTHER DAY—SOME TIME AHEAD—THEN YOU'LL GET THUMPED UPON INSTEAD."

"*Ah,*" said Iffleplum thoughtfully, thinking of his fist-fight with fat Podge, and the funglings who later thumped him to the ground. "Oh, Yes, I see—I've heard of that Reboundage Law before."

"ANYWAY, NEXT TIME—BEFORE YOU GO SCRAMBLING UP A HILL, JUST ASK YOURSELF—*COULD THIS BE A YAKKABOO OR A GNUMPF?* THEN TIPTOE CAREFULLY AS YOU CLIMB SO AS NOT TO WAKE US UP—OH! OH—" The Gnumpf's nostrils began to twitch. "EXCUSE ME, BUT I THINK I'M GOING TO HAVE A SNEEZE—AH–AH–AH—"

"Oh, please! Don't sneeze!" cried Iffleplum. "Your yawning's bad enough!" He backed away in alarm.

"*OHH*—BUT I'VE GOT A TINY TICKLE IN MY NOSE," said the Gnumpf. "IT'S BEEN NIGGLING ME SINCE YESTERDAY. *OH!* IT'S JUST A THOUGHT—I DON'T ASK MUCH; BUT MAYBE YOU COULD KINDLY SCRATCH MY ITCH FOR ME? IT'S IN MY LEFTISH NOSTRIL... OR SO I THINK. I'M SORRY TO BOTHER YOU. I WOULD DO IT MYSELF, ONLY—I DON'T REALLY KNOW WHERE IT IS. I'VE BEEN ASLEEP A LONG TIME, YOU SEE, AND I—WELL—I DON'T REMEMBER THESE THINGS VERY WELL." He laid his great chin on the ground, like a dozy dog hoping to be fondled round its ears.

"Oh, yes! I can help," said Iffleplum. "I could do it with my elven-net." He went and picked it up. Hesitantly entering his last-night's "cave" again, he began scrubbing the net-ring around the nostril's rim.

"OOH—THAT'S NICE!" cooed the Gnumpf. "BUT THE ITCHY-THING FEELS FURTHER BACK—JUST JIGGLE IT IN THE CREVICE THERE." Poking deeper with his elven-net, Iffleplum saw something flicker past him overhead. His heart gave a sudden leap. Oh, could it be? *Oh, yes!* It *was!* He could hardly believe his eyes. His elfin-heart was floating there! *It must have been in there all night long!* he thought. *No wonder I felt so cosy in his nose!*

"OH, *GOOD!* I THINK THE TICKLE'S GONE!" the Gnumpf rejoiced and gave happy snort "HAARUMPH!" At that, the elfin-heart shot out into the air. And Iffleplum went bowling over in the blast. By the time he scrambled to his feet, his elfin-heart was up and away!

"Oh, gripes! Not again!" he cried. Whirling about, he spied it swiftly flowing on towards the cliff-top, on a rippling cloud of smoke. He took off after it, waving the elven-net wildly.

"What's happening!" lisped the wolf excitedly, lolloping after him.

"My elfin-heart!" cried Iffleplum, dashing madly to the brink. "It's going off the edge!"

"Where? Where? I don't see anything!" yelled Fluff-Ruff. "Are you sure? Oh, for heaven's sake! Be careful, Iffleplum! The clifftop's crumbly over there!"

Just above the precipice, hanging like a bird upon the wind, the heart-wraith was now turning slowly in an eddy of the air. It lit up briefly, blazing like a heart of gold as the first rays of the rising sun shone brightly though it. A shaft of light shot down from it into Iffleplum. *Oh!* It pierced his empty heart once more, with a longing for that loving feeling he had lost.

Then, like a springboard, he felt himself leaving his body and bouncing back up into the whirling wraith. With a thrill he found himself filled with light! He was *made* of light! As golden as the sun! And suddenly—in great wonder—he was looking out of the elfin-heart at himself standing on the cliff! A strange-looking creature with sunlight shining in its big brown staring eyes! *Oh! Oh! Who am I? WHAT am I?* he thought. *Am I not that pearly pale body that now I see? Am I not an ifflepinn with an elfin-heart? No! No! I AM the elfin-heart—and the elfin-heart has ME!*

So thinking, in a moment more he was back in his body, much amazed. He gazed dumbly at the shining wraith, his nose a golden sheen. As in a dream he slowly raised his elven-net. But the elfin-heart was far beyond his reach. And curling up its wraithing veils, it turned away and spiralled slowly down the cliff.

"Oh no!" he groaned. He sank upon his knees. Despairingly, he watched it waft away on a gentle breeze beneath an overhang.

"Oh, rats!" winced the wolf, coming up beside him. "But don't despair! We'll find a way somehow, to get down there!" He patted Plumkin consolingly with his paw, then stopped and sniffed the air. "I smell smoke," he said, looking up, "and there's clouds of it up there!"

"AHUM! AHUM!" coughed the Gnumpf behind them. "EXCUSE ME FOR INTERRUPTING—BUT IF I'M NOT MISTAKEN—IT SEEMS THE MOUNTAINSIDE'S ON FIRE!" And so it was. The Gnumpf's great windy yawn had blown the embers of their fire all over everywhere. The scattered sparks had now slowly smouldered into life. Nearby bushes crackled up in a sudden *whoof!* of flame. Above them, crinkled autumn leaves began to catch alight and soon the trees around were all ablaze. Flames came quickly licking along the dried grass on the ground. A gusty breeze blew blinding heat and stinging smoke towards them.

The Gnumpf was forced to back away towards the precipice. He turned around, sweeping a wide swath across the burning ground with his heavy grass-grown lizard-like tail. It thrashed the burning bushes as it passed, sending showers of sparks up in the air. Some set alight the dead grass on his tail, without him noticing.

Extending his neck, the Gnumpf craned precariously over the precipice. "OH, YES—NOW THAT'S A POSSIBILITY," he mused, peering down the cliff, as the ground around began to creak alarmingly. "NOW THEN, LET ME SEE—IF I CAN MANAGE TO GET A GOOD GRIP ON THE ROCK DOWN THERE WITH MY CLAWS, I MIGHT EASILY CARRY YOU DOWN." He held up his huge five-taloned foot to show them, flexing his curving cat-like claws. But with a fearful sound, huge cracks began appearing all around them, zig-zagging past their feet.

"Oh, help! The clifftop's crumbling!" cried Iffleplum, staggering back. As the Gnumpf's great heavy leg came down, it plunged straight through the splitting ground. The clifftop gave a sickening lurch. And with a mighty roar, the overhanging shelf fell away, crashing downwards in an avalanche. Unable to stop himself, the weighty beast went with it, tumbling ponderously over the edge.

"Yikes!" yelped Fluff-Ruff as the Gnumpf went plummeting by. "Your tail's on fire!" With a desperate leap from the falling rock, the wolf bounded down onto the Gnumpf's great bushy back. Clamping his teeth around a branch he hung on grimly as they fell.

Iffleplum snatched wildly at a tussock of smouldering grass, as the Gnumpf's great overgrown tail went slithering past. It yanked him roughly over the brink. But the elven-net shot away from his grasp and went skittering down the slope. *Oh,*

223

Ühm! Without it he could never hope to catch his elfin-heart again. But he had no time to think.

The clump of burning grass came away in his hands. With a cry of despair he spun off sideways and went cartwheeling on his back down the smoothly sloping rock.

The Gnumpf's great claws screeched down the cliff face, scoring the stone with a trail of sparks. In a cloud of dust and rubble he skidded on down like a giant sled, his fiery tail shedding a column of smoke behind him.

"Help!" wailed Iffleplum whirling round. His cry cut short as he struck his foot on a ridge of stone. His ankle twisted painfully. But on he went sliding downwards in a spin. With a yell of surprise, he came to a sudden stop. Crashing full tilt into a cliffside bush, his breath was knocked away. He hung there, battered and breathless, in a daze, draped over a thorny branch.

A last quick glimpse of the Gnumpf and Fluff-Ruff was all he had, before they plunged way down into the misty valley glooms and vanished from his sight.

Not only his elfin-heart was gone again—but he had also lost his elven-net and his newfound friends as well!

His eyes grew wide. Now he realized the predicament he was in. He was hanging headfirst, halfway down the cliff. His dwemmer-coat caught on a prickly bush and his shoulderbag entangled in its thorns. If he moved, the bush slipped down a little more and lurched alarmingly.

Uh-oh! he thought. *The roots are coming free!*

He had never felt so much alone.

Part the Sixteenth

Morrigän

*In which Iffleplum meets the Morrigän of secret arts
and finds again his Elfin-Heart!*

here came a grating noise just below Iffleplum, to his right. It sounded like a large stone sliding over rock: which is exactly what it was. "What the flodding heck is all that racket?" said a girlish voice. A tangled head of bushy hair suddenly poked out from a hole in the cliff. Under it, a young girl with a smudgy face looked up.

"Was that you?" she said accusingly. "What you doing there?"

"Oh! What?" said Iffleplum, taken aback by her sudden appearance. "No—I—I didn't do it! The cliff fell down! There was a huge creature called a Gnumpf! It broke the cliff—"

"Oh, the *Gnumpf* was it?" she retorted. "Might have known. So he's up and about again is he? The dozy great brain-addled chump! Well, that's all right then! Never mind. No harm done."

"But he's fallen in the valley!" gasped Iffleplum. The thorny branch was pressing hard into his belly and making it difficult to speak.

"Huh! Don't worry for that!" the girl said dismissively. "The Gnumpf is *made* of mountain's bones! The very mountains quake when he's awake. He'll be right as rain, no doubt."

"But his tail's on fire!" winced Iffleplum, feeling prickles through his dwemmer-coat.

"No bother: there's a lake down there. He can easily douse himself. Don't you worry about him. It's *you*, you ought to worry about! You look in a right pickle, you do. Well, come on! Are you going to hang about up there all day? Or are you coming down?"

His jaw dropped: he didn't know what to say to that. Only now he noticed a narrow slanting ledge just below him, no wider than his foot. It ran on down beyond the hole the girl was peeping from. "I'm stuck," he answered plaintively. "And every time I move, I feel the roots come further out!"

"Oh, that," the girl said, clambering out of the rock barefoot. "Hold fast! " she ordered, sternly, as she sidled up towards him.

"I *am* doing!" retorted Iffleplum with clenched teeth.

"Not *you!*" she said. "The *bush!*"

She shook a branch of it alarmingly. "All right you, root up!" she ordered: "*Eterthalom!*" The hanging bush trembled

226

slightly, and then obediently slid its roots back deeper into a crevice in the rock.

Iffleplum was amazed to feel the bush hold firm as she unhooked him from the thorns. With his arm around her neck, the girl helped him hobble down through the hole and into a small cave. As she slipped inside, she glanced back up at the flowing smoke.

"Oh, ghòr's guts!" she muttered. "Looks like the hill's alight as well. Can't have that. Come on! Let's get up there!"

"But I can't walk," said Iffleplum. "I think I've sprained my ankle."

"Oh right," she said, swiftly kneeling down. "Sorry. Didn't realize." She held her hands in the air around his ankle, muttering some strange chant, in words he didn't know. He could feel a warming energy flowing round his foot. She stood up. "That'll have to do for now. We haven't time."

Surprisingly, Iffleplum found he could now walk on it without much pain. "It won't last long," she said. "So let's be quick." She raised up the lid of what seemed to be a horse-trough made of stone. A flickering shining light shone out. She scooped up a handful of tiny fluttering creatures from inside it. They looked to Iffleplum like flower-deeves with wings. But they were phosphorescent and shining from within. She set them down inside a lantern, where they brightly glowed.

"Faery lights," she told him. "Come on! Follow me," and set off up a narrow winding stair of rock. The faery-lantern lit their way with a shimmering golden glow.

At the top a boulder blocked the way out. "Shift!" she said, "*Sligerith!*" and the boulder obediently slid aside. Iffleplum looked at her askance, wondering what kind of wizardish creature this strange girl-being was. As they came out onto the hillside, a blast of hot air hit them. The fire was still raging everywhere.

"Aiee!" exclaimed the girl, throwing up her arm against the heat. She edged her bare feet back from the burning grass. "All right! All right! That's enough! Settle down." Fluttering her hands up and down towards the flames, she began to incant another strange song once again. And to Ieffleplum's astonishment, indeed, the fire gradually did die down!

"Fire-dousing song," she said airily, nodding at the blackened, smoking grass, as the last sparks died away. "Can't do with that," she said. "My pretty gauhns like to graze up here."

"Gauhns?" enquired Iffleplum.

"Yes, my little friends. You know—long-horned gauhns: speckled, spotted, and brindled. Want to see them? Come on down."

They returned to the stairway in the rock. At her command, the boulder closed behind them. Taking up the faery-lantern, she led him back down the winding stair again. Then, by a low round sloping tunnel, like a giant rabbit hole, they came to another level further down. It opened out into a roundish cave with a powerful cheesy pong, like the sickly-sweet smell of a cow-barn. The floor was lined with stone-lidded bulbous jars and pots. "Dairy," said the girl, waving her hand nonchalantly. Taking a quick peek as he went by, Iffleplum saw that some pots were filled with fresh milk and some with curd. And above them, round cheeses stacked on racks.

The cave entrance was hidden by an ivy-curtain hanging down the cliff. On passing through it they emerged onto a sunny mountain meadow. A herd of enormous cow-like creatures with long wavy horns, shaggy legs, and huge broad snouts were browsing in much greener, flower-speckled grass. Some were spotted and some were flecked and others brindled with fine stripes. Only a few of them were of a cattle-coloured chestnut brown, but most were of a greenish or a purple tinge, or a blending satin-sheen of both.

"My little pets," the girl said proudly. (Her "little pets" were twice as tall as she was.) "My name's Morrig by the way. What's yours?"

"Oh! Er—Iffleplum—but mostly others call me Plumkin."

"Ah, well, never mind, don't worry about it. I'm Morrigän, but Morrig's good enough. Anyways, the valley-folk call me the 'Morri-gauhn'—the cattle-keeper." She sniffed disdain-

fully, "Cattle! Huh! That's all *they* know." Then looking
down, she noticed that the iffepinn was limping once again.
"Ah, yes: your ankle. We'd better see to that," she said.
"Come on back inside."

*

Ifflepium lay at ease on a bed of dried grass, inside a recess cut
into the sidewall of the rock. He was happily tucking into a
bowl of blackberries and honey stirred in curd, while
Morrigän gently massaged his painful foot and leg. Although
her words seemed short and sharp, her touch was only
tenderness. And he could feel the Lightstream *Lûmentir* was
flowing through her heart. A soothing calm soon crept over
him from the gentle fluence of her hands. There was also
something very comforting about the feel of her sleeping cave.
Its shape was somewhat like the inside of an egg. From a
frame of sticks across the curving ceiling, bunches of dried
herbs hung down and others dangled on the walls. Many more
were stored in earthen jars on shelves around the cave or
standing on the floor. The mingled smells were heady, but
they made him feel quite sleepy and relaxed.

Finally the girl wrapped moist leaves around his ankle. She
then smeared all over them with a greeny paste from a jar,
which smelled a bit like sweet-warm mouldy hay or grass. She
rubbed some on the grazes on his knees and elbows too and
on the scratches down his ears. "That'll do the trick," she said.
"It'll dry hardish in a while. It pongs a bit. But keep it on a
day or two, until it all cracks off." She wiped her hands on her
brown and grimy well-patched leather jerkin and then rubbed
them down the sides of her wrinkled baggy breeches.

"Now then—what are you?" she demanded.

"Eh? What?" frowned Ifflepium, taken by surprise at her
sudden change of tack.

"I said, what *are* you?" she repeated. "For sure, you're not
a gnorf, or a dwarf, or any kind of gnome. I've seen bogles,
pixies; even tiny trolls your size, and ghòrs as well. But what
you are, I do not know."

"Oh *that!* I'm just an iffepinn."

"What?" exclaimed Morrig excitedly, "an ifflepinn? Truly, you're an *ælfÿnpinn*? You surely jest with me? But no—I see you tell me true. Then, can it be—you're an *ælfÿnpinn* of *Ælfÿlon*?"

"Why yes—I come from Ælfÿlon. Oh! then you've heard of it? But—what's all this about an *ælfÿnpinn*? Why do people always call me that?"

"You mean you don't know what you are? *Ælfÿnpinnü*—or *ifflepinns*, as some now say—are a fabled faery folk! People say you don't exist! In the Old Tongue 'elf' was written with an 'Æ' you see. *Look*—like this!" With a stick she drew the letters Æ–L–F on the sandy floor. "And *pinna* meant 'a child or playmate' or a 'friend'. So '*ælfÿnpinn*' means 'friend or playmate of the elves!'

"Hoo!" hooted Iffleplum. "So that's why my heart is drawn to elves and dwemmers and suchlike. But there are no elves in Ælfÿlon! And there's nothing faery-like about us ifflepinns. We're really very ordinary. I dreamed of meeting fabled creatures here in Ümmulon myself!"

"Ah! But you 'ifflepinns'—as you call yourself—are as rare as unicorns to us! Once upon a time, our stories say—the elves and *ælfÿnpinnü* were frolicsome friends, who lived somewhere over the hills and faraway in a secret land called Ælfÿlon. But one day a powerful Warlock-Wizard, grim and fell, came there and drove the elves away—or so the story-singing bards all tell. But when the Warlock went away, no longer could the elves go back. For once they came to the Land of Lün and set their eyes on Ümmûârkon's magic mountain peak, it held them in its spell. They could not leave its sight. And so, unable to return, they conjured up a spell themselves, to hide their ancient home from prying eyes. That way, the ifflepinns and ummal-folk stayed innocent, so they say. For the elvish magic kept them free from evil beings such as he.

"And so you see, that's why the '*lon*' in Ælfÿlon means 'hidden place or country,' don't you know?' And so the meaning of '*Ælf–ÿ–lon*' (three words in one) is actually: 'The Hidden Land of Elves.' But no one really believes in Ælfÿlon these days. They think it's just a faerytale—like castles in the air."

"Hoo-hoo!" said Iffleplum. "And I was never sure if the Isle of Ümmulon was real—a story on my book or just a hopeful dream."

"What do you mean—a dream?" frowned Morrig. "You *already* live on the Ümmal-Isle! Why do you think it's called Ümmulon? That's where you're from! The land where Ummals live! And your little land of *Ælfÿlon*—although it may be a hundred hidden miles away or more—is still somewhere, secretly, on *this* great isle within its shores."

"Oh, what?" gasped Iffleplum. "You mean—that Ælfÿlon's already somewhere *here* in Ümmulon? Oh, gripes! Then I—I already *live* in the 'Ifflepinn Island' of my dreams! Oh, good grief! Then—that must mean—that one of the fabled creatures that I read about, around the Magic Mountain's feet—was *me*?"

"Seems so, doesn't it? There's many a one thinks the grass is greener in some far-flung otherwhere. That's why we often miss what's magical in the land where we belong. I may sometimes dream of Ælfÿlon. But luckily, in my little cave, I'm happy where I am! We Angarslanders don't much like to travel beyond the borders of our realm. And for me, there's no greener grass than here, where I can feed my gauhns. Which reminds me: I must be off to see to them. It's already half-past milking time. You better stay here and rest your leg."

She bustled off and left him lying there, wide-eyed with wonder. It was a very thoughtful ifflepinn that slowly finished off his bowl of blackberries and curd. For once, he had even forgotten he was eating. It must have been the slowest meal he had ever had.

*

"Look what I found!" said a voice excitedly. Iffleplum awakened with a start. He looked up groggily. After finishing his breakfast, he had fallen asleep again, while waiting for the "Morrigauhn" to return. His empty wooden bowl and spoon lay on a stool beside him. Now Morrig bounced back into the cave, smelling of milk, ripe cheese and gauhn-hide breeches.

"Look at this! See what *I* found!" she cried.

Iffleplum sat bolt upright in shock. He shook all over. There it was! Beyond all hope: hovering in the air between her hands! A shimmering, heart-shaped wraith with softly wisping veils!

"My elfin-heart!" he gasped in joy. "Where did you find it?" He could still faintly see the little dots and flecks of print that speckled it, where the *Legends* book snapped shut. But impossibly, it was hanging there! Floating in the air between her hands! "I found it caught up on my dream-catcher!" she exclaimed. "Out on my balcony—the overhang, I mean— where I sun myself. There's a funny-looking fishing net out there on the ledge as well."

"Oh! That's mine too! But quickly! Give me first my elfin-heart! Come! Give it me!" She held it out to him. Eagerly he snatched at it, to try and drag it to his chest. But his hands passed right through the wraith, as if it wasn't there! "Oh! Oh! I can't hold it! It won't come to me!" he whittered plaintively. "How do *you* do that?"

"I don't know. I didn't think. My hands just gathered it. It must be Old Ühmkyn's fluence in me, I suppose. When I feel Ühmkyn flowing through me, I can do things—just like that! Sometimes it comes, sometimes it goes."

"It's not fair! It's *mine!* Why can't *I* hold it?" he complained. Frantically, he scrabbled through it with his hands, grabbing nothing but the air.

"It might be, there's still too much of Iffleplum in you, and not enough of Ühmkyn, I suppose."

"Well what *am* I to do then?" he cried. "Oh! Wait! I know!" An idea suddenly struck him. "Hold on! Wait there! Don't let it go!"

He hobbled out of the sleeping chamber and into the cave next door. It opened out onto a sunny parapet of rock, jutting outwards from the cliff.

232

Hanging from the low cave arch was a hoop of slender willow-wand, webbed within with criss-crossed spirals like the pattern of seeds upon a sunflower's head. Pearly beads bedecked the webbing like dewdrops, flashing and twinkling as the hoop turned gently in the morning sun. Spotted feathers, beads and bones and holes in stones dangled down from it. *Oh! So that's a dream-catcher*, he supposed.

Spying his elven-net on the edge of the ledge, he swiftly snatched it up. In doing so, a quick peek way down into the valley made his stomach turn. By now the mists had lifted. He could see the hazy meadowlands far below and a large lake glittering in the sun, with a rocky island in the middle. But there was no sign of Fluff-Ruff or the Gnumpf.

He hurried back and held the elven-net before Morrig's outstretched hands. "Quick-quick! In here! Put it in!" he urged. She slipped the elfin-heart inside it over the rim. Undulating like an eel, it seemed to snuggle down happily in the net. And to Iffleplum's delight it stayed there! The elfin energy-field entrapped it in its finely woven mesh. At last, he had it in his grasp! His heart beat wildly with its nearness as he hugged it lovingly to his breast. Pressing the net-ring to his chest, he shook the net-bag by its tip, hoping the elfin-heart would enter him. But nothing happened. The elfin-heart stayed where it was.

"Oh!" he wailed. "Oh, gripes! I've chased my heart for so long! And now I've got it, I don't know how to put it back."

"Nor I," said Morrig thoughtfully. "But I know someone who can maybe help. There's a man in Gauhngarth—a *Master*, I should say—who perhaps can tell you what to do."

"A Master?" said Iffleplum hopefully, thinking of the Ârkühm and his starry eyes.

"Yes. His name is Ælrik Athanôr—and he's *my* Master in the art of Ühmkyn's Way. He's the leader of the *Ühmkynü*— the followers of Ühm. But people don't know that. They think he's just an apothecary and herbalist."

"An *appotha-kree-anerbalist*? What's that?"

"It's a man who makes medicines and sells simple herbs and potions—you know, like *Simpler Simon* in the nursery rhyme. He has an Apothecary's shop down there in Gauhngarth— that's the market town down in the Vale. I gather herbs for him on the mountain, now and again—as you can see." She nodded up at the dried bunches hanging from the ceiling. "But his shop is just a front to hide behind. He's really a Master Alchemist: but alchemy is forbidden by the Law."

"An alchemist?" said Iffleplum brightening up, remembering the Magister Umbelliferous. "Does he bottle up elfin-hearts?"

"Oh, no! Nothing like that. I don't think so, anyway. He makes all the medicines, pills, and potions that he sells. Does experiments too! And invents all kind of things. Some say alchemists can make lumps of metal into gold, or something. I don't really know. But he's a good man. He knows lots of things. He may be able to help you in some way."

"What's gold?" asked Iffleplum.

"Oh, it's just a bit of shiny butter-coloured metal. Men seem to like it more than anything. Don't ask me why."

"Then why is—erm—*alkermy* not allowed?"

"I don't really know. The King doesn't like it, I suppose. But then, he doesn't like anything very much—except taxes—and carting people off to prison. All those the soldiers drag away are never seen again. And he's got spies and soldiers every- where. I don't know what he's so afraid of."

Iffleplum was shocked. "Prison?" he exclaimed. "Spies and soldiers! What kind of King is that?" This was not at all like the noble monarchs he had read about in his *Legends* book. Then remembering the fatuous Fungling King, he began to feel that perhaps kings were after all not such splendid beings as he had dreamed.

"Oh, him!" said Morrig disparagingly. "Prince Märûcha— now the Johnny-come-lately Changeling-King—Usurper Lord of Angarsland, Gûdârkaçh-Âhn, Beyond, Back of Beyond, all Lakenland—and half of Ümmulon, for all I know. And a bothersome brat he is! The gossips say he poisoned the

234

rightful Regent, to make himself King before he comes of proper age.

"However that may be, now he's taken the crown, he's a swaggering teenage tyrant. Always throwing tantrums and not well liked by common folk. They say he's not the real son of the Good Old King who vanished up the Mountain years ago and left the Regent in his place. Folks think that he's a changeling child, swapped by faery witches in the crib. They reckon that the real king's son was stolen clean away."

"But why? Why would anyone do that?"

"Search me. They say it's all to do with polly-ticks around the king. I've got enough trouble with cattle-ticks on my gauhns. But polly-ticks sound a sight far worse. I've heard the courtiers at the Castle go crazy, creating crafty wars to fill their pockets, when they're bitten by the polly-ticks. I wouldn't like to catch one. But there seems to be a plague of 'em around the palace!"

"Is the castle down there in the valley town?"

"Thank heavens, no! It's way over yonder there at Angarsburg—the city of the King. But I don't go there. Gauhngarth's far enough for me. Us Angarslanders don't like to go elsewhere. No, I keep well out the way of 'em all up here. Luckily, hardly anyone ever one comes up this way, cept for Mattylocks the Milk Boy, every other day"

"But don't you get lonely sometimes, up here all by yourself?"

Morrig shrugged. "No, not much. I've got my gauhns for company. But then—" she grinned, mysteriously, "I'm not always *here* myself. At least—not when I feel Old Ühmkyn moving me!"

"Oh! Yes. I meant to ask—what do you mean—'when you feel Old Ühmkyn moving you'?"

"Oh, *come now!* You surely know Old Ühmkyn's moving us, whether we're aware of it or no? Without Ühmkyn dreaming us, how could we be? How could the Spirit of the Land be not everywhere? Old Ühmkyn is but sleeping in the stones, and dozing in the plants and trees. Ühmkyn's yawning in the animals. And Ühmkyn's spirit springs awake bright-eyed each day, in folk like you and me! How else could we think, were it not so? Ühmkyn chuckles in the mountain streams and gambols in the clouds. And at times I feel Ühmkyn dancing in my skin! And when that happens—I don't even remember that I'm *me!*"

"Goodness!" said Iffleplum amazed by the sparkle in her colour-changing eyes, where something deep and mysterious seemed to shine. "Oh yes! I see! *Khämmârkaï* Tômukh-Ar in Dwêmòriæ told me that. He said Old Ühmkyn's looking out of me. I didn't understand, but I felt so full of joy! So I s'pose you can't feel lonely when you're *One* with the Spirit of all Ümmulon!"

"Too right," said she. "But, honestly—I don't always feel like that. I'm just an apprentice of the *Ühmkynü*—the followers of Ühmkyn's Way, that is—as taught to us by Master Athanôr. I'm only learning how to dance to Ühmkyn's tune. But when Old Ühmkyn's moving me—then suddenly there is no 'Morrig' anymore! So who is looking then? When 'Morrig' goes missing—then I feel Old Ühmkyn's *me!* Then I am Ühmkyn—the Dreamer, see? And then I know that this whole world is only Ühmkyn's Dream."

Iffleplum could only gape in wonder, astonished at her words. Her many-hued eyes were shining brilliantly, as prettily colour-changing as his nose.

"Ah—but when I come out of it," she sighed, "and I'm just plain old Morrig once again—then honestly, yes—I guess it's true—I feel alone again. Sometimes I do miss a little company. But then, the trouble is—I can't stand *people*, see? That's why I mostly keep away from town.

"But anyway, on the morrow, when the Milk Boy comes, I'll take you down in his gauhn-cart to meet Master Athanôr."

*

For most of the day Morrig was out and about, attending to the gauhns. But after all his adventures, Iffleplum was more than happy to spend a restful day with his leg up on a cushioned stool. Although from time to time, he found himself

236

casting an anxious eye on the elven-net hanging from a peg on the wall.

His elfin-heart was on his mind.

He was afraid it might somehow slip away again. Getting up, he hobbled over and tied the net neck tightly below the rim-ring, with a leather thong. He felt a little safer then.

*

The rest of the day he sat out on the rock-ledge that Morrig called her "balcony", gazing out across the mountain valley, or idly leafing through his *Legends* book. On turning over to the stained pages where the elfin-heart had been, a thrill came over him. A sudden idea leapt into his mind. Now he knew what to do to sooth his anxiety over the safety of his elfin-heart.

He limped unsteadily over to the net. Lifting it off its peg, he took it over to the open book. Untying the thong, he pressed the rim-ring flat upon the same pages that had held the wraith before. Gently shaking the elven-net by its tip, he carefully teased the elfin-heart down into the book. With a sound like someone slurping tea, the book absorbed it easily.

Just as he had hoped! Triumphantly, he quickly closed the pages on it and clicked the little golden snap-lock that held the covers together. To be doubly sure, he took the elven-net off its bamboo stick and stuffed the book inside it. Wrapping the net around the cover, he tied the ends and then buckled it tightly in his dwemmer-bag. He slipped the strap over his head and across his chest, hugging the bag to him. Now he felt somewhat more secure.

*

In the evening, Morrig lit a fire in a hollow of the cave wall. A chimney ran up inside the rock. In a smallish cauldron, she cooked up a homely stew flavoured with delicious-tasting herbs. As they supped in the firelight, she told him tales of Angarsland: of its kings and soldiery and their constant wars with dreadful creatures known as *Ghòrs*, whose bandit clans riddled many a mountain round the land. Then later, as his eyelids drooped, she laid out comfy pallet of hay. Covering

237

him with an old gauhn blanket, smelling sweet as a cowshed,
she bade him goodnight. Waving her hands gently over him
he fell at once into a deep and dreamless sleep.

*

Next morning, he awakened feeling much refreshed. He heard
the sound of milk-buckets clanking in the cave below. Morrig's
busy movements echoed up the tunnel. Now he found his foot
was fairly walkable, with hardly any pain. The leaves and
paste around his ankle had dried hard and slightly cracked a
little as he began to walk. Slipping on his dwemmer-coat, he
hobbled gently down, passing through the strong stinky-
cheese smelling dairy and out under the ivy curtain. It was
early dawn and the sun was still abed. The sky was grey. Thin
blankets of wispy mist hung floating on the hillsides here and
there. The gauhns were browsing in the dewy grass. Morrig
had already been out a-milking since first light.

"Ah! Plumkin! Just in time," she said on catching sight of
him. "Here comes Mattylocks the Milk Boy." The sound of
squeaky wooden wheels came to Iffleplum's ears. Around a
bend below, a gauhn-pulled cart came trundling slowly up the
track. As it arrived, the browny-backed great gauhn, with
one odd slightly twisted horn and greenish shaggy legs, gave
a wince-making bellow of relief. A sturdy lad with friendly
flour-smudged face and a head of unkempt whitish hair sat in
the driver's seat. His dirty off-white yokel-smock gave off
clouds of floury dust as he jumped down from the cart.

But if he was astonished to see an Ifflepinn, he gave no sign,
but greeted them both in a cheery way.

"Good morrow, Morrigän and matey there! Do you have a
visitor, is it?" he said. "Well met, my dear. Matty's the
name!" Before Iffleplum could touch his nose in greeting, the
Milk Boy clasped his hand and pumped it up and down. The
gesture surprised him. *Why does he want to wobble my arm?*
he wondered, somewhat taken aback. But he had no time to
understand the niceties of Man-folk greetings.

"Right, then!" said Matty, rubbing a cloud of flour dust off
his reappearing blondish hair. Iffleplum sneezed and rubbed

238

his eyes. "Oh, sorry about that!" the Milk Boy grinned. "I've been helping early, down at the flour mill. Come you, now. Let's get her loaded up in good time for market." Then the two of them set to, lumping pots of curd and milk churns onto the cart. Seeing nothing for it but to lend a hand, Iffleplum joined in as best he could, bringing out armfuls of big round cheeses. But he found the work well warming in the chilly morn.

Finally, Morrig brought down a sack of herbs to top the load and stashed it on a stack of cheese. At last the cart was full. Then Matty took a cleaver from beneath the seat and chopped some firewood. He soon had a small fire ablaze and they brewed up mugs of sweet herbs and honeyed tea.

And not too soon, thought Iffleplum grouchily. He wasn't used to doing *anything* before having Wakes, let alone *working* before his breakfast tum was full. But soon his tum was satisfied. They sat and breakfasted on fruity curd and fresh-baked chunks of crusty bread the Milk Boy had brought up.

Before leaving, Iffleplum fetched his shoulderbag, with the book and elfin-heart still snugly safe inside. Slipping the strap over his head he climbed up in the cart. Morrig stood up. She cupped her hands around her mouth and cried "Aiee-*yah!*" towards the gauhns. Then cupping her hand each side of her temples, like someone might behind their ears, she bent her mind towards them. The gauhns all raised their heads and nodded sagely.

"Just telling them I'll be back before evening and not to worry," said Morrig. Matty clicked his teeth and slapped the reins. With a snort and a loud bellow, the huge gauhn set off. The creaky old wooden-wheeled cart wound slowly down the winding mountain road, way down to the iffepinn's first big scary town and full of *Ühmenü!*

Part the Seventeenth

Gauhngarth

Although to hide himself poor Plumkin does his best,
but still the day turns out with his arrest.

he gauhn-cart lumbered into town, clattering over
the cobbles under an echoing archway in the huge
surrounding outer wall. The bored gate-guard
yawned widely as the weekly milk-cart went creaking past:
nothing of interest there. Besides, he had his eye on a stray
chicken in the road in hopes of a free supper.

"Do put your hood up, now!" warned Matty. "Best cover up
your snout and keep your head down. We don't want the
King's Men troubling us! They jump on anyone unusual."

Iffleplum cowered down, peeping out between the pots, agog at the colour and cacophony of the crowded streets. Tradesmen, farmers, sheep-herds, tinkers with handcarts and barrow-boys, peddlers and pie-men were bustling everywhere, coarsely shouting out their wares. He never thought so many *Ühmenü* existed anywhere!

Now and then, as they trundled down dark, narrow, twisty streets, between tall half-timbered, leaning-over houses, the milk cart stopped at little shops and food stalls, where Matty and Morrig handed down pots of curd and cheese. But all they got back in return were little piles of round brown copper discs. "So *that's* money?" sniffed Iffleplum disappointedly. It wasn't even pretty. "Why give away good food—nice curd and tasty cheese—for bits of metal that you can't eat?" he wondered.

Morrig laughingly tried to explain what money was about, while delivering their last churns of milk to inns and eateries. "In towns, no money means no food or bed," she said. The ifflepinn was even more bewildered. "But you already had food, anyway!" he objected. "And what have *beds* to do with it?" His companions laughed heartily at that.

On leaving the shadowed streets, they came out into a thriving sunny market place. There they stopped and climbed down from the cart, now empty apart from the sack of herbs for Ârkü Athanôr. Matty lifted it out and slung it over his shoulder. "We can't get the cart down narrow alleys to the Pothecary shop," he explained. He handed the reins and a copper farthing to a waiting urchin. The lad grinned, his teeth white against his mucky face. Clutching his booty, he happily led the gauhn-cart off into a carter's fodder-yard.

Now they made their way through the jostling throng, between lines of many multi-coloured stalls. All around them, townsfolk and farmwives were haggling over crates of chickens and baskets full of eggs and vegetables. Now and again, weaving in and out among the crowd, Iffleplum saw several cheery round-faced folk (more or less the same size as himself and dressed in similar garb).They had biggish lumpy-looking noses and mushroom-coloured skins. Most of them

241

were humping basket-loads of fodder or sacks of dung-bricks on their backs. Some were pulling tiny carts behind them, piled high with pots and pans hanging from an A-frame, along with ribbons, balls of string, soup ladles, and lots of shiny beads and dangly things.

"*Gnorfs,*" whispered Morrig, as she saw him staring. "Peddler folk: they travel wide and buy and sell all sorts of strange things from the Outer-Lands." *Ah,* he thought. So that's why with his snout, he had been mistaken for a lumpy-faced-looking gnorf. Noting that some of them wore hoods, the ifflepinn shrank gratefully back into his. He now felt his dwemmer-coat to be a good disguise.

Moving around the market-place, his mauven nose changed colour many times with pleasure, at the whiff of toasted muffins, griddle cakes and honey, strange spicy smells and hot pies from the oven. But as they passed another stall, a strong unpleasant stench assailed his nostrils. And his nose quickly dwindled to a smoky grey. "Fresh fish!" shouted the stall-keeper. "Fresh out the lake this mornin! Fresh out the lake! Just delivered! Still a-flapping!"

Rows of goggle-eyed scaly bodies lay dead upon a marble slab. A few of them still flopped about, their mouths slowly gasping in the air.

"Aiee!" cried Morrig, clasping her head and hurrying past. "I can hear their silent screams! The poor things are drowning in the air." She stopped and closed her eyes. "*Sleeeep,*" she said softly. And the suffering fish grew still.

At the far end of the merchant's stalls, they came upon the cattle market. There the sickly sweet mixed smells of dung and ale, wood-smoke, sizzling fats, and roasting meats was overpowering in the air. All down one side, many folk were quaffing beer or munching meaty-bones at stand-up eateries. Across the aisle, the cattle pens—or gauhn-garths—were full of bellowing and bleating livestock. Just above the fence tops, up on high stands, stood rival auctioneers, jabbering loudly over the noise in their speedy singsong way, selling off sheep and goats and spotted hogs and shaggy longhorn gauhns.

242

Morrig stopped and bent her mind towards the packed-in, penned-up beasts. A few of the gauhns nodded glumly at her in return.

"Oh woe! The poor things are too old for milking now," she said. "It seems a slaughter-man's been bidding for the lot. They reckon it's the butcher's hook or the roasting spits for them." The nearby gauhns lowed mournfully in agreement.

"Oh, gripes," said Iffleplum. "Is there nothing to be done?"

Morrig shrugged and sighed. "Not till folks stop eating every other living thing that walks, or hops, or flies," she said.

Iffleplum shuddered, remembering his close encounter with the hunters.

As they turned away, Matty bumped into a burly wagoner, busily humping crates of squawking chickens onto his cart. With his brawny arms wrapped around a stack of them, the carter could hardly see between the flapping hens.

"Get out of the flodding way!" he bellowed, stumbling against a wagon wheel and nearly dropping half his stock.

"And a good day to you too, Master Wagoner!" chuckled Matty, dodging around the crates.

"Ah, Matty Milko, is it? Look where you're going, next time, you shaggy-headed dreamer!"

"Might I say the same to you, squire! For as you so rightly say, the way indeed is perilous and full of *flodh!* One unguarded slip and you'll be up to your sweaty neck in it." As a parting shot, he added, "It might well improve your smell in any case!"

"Get gobbled by the ghòrs!" rejoindered the carter amiably.

"*Flodh?*" enquired Iffleplum, as they walked on. "What's that?"

"Ha! Don't you know that?" laughed Matty. He grinned at Morrig: "He doesn't know what gauhn-flodh is! Can't you smell it? Look you there, it's everywhere!" He pointed to a round green steaming mound in the middle of the road. "That's flodh! A pile of gauhn-dung, isn't it?"

"Oh, yuck!" said Iffleplum, sidestepping to avoid it. He wrinkled his snout in disgust, as his slowly yellowing nose

turned a mustard-colour like his dwemmer-coat. "Pooh! What
a whiff! What nasty stuff!"

At that Morrig cackled merrily. "Nasty is it? So what d'you
reckon's round your ears and ankle then?"

The Milk-Boy laughed along with her. "Arr! Gauhn-flodh
is a rare good medicine for cuts and sprains, like what you've
got. But by Ghòr! It's powerful strong when fresh. So do you
watch your step, or you'll end up smellin like a gauhn-garth—
or just like Morrig here!"

The girl punched him smartly on the arm, in mock-
annoyance. "Speak for yourself, boggy-breeks!" she retorted
haughtily.

The apothecary's shop jutted out on the corner of a narrow
cobbled lane marked *Leech's Alley*. On a gently swinging sign
above, was written: APOCATHARIUM—PROPRIETOR: ÆLRIK
ATHANÔR. It also bore a painting of a pair of scales, between
which rose a wingèd stick with two serpents twined about it,
on either side. Below, inside a many-paned bow window,
bowls of herbs and bottled medicines were on display, together
with a human skull, a large pestle and mortar and some kind
of huge stuffed lizard hanging in the air. But to their dismay
the shop was shut. Inside the half-glassed door the blind was
down.

A note upon it read: *Away until this Eventide.*

"Botheration!" snorted Morrig. "What a pestilence! Now
what are we to do?" She puffed out her cheeks in consterna-
tion. "I'm sorry, Iffleplum. But I fear we cannot stay until the
night. Matty has to take me back up home again, before the
dark or my little pets will fret." They wandered down the alley
to an ornate door, set in the wall about twenty paces further
from the shop. It was carved with ivy-leaves and impish faery
faces peering from the foliage. "That's Master's front door
there. If you don't see him in the shop after dark, then ring
the bell, and tell him Morrig sent you here."

They made their way back along the narrow winding alleys
to the busy market place. Iffleplum's rumbling tum had sorely
missed his mid-morning Minch. And even Muncheon time was

nearly past, as the sun was now sliding into afternoon. Just opposite the gauhn-garths, they finally found a small free table in a crowded, canvas-covered outdoor eatery. They ordered pumpkin pie and mash, and then sat there suffering the eye-watering smoke wafting from a nearby roasting spit as they ate. There were irritating flies all over the tables, but the wasps were even worse! One flew into Iffleplum's hood and buzzily crawled beside his ear. Swiftly throwing off his hood, he shook his head, flapping his floppy ears about. The wasp shot off and zoomed away.

Most of the other diners were too engrossed in stuffing themselves and boisterous chat to notice him: *except for one.* A pudgy-faced man with beady eyes and the red-veined cheeks of a butcher stared at him intently. Iffleplum caught his glance. He had the piggy eyes of a hunter. The ifflepinn hastily covered his head again, in spite of the heat. The man quickly gobbled up his meal and stood up, smirking slyly to himself. As he rose, a striped and bloodied apron belied his trade. Briskly he paid his bill and left the eatery without another glance. Iffleplum frowned suspiciously as he disappeared in the crowd.

A feeling like the Darkstream lingered on behind him.

Over the meal Matty and Morrig talked little, but listened quietly to the gossip all around them. At a large table next to them, the local townsfolk were astounding some yokels from outlying farms, with a strange tale they had to tell. It seemed on yestermorn, half the mountainside had fallen into the Gauhn Valley Lake, and a mysterious bushy island had suddenly appeared in the middle of it, where no island ever was before!

"When the mist all thinned away, all of a sudden—there it was!" said one. "We all saw it, plain as a pikestaff. Mind you, we dursn't go too near, not knowing what kind of magic brought it there! Anyroad, the fishermen saw giant *wolves* running about all over it. But then—just this morning, when we looked again—there it was—gone!" he said wide-eyed. "Vanished! Just like that!"

Morrig and Matty grinned at each other. They nodded knowingly at Iffleplum. "Told you so," said Morrig quietly. "He's off and away to find some quieter place to be." Iffleplum felt happier then, knowing that the Gnumpf was still alive and well. And it seemed that Fluff-Ruff was with him too. It would have pleased him to be seen as a scary pack of "giant wolves"! But at the same time the ifflepinn was saddened, not knowing where his new found friends had gone.

*

"Well, we'd best be off," said Matty, back outside beside the gauhn-garths. "The afternoon is getting on." He handed Iffleplum the sack of herbs and gave him three copper coins. "You can buy yourself a bit of scoff with that, later. A penny'll get you an apple pie, while you wait for Master Athanôr."

Iffleplum held up a dark-stained, dull copper coin. "They'll really give me a *pie* in exchange for *that?*" he laughed. He shook his head in amusement. *These Ühmen folk were mad as wild pigs.*

Back in the aisle, Matty handed the sack of herbs to Iffleplum to take to Athanôr. As they were saying their goodbyes, the butcher-man and two halberdiers came bustling through the crowd. People hastily stood aside when they saw the soldiers coming. They never knew who they would pick on next. The soldiers wore plumed helmets and blood-dark uniforms, crossed with bandoliers and sporting many shiny golden buttons.

"There it is! There it is!" cried the chubby butcher breathlessly, panting to keep up with the soldiers. He pointed a pudgy finger at Iffleplum. The civic guards strode over swiftly, stationing themselves before and behind the ifflepinn. They stood over him looking menacing. A crowd of gawkers gathered round to watch the excitement, now they knew the guards weren't after *them.*

"Stay right where you are, Sunshine!" demanded the senior-looking officer sternly, his mutton-chop whiskers and bushy white moustache bristling with officialdom. He nodded to his underling, "Corporal!"

246

"Right, Sarge!" said the Corporal, taking Iffleplum by the shoulder. "Where's your permit?"

"Permit? Wh–what permit?" faltered Iffleplum.

"Gnorfish Trader's Licence, that's *what!*" barked the soldier, standing to attention, his chin jutting in the air. Remembering his barracks lesson on how to talk with authority, he puffed out his chest, clasped his hands behind his back and recited: "*All gnorfs—within the Gauhngarth town limits— must, at all times, show, on demand, if requested—by any member of His Royal Highness' Armed Forces, namely, His Majesty High King Mārûçha (may he rule forever)—without which—*"

"He's not a gnorf and he's not trading!" said Morrig, interrupting his rigmarole.

"What's he got in the sack, then?" demanded the Sergeant. "And what is he, then, if he's not a gnorf?"

"Well, you might not credit it, but as a matter of fact—he's an ifflepinn," said Matty, "believe it or not—from *Ælfÿlon.*"

The corporal opened his mouth to guffaw—but as the Sergeant smartly whipped Iffleplum's hood back off his head— he stopped in mid-laugh. The corporal's face went white. He stared at Iffleplum in disbelief. "Ghòrs guts!" he gasped in awe. "It can't be true! 'Pear-shaped, floppy ears, mauvish-looking nose—' I thought it was a joke, pinned up in the barracks there! But ghòr's flaming guts, Sarge! If this isn't one, I'm a flodding dung-beetle! Flodding heck! If this doesn't mean promotion!"

Sensing big trouble, Morrig bent her mind again towards the gauhns. The great beasts began to thrash about and moo restlessly.

"I told you! I told you!" said the butcher. "Do I get the reward, then?"

Both soldiers immediately gripped Iffleplum firmly by the shoulders of his dwemmer-coat. "Right, Sunshine!" grinned the Sergeant, with great satisfaction. "You're under arrest! Come along with us!"

"On what *charge?*" demanded Matty angrily.

"Never you mi—" began the Sergeant, but he was cut off in mid-sentence.

Morrig had cupped her hands and gave out a trilling high shrill cry—"Heyaa!" At once, all over the market-place, every gauhn lifted its head. As one, they bellowed out with an answering angry roar. And in a trice, the beasts went wild. They jumped and stomped and kicked the fences down around them with their hind legs. Battens exploded behind the soldiers, as a drove of bellowing gauhns came bursting out through the shattering framework. A chunk of wood shot off the fence and whacked the back of the Sergeant's head, knocking his helmet off. He fell senseless to the ground.

In alarm, the corporal let go of Iffleplum and tried to jump aside. But the madding press of gauhns knocked him flying backwards into the butcher's stall. He crashed through the counter top as the stall collapsed around him and he disappeared beneath a rain of hams, dead ducks and sausages. And finally, a smelly bowl of offal slid down and tipped itself all over him.

The struggling mass of bystanders fell over each other in their haste to get away. The butcher turned about with a furious yell, attempting to fight his way through them to the wreckage of his stall. But the tip of a long horn scored his back, as the gauhns went sweeping past. And a purple gauhn with a crumpled horn got entangled in his apron strings. He gave a fearful scream as it yanked him off his feet. His chubby little legs scrabbled wildly in the air, as the great beast dragged and bounced him all along the road. Folk scrambled to the sides as the madly galloping gauhns stampeded down the twisty narrow lanes between the houses. In moments they were out of sight. But the butcher's wailing yells could still be heard, echoing faintly in the distance, as they thundered away to freedom.

Just as the gauhns burst out, Matty had quickly jumped up on a stall. He hauled Morrig straight up after him. "Run for it!" he yelled at Iffleplum on the other side of the stampede.

Flattened against the ruined fence, the bewildered ifflepinn hesitated.

"That way!" bawled Matty pointing down an alley. "Go! Go! While ye've got a chance!"

Iffleplum took to his heels, his dwemmer-bag and sack of herbs both bouncing on his back.

All over the market-place the crowd was scattering. More great beasts came bursting out all over. They went surging this way and that among the stalls. Even Matty's gauhn (still attached to the cart) had heard the call. It came careering madly down the aisles. Its curly horns and cartwheels snagged on awning poles and guy ropes, bringing many stalls tumbling down behind it. Baskets of bread and fruits and vegetables went rolling everywhere.

Matty and Morrig leapt stumbling into the cart as it came on by. "Yaa! Yaa!" cried Matty in encouragement, catching up the reins and slapping them on the gauhn's great rump. People hastily leapt aside as the cart raced on wildly, zig-zagging through the streets. Rattling over the cobbles, they swept out through another town-wall gate. The snoozing guards in the gatehouse woke up abruptly from their slumbers as the gauhn-cart clattered by. But by the time they had tottered out, scratching their sleepy heads and staring after them, Matty and Morrig were no more than a distant cloud of dust.

*

Twilight was falling before Iffleplum emerged from his hiding place. He had run haphazardly down the twisty streets and quickly lost his bearings in the maze of alleyways. Pausing to catch his breath, he had slid down into the shadow of a tiny humpbacked bridge. A small, swift stream swept past his toes, winding its crooked way between the houses. Draping his hood well over his snout, he had huddled there awhile, still shaking from his near escape, until his heart grew calm again.

He was about to set off once more, when half a dozen loud-mouthed soldiers came stomping down the street. He shrank back beneath the bridge, hiding himself behind the sack of herbs. From the snatches of their talk he caught as they passed by, it seemed they were looking for *him.*

"Well, they reckon it came down this way," said one.

"Flodding wild goose-chase if you ask me," said another. "Chasing faery-folk that don't exist."

"Well, I don't know about that—his Royal Highness seems to think it's something important," said a third.

"Yeh, well—he's got lots of bees in his bonnet, he has—" retorted the other as they clumped off out of earshot.

Iffleplum now felt it wiser to stay where he was. He wondered why they wanted him. *Not for something nice,* he thought, *they would have dragged me off to prison!* And for an hour or two he was afraid to venture out, whiling away the time by dreaming of the apple pie he daren't go out and buy. At long last evening came and twilight softly settled on the streets. A lamplighter with a long pole passed down the alleys, humming to himself and igniting lanterns here and there.

After he had gone, Iffleplum felt it safe enough to crawl out from his hidey-hole. But as he stood, a sudden a shadow loomed over him. A silent figure was standing on the bridge above! His heart leapt. The shadowed shape seemed suddenly to be a Grope! In shock, he stepped back into the stream, soaking the hem of his dwemmer-coat. The creature grinned. And in his fright, a fearsome row of sharkish teeth sprang forth in his mind.

"What you got there then, matey?" said the shadow in a friendly voice. Instantly, his phantom vision of a "Grope" transformed into a normal *Ühmen*-man.

"Oh! What?" said Iffleplum, taken aback. His heart was beating fast, as his fear-created image faded away.

"I said, what wares carry you?" asked the stranger.

"Uh? Wares? Oh—erm—yes, just herbs," said Iffleplum, keeping his head down and hoping he was taken for another gnorfish peddler. "I have to take them to the Apothecary shop. But I lost my way." He stepped out of the stream and up the bank.

"Herbs, is it?" said the inquisitive stranger. "There's not much trade in that, mate. Lucky you met me, old son. I can get you much better stock. Come on, I know the shop. It's sort of on my way." He clamped his arm around the ifflepinn's shoulder and ushered him over the bridge. "Yes, it's on the corner of Simpler's Street, off Leech's Alley. Just along Shoemaker Row."

As he led him down the shadowy dark and lamp-lit lanes, the stranger never stopped talking for a moment. "Oh yes, matey! What luck you chanced on me, my old gnorf! Trader-Jack's the name! Whatever you want, I can get it for you— *cut price!* Right? You won't get a better deal nowhere. You must have heard of me—I'm the famous Jack-of-all-Trades." He laughed at his own witticism. "You want goods: any kind—just ask for me. I'm Jack-the-lad! Salt or silver, bangles or butter, *flodh-a-gauhn* bricks or fancy goods—you name it, I can get you—"

But the sudden clatter and bang of hammers drowned out his voice, as they passed by a long low window near the ground. It was divided into many grimy panes.

"Ah now!" said the shyster. "We're in Shoemaker Row! Now this here's a *magic* shoe-making factory." He rubbed the grimy window with his fist. The huge cellar-like room below was filled with dozens of grey and white-bearded dwarves whacking away on the upturned soles of boots and shoes.

"Now looky there! Here's a chance for you. I can get you a whole stock of those magic shoes, that keep the wearer from any harm. All made by those wise old dwarves—half-*elves*, some of 'em. Now, lucky for you, I got contacts. I can get you a really good price on a whole cartload of boots and shoes. What do you say to that? *Eh?* What do you say?"

Iffleplum peered through the grimy glass.

"My goodness!" said he, seeing all the ancient-looking dwarves. "What a lot of *old* cobblers!"

"Ah yes, well," said Trader Jack, thinking he had been rumbled. "Right you are, squire! It's been nice knowing you. I'm off the other way now. You're nearly there. Go straight down Tinsmith's Lane and take the second left and first right into Simpler's Street. But as I say, if ever you want a better deal—just ask around for Trader Jack—and—"

"Yes, yes. Thank you—thank you very much," said Iffleplum and hurried off down the street.

Trader Jack watched him as he went. "Funny-looking gnorf, that," he muttered to himself. "Never seen one with a multi-coloured nose before. He doesn't talk like one either." Clutching his chin thoughtfully, he turned and went upon his way.

It wasn't far to Simpler's Street, as the Trader had said. But in the ill-lit alleyways, Iffleplum's heart jumped at shadows. He startled whenever a cloaked figure came looming up from out of the dark, or round a sudden corner. In his frightened eyes, they all took on the scary shambling shapes of Gropes, until the people passed him by without a second glance.

At last the corner shop came in sight. But it was closed, dark and shuttered. His heart sank. The sign above swung softly, creaking in a draught. Its squeaky sound was not encouraging. With a heavy heart, he turned down Leech's Alley

252

towards the ornate door. Tired and hungry, he set down the sack of herbs with a sigh of relief.

Not knowing what to expect, he stared at the dark doorway, gathering his courage. But the twinkling eyes of the wooden imps peeping from the gloom of the carven ivy foliage were a little frightening. As he stood, the hem of his dwemmer-coat dripped wetly down his leg.

Tremulously, he tugged on the bell-pull, and waited anxiously.

But no one came.

Just then, way up the hill on Simpler's Street, he heard a sound that filled his heart with dread.

The rhythmic clump of soldiers' boots!

The tramp of a troop of marching men came echoing down the narrow lane. And they were coming his way!

His heart hammering, he jiggled the bell-pull frantically.

Part the Eighteenth

The Alchemist

*In which Iffleplum learns of a prophecy
that he finds frightening and discovers the trouble
that having a little fat belly brings.*

small round flap suddenly shot open in the middle of the door. A wild-eyed, furry fat face poked out. Iffleplum startled in surprise. "Go away!" it hissed angrily, in a raspy little voice, showing its sharp and tiny needle-like teeth. It drew its head back in. And the flap slammed shut behind it.

Iffleplum stared up at the dark door in shock. The carven imps around the upper panel seemed to be winking and grinning at his discomfiture. He rubbed his eyes and shook his head. The tramp of soldiers' boots was drawing nearer still. By the sound of it they were already halfway down the hill.

Oh, great greeny gripes! he thought. *What now?* But then suddenly it came to him in a flash. That hairy-whiskered furry face he had seen had been a cat! A *talking* cat! An ummal-cat! There was still hope.

Desperately he hung on the bell-pull and banged on the door with his other fist. The muffled ringing of a bell inside could just be heard. A moment more and the peephole flap burst open once again. And the same furry ginger cat-face filled the hole.

"I said—go away!" it hissed. "Shop's shut! No hawkers or traders after hours! Master's occupied!"

254

"Oh, please!" pleaded Iffleplum, throwing off his hood. "Look! I'm not a peddler! I'm an *ummal*—just like you! I'm an ifflepinn! Morrig sent me! I've got herbs for Ârkü Athanôr." He held up the sack in evidence. "Quick! Quick!

The soldiers are after me! They're coming! Oh, please! Quickly! Open the door!"

"Just wait," hissed the cat wearily, withdrawing its head. The peephole panel slammed shut again.

*

"Heft-right! Heft-right! Pick your feet up there!" bawled the sergeant as the soldiers came stomping down the cobbled street. "Left—*wheel!*" he barked, as they turned the corner into Leech's Alley, not twenty yards from where he stood. They were almost upon him. Iffleplum shrank into his hood and froze.

Abruptly the door opened. Light spilled out into the alley. A man's head in a round cap poked quickly around the doorframe. Seeing the oncoming soldiery, his fist shot out and grabbed Iffleplum by his dwemmer-coat. With a swift tug, he yanked him inside. The door slammed behind him. Leaning back against it, he clutched the ifflepinn tightly, clamping a firm hand over his snout.

Uh-oh! Out of the frying pan into the fire! thought Iffleplum, his heart pounding.

But the sound of the soldier's boots went marching by without a stop. Then the man relaxed and loosed his grip. He hastily hustled him down a few stone steps. They passed under an arch and through a curtained doorway. Iffleplum stumbled into a long low room with a domed ceiling, half obscured by rising steams and acrid smokes. His eyes smarted. His nose went greyish-blue.

Before him, in the middle of the room, stood a massive tile-topped table, throbbing with extraordinary working apparatus. Coloured liquids bubbled in whirly tubes and bulbous glass containers, boiling gently over tiny flames of gas. Ambelics wobbled and rattled slightly on their tripods, spurting puffs of sweet and stinky smells. Iffleplum's nose wrinkled and changed colour several times, as sharp metallic reeks and itchy odours pricked his nostrils.

Dressers and worktops all around the room were piled high with pestles and mortars, potions, bottles of multi-coloured

256

medicines, scrolls and tumbled stacks of books. Gaslights lit the walls, which were covered with strange charts and diagrams. At both ends of the room, overstuffed library shelves groaned from floor to ceiling, with the weight of rare books and heavy ancient tomes. Between the curtains of two tall steamy windows in the facing wall, he could faintly see a few stars twinkling.

But now the man stood over him, dressed in a floor-length wine-dark gown and an under-tunic of burnt umber, with long deckled-edged pointy sleeves, that dangled from his elbows. His straggly shoulder-length grey hair escaped from under a round maroon-topped flattish cap, embroidered with a colourful band of mystic symbols round its edge. Slender half-spectacles perched upon his nose. And the light of the *Lûmentir* flowed through them, for the eyes that now looked down at him were soft and kindly.

Iffleplum felt reassured. Bravely throwing back his hood, he gazed up at the man. "I am Iffleplum of Ælfÿlon," he said, placing his hand upon his heart in the dwemmer way. "And I thank you for my rescue."

"Ælrik Athanôr at your service," said the Alchemist, inclining his head gravely. The symbols around the brim of his cap glimmered briefly in the gaslight as he moved. "And I do hope you will excuse my doorward, Sulphie," he smiled, with a toss of his head at the ginger cat. "She is inclined to be a little hasty, now and then."

"Hmmf!" sniffed the cat disdainfully, stalking off with its tail in the air, and hissing: "Answer the door yourself then, if you're not satisfied! And leave me by the stove!"

"I have to say, she *does* do a great job of keeping unwanted visitors away though, when I am working," said Athanôr loudly, with a wink to Iffleplum. But the cat deigned not to hear. It leapt up onto a cushioned stool and curled up huffily in a ball.

"Now—what brings you so fortuitously to my door?" asked the Alchemist.

"Morrigauhn the milk-maid sent me," said Iffleplum, holding out the sack. "She said to bring these herbs to you."

"That much I know. And much obliged," he replied, setting the sack aside. "But by the way, she's not a milk-maid," he corrected. "Nor a *morri-gauhn* as the people call her. She's far more than a cattle-keeper. She's a *morrigän*—a half human, Wicca-wise sprite, or witch-girl, you might say—and one of my best pupils," he said warmly.

Oh! thought Iffleplum. His eyes grew wide. *Now that explained a lot; her strange powers and all.*

"So—" said Athanôr, looking down upon him with some wonder, "My cat—Sulphie—tells me you are an ifflepinn?"

The ginger feline opened an irate eye. "I'm not *your* cat!" she growled. "I'm my *own* cat."

"Ah! Quite right," apologized the Alchemist. "Slip of the tongue. I stand corrected. And over there are my other two—er—*companions*, Merkie and Sally." He waved a hand towards a silvery brindled tabby cat sitting on the rounded top of a small furnace. Another white cat lay curled up below beside it. "Sulphie, Merkie, Sally: I present you, Iffleplum of Ælfÿlon." The ifflepinn touched his nose and dabbed his finger towards each one of them in turn. The cats slightly waggled their heads by way of recognition.

Now, despite the warmth of the room, Iffleplum suddenly found himself shivering with aftershock. After his Grope-filled fright in the shadowed alleys and the coming of the soldiers, he was now all atremble at his near escape. He imagined pale round mothy-eyes peering in at the windows and quickly looked away.

"Erm—are there Gropes around here in Gauhngarth?" he asked anxiously.

"Gropes?" frowned Athanôr, cocking his head inquiringly.

"Well—erm—they call them *Dhârkäsü* in the Elvish-speech. It's just—I keep thinking I see them *everywhere*."

"Ah! *Dhârkäsü* is it? You are plagued by *Dhârkäsü*—the Shadows of Fear? They are but phantoms of the mind! They have no power in themselves. They only ever appear where

258

fear abides. They are no more real than monsters in the wardrobe, or bogeymen under the bed. If you laugh at them they'll shrink away.

"But *who* is it thinks them up? You conjure them yourself, whenever you're afraid. You call up Shadowfolk, by the fancy of your thoughts. Like a lantern show, you project them from your fearful heart—for there you have already let them make their lair! But without you feeding them on your fear, they cannot even be."

"Oh! I see. But I never used to be afraid in Ælfÿlon. That is—not until my elfin-heart came loose. Oh, yes! It's true! When I began to be afraid in the faery-ring—that's when I saw them first! And now I think I see them everywhere. So, if they appear from a fearful heart, how can I keep them out?"

"How? Just look outside!" cried Athanôr, drawing aside the heavy velvet curtains from the window. "See? There is Night, sitting out there! Demon-dark and black!" He waved his arm dramatically, with fingers splayed.

"We are surrounded by shadows and darkness—yes? And what happens if we let the darkness in?" He opened the windows inwardly. "Stand back! Now see! The fearful darkness rushing in! Do you see it filling the room? Do you see the darkness swirling all around us now?"

"Erm—no... of course not—"

"And why not?"

"Because... because the room is full of light," said Iffleplum.

"Precisely!" said the Alchemist, smiling warmly. "Because it's full of light. And so—if your heart is full of light—how can the dark get in? After all, what is the dark? It is only lack of light. When the sun arises, darkness flees. So keep a sunrise ever shining in your heart; a love-light brightly burning there! And the Fear-Shadows will trouble you no more."

"Oh. Now I realize—the love-light *was* my elfin-heart. But then I lost it, wishing for a wilder way of life. Now I can't feel it any more. I chased it everywhere. Then Morrig's dream-catcher caught it in its web! That's why I came to you. She thought you might help me put it back. I have it here,

259

wrapped up in an elven-net." He pulled his shoulder bag around and held it up.

"Ah, so. I see. Remarkable," muttered Athanôr, "truly remarkable. This, will need some thought. Now, why were the soldiers seeking you, may I ask?"

"I–I don't know, but it seems it was on orders from the King."

"Hmm, there's more to this than meets the eye. But I forget my manners. Don't just stand there, dripping on my floor. Let's get you out of your coat and we'll see about some food."

*

They supped later in the Alchemist's cosy study, on toast and buttered corn-cobs, beside a fire. And the little Plumkin part of Iffleplum laughed gaily when he found there was apple pie for pudding! Two large helpings with custard made up for missing out that afternoon. Finally he pushed his plate back with a happy sigh.

Then Athanôr fell silent for a time, thinking deeply. He gazed awhile into the fire. At length he said, "I know not if I can help you in your quest, for I have no knowledge of replacing elfin-hearts. And I do not wish to risk it getting loose again. Not merely for the sake of my own curiosity, much as I would like. I must consult the books. Mayhap I will find something written there."

"Oh," said Iffleplum disappointedly. "I was hoping you might magic my elfin-heart back into me?"

"I'm an alchemist, not a magician!" retorted Athanôr. "Nor have I found the Philosopher's Stone for changing base metal into gold. I make practical experiments, not magic. My only 'magic' is to awaken witless folk to Ühmkyn's Way; whereby, I may at least turn a few cabbages into kings!"

"Oh, well, I hope you didn't make this King who's after me."

"Oh, him!" he snorted. "Märûçha the Changeling. That backward boy. I wonder greatly what he wants with you? I know nothing of the lore of ifflepinns, to account for it. Ah! Which reminds me..." He got up thoughtfully and passed into

260

his alchemery. In moments he was back, clutching a huge gilt-lettered leather-bound book, entitled *Beastiology.*

Blowing off the dust, he riffled through the crackly old pages, muttering, "Aardvark, Aardwolf, Abada, Accipiters, Acephalus, Adders, Ælfÿnkin... Ah! Here we are! Ælfÿnpinn! Let's see, now..." He pushed his half-lens spectacles up to the bridge of his nose and began to read. "Legende hath it of a long lost land whence came the Ælvenü—the Elvish people—a countrie mist-enshrouded, cloud-covered, its whereabouts unknown; called as Ælf-ÿ-lon; within the bounds of which, dwelleth Ummals known in myth, that speaketh as we do; one specie so-styled as Ælfÿn-pynnü—shapen in forme most likened to a peeled and legged pear—mauven snouted, much disposed to changing hue when feelings moveth them—ears adangle—' and so forth—mere description—but it doesn't really say—wait! What's this here below? A scribbled rhyme:

'*Whan faery Ælfÿnpinn to Khämmârkhond doth come,*
Angarr's Changelyng Kynge his doome shall fynde,
Highe yn yonder Dwæma-Lannde of Lün.'
Thus sayeth Mälkòrnäth the Seer.'

"That's *it!* Here it is! Plain as a pikestaff!" said Athanôr elatedly.

"*What?* What is?" asked Iffleplum in bewilderment.

"The *answer!* This must be a quotation from *The Prophecies of Mälkòrnäth* the blind Seer, of three centuries ago. It would appear he had a vision of the coming of the Changeling King and his downfall. Look what it says! '*Whan faery Ælfÿnpynn to Khämmârkhond doth come...*'

"I see it now! Khämmârkhond is the capital city of Lün—the land where Elves and the *Dwæmahîn*—or Dwemmers, dwell. It is the highest city in all of Ümmulon. Way up in the highest mountains surrounding Ümmûârkon, the mightiest mountain of them all. And there, traditionally, the Good Old King of Angarsland—and all the lands round—would always go, to preside over the famous Festival of Spring each year.

261

Now, Mälkòrnäth says that if an ifflepinn comes to Khämmâr-khond, then the tyrant King will get his comeuppance there.

"Methinks Märûcha must have seen the prophecy and fears for his life, should an *ælfÿnpinn*—or ifflepinn, appear. And mayhap that ifflepinn is *you*. For you are first I have ever seen in Angarsland. And from what you say, word may have reached the palace by now, that you are not a mythical creature after all. For at least the soldiers now know that you exist."

"Oh, gripes!" exclaimed Iffleplum. "But this is awful! What if he finds me?"

"Alas, I fear he will not wish to let you live. Only that way might he stop the prophecy from coming true. He must not find you. You must haste away. But you are safe here for the moment. Until we find out what's best to do. Meanwhile, let's find some place for you to sleep."

Athanôr drew back a curtain, revealing a bunk set in the wall beside the fireplace. "Here is my guest room," he smiled. "Sleep well. And remember—keep a bright sun shining in your heart: for there the fear-shadows cannot come."

Iffleplum climbed into the bunk gratefully and snuggled down. He hugged his shoulder-bag with his dwemmerbook and elfin-heart inside for comfort and clasped it to his chest. Sensing his unease, Sally, the white cat, came and curled up beside him. Velveting her paws, she softly kneaded him, soothingly purring in his ear. And the sun shining in his heart sank down slowly into sleep.

*

Next day, Athanôr said, "The soldiers are still all over town and questioning everyone. It is like a hive of bees out there. I advise you not to venture out until the hue and cry dies down. You may stay here awhile with me, as long as needs be. Keep out of sight and do not go out until I say."

So it was that Iffleplum stayed hidden in Ârkü Athanôr's Alchemery for many a day. On evenings when the shop was closed, the Alchemist taught him how to grind up minerals and healing herbs and pound them with a pestle in a mortar bowl. Some days he worked the bellows on the forge to keep the fire bright. With all his tasks he hardly noticed that a week went swiftly by.

When the weekend came, at twilight, Athanôr placed a "Closed" sign on the shop door. Yet oddly, the doorbell tinkled again and again. One by one, silent folk kept coming softly in from the darkling alleys. And without a word they slipped quietly down the back stairs of the shop, into a domed and roundish room below. There they gathered every week, to chant strange songs and hear Master Ârkü Athanôr teach them the secrets of Old Ühmkyn's Way.

But frustratingly, to protect him from being seen, Iffleplum was bidden to stay hidden in the Alchemery. In the next room he could sometimes hear the assembly chanting "Ooooom" in curious tones. (Athanôr told him it was the name of *Ühm* they sang.) He found the sounds and melodies strangely moving. And the deep and rumbling tones were soothing to his empty heart. It reminded him of Old Wossul's *Song of Spring* and the warming fire of home.

*

On other days when Athanôr was busy in the shop, Iffleplum would sweep and tidy up the Alchemery. Sometimes he opened up the *Beastiology* book, fascinated by all the weird and wonderful creatures therein. But there was never a mention of the Gnumpf. Often he mulled over the strange rhyme of Mälkòrnäth the Seer.

Can he really have meant ME? he wondered. The thought made the peach hair prickle on his skin.

*

As days went by, the safety of his elfin-heart began to prey upon his mind again. Even wrapped up as it was, it troubled him. He was often tempted up open up his *Legends* book, to make sure it was still there. But the risk of losing it again was strong. Understanding his anxiety, Athanôr offered him a small chest-like, brassbound box with a copper key. "It won't make any difference, but if it makes you feel better, you can put it all in this," he said. Iffleplum gratefully locked the shoulder-bag inside and pocketed the key. The Alchemist then hefted up the box and placed it safely on an upper shelf.

*

Weeks went by and still Athanôr had found no answers to Iffleplum's dilemma. "It seems I can be of little help in your quest," he said one evening as they sat beside the fire again. "There is nothing in the books. I can only say, that in Ühmkyn's Way, it's said that 'the thing that you desire most'—*that* you should offer unto others. It's a way of *freeing* us from forever holding on to things—things we cannot take with us when we leave and 'travel on'."

"I don't care for *things!*" retorted Iffleplum. Athanôr raised an unbelieving eyebrow. "Oh, well—perhaps my *Legends* book. But I *need* my elfin-heart," he sniffed tremulously, glancing up at his brassbound box. "That's what I want the most. How could I give *that* away? And why? And what would be the use of that?"

The Alchemist shrugged and splayed his upturned hands. "I know not. One only knows a deed's value when it's done. And even then—we of Ühmkyn's Way are not concerned with that. It's only how we *feel* when we have given our last desire away that counts. As for your path, which way you must go, I cannot say." He stared awhile into the fire.

Iffleplum spoke softly. "Whichever way, I must go soon. I feel Ümmûârkon calling me. The mighty Mountain I have always yearned to see. Perhaps that's where I'll find my destiny. I am well with you Master Athanôr, but I feel an urge to travel on. And—I need to smell the *woods* I love again! Woods and ferns and *grass!* I stifle in these walls."

"Then the time has come. I will consider ways to smuggle you out of Gauhngarth, past the Gate-Guards. They have doubled the watch on all ways out of town. And they're still checking all who come and go. Perhaps we can hide you as you came, in Morrig and Matty's milk-cart, come next Market Day."

*

The next afternoon Iffleplum was thrilled to discover a cupboard full of maps of the many different lands all over Ümmulon. Maps were something mysterious and magical to the ifflepinn. Despite dreaming of returning home to Ifflenook, they thrilled him with the thought of lands unknown and paths untrod. Gazing at them awakened his adventurous heart again. One large map he unrolled on the bench-top, showed the whole of Ümmulon! He pinned it down on its curly corner with a huge fat candle on a sconce. Sulphie jumped onto the bench and obligingly curled up on the other side.

Evening was coming on and the gaslights were dimming down. Iffleplum lit the candle above him on the sconce, the better to see by. In the pool of candlelight, he gazed in fascination upon the many strange-named shires and little lands spread out for miles in every direction around the mighty mountain's feet. Goodness! Ümmulon was enormous! An island continent it seemed. But an island all the same, for the Silver Sea hemmed it all around. Here and there, in the southern lands, uncharted empty spaces were marked both in the Common Ummal-tongue and Elvish, "Desert Wasteland", or "Here be Dragons", or "Ware Ghòrhîn"—in brackets "(Ghòrs)" written in browny-reddish ink.

Then his eyes fell upon a river marked the *Ælventir*. His heart skipped a beat. *Ælventir?* A wonder sprang into his mind! He thought of Merryvale and the river *Elventear*. Scouring the map, he now saw that every other river was written as *tir* in the Elvish script, like *Sylvantir* and *Tir-Nhannogh*. It seemed that *tir* meant 'river' in the Elvish tongue, then the *Elventear* of Ælfÿlon was really *the River Elven*, flowing all the way from Ümmûârkon in the centre of the land! Excitedly, he traced it with his finger, snaking away from the mighty Mountain, through strange-named lands and little shires to somewhere west of north. And there, mysteriously, it vanished, in a bare patch marked "Unfound-land—whereabouts unknown".

Is that the hidden land I'm from? he wondered, shifting Sulphie's leg aside to see it properly.

While poring over the map, Iffleplum never noticed that a stack of scrolls sticking outwards from the shelf above his head, were browning in the candle flame. Not until a stronger smell of scorching reached his nose—*a little late!* Suddenly the scrolls burst into flame with a crackle and a roar. A flake of burning parchment dropped down upon the snoozing cat.

Sulphie screeched and leapt off the bench. Without a stop she fled out through the cat-flap in the corner door, yammering off into the dark.

Iffleplum leapt up, horrified. Grabbing his dwemmer-coat off a peg he flapped it wildly at the flames. A spray of Sandman's dust from the shores of Dwêmòriæ shot out of the pocket and sparkled in the air.

At that moment the Alchemist came downstairs from the shop. "What's this?" he thundered in amazement.

"I'm sorry! I'm sorry!" cried Iffleplum. "The candle set the scrolls alight! I wasn't looking!"

"Never mind the scrolls!" said Athanôr, offhandedly throwing a jug of water over them. "What's this starry dust that sparkles in the air?"

"Oh! that! I had forgotten it. It's just some sand I picked up in Dwêmòriæ."

"Sand?" exclaimed Athanôr. "Sand of Dwêmòriæ? Show me!"

The scrolls now fizzled out, leaving a smell that tinged Iffleplum's white-frighted nose to greyish-brown. Taking a tiny handful of the Sandman's sparkly dust from his coat pocket he held it out. The Alchemist took his wrist and steered him to the central table, tipping the soft silvery grains gently into a bowl.

"I saw the Sandman fill his hourglass with it," said Iffleplum. "I think it's what he throws into the eyes of little children to send them off to sleep."

"Is it now?" answered Athanôr. "Let's see." He took a tiny pinch between his thumb and finger and sprinkled it over the wide-eyed Sally Alley-cat. Immediately the cat yawned hugely. Her head dropped down and in a trice she fell even faster than fast asleep. "Fascinating," murmured Athanôr. "Now then, Merkie! Come—and spit in that."

The tabby cat grimaced. "Not again?" he growled resignedly and padded over. Jumping onto the table, the cat hawked impressively and spat into the dust. Suddenly it all went liquid and runny, like quicksilver.

"By Ühmkyn's beard!" exclaimed Athanôr excitedly. "That's it! At last!" he cried. "This time we've done it! The noble metal! By Ühm! My boy! You have found it! The Philosopher's Stone!"

"Stone?" queried Iffleplum. "I don't see any stone?"

"Ah! 'Tis not a stone as such. We alchemists call it that because it's 'fixed'—unchangeable—like stone. That is—until it's mixed with mercury! And Merkie's spit has done the trick! This 'stardust' of Dwêmòriæ is truly it! The sacred Stone! All kinds of powers it can give! It's a tool of transmutation! Just a drop of it can change crystals into precious gems, more dazzling than diamonds. Or change a lump of lead to gold! A touch on the tongue brings healing to the sick. And a dash of it in milk exhilarates and gives great energy! By Ühm! With this, I can do great good to *all* who come to me! Far more even than my herbs and all my medicines."

*

That night Athanôr elatedly stayed up until the early hours, experimenting with the silky stardust sand. And by his cries of joy at intervals—which kept Iffleplum awake—he knew that the Alchemist was having great success. He had stayed up as long as he could, watching a gold flush creep over a lump of greyish lead in Athanôr's first experiment. "Pure gold!" exclaimed the Alchemist delightedly. But Iffleplum was mystified. *So, now it's golden*, he thought. *A buttery yellow instead of grey. But what's so exciting about that? I could have painted it much quicker*. It had taken several hours just to "prettify" a lump of lead. So sleepily, instead of watching more, he had staggered off to bed. Not that he got much sleep.

*

Next day Athanôr was in the shop as usual, bleary-eyed, but enthusiastically dispensing liquid drops of stardust in little blue bottles, marked "Heal-All Elixir of Life"—as he now called his "Philosopher's Stone" concoction. With the tiny amount Iffleplum had given him, it seemed he could make as much as he needed. It was not long before sick people found themselves soon becoming well and rising from their beds. Word quickly spread around the town. By the end of the week, the Apothecary shop had gained great renown among the gossips for its "magic medicine". And clamouring customers came pouring in.

"I fear we are attracting too much attention to ourselves," said Athanôr. "Alas, I was too keen to make all people well. It is not wise to go overboard with anything." Too right he was.

That very day, two soldiers belligerently burst into the Apothecary shop—in the company of Trader Jack. They glared menacingly at a couple of timid customers, who quickly found themselves back out in the street. Merkie, who was curled up on the counter, sat up suddenly sensing trouble. His fur bristled.

"It has come to our notice," said a square-jawed officer, "that you have had dealings with a fugitive from the Law. A fugitive, fleeing from the justice of His Royal Highness King Mărûçha (may he live for*ever!*)—notably, one mythical creature with a multi-coloured snout, designated as a hifflepinn." The other solder, who was clutching a pikestaff, sniggered at the description.

"Oh? A hifflepin, is it?" said Athanôr, glancing a quick warning at the cat. "I know of no such creature." Merkie slyly winked and nodded. Stretching and yawning exaggeratedly, he dropped off the counter and padded nonchalantly down the stairs.

"Now then! Now then! I reckon you do know something about it, matey!" said Trader Jack, with a knowing grin. "I talked to it only the other week, didn't I? Funny looking geezer it was. And when I thought about it afterwards, it weren't like any kind of gnorf I ever saw. And now these blokes are looking for something of the sort. And it said it was coming here, with a bag of herbs."

"And what's all that then?" said the soldier, waving his pikestaff at the shelves. "Pots of herbs, isn't it?"

"So we'll just take a look-see, if you don't mind," said the Officer, heading towards the back stairs.

"It so happens, I *do* mind!" objected Athanôr, barring his way. "I have delicate medical experiments in progress downstairs! They must *not* be disturbed. And besides—do you have a search warrant?"

"Oh? Obstructification, is it?" said the Officer. "Corp!" he barked, with a jut of his chin at the pikeman.

"Here you are, then!" smirked the pikeman. "Here's your warrant!" and abruptly slammed his pike against Athanôr's head. The Alchemist staggered back stunned against the wall. "With his Majesty's compliments!" guffawed the pikeman.

Roughly elbowing him aside, the soldiers barged on by and stomped their way downstairs.

Merkie hurtled through the roundy-room into the Alchemery. Iffleplum was washing up decanters at the sink. "Soldiers!" shrieked Merkie. "Run! Run! They're coming! Slip away! Go–Go–Go!"

Iffleplum spun around in confusion, hesitating. *Which way? Where?* There was nowhere to hide.

"This way! Follow me!" screeched Merkie, dashing through the oversized cat-flap in the door.

In panic, Iffleplum ran after him. But the door was bolted shut. He struggled with the bottom bolt. It suddenly shot back. But oh-oh! there was another bolt blocking the top! It was far too high for him to reach. And there was no time to fetch a stool.

The heavy boot-steps of the soldiers came clumping down the stairs.

Desperately, Iffleplum plunged headfirst into the cat-flap. He was halfway through, when—oh, gripes!—his little round belly got stuck in the frame! He huffed and he puffed and wriggled and squirmed to no avail. Now he wished he hadn't been so fond of food. With a final frantic effort, he sucked his stomach in. Kicking his legs and scraping the skin off his sides he popped out like a cork from a bottle. And made it just in time! He was out and free!

The soldiers stormed officiously into the Alchemery. But no one was there.

Only the cat-flap was swinging gently to and fro.

Part the Nineteenth

Of Fish-Pong
and the Ferryman

*In which, our hero is caught and gets away, loses his home
and elfin-heart and escapes again the following day.*

eyond the cat-flap the ground suddenly fell away.
And Iffleplum went tumbling head over heels down
a short steep bank. With a mighty splash he fell into
a cold and swiftly flowing stream. It carried him off in a
twinkling, ruckling and frothing along between the tall
higgledy-piggledy houses hemming it in.

In seconds he had whirled around a corner out of sight.
Merkie, having jumped across the stream as usual, gave an
anguished yowl of fright as the ifflepinn disappeared from
view. Water was a very scary thing for cats. But bubble-
bellied ifflepinns can bob about like corks upon it. So Iffleplum
was not afraid for that. At least—not until the speeding
stream suddenly swept him underground. And plunging into
sudden dark—now that was *really* scary!

As he sped along, garbage and flotsam oozed out from
unseen holes along the way. Slimy things slapped up against
him. Not nice at all. But worse was yet to come. Swirling
around a bend, a scurry of scrabbling feet came echoing out
of darksome tunnels on either side. A chittering chorus of
squeaky voices filled the air. And the chilling eyes of a horde
of hungry creatures glittered all around him in the gloom.

Rats! A mass of them came plunging after him. By the sound their splashes made, the rats were all the size of cats or more! Giant rats! As they swam up to attack, he saw some were almost as big as himself! No wonder Merkie had screeched! He well *knew* where the stream was taking him.

Sharp teeth nipped at him on every side. He yelled and lashed out with his fists, thrashing the water like a netted fish. By now the stream was growing stronger, gaining speed. He felt it fiercely sweeping him along. Then with fearful shrieks, the frantic rats abruptly let him go. He had no time to wonder why. Suddenly he was falling through the air. The stream had swept him over a foaming weir. And rolling wildly he toppled down another one.

Squeals of rage and chittering echoed from the stream above.

But Iffleplum went swiftly floating on.

In disappointment, the slimy giant rat-things splashed away back into their own dank and darksome holes.

Very soon, around another bend the tunnel ended. Quickly coming out into the light, the brightness hurt his eyes. He shut them tight, as he sailed out from underneath a bridge.

"Hey look! What's that?" said someone crossing over it. "Ah, dead pig," said his friend, with a glance at Iffleplum and continued walking on.

Luckily, no one else noticed him. Bobbing along between the houses he floated right down to the rippling shore. There the stream finally found its end and spread itself out in Gauhngarth Lake. Iffleplum let the current carry him further on out. In the deeper waters he rinsed himself free of sewage smells. By now, the fearful thumping of his heart had slowed again. He began to breathe more easily. And with arms outstretched he floated on his back, relaxing, gazing at the sky and squinting with the sun. But something niggled him at the corner of his mind.

Only then he realized. A dreadful shock! He had left his elfin-heart behind! And his dwemmer-coat was hanging on peg! He was out of his disguise. Now anyone could know him for an ifflepinn. *What am I doing here?* he thought. *And what of Athanôr? I hope the soldiers didn't do him harm. I must go back!*

Just then, a net fell over him.

Roughly he was hauled up into a boat. "We got it!" cried a voice. He tumbled into the bottom onto a pile of eels and slithery fish. The smell was strong. His nose went quickly grey. A grizzled old fisherman and a young lad looked down on him in astonishment. Carefully, and a little apprehensively, they unravelled him from the net.

"By ghòr! What have we here?" said the old man in a cap.

"It's one of them there faery iffle-things, that's what!" said the boy excitedly. "I seen a drawing of it on a 'Wanted' poster, on a wall! It's all over town! The King's men are after it. And there's a smart reward for catching one, and all!"

"Is there now?" said the old man thoughtfully, gazing at the ifflepinn in wonderment.

This time Iffleplum was wiser to the ways of *Ühmenü*. He decided not to speak or show he understood. Not until knew more about their attitude.

"Aye!" said the crafty-eyed youngster, hastily throwing the net back over the ifflepinn. "Better wrap it up again smartish! Don't want it jumping off the boat, do we? The Treasury might pay us well for catchin it. Why—us might even get honour from the King!" His eyes gleamed proudly at the thought. The old man said nothing but "Wind's coming up!" and tended to the boat.

Tugging the net tight around Iffleplum the fisher-lad tied it off.

Sun-edged clouds were scudding overhead, but darkling with the threat of coming rain. Briskly hoisting up a single sail, they blew back across the lake, bobbing swiftly into dock on the rising waves. Several other small fishing boats were rocking there. Much activity was going on. Noisy fishwives were gutting the catch on marble slabs. Shouting men were humping crates of fish and loading them onto gauhn-hitched carts. The great beasts were bellowing, smelling the coming of the storm.

"Better us not let the others see, for now," cautioned the young man. "Don't want 'em getting jealous, do we now? They might want to be in on what we get. Best keep it to ourselves." The old man nodded.

They stuffed Iffleplum into a basket and covered it with a reeking sack. He nearly fainted from the smell.

Hauling it up onto the quayside, they carried it to a nearby row of rickety, tarred-tin tackle shacks. In one of them, they left him tied up to a table-leg and locked the door. And off they went to unload the catch. No matter how he wriggled he could not free himself. Stacks of baskets, coils of rope and hanging nets, all stank overpoweringly of fish. And the makeshift shack shuddered and rattled alarmingly all around him in the rising wind. After half an hour the fisher-folk came back.

"Do keep an eye on it," said the shifty-eyed young lad, "whilst I fetch a King's man from the dockside taverns roundabout. I'm bound to find one there."

274

"I wouldn't do that," said the old man. "Better you nip up to the garrison in the town, that's what. And don't you talk to anyone but the Chief Commander there. Shouldn't wonder he'll give you a right *royal* escort. But a common soldier might just cut you out and take the booty for himself."

"Ah! Right you are!" said the young man, tapping his nose at this advice. Poking his head outside, he saw the sky was growing dark. The wind was gusty and thunder grumbled overhead. Spots of rain began to fall. 'I best be sharpish, then!" said the lad and set off smartly for the town.

As soon as he had gone, the old man took off his oilskin jacket and cap, revealing a half-bald shiny head and straggly grey hair like a shaggy dog's ears on either side. Bending down he blew life into a tiny charcoal stove and put a kettle on the top. Then gently he unwound the fishnet from around Iffleplum's head. He sat down and stared in awe at the ifflepinn.

"So—they *do* exist," he muttered to himself. "Just like my old Ma said. Can this really be an *ifflepinn*? I never dared to quite believe in 'em, but I always hoped it so. And now, glory-glory! Here one be, if my old eyes are seeing right."

In his joy, his eyes were shining wondrously. Suddenly they moistened and brimmed with tears.

Iffleplum then felt the feeling of his heart and softly said, "An ifflepinn I am. And we are Ummals, so we speak." The old man clutched his chest and caught his breath. "Oh! Oh!" he said delightedly. "Oh, glory be! Glad I am to have lived to see this day! My old mother told me bedtime tales of ifflepinns, when I was but a tiny sprat. Now my faerytales have come to life. Never I thought such a thing would happen to little old me! You do bring light into my old heart. But come! Let's get this offen you!"

So saying, he quickly unwrapped the net from Iffleplum.

"I'm sorry for allowing that. But if I'd've done otherwise, my prentice lad would've reported me to the Guard. That's how he is."

Just then, the kettle sang. "Ah, right!" said the fisherman. "You must be proper chilled! I'll make us up a pot of tea. If ifflepinns are a-drinkin that?" Iffleplum nodded numbly. The old man poured the hot water into the teapot then rubbed him down with a bit of grimy towel. It dried him off, but still left silvery trails of smelly fish scales on his back and arms from tumbling in the catch.

"Now tell me—so what's the soldiery want with you?" the old man asked.

With his numb hands wrapped around a mug of the warming brew,

Iffleplum hastily told him all he knew from Athanôr and the *Book of Beastiology*.

"Oh? Prophecy is it?" said the fisherman thoughtfully. "Well, I'm up for anything that might make that brattish tyrant fall. His soldiers make our lives a proper misery. My prentice thinks the King's Men and their uniforms are something splendid. He wants to be a soldier when he's old

enough. He's got his head on back to front. But don't you worry now, I sent him longways to the Garrison. The fat Commander there's a sly old pig. He'll keep the lad there for questioning. I know him, old Belchbottom. He'll send the soldiers down to pick you up and get the credit for himself."

There came a sudden crack of thunder overhead. Lightning flashed. The last few fishwives shrieked and fled, holding their aprons over their heads. Men yelled, leaping to their carts. Hastily humping in crates of fish and whipping up the gauhns they sped away in all directions. The lake turned black. Rolling waters came bashing up against the quay in explosive bursts of spray. Heavy rain came rattling down on the shack tin roof. It rippled shakily with every gust of wind.

"At any rate, they'll not be coming down in this awhile!" said the fisherman happily, standing up. He pushed up at the loose tin roofing with his hands. It jiggled up and down. "With a little help, the roof might just blow off in the wind. And then I'll have some tale to tell."

He went on in a whiny voice, "Oh, dear, I'm sorry Sergeant! I was all confuzled—see, my roof blew off! And while I was chasing it, that faery creature must've got blown away and all!" He grinned and winked at Iffleplum.

Dressing him in a tattered oilskin jacket and a cap (both stinking strongly of fish) the old man gave him directions back to Simpler's Street. "Cross the bridge beyond the quay. Then just keep Simpler's Beck always to your right. Point your nose uphill and you'll find it easily. There'll be none about to see you in the storm. May Ühmkyn guide you on your way. Farewell!"

By this time night had fallen with the rain. Iffleplum staggered his way back along the blustery ill-lit streets, tottering in the wind. Rain lashed against his face. It was still falling heavily as he trudged up to the Apothecary shop. But as he neared, he saw again the lights were out. His heart sank.

Worse still, two planks were nailed criss-cross before the door!

An official proclamation was plastered on a board above:

Oyez! Hear this, all Citizens.
On His Majesty's Pleasure, King Märûçha
(May he live forever)
the traitor Ælrik Athanôr has hereby been
Apprehended on charges
of Harbouring
Enemies of the Realm
and Unlawfully
Practising the Black Arts of Alchemie.
Signed: Quinsley Belchbottom
Commander-in-Chief of Gauhngarth Garrison.

If Iffleplum was wearing boots, his heart would have fallen into them. He slumped down wearily, banging his head against the bow-bay windowpane. Tears and raindrops trickled down his face. *What now?* he wondered. A ghostly form with yellow eyes jumped suddenly in front of him. It yowled. He leapt back startled. Oh! It was only Sally alley cat standing in the window-bay! She mewled at him through the glass. "Go round!" she mouthed and waved a bent paw up Simpler's Street. "Slip down the next small alley to the stream! And come in from the back!"

Iffleplum hurriedly followed her advice. Down a dark and narrow arched passageway he came upon the rushing stream. Slipping and sliding along the rind-narrow bank he soon came upon the Alchemery door. Shedding the oilskin, he wriggled tightly through the cat-flap once again. This time it was a little easier, as he hadn't eaten anything all day. He dragged the jacket in behind him. But it was dark inside. Getting up, he stumbled over tumbled objects on the floor. And something scrunched like broken glass beneath his feet. Something was very wrong.

Groping a candle from the cupboard store he lit it with a tinderbox. Holding it up, he looked around him in dismay. Shattered jars and bottles lay littered on the floor. The central table now was bare. And Athanôr's precious instruments had gone and some were smashed. On every side, as he looked about, the whole Alchemery was trashed! Many things were missing. And—oh, gripes! His eyes darted to the upper shelf. He raised the flickering candle.

Oh, no! The box that held his elfin-heart was gone!

His knees gave way and with a groan he sank down in despair.

Two cats came bounding down the stairs. At the same time a bedraggled Merkie pushed in through the cat-flap. The three of them ran happily up to Iffleplum.

"Mmm, you smell nice," said Sulphie, sniffing him. "Fish."

"Never mind that," growled Merkie, shrugging raindrops off his fur. "What happened to you? I chased all round the houses down the stream, but never found you more. I've been searching for your scent for hours. Did you get safely past the—Rats? If you'll excuse the word," he apologized to the other cats.

Iffleplum hastily recounted his adventures: "—then the kindly fisherman let me go," he ended. "But tell me—what of Master Athanôr?"

"The soldiers set upon him! Knocked him down the stairs! They sacked the shop and stole his instruments. They barred the doors and shackled him. Then shuffled him off in leg-irons to the Garrison," said Sally angrily. "We'll find out more tomorrow when the storm dies down. There's nothing we can do right now."

The news was too much for Iffleplum. Exhausted and sick at heart, he picked his way over the rubble to the study. The fire was cold. Chairs were overturned and his bedding was strewn about the floor. Wearily, he stuffed it back into his bunk bed and clambered in. He was too tired even to think of food. The three cats leapt up and snuggled him for warmth.

And soon he fell asleep to a soothing lullaby of purrs and the fish-loving licks of three raspy little tongues.

*

Next morning Merkie nuzzled him urgently awake. "Come on!" he hissed, "No time! My friends, the rooftop Toms, say

Master's head's stuck in the in the stocks! It's Market Day. And the soldiers are saying Athanôr's a traitor to the King! So the townsfolk are pelting him with stinky fruit and eggs! Folks say they're taking him away to Angarsburg today! And those the soldiers take away are never seen again!"

Market Day! thought Iffleplum, with a spark of hope. *Then Matty and Morrig may be there too!* Rubbing sleep from his eyes, he scrambled hastily out of bed. In the wrecked Alchemery, he was happy to stumble upon his dwemmer-coat in a bundle on the floor. And bending down he saw a little blue bottle rolled under a bench. Stardust-stone Elixir! He snatched it up and slipped it into his coat pocket. "Come!" hissed Merkie urgently.

Not even a bite of Wakes, thought Iffleplum with a wistful glance at the open pantry door. *Ah, I see the soldiers have rifled through it anyway.*

Hurriedly following after Merkie, he squeezed out through the cat-flap once again, pulling his clothing after him. *Easier this time; I'm even thinner today.* Outside, he donned his dwemmer-coat and wrestled the oilskin over the top. Stuffing his ears up inside the fisherman's cap, he tipped it down over his snout. Then he and Merkie headed for the Market Square.

The day was grey and misty. After the heavy rains a thin fog lay on the streets. Coming out of the narrow alleyways, the noise of an angry crowd caught their attention. Merkie's ears pricked up. "They're calling Master's name!" he hissed. "In Main Street! Come! Keep up!"

Quickly they wormed their way through the milling throng. Some sort of procession seemed to be going by. They squeezed between the people to the front. A canvas-covered military supply wagon drawn by four white horses trundled slowly down the main thoroughfare. An escort of eight King's musketeers in blood-dark uniforms marched along beside it. The soldiers stonily stared ahead without expression.

An open wagon followed on behind. Three more soldiers sat up on the driving seat. Behind them loomed something like a huge, stout wickerwork lobster pot or birdcage with a rounded

280

top. It was tied securely to either side with ropes. Inside it stood the Alchemist clutching wearily at the bars. His face was bloodied and smeared with mouldy fruit. All around him, the wagon was piled high with Athanôr's alchemical apparatus and a stack of other things from the Alchemery. And sticking out on top of them, Iffleplum espied his brass-bound box!

"Athanôr! Athanôr!" some folks were crying out, and one or two shouted "Master!" Some cried in anger, some in sorrow. A handful of street-urchins laughed and jeered. A young lout threw a rotten egg. Several townsfolk set upon him angrily. Then fights began among the crowd. Others shouted out in rage against the soldiers and stepped out in their path. "Why take you our Apothecary?" cried one.

"Order! Order! Get out of the way!" the soldiers bawled, thrusting the angry folk aside. "Or you'll end up in the cage yourselves!"

A pack of street dogs came barking after the wagons. Suddenly they spotted Merkie beside the road. Yapping excitedly they hurled themselves towards the cat. Merkie screeched and fled back through the crowd. The dogs tore after him between the people's legs. And one or two fell down.

Iffleplum spun around, not knowing what to do. He was lost without the cat's advice. But Athanôr and his elfin-heart were fast disappearing down the street! Which way to turn?

Follow your heart, the Ârkühm had said. He turned about.

But a surging throng now followed on behind the prison wagon, some laughing and others waving fists and shouting angrily.

Desperately, he pushed his way through the crowd. At the end of the street, the wagons were rumbling on out through the echoey tunnel of the town wall's guarded Western Gate. Iffleplum anxiously watched them fading into the thickening country fog beyond.

As he neared the gateway, a powerful whiff of dead fish turned his head. The smell was even stronger than his clothes. A busy fishmonger's stall was set up against the town wall.

281

An idea popped into his head. He went closer. Taking in a strong sniff (which made his eyes water) the ifflepinn's very obvious mauven nose at once dimmed down to a safer shade of grey.

At that moment, a party of chattering gnorf-porters, humping great loads on their backs were passing out under the archway. Beside the stall he spotted a broken fish-basket with a few old bits of rope inside it. Grabbing up the basket he hoisted it onto his back. He pulled his cap down over his nose and hastened along behind the gnorfs. The gate-guards were busy watching the prison wagon trundling off into the mist. They never noticed him at the tail end of the porter-gnorfs' party.

And so it was that Iffleplum escaped from Gauhngarth unseen by anyone.

As he remembered from the maps, the road to Angarsburg ran for a mile or two along the western lakeshore before it veered away over a ford towards the mountains. Still carrying his basket, Iffleplum trudged along head down, a little way behind the gnorfs. His thoughts were as gloomy as the weather.

What am I to do? he wondered miserably. *Even if I catch up with the wagon, what can I do with all the soldiers there?* But even so, without supper, Wakes or breakfast, he gritted his teeth and willed himself to carry on. Filling his belly seemed less important now. Athanôr needed help. And his elfin-heart was calling him. Even without food, a new strength was growing in the ifflepinn.

Looking up, he found the gnorfs had vanished into a cleft between a rocky promontory and a cliff. He hurried on through a short gully. On the other side he came upon the porter gnorfs all in a huddle, hardly visible in the mist. They were dumping their burdens down before a wide and frothing stream. After the recent storm the waters were in spate.

One wagon was already over the ford. And ho! What luck! Halfway across, there was the prison-wagon, stuck! Its front wheel hard pressed against a rock. It gave a sudden lurch to

282

one side, as two wheels sank into the mud. A rope snapped and the wicker cage with Athanôr tilted alarmingly. The soldiers yelled, thrashing about in the water. Cursing foully, they floundered around attempting to rock the wagon free. The gnorfs clapped their hands over their ears, unused to such colourful language. "We'd best be getting on," they said. "We'll not be crossing Gauhn Ford in this state." Picking up their bundles, they noticed Iffleplum forlornly standing by.

"Greetings, stranger," said one. "Are you new in these parts?" Iffleplum nodded wanly. "Well now, don't fret for this," the gnorf went on, nodding at the river. "A couple of furlongs further downstream you'll find a ferryman, by name of Dogmother. Bit of a funny customer. Now don't upset him or he'll not take you on. He's a bit you-know-what," he said tapping the side of his head. "Just humour him."

Iffleplum thanked him for this advice, but told them he would rest a bit before he travelled on. The gnorfs nodded, hefted up their baggage loads and cheerily waved goodbye. As a parting shot, one called out, "If you catch us up, we'll be camping in the Mutterhorns tonight!"

Whatever that is, thought Iffleplum, wistfully watching the friendly folk disappearing downstream in the gloom.

Meanwhile the soldiers were still shouting and wrestling with the wagon. Some were tugging fiercely at the horses' heads. One was plunging in (on severe orders) to try and shift the rock. Whilst they were occupied, Iffleplum hurried down to the water's edge. Taking off his fisher-cap and throwing back his hood he waved his cap wildly at Athanôr.

The Alchemist saw him at once.

Get away! he shouted silently, frantically shooing at him with his hands through the bars. *Save yourself! Cover up!* he mimed. Iffleplum put up his hood, but resolutely shook his head. He shrugged and raised his hands in a what-else-can-I-do? kind of gesture.

Athanôr upraised his hands and clawed the air frustratedly. *Go! Go!* he mouthed, flicking his fingers furiously. But Iffleplum still dithered at the water's edge. He had no notion how to rescue him. But he could not leave him to his fate. In exasperation, Athanôr's leg abruptly shot out through the bars. With a hefty kick he booted Iffleplum's brassbound box straight off the tilted wagon. It tumbled through the air and splashed into the stream. With all their noise and shouting the struggling soldiers never noticed it.

But then—*Oh, gripes! Now what?* Iffleplum had no choice. The box was half submerged and swiftly floating down the stream. Clasping his hands across his heart he bowed his head to Athanôr's artful ruse in sorrow.

Swooping down he snatched up a handful of rope from the broken basket and slung it over his shoulder. With a brief gesture of farewell he turned away. Hastily he scurried along the riverbank after the quickly disappearing box.

Once more he was chasing his wayward elfin-heart.

But the more he ran, the less he could see of his precious chest. A heavy mist lay over the ever-widening stream, which was now rapidly growing to river-size. He began to sweat inside his clothes. Throwing aside the oilskin and his cap he hurried on. As the waters eddied and curled around the rocks, the old chest swirled and batted about among them. It was gradually drifting further out and over towards the other shore. He heard a sudden soft clunk over the water. *Was that it, stopped?* Straining his eyes, he thought he could see it bumping in the branches of a fallen tree. But the current there was still far too swift to cross.

He turned his head at the muffled clanging of a bell. Some way downstream he could dimly see a lantern glowing in the fog. *Ah! The ferryman!* He hastily made his way towards it. In the gloom the shape of someone sitting in a boat loomed up. A lighted oil lamp hung from a scaffold sticking up in the stern of the boat. A bell behind it gave a dull clang as the waters rocked the skiff. Iffleplum trod carefully onto a short ramshackle jetty. The boatman had his back towards him.

"Knew you were a-coming," he said, still staring straight ahead.

284

"Erm—are—are you the ferryman? Mister Dogmother?" asked Iffleplum hesitantly.

"Aye. I'm your ferry Dogmother. Cross my palm with copper coin. And I'll grant you three witches."

"Three—*witches*?" said Iffleplum. "Don't you mean three *wishes*?"

"I knows what I said," said the boatman turning round. His eyes were strange and looked in two directions. "And *witches*, it was."

"What—what would I want with three witches?" queried Iffleplum apprehensively. "It's very kind of you, but that's not exactly what I need."

"That's as may be," replied the ferryman. "But that's all I gots to offer. Now do you want to cross or not? One copper coin is all."

Iffleplum remembered what the gnorf had said: "*He's a bit you-know-what. Just humour him.*" He dug into his dwemmer-coat pocket and found the apple-pie pennies that Matty had given him. He paid the boatman and stepped into the boat. Without another word the wall-eyed ferryman rowed steadily out into the gloom.

Three witches! thought Iffleplum. *And I let myself be ferried by this loon? Which one of us is madder? What am I doing here? Where am I going?* Not for the last time did he wonder that.

A chill of foreboding crept into his heart.

As the boat bounced over the dark water, the bell above him clanged mournfully all the way.

Part the Twentieth

Madness in the Mutterhorns

*In which Iffleplum feels himself alone, unhappy, and forlorn,
and finally falls foul of soldiers in the Mutterhorns.*

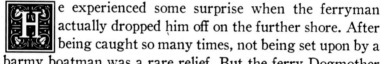e experienced some surprise when the ferryman actually dropped him off on the further shore. After being caught so many times, not being set upon by a barmy boatman was a rare relief. But the ferry Dogmother simply turned the boat around. Then, with a knowing wink and nod, he held up three fingers and silently rowed back into the mist.

Iffleplum hastened back upstream. On this side the riverbank was wooded to the water's edge. He scrambled and stumbled over the roots of trees, panting heavily. Finally he came upon the fallen tree in the water. But the brassbound box was nowhere to be seen. "Oh, river, river! Where has it gone?" he wailed unhappily. He was sure it had not floated past him as he hurried along the bank. *What if it has sunk to the bottom?* He weakly fell down on his knees at the water's edge, attempting to peer into its inky depths.

A sudden thirst came over him. In his haste he had neither drunk nor eaten since the day before. Cupping his hands he dipped them in the stream—then stopped. His jaw dropped. Below him, a greeny-golden light bloomed beneath the surface, glimmering. Steadily it grew brighter still. A glowing

287

ghostly face came up towards him. The water bulged. Slowly
it rose upwards, forming itself into the head and shoulders of
a female river-sprite.

She stared at him out of greeny-golden cat-like eyes. "Do
not drink!" she warned him sternly, in a rippling liquid voice.
Iffleplum knelt there petrified. The water drained feebly from
his fingers.

Her fluid figure rose up waist-high, transparent, and of only
water-made. A strangely beautiful being, she sparkled from
within with specks of greeny-golden *lûmenü*. They flowed
around inside her like glints of moonlight on a rippled running
stream. He gazed astonished. And doubly so, for there, in her
watery arms, she cradled Iffleplum's bobbing brass-bound box!

"Oh! Excuse me! Please. You have my box!" he cried,
stretching out his hands towards her.

"Yours?" replied the water-sprite archly. "Know you not to
whom you speak? I am Undine-Ellòra—Water-Witch! And
what is given to the river is always mine!"

Oh no! thought Iffleplum, remembering the ferryman. *Three
witches!* he had said. *And here's already One!* "Oh! Good

Water-Witch!" he pleaded, "you can keep the box! But *please*—my elfin-heart's inside!"

"That, well I know," replied Undine-Ellòra, "for I too am an elfin-heart of all waters fresh and flowing everywhere! A guardian am I, of rippling beck and rushing stream and rolling river wide. And little need for a floating brassbound box have I. But what's inside well pleases me, I don't deny. It has come to me in time of need, right now! For my river is befouled!" she growled in a gurgly way and rippled frowns formed upon her brow.

Waving a watery arm she fumed, "Away upstream I feel the maddened minds of soldier-men! Their cursing anger now comes surging down. My river quivers with their thoughts! They're soiling all the waters as I feel them flowing by. And mind-sullied water is not fit for even hogs to drink. It would sit too heavy in your belly. Curse-riddled as it is, 'twould do you harm."

"Oh! Is water touched by what folks think?" asked Iffleplum amazed.

"Thundering cataracts!" exclaimed the Water-Witch. "Are even *Ummals* unaware that Water is a *living* thing? *Of course* it's touched! All liquid-forms are changed by *thought!* Like crystals, we hold *memory!* We are but flowing crystals, after all. Do you not recall when winter comes, we crystallize in ice? Of *course* Water remembers *everything*, you foolish Ummal! It soaks up all that every creature near us *feels or thinks*. And yet, all beings drink us down unthinkingly. For little do they know of all the memories we carry to their blood. Know this— *dark thoughts deeply densen us.* And those who drink such draughts are densened too! While bright thoughts revitalize every water-drop. And thus, so energized, we better serve all those who drink of us."

"Oh, Water-Witch! I understand! I *only* do! I drank from light-filled water in Dwêmòriæ! And it made my sad heart happy for a while."

"Aye, so it would," she chuckled like a trickling brook. "Heart's-warmth and gratitude are what we Waters need.

Not thoughtless guzzling! And right now—what's in this box
is pulsing out warm-hearted waves to every drop of us.
Feelings such as this elfin-heart sends out, now soothes my
soldier-sullied waters on their way. Can *you* do more than
that?"

"Well, I–I don't think so," stammered Iffleplum. "I couldn't
really say. 'Cause I never realized my elfin-heart could radiate
that way.'

"But *every* elfin-heart can do the same, you silly sort-of-
thing on legs! If only folk would well-wish their heart's-
warmth out to all others, then—what a strifeless wonderland
would your wetless world become!"

"Oh yes!" agreed Iffleplum, "my friend Çhelône said something of the same. I had forgotten it already. Well, then I
humbly *promise* you, I'll think *very* loving thoughts to every
drop of water that I drink from now. And—I'll do the same
to every pond, and stream and lake I find. Oh! But, oh!
Without my elfin-heart, my heart's becoming cold and sad—
and growing colder by the day. And the best of my heart's-
warmth is there—inside that box you hold."

"Then, you shall take it back again," said Undine-Ellòra,
softly gurgling, like a streamlet over stones. "If keep you to
your promise made. But wait awhile, till I am done." So
saying, she sank down slowly with the box beneath the
stream.

Iffleplum held his breath, unsure of her return. As he waited
anxiously, the muffled cries of shouting men came dimly
downstream to his ears. He vainly gazed into the gloom,
wondering if Athanôr was safe. Or had he tumbled with his
cage into the ford?

Then out of nowhere, a majestic wide-winged heron came
silently gliding over the water and vanished downriver in the
mist. It touched his heart as if an omen for the good.

A moment more and the Water-Witch rose up again. She
was smiling: "At last!" she gurgled, "the soldier-men have
scrambled from the ford. A cattle-tang of many sweaty beasts
and frightened horses came of a sudden streaming down. But

it has passed us by. And now the river's flowing *thought-free* once again. Look-see!" said she and raised the dripping box, which floated on her breast. "Your elfin-heart has energized the water swirling here around this fallen tree. So feel you now quite free to drink!"

Iffleplum dipped his hands in eagerly. He closed his eyes and deeply drank, with heartfelt gratitude to the stream. And the elfin-heart-warmed water seemed to fill him more than food. His thirst quenched, he looked up to find the Water-Witch was gone.

But his box was rocking at the water's edge. Grasping one of its handles on the side he hauled it to the bank.

Clammily clutching it to his chest, he sat down beneath a tree. A little fearfully, he wondered if his *Legends* book was waterlogged. He had to see. Quickly rummaging through his pockets, his fingers found the little blue bottle of Heal-All Elixir, two pennies, some silky dust, and fluff.

But nothing more.

Oh what! It can't be true! Oh no! His heart beat frantically. He scrabbled in the pouch-pockets of his skin. Nor was it there.

Only a tiny trickle of Sandman's dust.

He emptied everything and searched his dwemmer-coat thoroughly. No, there was nothing more. All pockets bare.

Oh, great greeny gut-wrenching gripes! he wailed. He had lost the key! He *only* had! *It must have happened when rolling down the weir in Simpler's Stream,* he thought, *when escaping from the rats! I should have tied it on the conker cord around my neck. I could have kept it there like Ifflepaw's Hat-Trunk key.*

Lifting the conker on its string, he gazed upon it wistfully. It reminded him of Ifflemother's chestnut-coloured eyes and loving hugs. And of mellow autumn days in Ælfÿlon and the conker contests he had won among his friends. And he thought of Ifflenook, the cheery fire of home and Granpaw, Ifflepaw and Erf. And then again, of Athanôr—all smeared and bloodied in a cage! He felt guilty for leaving him. *But what could I have done?* he told himself. *And what now? What must I do?*

Alone and miserable, he sat glaring wretchedly at the sodden box.

He had found his elfin-heart again, but it was still far away from his grasp. Dejectedly, he sat there staring out unseeing at the mist, as the morning slowly wore away.

*

In a long unhappy, bitter while, he sighed and lurched to his feet. The mist was thinning now and rising off the river, gleaming whitely from a hidden sun shining somewhere high above. Knotting the bits of smelly rope together around his sodden box he slipped it through the handles and strapped it awkwardly to his back.

Again, he thought of Athanôr's kindly trick to save him and his elfin-heart. He was deeply touched. His eyes misted. The Alchemist's weary face kept coming back to him. And the words "those the soldiers drag away are never seen again," as Merkie and Morrig had said to him.

"I must get back to Athanôr," he muttered, falteringly. "I have to help him. But I don't know how." There was no way along this side of the riverbank. Here the forest was thick and tangly, with brambles hanging over the water's edge; it was impossible to follow the river back upstream. He attempted to thrash his way through the undergrowth, but soon the thickets thwarted him. Dense bushes blocked the way. Cobwebs clung upon his face and spiky branches kept snagging on his dwemmer-coat and hood.

With a heavy heart, he struggled back over the tree-roots to the soggy moss-grown track where the ferryman had left him. Hoping to find a way around the forest, he squelched on through the rutted ooze. But the dim and winding path between the trees seemed to have no end. And no birds sang in this dark and dismal wood. Only a few thin shafts of sunlight stabbed down here and there. In a gloomy mile or two the fog and the dreary forest thinned and the track began to harden. Finally he came out into the sun. But even then, he found a huge swamp on his left with no way to get across. Grumpily, he shuffled on.

After a while, he came out upon a cart road and soon found himself in more open countryside. The sun was now shining fitfully through patches of fading mist. Dewdrops glittered lacily on cobweb-covered hedgerows beside the road. This was farming country. There were fields and cultivated land on either side. And that meant *people*. He pulled his hood down over his eyes and bent his back.

And soon enough, on passing by a field of sheep, he was suddenly aware of two farmer-folk beside a gate. One was sitting on the top of it. The other in a battered hat leaned over it, puffing idly on a pipe.

Iffleplum shrank into his hood. He trudged on by with his nose towards the ground. But the gate-sitter took him for a gnorfish peddler. "Hoy there, old slugfoot!" he cried. "You're way behind your lot! They went by some hours gone! They'll be halfway up the Mutterhorns by now."

Iffleplum made no reply. Not looking round, he kept on walking. But the yokel hopped off the gate as he passed them by and shouted after him. "Anyroad, what's your merchandise? What are you carrying?"

"My *heart*," said Iffleplum wearily, too tired to care. His head still bowed, he plodded on.

The yokel turned back to his friend. "Rum fellow, that," he said. "Keeps his heart in a box."

"Ah, some do," his friend replied. "Some do. I've come across one or two like that, in my time."

*

Night was falling when the less-used ferry track finally joined the fording road to Angarsburg. A few bright cold stars came out: just enough to see by. But the well-rutted road was empty. He was the only lonely traveller. He tramped on half-asleep, his eyes adroop. After a while his little legs could feel the road was rising. The trail began to climb steadily up towards the mountains. The *Mutterhorns*, as the yokel called them.

Iffleplum trudged wearily on, looking for somewhere to lay his head. But here among the rocks and boulders, he found no sheltered spot to rest. A gusty wind was whistling strangely way up in the higher peaks. As it blew down from the hills, it sounded like a host of ghostly phantoms muttering unknown words among the stones. *Ah, that's why "the Mutterhorns",* thought Iffleplum, shivering at the eerie sound.

He paused for breath and sat down beneath a rock. Throwing back his hood he eased the old chest off his back. The rough, fish-scented ropes were chafing his shoulders, even through the dwemmer-coat. With his elbows on his knees, he put his thumbs in his ears to shut out the ghostly whispering. It brought to mind Çhelône's advice on how to hear the *Song of Ühm*, to keep his heart from dread. His stubby fingers couldn't reach his snout, so he palmed his eyes instead. But still, all he could hear was only a dull and rumbly thundering sound inside his head.

On opening his eyes, he now saw that he was much higher than he had realized. In the light of a misty moon, rising far across the farmlands, he thought he could see the glimmer of

Gauhngarth Lake. But it was no time to sit about. Despite the sweat of the climb, he was now feeling cold and hungry and slightly faint. And irritating bursts of wind batted his dangly ears about, like the dab of a playful kitten's paws.

Looking up he saw dark wind-driven clouds rolling across the stars. A few spots of rain begin to fall. "That's all I need," he muttered glumly. "Jolly, jolly." His stomach grumbled like the clouds. Not only was he ravenously hungry, but now he realized how thirsty he was again. Tipping his head back, he tried to catch the raindrops in his mouth. But that did little to quench his thirst. And the rain clouds passed on overhead, thunderously loosing their load upon the higher hills before him.

Humping up his box, he doggedly set off again, trying to ignore the scary mutterings of the wind between the rising craggy cliffs. Here and there beady eyes peeped out at him among the stones. But as he neared they bobbed away, skittering over the rocks and snickering like malicious imps, which is probably what they were. Around many a hairpin bend, the rocky road still climbed on up and up. And chilly air came gusting down. Before long he felt he was walking in his sleep. But whenever he began to nod and falter, a distant lightning flash and rumble would awaken him. And he would struggle on a few steps more.

Hardly able to put one foot before the other, he staggered up over a rise and came down into a long, low, undulating deep dark valley, smelling fresh with rain.

At the end of his strength, he was about to fall down wearily on the road. Then a sudden light blazed out some way ahead. The flame of a camp-fire flared up in the dark. His heart leapt up in sudden hope. *The gnorf-camp!* he thought in great relief. *I was invited there! They must have settled for the night.* He was freezing and shivering in the weirdly whispering wind. But the thought of friendly folk and maybe *supper* heartened him. With a final effort, he stumbled off the track towards the campfire's cheery glow.

But without warning, what he had taken for a boulder or a tree stump suddenly jumped up before him.

"Halt! Who goes there?" cried a rough voice. His heart sank. He could have wept. Soldiers! After all his efforts to escape, he had stumbled straight into the soldier's camp. A sentry in a rain-cloak towered over him, with a musket pointed in his face. "What's your business here?" he snarled.

Iffleplum hunched over, hiding his face and clutching himself for warmth. "P–p–peddler!" he stuttered with the cold.

"Oh, right!" said the sentry. "Gnorf camp's over that-away!" He waved his arm towards another campfire he hadn't seen before, hidden in a dip. "Now, get off with you! You gave me quite a turn, you gormless gnorf! Why can't you carry a light, or something? Or blow your horn and tweeters when you're coming—like that other lot over there? Go on, shove off!"

Iffleplum could hardly believe his luck. His heart thumping, he tottered over to the gnorfish camp, shaking with relief. There he was welcomed heartily by the kindly porter-gnorfs. They remembered him waiting at the ford. Accepting him as one of themselves, they set him by the fireside in a blanket until he had thawed. And soon a wooden bowl of steaming stew and a chunk of crusty loaf sat on his lap.

The gnorfs then all spread out to find somewhere to sit alone. They reverentially ate their meal in silence, as was their custom. Iffleplum sat by himself upon his box. He leaned his back against a mossy boulder (having checked it first for eyelids).

Clasping his hands gratefully around the warming bowl, he sniffed its appetizing aroma. His nose grew rosy pink. But before he could even take a sip, he nearly dropped the bowl in shock. A pale green light began to glow inside the stew. *Uh-oh! What now?* He blinked in disbelief, as a tiny figure rose up out of it. The water sprite sternly looked at him with lime-gold eyes. "Remember your promise!" she gurgled.

"Undine-Ellòra!" gasped Iffleplum. "How come you're here?"

296

"Why, wherever there is water, there am I. Mist rises off the lakes and streams. It gathers up as clouds: then falls as rain. And I am the elfin-heart in every drop. *Soup* is still water, even tastified! Forget me not. Drink me down lovingly, as you vowed." She smiled then, and gracefully sank back into the stew.

Stupefied, he stared awhile at the liquid before he dared to drink. How *could* he drink the Water-Witch? But then he realized he had been drinking her all his life without respect. He now gazed with love and gratitude upon the bowl of chunky stew. Sipping it gingerly, he felt its warmth flow through him. A sudden new strength stirred within him, even to his bones. His peach-bloom hair stood on end and prickled everywhere upon his skin. *These gnorfs can make a mighty stew!* thought he, and scoffed the veggies down with glee.

When the meal was done, the gnorfs made merry round the fireside, making music on many strange instruments. As if to make up for their silent meal, they were now as boisterous as could be. They danced and sang, or rather mostly *bawled*, to many a loud and rollicking country song, while others blew on horns and tweeters. Jokingly, they slapped each other on the back as they drank their ale, so they snuffled it up their noses. They seemed to find this hilarious, the more often it was done. And they fell about upon their backs with laughter, kicking their legs up in the air, like children at a party.

But heart-warming as it was, Iffleplum was in no mood for partying. He was now wide-eyed and no longer tired or ready for bed. The Witch-water stew was working its magic in his blood. No more a timid ifflepinn! No more a child. Iffleplum was growing up fast. His face grew grim. He hardened his resolve. Somehow he had to rescue Athanôr, no matter what. *As he saved me, so must I save him,* he determined.

Backing away from the firelight, he passed through the cluster of circular hide-covered tents the gnorfs called *gnurts*. He peered out into the dark. The wind had dropped. Mist was now creeping down the hillsides and gathering on the valley floor. "Oh, thank you, Undine-Ellòra," he murmured. "Just what I need. I may get by the sentries under cover of your cloak."

Unwilling to be parted from his precious chest, Iffleplum once more roped it to his back. Leaving it behind would be too troubling to his mind. *Who knows what might happen to it if I'm caught?* he thought—then stopped. His eyes grew wide. *If I'm caught? Then that's the end of everything!* A sudden frightened chill fell on his heart. He remembered the hard and stony faces of the guardsmen who marched beside the prison wagon. In a moment, his resolve and his wobbly knees gave way. He sank to the ground.

Then "the bravest knight is he who fights the foe afraid," he heard himself telling Ifflemother. Long ago it seemed. *Whatever happened to bold Sir Plumkin of the Vale?* he thought, ashamedly. Steadying the beating of his heart, he gathered his courage. He took a determined breath. And crawling on his belly like a slurmy snail, he stealthily slithered off into the fog. Guided by the light of their bright campfire, he managed to squirm between the boulders, bushy scrub, and the sentries without a challenge. His cleverness at worming his way into the camp encouraged him.

Nearing the ring of tents he paused. In the centre, only a single musketeer sitting sideways on to him was poking idly at the glowing embers with a stick. Otherwise the camp was quiet, but for the snorts and whickering of horses stamping somewhere in the mist. It seemed the weary foot soldiers were all abed.

Lanterns glimmered softly at the entry-flaps of several tents. He could just make out the prison wagon, standing slightly upslope on a rise beyond the fire. It looked like some great beast with horns, with its cart-shafts stuck up in the air. A row of soggy uniforms and leggings hung listlessly on a washline strung from one shaft to the corner of the barrack tent.

But where was Athanôr? Upon the heap of the alchemist's apparatus, the huge lobsterpot-like wicker cage had fallen

298

down. It was lying on its side with a mouldy canvas carelessly slung over it.

Was Athanôr asleep in there? Had they just left him covered for the night, like that? Or had they tied him up somewhere in a tent?

His heart beating, Iffleplum decided to investigate. And slithering through the wet grass, he stealthily worked his way around behind the tents. There was not a sound from the first one he came to. Hesitantly, he lifted the canvas and poked his head inside. It seemed no one was there: only boxes and barrels. But he crept inside in case Athanôr was lying somewhere tied up in a corner. He sniffed: a funny but familiar smell. He could just make out a stack of muskets and a pile of smallish kegs: one was split and spilling powder on the stony ground. By a beam of lantern-light falling through the tent flaps, he read the word roughly painted on every keg.

Gunpowder!

Now he recognized the sulphurous smell from Athanôr's alchemery. "I call it *Guanpowder*," the Alchemist had told him, when teaching Iffleplum how to grind it in a mortar, "because it's made with *guano*—bat droppings—plus one part willow-wood charcoal, one part sulphur and six parts saltpetre. You must grind it very fine." He had seemed to need a lot of it each day, but he gave it all away to the townsfolk after meetings, who hid it underneath their cloaks at before they left. "What's this kind of medicine for?" Iffleplum had asked him. "Ah, oh—erm—it's very useful for removing obstacles to people's happiness," he had replied. "Or *will* be, I hope," he added, to himself.

Stealthily Iffleplum crawled out again.

In the next tent he now heard voices raised excitedly. The shadows of men sitting at a table were silhouetted on the canvas wall. The tent was well lit up inside: obviously Officer's quarters. While the lesser ranks were sleeping, the officers were still awake. And arguing, it seemed. Iffleplum crept close and pressed his ear against the tent side.

"—it *was* a banshee, I tell you!" cried one impatiently. "How could we have dealt with that?"

"Too right, Sarge!" said another. "Out of *nowhere* they all came! Knocked us all for six, didn't they? What else but a banshee could ride bareback on a herd of wild gauhns like that? And that cry it made: *Heyaa!* Scary, what? It gave me goose-bumps all over!"

"Yes," growled the Sergeant. "Like he says, they came out of nowhere—straight in the ford! All thrashing round the prison-cart! What could *I* do? Those flodding longhorns tossed me head-over-heels in the drink! Before we had time to turn about, they'd snatched him off and scarpered in the fog! Uncanny that! Like magic!"

"Indeed. Quite so," said a more cultivated voice. "It's most unsettling. It happened far too quick. Alas, from the other bank, I could hardly see what happened for the mist. But as they turned about, your 'banshee' seemed to me nought but a scraggy-headed young girl, I thought."

300

"Aw, come on, Cap'n! Don't say that. We can't tell the King we lost the prisoner to a scraggy-looking girl! He'll have our guts for garters! We're in for a Court Martial as it is, for losing the prisoner. Anyways, that's just how banshees look! Like ghostly white-faced girls."

"Yeah, right, Corporal!" said the Sergeant enthusiastically. "And they make a wailing cry like that when some poor beggar's about to snuff it!"

"Exactly, Sarge!" agreed the Corporal. "Perhaps the traitor's time had come! What about that ghostly geezer with the cleaver then?—all in white!—who chopped the cage in half? That must've been the *Deathly Reaper*—come to drag him off into the Otherworld."

Iffleplum gasped at what he heard. His head bumped against the tent side. A vision of Matty's white smock and flour-dusted hair flashed through his mind. Had he and Morrig *already* rescued Athanôr?

"What's that?" yelled someone from the tent on hearing him. A shadow leapt up from the table. "There's someone listening out the back!" cried another, as the officers dashed towards the tent flap.

Iffleplum took to his heels. He tore past another tent smelling strongly of wet and humid soldiery.

A bell rang out frantically. *Alarm! Awake! A spy in camp!*

He heard the cries behind him. He raced past the washline, his heart-chest bouncing on his back. Skirting the prison-wagon, he stopped abruptly. The back of a soldier busy buttoning up his breeches, loomed up in the gloom ahead. Iffleplum swiftly scrambled up the cart-side, before the trooper turned about. At a glance he saw the broken wicker cage was empty. Jumping down among the debris to hide, a bottle rolled away beneath his foot. With a stifled cry, he fell among the apparatus with a crash. Then the whole wagonload began to slide.

The tailboard tumbled off its catch. Decanters, bowls and bottles, tripods, books, and scrolls all went cascading to the ground. Iffleplum went sliding with them, upside down. With a crunch, he landed backwards on his box, which nearly broke his back. But the lid burst open! And the paraphernalia rained right down on top of him.

With the sudden shift of weight, the wagon lurched forward with a jolt. It began to trundle down the rocky slope towards the fire.

Half-dressed sleepy soldiers came stumbling from their tent. But as the wagon picked up speed, the clothesline tied to its upright shaft ran with it. Swiftly growing taut it tugged against the tent-pole to which the other end was tied. With its weight of soggy uniforms, it smashed into the soldiers and scythed them down like corn. And one end of the barrack tent came crashing down along with it.

The wagon went hurtling on straight over the fire. The musketeer leapt aside as it shot past. At full speed it walloped into the munitions tent, sending the entry lantern flying off its hook. There came a crash and tinkle as it smashed inside. Picking themselves up, the shocked soldiers froze in dread. The flaming lantern rolled across the powder spill and struck against the keg.

A moment more and the tent erupted with a mighty roar. The wagon blew up in the air. Wheels and bits and pieces rained down everywhere. Powder kegs exploded like fireworks. Explosions lit the night. Bits of burning canvas floated down upon the tents. And the yelling soldiers slapped at their sizzling hair. Horses shrieked and broke their tethers, running off in all directions.

Boom! Boom! More kegs exploded.

In the confusion, Iffleplum wrenched his dwemmer-bag from the broken box and looped it over his head. He turned and fled into the dark, half-blinded and deafened by the blasts. The soldier with the half-buttoned flies had stood there stupefied at these events. Finally, his wits awoke. "Oi! There he goes!" he screeched. Two other soldiers took off after him, firing shots. The ifflepinn ran madly down the valley in pitch dark, not seeing where he went.

Suddenly the ground fell away before him! He stumbled forward and tumbled into a rushing rivulet running down the hillside. Like a phantom he vanished from the soldier's sight. The swift stream slippily swept him off in a gushing muddy flow, jolting and bouncing all the way. Down and down he went without a stop. At the end of a speedy slither, it dumped him onto a road below, over a sudden short drop. The water cascaded over him and spluttered and frothed across the track.

He lay there moaning, soaking wet. No tent. No chance of a gnorfish gnurt for the night. No hope of bed. And no idea where he was. But at least he had lost the soldiers—or hopefully, they had lost him.

Then to his dismay, he heard the clip-clop of horses' hooves from further down the track. He flung himself into a ditch against the bank. But soon to his ear came the merry jingle of harness bells. A guardsman's horse would never jingle. That, at least, was comforting. And now he could hear the creak of wagon wheels. A misty lantern light began to blossom in the fog. As it neared, a merchant's covered wagon emerged slowly from the gloom.

His heart leapt up. *Rescue!*

Iffleplum staggered to his feet and weakly flagged it down. The wagon halted before him. A fat wagoner glared at him suspiciously.

"What d'you want?" he growled. Anxiously, he stared about him at the hillside.

"Can I ride with you—*please?*" pleaded Iffleplum.

"What is it?" yelled a rough Angarsland voice from the back of the wagon. "Why've you stopped?"

"Naught but a gnorf!" shouted back the driver. "Are you by yourself, gnorfling?" he demanded. Iffleplum nodded.

With toss of his head the merchant grunted: "Get up at back then! It's five and a ha'penny-worth to Angarsburg, if you want a ride. And get a move on! We're late! Sounds like a storm's comin up! Did you hear that heavy thunder in the hills? Oy! You at the back there! Help him up!"

Iffleplum hastily trotted round to the back of the wagon. A brawny arm shot down. A huge hand grabbed him by his dwemmer-coat and hauled him up over the backboard. As the wagon jolted off, he tumbled in onto a pile of stinking pelts. The reeking skins of fresh-killed deer and bear and wild goat and smaller furry animals piled up around him. The smell stung his eyes and his nose grew mustard-green.

"Well, well, well," said a familiar voice from the gloom, "if that ain't nice of you to drop in on us."

Iffleplum scrambled up aghast. A huge huntsman with a black beard grinned down at him. His smaller companion jumped to his feet.

"Ghòrblimey! If it ain't the ifflepig!" said Floppy-Hat.

Part the Twenty-first

Ümmûârkon

In which the hope of reaching Ümmûârkon nears,
when travelling with a bunch of merry Mattockeers.

Iffleplum awoke in great discomfort, cold and aching. Despite his desperate position, having been tied up by the hunters and bone tired after all his exertions; somehow he had fallen asleep with the jolting of the cart. Late in the night he had awakened, aware that the merchant's wagon had stopped. But he was unable to move. He found his body bound up in some kind of wrap-around stinking hide. The smelly skin was tied down over his eyes. And a cord ran tightly around his snout, preventing him from calling out. He could see nothing. But he had heard shouts and doors banging, a dog barking and a clatter of hooves as the cart-horse was led off to the stables of some kind of wayside inn.

"And make sure you wake us early!" came Blackbeard's voice as he went inside.

"Oh, don't you worry about that!" chortled the innkeeper. "My alarm-cock will crow off at the crack of dawn." The inn door closed behind them. Then all was quiet. Iffleplum was left alone in the reeking wagon's dark. He struggled with his bonds awhile, but they were far too tight for him to wriggle free. Exhausted by his efforts, he had finally drifted off to sleep once more.

Somewhere close by, a cock crowed loudly in the half-light of a chilly mountain dawn. Its carolling woke Iffleplum. And set off a cackle of chickens. He could hear them clucking and

305

flapping about the yard. Inside the inn, an impatient dog was whittering and scratching at an outer door. Iffleplum heard the door creak open. "Go on then! Get off out, you stupid git!" came a young lad's amiable voice. The dog came rushing out and ran around the wagon, sniffing excitedly at the iron-rimmed wheels. Raising its hind leg in salute it gave the spokes a good washing. A fascinating mix of strange smells came wafting down from the wagonload of hides. The dog's nose prickled. Standing on its hind legs, it scrabbled at the backboard, desperately woofing to try and see inside.

The stable doors banged open and the sound of hooves clip-clopped across the cobbled yard. The wagon gave a jolt as the stable boy hitched up the horse to the cart-shafts. By now the dog was jumping up and down and yipping in frustration. "What are you about, Tiggin?" came the lad's voice. "Leave it be! There's nothing there for you!" His footsteps came around the back, to see what so excited the dog. Pushing aside the backflap, he glanced curiously over the tailboard. All the boy could see was something stirring in the dark. Iffleplum wrestled in his bonds, trying hard to sit up and speak. But the cord around his snout allowed him no more than a noise that sounded like a growl.

"Wolf!" gasped the boy and fled into the house.

In moments he was back with a serving-maid in tow. As they crossed the cobbled yard, she was saying, "You'd better not be pulling my leg. I've not got time to muck about. I've got to clear the breakfast things, behind those three smelly customers."

Lifting the canvas flap she peered cautiously into the wagon's dark. Her nose wrinkled at the whiffsome hides. With a start she caught her breath and jerked away as a pair wolf-ears shifted in the gloom. But then, unsure of what she had seen, she ducked back in and took a second look.

"That's no wolf," said she. "Look you! It's got chubby legs underneath that wolfskin! And it's all tied up! See? The wolf's face is tied down on its snout!"

A wolfskin! thought Iffleplum. *Oh, gripes! I hope it isn't Fluff-Ruff!* He shuddered to think he might be wrapped up in Fluff-Ruff's hide. With a whimper like a beaten pup he wriggled in his bonds.

"Oh!" said the young woman, her warm heart touched, "It's some poor creature they've got tied up there. Poor thing's been there all night without a drink or sup. That ain't right." She hoisted herself up into the wagon. "Phew, what a pong!" she muttered as she clambered over the hides. "It's a wonder the poor thing didn't suffocate with all this stinky stuff!" Loosening the cord around his snout, she peeled back the wolf's pelt from his eyes. She looked at him in puzzlement. His nose had gone pale green-grey-yellow with the smell.

"Well, what kind of creature are you, my pet?" she wondered to herself. Her face was kind and comely, surrounded by a halo of fair-hair bunched out in ringlets. Iffleplum liked her right away. "A Lightstream lady", he decided: someone he could trust. A teardrop tumbled from his eye at the warmth in her voice. "Thank you," he whispered weakly.

"Lawks! It *talks!*" the girl exclaimed. "You're not an animal, then?"

"Of course not—I'm an ifflepinn: an Ummal from Ælfÿlon."

"Is it?" she replied somewhat amazed. "You're a faerytale come true, then. I heard there were ummals outside of Angarsland. But I haven't been anywhere but Kingstown—Angarsburg, that is. Well, we called it 'Kingstown' before that tick Märûçha took the throne. Anyways, what are you doing, tied up here?" From the way she spoke, Iffleplum realized she was no supporter of the Changeling King. Hurriedly gave a brief account of his capture by the hunters and the fact that Märûçha's soldiery was after him.

"Then you mustn't go near Angarsburg. The Gate-Guards are inspecting every wagon that comes into town. And I just overheard that fat merchant and the hunters talking over breakfast. They were arguing about how much each would get when they sold their 'special merchandise' to the Kingstown commandant. And now it comes to mind, that 'merchandise' is *you*. Come now. Quick! Let's get you untied."

But as she reached for the knots, they heard the inn door open. A burst of raucous laughter followed, as Iffleplum's captors came out into the yard.

"Martha!—the men are coming!" hissed the boy. The maiden shrank back. "No time!" she whispered, quickly looping the cord back loosely round his snout. "Listen. My swain's a *mattockeer*," she said. "He's shepherding his flock to winter pastures, way past Angarsburg. Today, his camp's way down by Blunder's Gorge. Don't worry now. He'll look after you. I'll send a message by his dog."

The merchant and the hunters were making coarse jests, while relieving themselves against the cowshed wall. The inn maid just had time enough to scramble down unseen. She and the stable lad slipped back indoors, dragging the inquisitive dog along behind them. Once inside: "Quick now! Find me a quill and ink!" she told the boy. He drew out pen and paper from a drawer. Hastily she scribbled a note to her mattockeer man. Drying it over embers in the fireplace, she stuffed it into a small leather drawstring purse. Tying it to the dog's collar,

308

she let him loose from the inn's back door. "Go, Tiggin!" she urged. "Find Berric, boy! Find master! Go! Go!"

With a yelp of delight the dog joyfully raced off, quickly disappearing down the misty track.

Satisfying themselves that the ifflepinn was still securely tied, the hunters slung their packs and Blackbeard's shotgun in the back. They clambered up into the driving seat beside the merchant, without giving him another thought. The wagon steadily rumbled off into the mist. Iffleplum felt a dull ache from something digging in his side. With great relief, he realized it was his *Legends* book! What luck! In their haste to wrap him up, they had left Çhelône's shoulder-bag still strapped across his back. As the wagon jolted over a rut, he tumbled sideways and fell against Blackbeard's baggage. A buckle on the hunter's pack caught on the loose cord and snagged it off his snout.

Scraping his face down the wagon-side, Iffleplum wrinkled up the wolfskin just enough to see beneath.

He looked around unhappily. It was not a pretty sight. The hunters had been very busy, killing all kinds of creatures. Piled up all over the merchant's wares, were the pelts of marmots, squirrels, rabbits, deer, a mountain goat, a furry bearskin (not to mention *wolf*) and other beasts he knew not what. And also a huge, shaggy, evil-smelling hide that lay along the whole length of the wagon. It had a hideous-looking head.

Could that be a troll? He shivered at the thought. He was still in dangerous country.

*

After a couple of crawling hours uphill, the wagon came out onto a perilous ledge-road on the edge of a precipice. It hugged an overhanging cliff, far above a deep ravine that rumbled in its depths. The hoarse *kraark! kraark!* of swirling crows bounced in echo off the nearby crags. To their right was a frighteningly long drop down to a raging river far below. The thunder of water came up to Plumkin's ears.

This must be Blunder's Gorge! he thought, remembering the inn-maid's promise. Here and there the unprotected road edge had crumbled away. So the merchant urged the horse to hug the ditch-side beneath a lowering cliff. The wagon now heeled over sharply to the left. On that side, the overhanging bluffs were slowly descending, giving way to thickly wooded hillsides.

They were nearly out of the far end of the roaring gorge, when the merchant pulled sharply on the reins. The wagon stopped with a lurch. The horse shied. Rearing up on its hind legs it whinnied in fright. With a sudden jolt Iffleplum was thrown against the backboard.

"Ghòr's guts!" cried Blackbeard, falling backwards onto the pile of hides. He scrabbled for his shotgun.

Three enormous stumpy creatures had suddenly stepped out from the trees and completely blocked the road.

"Trolls!" squawked Floppy-Hat in panic.

Sure enough, two of them *were* trolls. But the other was a huge shaggy-headed, three-eyed ogre! Giant-size, they towered head-high over the wagon top. One flat-faced troll was as ugly as a pug-dog with protruding upright fangs. The other was more goatish-looking with three ram's-horns curling from its head.

"*Skrahbban dorksgob!*" exclaimed the pug-faced one excitedly. It grabbed the horse behind the ears in a paralysing grip. The cart-horse fell to its knees.

"What?" growled the ogre. "Stop talking Trollish. Talk what *I* can understand!"

"*Horse!*" said the troll. "I likes horse. Can I have it? I'm fed up with mattock and boiled gnomes. Cept for breakfast."

"Yaah," grunted the ogre. "All right! I'll see what's in the back." Gleefully, the troll wrenched off the horse's harness with its massive hands, snapping the leather straps like cotton. Blackbeard scrambled to his feet. But as Pug-Face roughly dragged the horse off from the shafts, the wagon jerked backwards throwing him off balance. He fell forward, banging

310

his head on the driving seat. Seeing stars, he lay there stunned awhile, cross-eyed.

Pug-Face humped the limp cart-horse over its massive shoulders. Clutching its legs, he set off down the track, chortling a trollish nursery-rhyme to himself: *Horse for pudding, horse for lunch, horse's bones is nice to munch!*

Meanwhile Ram's-Horns loomed over the driving seat. The fat merchant fearfully slashed at it with his whip. With a snarl, the giant troll reached over and grasped him and Floppy-Hat by their necks. They yelled in fright, arousing Blackbeard from his stupor. The troll smartly banged their heads together. They both fell senseless across the driving seat.

In the wagon's gloom there came a flash of light as the back-flaps opened. Blackbeard blearily looked around. An arm like a tree trunk reached in. It grabbed up Iffleplum and hauled him out, dangling him the air. The ogre regarded him greedily with its three huge rolling eyes. "*By ghòr!* You're a tasty gobbet, I shouldn't wonder!" it boomed. "Once you're skinned, that is." It roughly ripped off the rope and wolfskin wrappings and tossed them down the ravine. Pinching the ifflepinn's chubby legs it licked its drooling chops with hungry interest.

Blackbeard thrust his head and gun out through the flaps. "Hey! Get off my merchandise!" he bellowed. Abruptly, the ogre slung Iffleplum in the ditch and swung around. With a fist like a leg of ham, it slammed Blackbeard in the face. The gun exploded. Blackbeard went flying backwards over the hides. And the three-eyed ogre fell stone dead, with a bullet through its middle eye.

Ram's-Horns came bounding to the back to see what made the bang. It glanced down at the dead ogre spread-eagled on the road. "Humph!" it sniffed disdainfully. "Kshnuffed it!" Flinging aside the back-flaps with both brawny arms, it glared into the wagon. Then, the trollskin caught its eye. Blackbeard glanced fearfully from Ram's-Horn to the trollskin. He scrabbled backwards, his face white.

311

"Trollskahn!" roared the Ram's-Horn troll. With a howl of
rage it smashed its horned head into the wagon, slewing it
sideways and flinging Blackbeard into the hides. The wagon
lurched as the back-wheel skeetered over the edge of the
precipice. Then the troll went berserk. Banging furiously with
its head all along the side, it rocked the wagon alarmingly.
Reaching the front, it grabbed up the cart-shafts. With its
312

massive strength and a maddened roar, it shoved the whole thing backwards with a mighty heave.

The cart-shafts shot up in the air as the wagon hurtled straight over the cliff.

As it fell, a flailing harness strap snapped back like a whip. Lashing across the troll's horn, it swiftly snagged around it in a coil. And with the falling wagon's weight, it yanked the huge beast off its feet. The troll roared out in rage as the strap tugged it topsy-turvy over the edge.

Turning over in its flight, the wagon seemed to tumble in slow motion through the air. Floppy-Hat and the merchant were flung out wide like sacks of grain. The strap unravelled from the ram's-horn and the ugly brute was slung off upside down. With a blood-curdling scream the troll went plummeting down the gorge.

Suddenly all was still. There was a shocked pause and a ringing silence. Then a mighty *crack!* was heard as the wagon hit the running river far below. A whoosh of waters echoed up the cliff. Iffleplum tottered to the edge. Dizzily he peered down over the brink. The wreckage of the sinking wagon was speedily rushing away in the roaring muddy flood.

There came a furious bellow from down the track. Iffleplum looked up. Pug-Face had turned about. Still clutching the cart-horse on its back, the troll came menacingly striding back.

Iffleplum was too weak to run. His knees gave way and he fell down in a faint.

*

He was out of it for quite a while. But gradually he was coming round. He awakened groggily to the sound of soft voices in his ears. There were people talking all around him. The smell of mountain-berry tea and sweet cooked apples drifted to his nose. *That doesn't seem like something on a troll's menu*, he thought. A warming pink flush flowed across his mauven snout. He squinted carefully through his lashes. Thankfully, he saw he was *not* in a troll's den, but in the open air.

He was covered in a clean warm blanket and lying on a mat of straw. A mixed group of young men were sitting in a circle close beside him. Some were bearded, some clean-shaven, some with loose-flowing hair at shoulder-length and others with hair tied back in horsetails. They seemed a friendly-looking, happy, and contented bunch: just quietly chatting. Not threatening. They were sprawled around the dying embers of a campfire, sipping mugs of rich red mountain-berry tea. Iffleplum recognized the smell from his breakfast on the *Boat of Hearts*. That seemed a hopeful sign.

Opening his eyes a little more, he gazed around cautiously. Beyond the circle of tea-drinkers, he could see a herd of huge, ungainly-looking beasts standing about on the boulder-strewn hillside. Those lolling in the grass looked much like boulders themselves: greenish near the grass and greyish on their backs. The ones standing stood about the size of gauhns. But to Iffleplum they looked more like giant snails with legs that had somehow lost their shells. And similarly, their tiny eyes came in and out on stalks above the longish grass. Their bloated bodies were twice the girth of an over-fattened horse. In fact, they looked as wide as *two* fat horses side by side. Short forked horns, like the end of a crowbar, sprouted on their broad and bulbous snouts. These seemed to be for grubbing in the ground for roots, by the way they were turning up the clods. They waddled about like drunken ducks on short and stretchy legs, tearing up the grass and chomping loudly as they browsed.

Iffleplum now became aware of a blonde-bearded, wind-burned young man beside him. The fair-faced fellow was watching him with interest. A longbow leaned upon his shoulder and a quiver of arrows was slung across his back. Their eyes met.

"Greetings," said the young man warmly. "How are you feeling now? Do not be afraid. You are safe with us. I am Berric—Master Mattockeer. We are herders of the Grubbing Mattocks you see over there." He waved his arm towards the

314

boulder-looking beasts. "My Tiggin brought me Martha's note."

"The inn-maid?" responded Iffleplum. "Oh! She told me you would come." He gave a sigh of relief.

"Aye, I'm only sorry we didn't get there sooner," Berric said, pulling at his wispy beard. "It might have gone bad for you. But those thieving trolls had made off with one of our mattocks in the night. So we were tracking them already. We found their camp all right. But the poor old mattock had already been half eaten. So we stopped and cut up what was left. We can't be too careful for provisions on a march. Anyroad, that's when Tiggin came bouncing up to find me. Luckily, he sniffed out where the trolls had gone. So we got there just in time."

A horse gave a sudden snort and whicker behind them. Iffleplum looked around. The merchant's cart-horse was tethered to a tree. "Oh, you saved the horse! What happened to the troll?"

"I don't reckon he's feeling too well!" laughed another lad.

"Nay, not with two arrows in his head," grinned Berric. He patted the longbow over his shoulder. "Luckily, we got him before he got you. Seems he fancied a swim down Blunder's Gorge. His ogre pal took a nosedive too–with a little roly-poly help from us." The lads chuckled. "Too bad about the merchant and the hunters though," said one.

"Ah, right," agreed Berric, pushing up the twisted red-rag sweatband twined round his brow. "They got their come-uppance right enough. Anyhow, if they didn't hit the rocks, there's still a chance they might survive. A good wetting and a river-ride back from where they come's no more than they deserve."

Taking a dish and spoon from a warm stone beside the fire, he handed it to Iffleplum. "Gingered apple-bake," he smiled. "Martha's special. All else is packed. We had our breakfast long before. Sup up! And then we must be on our way. That there troll-hunt's set us back an hour or three. And it's a bit too chilly to sit about. We'll strike camp and set off soon as

315

you've done. That is, if you feel well enough? And you'd like to come along of us? We're off to Ümmûârkon, by the way."

Ümmûârkon! Iffleplum felt his heart leap up. He nodded gratefully, too moved to talk. And anyway, the second spoon of hot apple-bake was already in his mouth.

*

With shouts and yodels, the herders got the reluctant mooing mattocks to their splay-toed feet. Piles of baggage, tents, and tackle were tightly strapped upon the creatures' backs. The superstitious mattockeers had attached posies of dried herbs to the neck halters of the baggage-beasts, in order to ward off calamities on the way. All fastenings were double-checked before the cattle-drive began. The mattocks made a racket, complaining loudly, as girths were tightened here and there. But the rough roads and narrow trails were much too dangerous to risk a slipshod packing of their loads. Berric hoisted Iffleplum up into a seat on his own mattock's back. It seemed the largest and the leading mattock, at the head of the herd.

Inside a sort of comfy wicker saddle-basket, Berric sat cross-legged with the ifflepinn in front of him. Giving a loud cry, the Master Mattockeer slapped the reins. And with a mighty roar of beasts, the cavalcade set off, nigh on forty mattocks strong.

"I call my mattock, 'Martha'," Berric grinned, patting his steed. "But don't you tell my dearest that. She wouldn't be amused."

*

And so for the next few days, endlessly climbing uphill and down again in dales, the ifflepinn travelled with the merry band of mattockeers. They passed through fantastic scenery, below red-rocked and tree-clung craggy misted mountains higher than he had ever seen. Everlasting snow lay on the peaks. Some lads walked beside the herd, while others perched upon the baggage on their backs. The grubbing mattocks moved ponderously up the mountain tracks like a slow-moving stream of short-legged giant slugs. But with their splay-toed, sticky gecko-like feet they clamped on rocks and boulders, flowing over them without a slip. And they clambered over fallen trees along the narrow trails with ease.

Iffleplum had come to notice that their skins changed colours like shot-silk, according to the landscape they were in. Alongside red rocks they turned a rusty brown. In forests they speckled greeny-gold like sunlight on the leaves. Among boulders their hides grew grey and mossy-green. When they were sitting down, it was hard tell the mattocks from the rocks.

The first night, around the campfire, Iffleplum was shocked to see the mattockeers roasting slabs of mattock-meat and eating them with relish. He wondered mightily at that. Remembering the hunters, it troubled him at first. But slowly he began to realize not all flesh-eating folk were monstrous men or Darkstream types. The mattockeers were all good-hearted lads. They had just never thought about what they ate, having grown up eating slaughtered beasts.

But when the mattockeers saw the ifflepinn's nose grow sickly green, they kindly fed him griddlecakes; potatoes roasted in the embers and melted buttered cheese instead. Next day they loaded him with pockets full of apples, nuts, and dried fruit for nibbles on the trek.

*

The days and nights grew chillier as they travelled on. They had met no one on the trail for days, apart from a party of porter-dwarves coming up the other way. They had large loads on their backs. And all were wet and rather grumpy from a shower of rain. They were not inclined to talk and passed by with only a few grumbled words about the chilly change of weather "all too soon".

On the third night the air grew colder still. Extra blankets were handed round and the mattockeers huddled in their gnurts. Next morning when they awoke, hoarfrost glittered on the grass and trees. "Ghòr's guts!" groaned Berric. "The frost-giants have been out already in the night, breathing their frorebreath everywhere. Winter's coming on us sooner than I thought. This can't be right." After a scant and very hurried breakfast, they struck camp and got the mattocks moving much faster than before.

It was past noon when they began their descent from the high wooded hills. By a long and twisty track, they wound their way slowly down towards the vale of Angarsdale. Flocks of birds flushed from the trees before them with a whirr of wings. And many a time striped squirrels or wild pigs skittered from their path and vanished into the bush on either side. Halfway down the hillsides, a bunch of grim-gnomes from the pinewoods crossed the track in front of them. (Grim-gnomes were the only kind that would live among the gloomy pines.) But they trudged on by with their faces hooded and their heads down. Without a glance at the mattock-train, they silently slipped away into the woods.

Long before they reached the valley floor, they saw a fair amount of two-way traffic moving on the Kingstown highway far below. At length, in half an hour or more, they came down onto level ground, to where the Gauhngarth trail soon joined up with the busy road. Now there were many folk on foot and several farm carts and wagons trundling to the town. Smart carriages weaved in and out among them, passing to and fro along the highway. In the dim light of a greying day the great walled town of Angarsburg was visible way down the vale. And arising from the middle of the town, high up on a distant cliff, a many-towered castle stood,

The mattock herd ambled on towards the town, causing chaos in the traffic and collecting curses from the carriage drivers. A furlong from the town-gates, a fanfare of trumpets rang out from the walls. A troop of soldiers came marching smartly from the gateway underneath a mighty arch.

Iffleplum looked troubled. He glanced up anxiously at the Master Mattockeer.

"Don't you fret," said Berric. "They'll not know that you're with us. But get in under my coat, just in case" He wrapped his patterned greatcoat around the ifflepinn. "Anyroad, doesn't matter now. They don't allow the mattocks through

318

the town any more. So we can't take the King's High Road on the other side. We turn off here and take the *Drover's Way*." He pointed to the nearby mountains on their left. "See! Up there it goes. Zig-zagging way above the town. We go up and over Angarsburg. And after that we cross the mountain range they call the Wilderhorns. And in a day or two, just after the Ârkon-ârkü Pass, we drop down to the Meadowlands of Lün, at the feet of the mighty Ümmûârkon."

"Oh! Ümmûârkon! I've always wanted to see Ümmûârkon right up close," said Iffleplum eagerly, peeping from the folds of Berric's coat. "I've only seen it on the cover of my book."

"Is that right?" said Berric. "Well, don't hold your breath. There's very few who've ever seen it clear. Most times its cloud-covered all around; as hidden as the *Faeryworld of Ælfÿlon*—as we call it, begging your pardon. But some folk reckon Ümmûârkon only lets itself be seen by those it wants to welcome to the Lands around its feet. It's said that only simple honest souls can ever get a glimpse of it—from the Ârkon-ârkü Pass, that is. That's the last cleft in the mountains. Then from there we wind the longways down to the winter pasturelands of Lün. I've been through there many a time and only saw it once. Ho! But a rare sight and all it is.

"Ah, Ümmûârkon!" he breathed. "It's a wonder right enough." His eyes shone as he remembered it. "My drovers reckon it brings back luck if they don't see it from the pass. They're a superstitious lot. Mind you, sometimes I think they're right."

The mattock-train had turned aside and was now nearing the foot of the mountains. The soldiers had long gone marching past. But looking back, Berric saw they had left the Kingsroad and now were striding up the Gauhngarth trail.

Another near escape for Iffleplum! he thought. But he said nothing, not wanting to trouble him more.

Now, following the rocky, rough-tracked Drover's Road, the herd began to climb. Slowly they wound their way up around the seemingly endless hairpin bends. In an hour or more, they steadily rose high above the valley. Pausing to get their cloudy breath in the chilly air, they looked down upon the town. And a breath-taking view it was. From where they stood, the carts and carriages seemed the size of crawling bugs and the teeming townsfolk looked like milling ants. Berric pointed down to where a rocky ridge ran out from the mountains to the middle of the town. Upon its cliff edge, a great towered and turreted castle clung, a thousand feet above the rooftops of the houses far below.

"There's Märûçha's stronghold, stolen from the rightful King," growled Berric. "May he rot in his boots."

"Who is the rightful king?" asked Iffleplum.

"The old King's son," said Berric. "We don't rightly know who he is. But tale tells he was whisked away at birth, nigh on sixteen year ago. And it was whispered that Prince Märûçha was laid into his crib instead. He's a 'changeling child', 'tis said. For he's nothing like the kind old half-Dwemmer King we had before. The Old Man left in sorrow when his wife died and left the kingdom in the Regent's hands. He went off up the Mountain—Ümmûârkon that is—and was never seen again. Just like the Dwemmer-folk.

"When we say 'Gone up the Mountain', we mean that someone's died. Cause when it's time for Dwemmers to leave this world, they take a boat across the River Ringlet, as runs all round the feet of Ümmûârkon. Then they just walk on, up and up the Mountain till they disappear. Their bodies fade and they just *dwem* away. They vanish in the Everlasting Mists on High. I guess that's why *Dwemmers* is their name.

"Anyways, be that as it may. We are *true* King's men. And we look to see the day when the real King comes again. For word has it, that the old King's son still lives! There is an Oracle in Khämmârkhond—a wise and aged Seer—whom folks say has seen it in a vision, or so the whisper goes. So we believe that somewhere, someone's looking after him. That gives us hope. And there's many folk like us just waitin for a day when we might rise up and—oh, flodh it!" he exclaimed suddenly, looking up.

320

Iffleplum felt something damp settle softly on his snout. He looked about him in surprise. Snowflakes were falling gently from a darkling sky. Thousands of white swirling crystals speckled the air and drifted slowly down upon the town.

"Hey-o!" cried Berric, urging his mattock forward. "This isn't right! This bodes *not* well!" He turned and yelled back down the line, "Move 'em on, lads! Move 'em on!" The straggling herders strung out behind took up the cry.

"Haa! Haa!" they bellowed and set the mattock-train moving at a faster pace. The sky darkened even more. And the snow came whirling down. As they climbed, snowflakes furred their beards and eyelashes and clung upon the fine hairs of Iffleplum's face. He shrank back into Berric's coat and huddled against the Master Mattockeer for warmth. The mattock train struggled up and on, until they reached the mountain crest. There they came out onto miles of weary snow-draped plain that seemed to have no end

*

That afternoon they made no pause for tea-and-tiffin time. "Oh, flodh it!" gruntled Iffleplum gloomily to himself, mouthing the Angarslander's favourite oath. It seemed that Berric was anxious to press on before the weather worsened up ahead. If heavy snow had fallen in the Ârkon-ârkü Pass, it could completely block their way to the winter browsing lands. High snow between the canyon walls could freeze hard until the spring.

As early darkness came, they passed on through the narrow clefts and canyons of the high, stark Wilderhorns. Gusty whirling winds moaned eerily above them in the frightful towering crags. Sharp snowflakes spun down and stung like knife-nicks on their faces. At times it seemed like snickers and cackles of evil laughter came carried on the wind. After a while Iffleplum could no longer bear it.

"What *is* that sound?" he asked, wide-eyed. "Is that laughter or the wind?"

"*Ghòrs!*" growled Berric. "Gore-loving brutes! Some Ghòrish clans have claimed the lands twixt here and Ümmûârkon.

There's a realm called *Ghòrkol-Âhn* somewhere under the Ârkon-ârkü Pass. Sometimes they set on lonely travellers there. But they'll not trouble us. We're far too strong for them. And anyways—not in this! The ghòrs like it oven-hot."

Even so, that night they made a cheerless camp without cooked food or fire. Berric posted watchmen all around. Luckily the wind and snow died down awhile before they stopped. Taking the opportunity, they swiftly set up their gnorfish gnurts in a wide and sheltered canyon cleft. There the snow was only ankle deep. The mattocks had now all turned whitish like the snow. They settled down around the gnurt-camp in concentric circles. Beyond them, the mattockeers stuck flare-poles in the snow, tipped with a gaseous fire-rock that strangely burned brighter the damper it became. Touched constantly by steadily drifting snowflakes the torches spluttered and flamed on until the dawn.

*

When they awoke, the air was still and the land snow-silent. But the sky was dark again with heavy threatening clouds. The mattockeers briskly brushed down their half-buried beasts. They shook snow from the tentings and hurriedly packed them, wet and heavy as they were. The mattocks were fed a meagre meal of roots and grain from their carry-sacks. Frorebreath steamed around their snouts. The lads set off in all haste, though breakfastless themselves.

No breakfast? thought Iffleplum in shock. *I've not even had my Wakes!* Grizzling glumly to himself, he climbed back up into the wicker saddle-basket. But weather-wise there had been no time to eat. And luckily they had moved on, for soon after setting off, the snow came eddying down again.

Berric once more wrapped the mantle of his mountain greatcoat round Iffleplum, who sat clutching his shoulderbag on his lap. Only the ifflepinn's pale pearly nose peeped out through the folds. But he felt a comforting warming from his booktrapped elfin-heart, like a soft hot-water bottle close against his chest.

322

It began to grow dark again. The mattockeers lit up their flare-sticks, to not lose sight of their companions in the swirling snow.

"How do the flares keep burning in the wet?" asked Iffleplum.

"Oh that! They are tipped with fire-rock. Strange stuff that. The more it's wetted, the more it flares from a gas the wet sets off. It comes up from *Gûdârkaçh-Âhn*—where the tribes of Desert Ghòrs abide. Somewhere way down south. So it's mighty hard to get hold of and costs a pretty penny and all."

Very soon the mattocks were trudging through snow-mounds belly-deep. They brayed and groaned with the effort. By the afternoon, short-winded in the rarefied air, they had slowed down to a crawl. The mattockeers were desperately urging them on in a final push. They were hoping against hope that the Pass was not already blocked against them. Exhaustedly they stumbled on, a bitter north wind flinging snow in their faces. Agonizingly slowly they ploughed their wind-battered way across the rolling plain of a bleak high plateau.

"These ought to be green-grass fodder plains this time of year!" muttered Berric worriedly through gritted teeth.

As they neared the canyons of the Ârkon-ârkü Pass, the mountains closed in on them again. The weary beasts were struggling hard. Their forked snouts were ramming their way through snowdrifts higher than their heads. But the wind had worsened. And the sky grew darker still. Thickening snow-flakes came swirling down with double strength. It was now difficult to see more than a yard or two ahead.

"Ho! Berric!" cried a scarf-wrapped, hooded lad, bringing his mattock up alongside. "We can't go on in this here blizzard! We can't see fore nor back! We be like to lose the stragglers in this murk!"

Berric dashed the snow from his moustache and beard before replying. "Nor can we stop!" he bawled. "There's no shelter in these here parts, Darren! We're in the Ghòr-lands! We have to make it the through the Pass! Close in and pack

323

together for warmth! And keep the rock-flares high!" The order was shouted back down the line and sputtering fire-rock torches gathered round them like fog-lights in the gloom.

"The beasts are flagging!" yelled Darren. "They're exhausted. They'll not last out much more!"

"I know! But what to do?" cried Berric desperately. "We can't camp out in this! Look! The cliffs are closing in! We must be at the Ârkon-ârkü gully now! We should be on the last slope down into the pass!"

"Can't tell where we are!" yelled Darren. "The snow's too deep! It's running up ahead, not down. Look you! It's piled way up ahead of us." The torches revealed what seemed a mountain of snow piled up between the narrow cliffs.

"Work of the Warlock!" growled Berric. "The Pass is blocked! If we don't get over it, or under it, we'll be stuck here, fodderless, in the snow till spring! The mattocks all might die of it. Never mind about us! There's something strange in this! 'Tisn't natural, this weather, coming on so soon! *Press on!*"

"STAY JUST WHERE YOU ARE!" a chilling and commanding voice crackled out ahead: a voice like the sound of someone crunching ice-cubes between their teeth.

The mattock-train stopped dead.

A long tall figure loomed up, seemingly out of nowhere, dark against the falling snow. It raised its arms. And as it did, a wall of snow rose up behind them from the ground and thundered way above their heads. It went soaring over them with the roaring terror of a wild wave from the sea. The mattockeers crouched down instinctively, flinging their arms above their heads. But the white wave rolled right over them and plunged down some fifty feet ahead. It fell thudding to the ground with the walloping weight of heavy snow. The figure waved its arms again. And instantly the snow solidified, freezing hard. With a crunching crackle the ice-cavern covered over with a sudden sparkling sheen of frost.

They were shut off from the blizzard—but also from the world.

Trapped inside a suddenly silent dome of solid snow and ice.

324

"YOU GO NOWHERE, UNLESS I SAY!" hissed the crispy voice. Fine snow-dust drifted down upon them from the ceiling dome. Brushing it from their lashes, the mattockeers rubbed their eyes and stared.

A tall and slender figure in frosted robes now shone whitely in the snow-dome's gloom. Pale and pearly-faced, but beautiful, a woman-like creature stood before them. A diadem of icicles like star-rays crowned her head and a raised collar of spiky icicles splayed out from her shoulders. She held them in her frigid gaze, her eyes as cold as a snake's. Even mounted on their mattocks, she still stood eye to eye with every rider.

"An Ice-Witch!" gasped Berric hoarsely.

Oh no! thought Iffleplum. *Not again! The ferry Dogmother told me true! Now here's witch number two!* He leaned back, hidden in the Mattock Master's patterned coat and feeling rather faint.

"INDEED!" rasped the Ice-Witch, with a grimace that may have meant to be a smile, in a mouth much unused to smiling. "HOW *NICE* TO KNOW THE COMMON FOLK HAVE NOT FOR-GOTTEN US." She spoke slowly in her throat, still sounding like the scrunch of footsteps over frosted fallen leaves.

"Wh—what is your w—w—will with us, Mistress?" Berric stuttered, his teeth chattering in the waves of cold radiating outwards from the Ice-Witch's heart.

"*I* HAVE *NO* WILL IN THIS," she snarled. "*I* AM SUMMONED *EARLY* FROM MY SNOWBOUND SLEEP BY A GREATER POWER. MY MASTER IS *KHÂDHÂRKÂS* THE WEATHER WARLOCK—THE GREAT *ÂRKÛ* OF WEATHER, WIND, AND TIDE—WHO HAS NEED OF WHAT YOU CARRY WITH YOU. AND *UNTIL* YOU DO DELIVER IT, NO FURTHER SHALL YOU GO."

A forest of flaring fire-rock torches gathered round as the mattockeers urged their beasts up closer to learn what was amiss. Clouds of frorebreath misted round their mouths and their mattocks' breath was frosting on their snouts.

"We have many k—k—kinds of m—merchandise, M—Mistress," said Berric, now shivering and hugging himself against the growing cold. "Is this a toll for p–p–passing through your realm? T–t–take what you w–will and let us be."

The Ice-Witch grinned like a snake about to strike. "WHAT MASTER WANTS IS THERE!" She pointed sharply with her finger and an icy wind blew Berric's mantle wide, exposing Iffleplum.

"The *ifflepinn?*" Berric croaked. "Nay, Mistress! H–he is in m–my care! Aught else, b–but never he!"

"THEN ALL SHALL SURELY REST WITH ME!" she snapped, flicking her bony fingers at Berric's head. A rush of freezing air smote him. His face frosted over and a white glaze spread swiftly down his body. In an instant he was frozen solid in his seat.

Iffleplum wrenched himself forwards. His dwemmer-coat made ripping sounds as it tore away from Berric's icy clothes. A roar of rage erupted from the mattockeers. They surged forward. And with them came a rush of heat from nigh on forty flaming torches.

The Ice-Witch staggered back giddily in alarm. Splaying her fingers she swiftly whirled her arms about her head. A surge of icy stalactites came swiftly spearing down from the cavern roof in a circle all around her. Inside her protective cage of icicles, she smirked in satisfaction at the mattockeers dismay. But they urged the mattocks forward. Thrusting their rock flares before them, the ice-cage began to steadily melt away.

As the burning brands came near, the Ice-Witch's eyes widened with fear. She raised the back of her hand to moisture on her brow. "WHAT IS THIS?" she rasped in a feebler voice, "*I BLEED!*" For one who had slept through many a summer in caves of Everlasting Ice, heat was something she had never known. Sweat-like droplets trickled down her face. She clutched her head fearfully, near swooning with the suffocating warmth. The icicles on her head and shoulders had begun to melt. "WHAT *IS* THIS WEIRDLY *WEAKENING WEATHER* ON MAGIC WANDS YOU BEAR?" she gasped. Her long, lithe body began to wilt like a candle melting in a flame.

326

In sudden realization of her danger, her eyes rolled wildly round and round. "OH! STOP IT! *NOW!*" she cried. "STAY BACK!"

She raised a shaking, spindle-fingered hand towards Iffle-plum. Without thinking, he held up his shoulder bag before his face, to shield him from her flow of frost. But the Ice-Witch fell back with a gasp. Her eyes widened in wonder at a growing glow within the bag. Iffleplum's pulsing elfin-heart was radiating warmth and light! A sudden beam shot out of it and smote the Ice-Witch in the chest. With a dreadful hiss of steam the warm ray passed straight through her icy heart. She screamed. But even reeling, still she stood. She looked down unbelievingly at the gaping hole in her midriff, dripping like icicles in the sun.

"SPARE ME!" she pleaded and sank down wilting to her knees into the melting snow.

"First undo what you have done to him!" growled Darren fiercely, pointing at Berric's frozen form.

"*THAT* I CANNOT DO," she rasped weakly. "HE MUST LIE BENEATH THE GOLDEN WEATHER EYE IN THE SKY FOR THAT."

"The golden what? Oh, ah! The *sun*, is it?" said Darren. "Then free us from this snow-cave wizardry!" he snarled. "And then perhaps, we'll let you be! Or else we'll puddle you to nothing with our magic weather-sticks!" He thrust the firebrand at her face.

"I WILL! *I WILL!* I PROMISE YOU!" wailed the Ice-Witch, backing away. "*GREATER* WEATHER WIZARDS YOU ARE THAN EVEN *MY* MASTER! BUT I BEG YOU, *BACK AWAY!* OR I CANNOT WORK MY WILL FOR YOU."

Darren waved the mattockeers back.

Suspiciously, they widened the semi-circle, easing the great beasts further off. With the lessening of heat, the Ice-Witch seemed to gain a little strength. She ran her hand around the emptiness between her navel and her chest. And the hole filled quickly over, spider-webbing with an icy crackle, like frosting on a winter leaf. In a moment more she had made herself whole again.

As one, the encircling mattockeers stepped forward, lowering their burning brands menacingly towards her. But the Ice-Witch held up her hands and backed away. "WAIT! WAIT! I KEEP MY WORD! GIVE ME SPACE," she grated. Turning about, she whirled her arm in a widening spiral. Way down ahead the dome wall collapsed in a flurry of snowdust. A sloping tunnel now opened before them between the icy canyon walls. With another sweep of her arm, a sparkling ice-road sped sheeting across the snow "NOW GO!" she croaked.

She slashed her flattened palm sideways, and the whole mattock-train was suddenly sliding at great speed down the ice-sheet slope. They seemed to slide on endlessly as if in a dream as the narrow walls whizzed by.

Suddenly they shot out into blinding light! The mattocks slammed straight into a bank of tumbled snow. They collided in confusion, piling up against the mound. Martha Mattock hit the snow headfirst. Iffleplum was flung off head over heels. Berric stayed frozen to his seat. The ifflepinn landed halfway up the drift, upside down. Unhurt, the mattocks untangled themselves, grunting and shaking the snow free from their baggage packs.

Staggering to their feet, the mattockeers looked up. Only a windblown snow-bridge roofed them overhead, spanning the final gap between the canyon cliffs. But they were out! They were at the tunnel's end! They gazed out amazed at the blizzardless, bright blue and sunny sky! Their hearts lifted. They had made it!

They stood between the final rock-walls of the Ârkon-ârkü Pass!

Way down through the clear air they could see the pasturelands of Lün spread out before them, far below.

But the mighty Ümmûârkon was nowhere to be seen. It was, as usual, hidden in a distant veil of mist. "Ah! Bad luck again," muttered one of the mattockeers. "Bad luck for our Berric, right enough," growled Darren.

The lads now anxiously crowded around Berric's mattock. The Master Mattockeer still remained ice-welded to the saddle-basket.

But the sun was warmly shining down. Anxiously they waited. They relit their sputtered fire-rock torches and held them up around his head. In a while, with a soft splitting sound the frosted ice began to crack off slowly from his face. Berric's eyes opened suddenly. He stared about him in a daze. "Did I fall asleep?" he croaked bemusedly. "I thought we were lost in a blizzard? I dreamed we'd all been turned to blocks of ice." He stiffly stretched his arms and the frosting crackled on his clothes. "Ghòr's guts! But I'm as frozen as if I had been!" The lads all chuckled in relief.

Iffleplum had now clambered up the heap of snow. Looking out over the top of it, his eyes widened in amazement. His nose went snowy white in shock! It then slowly softened to a wondrous warming rose. "Look!" he croaked in awe. It seemed as if a misty curtain was slowly drawn across the vale, as the majestic form of the mighty Mountain now came looming into view.

Ümmûârkon the Unbelievable!

Iffleplum fell to his knees, astounded by the sight. So did the mattockeers around him. The Mountain was overwhelming. It seemed to soar on forever, up and up into the sky. On and on it went, to way beyond where one would expect to see the sun or moon. But its lofty peak remained unseen, its inconceivable heights vanishing into the pale and misty blueness of the sky. Looking up at it, Iffleplum felt dizzy with vertigo. The clouds drifting across its face gave the impression that the Mountain was about to lean over and topple down on him.

He gasped in stupefaction. But then wonder, joy and laughter welled up in his empty heart.

"Yaay!" he cried, throwing up his arms.

"No!" hissed Darren in alarm. "*Never* cry out in the snows! You could cause an ava—"

But it was too late.

There came a crack and rumble from above. With the shock of Iffleplum's shout, the shelf of snow-bridge split off the cliff-walls overhead.

And with a muffled roar, the avalanche thundered down upon them like the raging claws of a polar bear.

Part the Twenty-second

The Grand Ghòrish Games

In which, for Iffleplum, no hope gleams,
when forced to face his wildest dreams.

he mattockeers yelled out in fear as the shattered snow-bridge came hurtling down upon them. They and their startled beasts leapt back in haste. Iffleplum looked up aghast. He was standing right below it! Hurling himself frantically down the mound, his leg plunged deep in snow. Thrown off balance, he stumbled wildly and fell forwards on his face. Then *whumpf!* a deluge of heavy snow crashed down upon him, knocking all the breath from his body. Exploding on the trail, it burst over the cliffside like a waterfall. And Iffleplum went with it! He vanished in a snowy cloud.

The mattockeers cried out in dismay. They rushed forward. But in seconds he was gone!

Snow was in his eyes and ears and up his nose. He couldn't breathe. His heart was pounding, his chest bursting. The rushing speed of the snowfall blocked his lungs. Smothering, his mind went blank. He was whirling and tumbling, but didn't know it. About to black out, he found a crevice suddenly opening under him. And the snow-stream sucked him down inside the mountainside. Bumping and slithering down a narrow snowy chute, he snatched a gasping breath. But a burning smell of soot and smoke choked in his throat.

He slithered to a sudden stop on a pile of steaming slush. A hissing cloud of smoky steam shot up. And a whacking great dollop of dirty snow fell down on top of him. He sprawled forward, tumbling into a tiny cave.

Dazed and breathless, he dragged himself out of a heap of hissing snow. He felt faint from lack of breath. Rubbing his smarting eyes he snorted soot and snowdust from his nose. Groggily he tried to focus. His bleary eyes picked out a stone table and two boulders serving as seats against the wall. A burning wick in dish of oil flickered on top of it. By its feeble light, he suddenly saw he was not alone.

An ugly little pig-faced ghòr-child was sitting on a pottie, in front of him. It was eating a salamander sandwich (a ghòrish delicacy). He could see its newt-like tail and one leg hanging out between the bread. The ghòr-baby goggled with widened eyes. Its lip trembled, about to cry.

"Dah-dah!" it shrieked, showing its bright red tongue and curvy fish-like teeth. *"Dah-dah! Snabbid iggidagh lâr kumbul iggun zyutlyn! Snapfek flôhdun ekka mahg-mah!"*[15]

16 "Father! An ugly bogey-thing came down the chimbley! It put the flodding fire out!"

"Hunh?" snarled a rough voice. A large and nearly naked, leathery-skinned ghòr, wearing a tattered grey tunic, shambled into the cave. It was no prettier than its pig-faced child. Its skull-cropped stubbly hair ran down its fat neck and spiked out across its shoulders, like a close-shaved hedgehog. Its reddish eyes glared at the snow-covered ifflepinn. Its knotted brow darkened. "That ain't a bogey, nipper!" he growled. "Looks like some sort of flodding snow-troll brat! What's it doing here in Ghòrkol-Âhn?"

Iffleplum was still too stunned to respond. His head was going round. *Snow-troll? Ghòrkol-Âhn?*

The huge ghòr grabbed him by the scruff of his dwemmer-coat and hauled him across the floor. A dollop of snow caught in his hood slithered icily down his neck.

"Kill it, Dah-dah! Kill it!" squeaked the ghòrish tot on the pot. "Stomp on it!"

The ghòr swung Iffleplum around as if to dash him against the wall. Nipper's pet horned cave-cat devil up in its wall-cage thrashed about in excitement, hoping for a meaty snack. (It was used to having fresh wall-smashed fodder.)

But then, the ghòr hesitated for a moment, scratching his hairy ear absently. Thinking better of it, he gave an evil grin. "Now!" he said. "I'll tell you what! It'll be more fun to watch it get eaten at the games! I promise you!"

Get eaten? That much Iffleplum understood. He squirmed wildly in the ghòr's claw-like grasp. "Keep still, you slimy little snow-toad!" bellowed the ghòr, cuffing him round the head with his free hand. "It's the lock-ups for you!"

The hedgehog-necked ghòr dragged him down a short passage. Brushing a sack-cloth curtain aside, they came out into what seemed a main underground thoroughfare. Along a smoke-filled smelly tunnel, a straggle of ghòrs were passing to and fro, carrying flares of flaming pitch. Most wore greyish clothing, one ghòr in dirty yellow and two others in dark red, worse for wear, went staggering by. The red-clad ones looked like pirates dressed in rags, carrying two-pronged spears and swathed in chunky jewellery. "Out of the way!" cried a rough voice, as a squad of soldier-ghòrs in grey uniforms, stomped by, thrusting everyone aside. Behind them rolled a solid wooden-wheeled squeaky cart, drawn by what looked like a giant lizard. Or perhaps a fire-drake with its wings cut off to stumps. It rolled on by. Then "Dah-dah" recognized the driver.

"Hoy! Snykyn!" he shouted after him. The skinny hairless ghòr looked around, jerking on the reins. The lizard-thing snarled in annoyance, spouting a sulphurous gout of smoke to the roof of the tunnel. A fire-drake it was. The cart stopped.

"Ho! What? Oh it's you, Bòrgäkk! What you got there?"

"Some sort of flodding snow-troll brat with its fur skinned off—or something like! Fell down my flodding chimney, so it did!"

Bòrgäkk gave a smarmy grin. "Come on! Give us a lift down to the lock-ups, will you? I just got time to put this in for the Games, tomorrow. It'll be a bit of a laugh for starters, before it gets eaten."

Snykyn sneered. "Bah! That's too titchy for the Games. There isn't anything his size to fight with. And snow-trolls are totally wet. They won't even put up a fight."

"This one will," grinned Bòrgäkk. "They've got a wildcat and a starving wolf in the lock-ups, that haven't been fed for a week. That'll do. They're about his size. That ought to make him jump about a bit! Anyways, should give us a bit of a show. Or perhaps something for a bit of light relief. You know, something for the kids to watch get shredded in the Interval, while the fighters take a breather."

"Hop up then! I'm taking a load of waste fodder down to the stink-pens to feed the prisoners, anyways."

The grey-clad ghòr slung Iffleplum onto the cart and climbed in. They squeezed themselves between a few open-topped barrels of unpleasantly smelling slops. Iffleplum cringed. A large dead eyeball stared mournfully out of the sludge.

Food for the prisoners? Yuck! He shuddered and began to tremble.

*

Ghòrkol-Âhn was a large underground realm of the Grey-clan ghòrs. All its tunnels led on down to a central cavern arena they called the Gorghòrond, where the Grand Ghòrish Games were played.

It was suffocatingly hot in the smoky thoroughfare. As the ghòr-cart passed a series of side-caves, a mind-numbing din of hammering and the blasting roar of furnaces echoed off the tunnel walls. Roasting hot air and eye-wincing clouds of black smoke came billowing out. The hot fumes made them cough and choke. The furnaces were being fed with huge logs of wood, hurled in by hulking great ghòrs in mould-coloured coveralls. Sparks were flying everywhere. A team of ghòrish smiths were busy beating redly-glowing iron bars into spear-heads. Others plunged sizzling scimitars into murky, acrid-smelling vats, raising clouds of foul-smelling steam.

The fodder-cart went trundling on down into Ghòr-town. They entered the ghòrish bazaar, a great covered market-cave lit by flaming torches. The air was thick with the stench of burning pitch and smoke. A packed and boisterous flea-market surrounded them, swarming with wild and weapon-carrying fiendish-looking folk. They looked like overgrown imps from the infernal regions. And the sense of the unseen Dhârkästir— the Darkstream—flowing through them all was stifling. It filled the cavern like a pool of ink, making Iffleplum feel sick.

But the ghòrs were in high spirits. The bazaar was alive with a raucous, festive air. Different ghòrish clans had come in from all over the mountains for the Grand Ghòrish Games. Drunken fights were breaking out merrily here and there, to the cheers and encouragement of the crowd. The whole bunch smelled like a pack of wet dogs rolled in rotten fish.

Snykyn cursed the milling throng that got in his way. He angrily flicked his lash at those not quick enough to jump aside. The crowd laughed gleefully at those who felt the lick of his whip. The fire-drake jerked its head and snarled in fury at every crack. It spat out a jet of flame that set the canopies ablaze above two stalls. The bystanders found this hilarious. Then a bleary-eyed Red-clan ghòr from Nhârghòrmûhl-Âhn stumbled out of a grog shop across the fire-drake's path. With a savage lunge, the fire-drake bit off its head. This caused a burst of laughter and much merriment among the Grey-ghòr crowd.

There was little love lost between the clans.

Iffleplum cringed down between the barrels and covered his eyes.

"Stupid Red!" sneered Snykyn. The fire-drake shoved the headless body aside with its hind leg and the fodder-cart trundled on. Weaving its way under ragged awnings down crooked alleys of reeking ramshackle stalls, it came to a stop before a pair of metal-barred gates, enclosing a dimly-lit tunnel beyond. A carved archway over it was decorated with leering gargoyle faces. A couple of bored gate-guards slouched on either side.

"Fodder!" yelled Snykyn. The guards sluggishly swung open the squeaky gates. Passing under the arch, the creaky cart rolled into another smoke-filled, eye-watering tunnel, lit by flaming torches. The firebrands spat out hot pitch on the walls and passers-by. Strange scary howls and gibbering from unknown beasts came echoing down the tunnel.

At the end of the passage was a huge cavern—the Gorghòrond. Its roof was held up here and there by stalactite pillars descending into stalagmites on the ground. As Bòrgäkk lugged him from the cart, Iffleplum fell to his knees. He had a quick glimpse of a large arena, with rock-hewn layers of tiered seating hacked out around the cavern sides: the Gorghòrond, where spectators would sit or stand. A high protective barrier wall ran all around the perimeter, with rough slogans scrawled all over it. Beyond a stone pillar in the centre, he spied another huge gated tunnel. *Big enough for giants!* he thought, running out on the other side.

Snykyn whipped up the fire-drake with a harsh cry. He drove out into the arena to deliver his barrels of slop to the feeders of the hungry howling beasts. Bòrgäkk grabbed Iffleplum by the neck and hauled him into a side-cave off the

336

tunnel. A fat and greasy Ghòr-official sat behind a desk. Bòrgäkk shoved Iffleplum forward.

"Late entry, here!" he sniggered.

The Jail-warden didn't seem impressed. "What's the fun in *that?*" he growled. "We already got a full menagerie! And there's top gladiators coming in from all the Clans. They'll laugh their fangs out at that thing!"

Bòrgäkk's brow knotted angrily. He thumped the desk and jabbered fiercely in the local ghòrish speech. A heated argument started up. But after a few more snarls and thumps on the desk, Bòrgäkk seemed to get the upper hand. Finally, the Jail-warden sulkily pushed a ledger forward. Bòrgäkk signed it with a quill.

He smirked at Iffleplum. "You're *in*! Have a nice *stay*," he snickered. And with a satisfied grin he left, clutching two free tickets for tomorrow's Games.

"Skabba!" yelled the Jailor. A sneery, dragon-faced grunt of a guard with a spear came in. The Jailor disdainfully flicked his flabby fingers in the air. Without a word, Skabba grasped Iffleplum by his dwemmer-hood and frog-marched him out. Faint with fright and sick with the smell, the ifflepinn stumbled to the ground. The ghòrish guard never slowed his pace, but strode on, dragging him down a gloomy corridor on his knees.

Opening a thick wooden door, he flung him into a dwarf-sized, dark and smelly cell. The door crashed shut behind him. The only light came in through a tiny grill in the door from a smoky pitch flare flickering on the wall outside.

Iffleplum choked. His eyes watered with the smell. The cell stank of foul creatures that had squatted there before him. He could hear unknown savage beasts roaring and stomping in other cages around the arena. Some were howling, while others whined in misery.

Oh, Ühm! sniffed Iffleplum. *Captured by ghòrs! Food with eyes! Then what? A fight to the death with wild beasts? And— oh! Oh, Ümmûârkon! There's no one who knows where I am!*

Could things get any worse?

Yes, alas, they could.

And then it hit him. His elfin-heart!

He had lost it! Again! *And* his *Legends* book!

They had both vanished in the avalanche! All was hopeless. All his efforts had been for nothing. The thought enfeebled him. Hugging his knees for comfort, he laid his sorry head down upon them. Tears stung his eyes, not only from the smoke. Far, far away was bold Sir Iffleplum of the Vale. Where now, his desire to be seen a dashing knight? And little Plumkin awoke in him once more, as the Ârkühm's words came flitting though his head. "Did you not say you would *give your heart* to sail on such a ship as this? To fight with monsters and suchlike and slay them merely for the sake of honour from a king?"

Oh, my! I did! he thought tremulously. *It's true! I did! I did! I've brought it on my silly self, by the things I wished to*

338

do. Oh, what a fool I am! I've brought reboundage back on me. How stupid can I be? Oh, why wasn't I satisfied to just be me? Just as I am?

Huddled in a corner of his lightless cell, he wept until his heart grew still. His tears had dripped down upon the conker hanging on a thread around his neck. He rubbed it dry on the peach-bloom hairs that fuzzed his chest. He could hardly see it in the gloom. But its chestnut colour reminded him of his mother's eyes. "Oh, I want to go home—" he whimpered to himself, thinking of those who loved him and treated him so kindly, back in cosy Ifflenook. And slowly, he dried his tears on memories of his home and family—of Mumkin, Ifflepaw, Granpaw, and Erf—and his carefree days in Ælfÿlon.

They'll never know what became of me, he thought sadly. And now he fondly recalled all his other friends and helpers— Çhelône and Fogdish, cheery Fluff-Ruff, and the Gnumpf. *Oh! Whatever happened to them?* And Matty, and Morrig, and Athanôr; and Berric and the mattockeer boys. *Did they all get swept over the cliff as well?*

In a rush of love, his heart embraced them all. Then its emptiness didn't feel so bad. But the rough voices of the ghòrs and the shouts outside echoed in his head. And the nasty way they spoke left hurtful feelings in his heart as well.

I never imagined there were people as horrid as this! Why do they act that way? he wondered. He remembered now how Mumkin and his friends would speak to him. *When people love you,* he thought, *they say your name in a different way: then you know your heart is safe in theirs.*

And thinking so *ping!* went something in his ears. Quickly he plugged them with his thumbs. With his elbows on his knees, he placed his fingers across his eyes as Çhelône had shown him how. He listened carefully. Gradually, under the thundering of his eardrums, he heard a high-pitched ringing sound. *Oh, could it be?* he thought. *Oh, yes! It is! It ONLY is! The SONG OF ÜHM is Singing me!* What was it that the Ârk- ühm said? "whenever you feel yourself all alone and full of fear: just listen well. For rising from your heart you'll hear a

339

singing-sound, like something ringing in your ears—the *Song of Ühm*—'twill be! And then you'll know, you're not alone, for Ühm is there. Ühm is the Singer and the Song and all that's Sung as well."

And he began to feel it so. Entranced, he listened long, as the Song grew strong inside him. And indeed, before long, it was no longer in his ears. He could feel the sound resounding in his empty heart. And his heart grew warmer then, as the Ühm-Song slowly soothed away his fears. Despite his situation, a quiet joy stole softly over him. And the sickening smells and cries of other cage-bound creatures all around now faded from his thoughts. Lingering long awhile in the singing-ringing sound, he steadily slipped away. Oblivious to the unseen creepy scuttling things on the cell floor, he lost himself unknowingly and fell into a deep and peaceful sleep.

*

Crash! A slot near the bottom of the door slammed open. A ghòrish guard pushed a bowl of slops inside. It was morning. Not that you would ever know. It was always night in Ghòrkol-Âhn, lit only by the flares of burning pitch and sulphur. But there was much activity going on outside the cells. Ghòrs were shouting roughly in the passageways. Many times he heard the metal entry-gates clang open and shut. And wagon wheels often went creaking by, up and down the tunnel. The bellows of fire-drakes echoed in the passageway. All was in excited preparation for the opening of the Winter season of the Grand Ghòrish Games, that very day!

Iffleplum sniffed suspiciously at the breakfast bowl. His lilac nose wrinkled in disgust. It quickly turned to the sickly shade of yellow-green fresh gauhn-flodh in the gloom. He couldn't see what was in the bowl, but the smell was quite enough. He pushed it away in distaste. He was ravenously hungry. *But I won't risk eating anything that might once have had eyes*, he thought.

He poked his nose out of the food slot, hoping for a sniff of fresher air.

"Get your snout in!" shouted Skabba, aiming a savage kick at the door-flap as Iffleplum leapt back.

The lock clicked and the cell-door was flung open. "Want to see what's going on, do you?" the ghòrish guard leered at him. He glanced at the untouched bowl of slops. "Well now, you nosey little blighter! Since you don't seem to care for our hospitality, I can give you a ringside seat instead. Just so you can have a taste of what's in store. While you wait your turn, that is," he leered. "Get up!" He jerked Iffleplum to his feet. Before he knew what was happening, the ghòr rubbed bright-red berry juice all over his nose. Then, with a stick of charcoal, he roughly drew black circles round his eyes and crosses over his lids.

"Hah!" he laughed oafishly, admiring his work. "Now you look the part! Proper little clown. You're going to give us clownish performance, I don't doubt."

The guard bent down. He unlocked a smaller round-topped door in the side-wall of the cell that Iffleplum hadn't noticed in the dark. He shoved the ifflepinn roughly through it and locked it behind him. Iffleplum found himself in a low-arched runway like a caged tunnel. He crawled along it towards the light. It ended in a metal-barred door looking out on the brightly-lit arena. All was hustle and bustle out there. The audience was already coming in.

Hordes of noisy ghòrs were filling up the tiered rock-seating around the Gorghòrond. Various ghòr-clans ganged up in different stands. Hucksters with wicker trays around their necks were weaving their ways among them, selling unspeakable ghòrish delicacies. Some of these delicacies were still alive and jumping from the trays, much to the amusement of the crowd. A seller snatched one up by the legs and smashed it senseless on his knee, before smugly putting it back on his tray.

In the massive oval-shaped arena, huge ghòrs in mould-coloured uniforms were raking the sand free of bat-dung and debris. A vast horde of smoke-grimed, huddled bats hung from the Gorghòrond roof on stalactites. In the centre stood a huge pillar, supporting an enormous cauldron of flaming oil. The flames reflected off metal mirror-sheets fixed to the cavern ceiling and threw light down on the combat area. The off-white, battered and bloodstained, high barrier walls were also hung with rows of flaming torches, each one on a sconce. A Mould-clan ghòr was lighting them with a blazing blob of pitch on a bamboo pole. By their flickering glare, Iffleplum could read some of the crude slogans scrawled on the walls.

Some were in the Ghòrish tongue and others in the Common Ummal-tongue. Those he could read, like *Ghòrkol-Âhn Rules, all right?* And *Up the Ghòrkol ghòrs!* Or *Marsh-ghòrs stink of Boggshrike's breath!* And *Get gutted, Gûdârkaçh ghòrs!* and similar heartfelt sentiments.

All around its perimeter, behind barred gates large and small, all kinds of creatures fretted and bellowed, or crashed against the bars in fury. The noise was maddening—and a frightening taste of what was to come. Iffleplum began to shake.

Suddenly trumpets blared and drums began to roll. The rowdy crowd roared with pleasure, as the Grand-Master Ghòr of the Grey-clan of Ghòrkol-Âhn—the ponderous Baron Bûl-Òrhkû—waddled to his seat, plonking himself down beneath a tasselled canopy. He punched the air with a triumphant fist at the cheers of the crowd. A thousand bats dropped off the cavern ceiling, awakened by the sudden din. They swirled about in flurries in the air, squeaking in annoyance. Ghòrish brats took pot-shots at them with their catapults. One or two fell stunned and flopped upon the ground. Sweepers ran in to quickly brush them off.

Then the trumpets sounded once again. There came a thundering applause and the audience roared. A herald with a scroll ascended a pedestal near the Baron's throne. Loudly he boomed out a welcome in the guttural local Ghòrish, a language which sounded as if he was being strangled, while munching on a bag of glass. Then, for the benefit of the tribes from other regions, he sang out in the Common Ummal-tongue, "Ghòr-folk of the Outer Clans, our noble Clan Chief, Baron

Bûl-Òrhkû—Senior War-Master to King Mûhl-Äddârh-Òrm
—(forever bless his toeless feet!)—our sovereign Great Ghòr
of Nhârghòrmûhl-Âhn—(the Root-Realm under Ümmûârkon!—for you ignorant squats from the Outer Reaches)—
who bids you welcome to Ghòrkol-Âhn and our Grand
Ghòrish Games!" The ghòrs cheered and clashed their shields
and stamped their spears and axes on the ground.

"Now then! Now then! Settle down!" cried the herald. "As
a mighty warm-up, our first challenger is Khòrättanäkh of
the Black-clan of Gûdârkaçh-Âhn—from the Back of
Beyond—who will fight the deadly boggshrike from the
swamps of Dräkhkännòr-Âhn! "So now! Let the Games
begin!"

Horns rang out. The crowd cheered wildly. Drums began
thudding with a steady and ominous beat. A huge half-
armoured Black-clan ghòr slipped out through a postern gate
and strode across the arena, swirling a metal mesh-net
arrogantly around his head.

He seemed well-known to the crowd. They greeted him with
roars of approval and applause. But scattered cat-calls and
coarse comments were shouted out from the rival clans. With
a snarl, Khòrättanäkh shook his fist defiantly at his opponents.

The drums thrummed to a crescendo then stopped. Silence
fell. Baron Bûl-Òrhkû heaved himself out of his throne. His
raise his arm. "Commence!" he proclaimed. All eyes now
turned to the Beast-Master, who sat perched on a rounded jut
of rock-shelf high above the menagerie. Lifting a horn-bone
megaphone to his lips, he boomed, "Release the boggshrike!"

A cage-gate crashed open down below him. And a creature
like a huge armadillo, thundered out across the sand. Its wide,
squat horny head and one-horned snout thrashed from side to
side, as it stared about with its aggressive red eyes. A great
aah! of anticipation went up from the crowd.

The fight began at once. As soon as it saw the Black-clan
ghòr, the boggshrike hurled itself straight at Khòrättanäkh.
It leapt upon him furiously with slavering jaws. But the huge
ghòr dropped flat upon his back and kicked it briskly over his

343

head. The crowd roared in delight. He scrambled up quickly and ran back to the attack. The boggshrike was a formidable beast. But Khòrättanäkh was a seasoned warrior. For all his size, he ducked and danced in pirouettes, swirling and stabbing with his trident, to the *oohs* and *aahs* of the crowd.

The boggshrike was gradually weakening, losing blood. But on staggering back from the lunging beast, Khòrättanäkh lost his step as an unswept bat squished under his foot. The boggshrike then suddenly spun around and whacked him with its head. The Gûdârkaçh-Âhn ghòr went flying backwards, crashing to the ground.

At this, the Marsh-clan ghors of Dräkhkännòr-Âhn jumped to their feet, cheering derisively at his fall. "Yaah! Go home and fight pussy-cats, you faery-footed dancer!" they jeered. "Leave boggshrikes to the Marsh-Clan boys!" Several other clans hooted and sniggered gleefully at his overthrow.

But as the boggshrike pounced upon him, Khòrättanäkh spun about. Furiously he snagged his mesh-net over its snout-horn. He wrapped it tightly around its mouth with his mighty arm. Then leaping up, he thrust his trident deep into its neck. Blood spurted and the weakened boggshrike crashed writhing to the ground. Its legs scrabbled feebly as the mighty Black-clan warrior finished it off in a flurry of stabs. The crowd leapt to its feet cheering madly.

"Ten points to the Black-clan ghòrs!" cried the herald.

The Marsh-clan ghòrs booed and jeered, "Yaah! Fluke! You fluky black pile of boggshrike squat!"

"Gûdârkaçh-Âhn! Gûdârkaçh-Âhn!" roared Khòrättanäkh, screaming his clan-name triumphantly and jabbing his blooded trident in the air.

"Dräkhkännòr-Âhn! Dräkhkännòr-Âhn!" yelled the Marsh-lander ghòrs, pounding their chests and greeny-grey shields pugnaciously.

Khòrättanäkh stormed off, saluting the cheering packed arena. He turned and made derisive gestures with his trident at the Marshlander stands.

So—as it began, so the Games went on, with roaring crowds and fights galore. Champions from the many clans and ghòr-tribes of the land first battled the beasts. The winners then fought each other, for scoring clan-supremacy. Soon the sand was soaked with blood.

After the horror of the first combat, Iffleplum could watch no more. He sat with his back against the metal grill. Plugging his ears and eyes he tried to lose himself again in the *Song of Ühm*. But the roars of the crowd kept breaking through. He sat there in despair, awaiting his certain doom.

*

To his surprise he found he had almost nodded off, when the moment he had been dreading came. A bolt shot back behind him and the cage-door swung open wide. He fell backwards into the arena. The audience tittered in appreciation.

The prison-guard Skabba stood over him with a whip. "Your turn!" he growled. Up on the pedestal, the herald cried: "Now then—for a bit of light entertainment—the furless Snow-Troll Clown will now fight the Starving Wolf!" A burst of circus-like music started up. With a smirk and a sneering bow, Skabba thrust a net and a trident into Iffleplum's hands. "Now, get out there, Snow-Troll warrior!" he ordered. Iffleplum hesitated and stayed where he was. "Go on! Get off with you!" snarled the ghòrish guard, slashing at him with a whip.

Iffleplum cowered back. Painted up like a red-nosed clown, he tottered out into the arena. The crowd roared with laughter. A scattering of ghòrish brats gleefully shot at him with their catapults. The pellets stung and hurt, even through his tattered dwemmer-coat. His little legs trembled and his knees shook like jelly.

"Release the wolf!" shouted the Beast-Master. The gate to the wolf-pen opened up. There was an anxious pause. But no wolf appeared.

"I said 'Release the wolf!'" bellowed the Beast-Master through his megahorn.

"It won't go out!" cried a voice somewhere inside the dark wolf den.

"Well, spike the flodding thing then!"

There was a sharp yelp and the wolf came hurtling out. It skidded to a stop, blinking in the sudden glare. Bewilderedly, it stared around at all the seething crowd. Then it spotted Iffleplum. With a wild howl it streaked across the sand and threw itself upon him. Iffleplum staggered back. His net and trident tumbled to the ground. The ghòrs leaned forward in gleeful expectation, hoping to see his head bitten off.

Then many mouths fell open in disbelief. Cackles of raucous laughter echoed across the cavern. The ghòrfolk fell about in merriment, slapping and punching each other in mirth.

The wolf was joyously licking the snow-clown's face!

"Plumkins!" whooped the wolf.

346

"Fluff-Ruff!" cried Iffleplum in joy. "What are *you* doing here?"

"Oh, Pestilence! They nabbed me in their nets! I was just enjoying myself—chasing piglings in the woods! When suddenly *whoosh!* I was whisked up in the air in a net—and hung up in the trees. Then the ghòrs came and cut me down. Nasty beasts! All teeth and claws. They stuffed me in a sack and slung me in a *disgustingly* smelly cell! These are *not* nice people. Not nice at all. But why are you dressed up like a clown? Oh! But your nose tastes nice! Like bush-berries."

"Never mind that, you silly thing!" said Iffleplum, hugging him in delight. "What are we going to do? They're expecting us to fight."

"Well, I'm *famished!* Your nose tastes delicious! I've not had so much as a snack for days! I'm all skin and bones. They stuck a bowl of *intestines* and cow's *eyeballs* in my cell! Disgusting! No self-respecting wolf would eat such stuff. Especially us vegetarians! And because I wouldn't scoff it up, they gave me nothing else to eat all week."

"Do they know you're an ummal?"

"*Of course not!* It might be worse if they think I understand the things they say. I've not spoken since I was captured. Just listening. That's how I discovered the middle passage over there—the giant one—leads out onto the mountainside. *It's the quickest way out!* Just in case we have a chance to escape!"

"But how can we—" Iffleplum stopped, suddenly aware of the growing angry murmurs of the crowd around. The ghòrs were getting restless. Stamping their feet they started chanting all together: "Fight! Fight! Fight! Fight!"

"Let out the scalykrake!" barked the Beast-Master.

A thickset Grey-clan ghòr on a nearby ledge pulled back a lever and a dagger-toothed portcullis-gate below rose up into the rock. Out stalked a scaly lizard-thing, like a giant crested newt, with a spiky face. It stood as high as Iffleplum. Rows of knobbled crests ran all along its sides as well as down its back. Swinging its flat head from side to side, it surveyed the arena with cold reptilian eyes.

"Aah!" cried the crowd. This was more like it!

Locking its gaze on Iffleplum and the wolf, the scalykrake let out a venomous hiss. Its lips drew back in a hideous grin, showing rows of incurved teeth in a mouth as wide as scythe-blade. Stealthily it stalked towards them, like a panther creeping up on its kill.

"This is definitely not an ummal," whispered Fluff-Ruff.

"Where's the Gnumpf?" said Iffleplum, hopefully, from the corner of his mouth.

"Sleeping. As usual. In the next valley. I wish *I* was! Maybe I am?" he said brightly. "Perhaps this is just a bad dream I'm having. Please—wake me up and tell me I'm asleep!"

Sleep! A memory awoke in Iffleplum. Sally-cat and the Sandman's dust suddenly flashed into his mind. *That's it!* he thought. But would it work on a scalykrake? It *only* might!

He scrabbled hurriedly in his dwemmer-coat pocket. The scalykrake came swiftly bounding over the sand. As the reptile leapt into the air, his fingers found a pinch of stardust. Hurling himself backwards, he flung it in the creature's eyes.

Fluff-Ruff's hackles rose and his ruff stuck out like a hedgehog's spines. With a snarl he pounced and clamped his jaws on the scalykrake's hind-leg. The reptile whirled about to shake him off, sweeping the wolf's feet off the ground. Fluff-Ruff spun around in the air, but held on firmly with his teeth. But now the scalykrake began to falter. It slowed down, dreamily shaking it head. Its eyes began to glaze. Its shark-like mouth widely opened in a sudden yawn. It turned about more sluggishly, now dragging Fluff-Ruff in the sand.

It's working! thought Iffleplum delightedly. The scaly-krake's head was nodding in a puzzled sort of way. It tried to remember what it was doing. But it was growing *so* sleepy. It yawned hugely once again and wobbled on its legs. Abruptly, it keeled over and crashed down on its side, giving out a gentle snore.

Fluff-Ruff was overjoyed. "Look! Look! Plumkins! I van-quished the scalykrake! I'm not a scaredy-cat any more. There'll be no more taunts about being a pussy-cat from the

348

wolf pack. Oh, I wish they could see me now! Fluff-Ruff the Ferocious—is back!" He plonked his forepaws on the scaly-krake's rump and let out a victory howl.

"Yaah! Get on with it!" yelled the ghòr-folk, jumping up and down in impatience. This wasn't what they came for. "Kill! Kill! Kill!" they chanted, throwing rubbish and half-eaten things with legs into the arena.

"Give 'em a proper beast!" cried a loudmouth in the crowd. "Yaah! Give us a show!" bawled others, brandishing their weapons wildly. "Let out something *big!*" they cried.

Baron Bûl-Òrhkû gestured furiously at the Beast-Master to do something—quick!

Flustered, the Beast-Master rapidly chose. "All right then!" he bellowed angrily. "Let out the Yäkkh-Ârbhû!" A couple of mould-clad ghòr-guards with spears slipped in from the side posterns. They ran to one end of the arena and unbarred the hugest beast-barred gates of all. Quickly they pulled them open and hid behind the bars. But no ferocious beast came out. The ghòrs began stomping their axes and spear-butts on the ground in anger. Nervously, one of the guards crept out. He peeked inside the creature's pen. "It's asleep!" he shouted, in some relief.

"Well, scare it out, you stupid dungling!" snarled the Beast-Master through his megahorn. The ghòrish guard fumbled in his belt pouch and pulled out a wiggly-string of fireworks. Lighting it on a flaming wall torch he hurled it in the den. A scatter of explosions echoed in the cave. Ghòrish fire-crackers burst around the sleeping beast.

With a furious roar, the massive creature came crashing out. Its enormous knobbly body, like a pebble-dashed hill, was flecked with many shades of greeny leafy-like patterns for camouflage in the woods. Even the Yäkkh-Ârbhû's wide snout was patterned like a stylized tree. It opened its huge mouth and brayed in rage at the ghòrish crowd. The ghòrs flinched back in their seats, happily thrilled.

This was more like it!

Iffleplum's eyes widened as he swiftly made connections.

349

Yäkkh-Ârbhû! He had seen the face of one in Athanôr's
Book of Beastiology! Now he remembered a snatch of the love-
song the Gnumpf composed jumped into his mind—

> *I'm sure I saw a yakkaboo*
> *As plain as it could be,*
> *It grubbed about*
> *With its massive snout*
> *And its face was like a tree.*

"Fluff-Ruff!" cried Iffleplum. "The Yäkkh-Ârbhû! It's the
Gnumpf's lost lady-love—the Yakkaboo he's long been
looking for! We've got to get out somehow and let him know!"

"Yikes!" yelped Fluff-Ruff, as the Yäkkh-Ârbhû came
galumphing furiously down towards them. "Stand back! Let's
hope it doesn't crush us first!" Iffleplum and the wolf shrank
back. They flattened themselves against the central pillar,
below the flaming cauldron.

The Yäkkh-Ârbhû thundered around the arena, kicking up
sand and roaring at the ghòrs. She was big—only half the size
of their friend the Gnumpf—but quite scary in a rage. After
her second lap, the Yäkkh-Ârbhû now noticed them. She
stopped her ramping and raging and eyed them with interest.
They were not ghòrs. And not warriors. Deciding to take a
closer look, she plodded over towards them, nudging the
scalykrake aside with her snout. The reptile yawned and rolled
over with a snort, its legs up in the air.

The Yäkkh-Ârbhû regarded them quizzically, as if
wondering what they were. "Erm—friends?" ventured Fluff-
Ruff, nervously.

"—of the Gnumpf," added Iffleplum.

"Ummals!" said the Yäkkh-Ârbhû gently, with a sigh. Her
long eyelashes fluttered in surprise. Her angry eyes softened
and moistened. "I've not seen ummals for many a while. I
weary of the Ghòrish tongue and of their foul ways. Long
have they penned me underground. And longer still since I
heard a friendly voice—or smelled the woods again." A tear
350

dropped down her face. "Alas, too soundly did I sleep. For the ghòrs crept into my secret forest glade. And somehow they dragged, or carried me away. And I wakened in this foul den. Many times they sent in warriors to test their skills on me. It was—oh, never mind—you say you have seen the Gnumpf?"

"Yes—" began Iffleplum, but his voice was drowned out by a violent crash of cymbals, the blare of Clan conch-horns and the screams of angry ghòrs. The Gorghòrond was in an uproar. Clouds of squeaking bats swooped everywhere. The crowd was wild with impatience. "Get on with it!" they yelled. "Make the flodding thing *fight!*"

Baron Bûl-Òrhkû made the thumbs-down sign. "Spike it!" he thundered.

Half a dozen ghòrish warriors came racing out from the giant gateway. They flung their spears at the Yäkkh-Ârbhû. Some bounced off her knobbly skin, but others plunged into her hide. She bellowed deafeningly. Spinning around she knocked the ghòrs down like skittles, sending them flying on either side. Her huge thick tail crashed against the cauldron column with a mighty wallop, knocking a round stone segment out of joint. The pillar shook. On top, the blazing cauldron gave a lurch. A wave of flaming oil sloshed over the brim like a blazing waterfall. It drenched down on the warriors, setting several ghòrs alight.

Fluff-Ruff leapt out of the way as the splash of burning oil-drops splattered everywhere.

Meanwhile, the scalykrake had awakened. It opened a greedy eye upon the nearby wolf. Stealthily it staggered to its feet.

But Fluff-Ruff's eyes were turned elsewhere, as he spied the open gate.

"Plumkins! The gate's open!" he whooped. "Let's make a run for it!"

"Look out!" shrieked Iffleplum. Too late! The scalykrake had leapt up like shot!

Quick as a flash—its jaws as strong as a steel-sprung trap—it snapped up the wolf in its scythe-wide mouth! Like a cat

351

with a rat, it shook its head and tossed Fluff-Ruff in the air. He fell back with a yowl, as limp as a sack. The scalykrake caught him again on the prongs of its thousand spiky teeth!

Iffleplum cried out in horror.

He scrambled for his trident. But before he could get to his feet again, the scalykrake was up and away!

"Plumkins! Save yourself!" wailed Fluff-Ruff, as the scalykrake sped across the arena. It bounded out through the open gate, knocking the startled sentries aside. The yelps of Fluff-Ruff faded away down the passage as the ravenous reptile carried him off.

Iffleplum stood rooted to the spot in shock.

Part the Twenty-Third

The Terror
of Ghòrkol-Âhn

In which Iffleplum faces death and Ghòrish leers.
And Ghòrkol-Âhn tumbles round his ears!

he ghòrish warriors ran back, dragging their
scorched and fried fellow ghòrs across the sand. With
a crash, the iron gates slammed shut behind them.
Huge beams slid across and barred them tight.

Iffleplum's last chance to escape had gone!

Frozen with dread, he stood staring blankly into space, too
stunned to move.

But the scalykrake with a mouthful of wolf was by now well
away. Like a cat with a mouse, it sought somewhere secret to
devour its prey. Bursting past the ghòrish guards at the
tunnel's end it shot out, streaking its way to freedom and the
light of day.

In a thoughtless daze, Iffleplum shook his head, hoping it
would clear.

And *ping!* he heard the *Song of Ühm* again, resounding in
his ear.

He closed his eyes and sank into its ringing sound. *But oh,
Ühm sings in me!* he realized. *And so—even ALL THIS is
Ühmkyn going on! I'm not alone!* As he listened deeply to the
high-pitched sound, the coldness in his breast grew warm
again. He took a few long breaths. As his heartbeat softened

353

down his fearful feelings slowly dwemmed. He opened his eyes and dared to look around.

The Yäkkh-Ârbhû lay forlorn with her head upon the ground. Her hill-like body leaned heavily against the cauldron column, which now listed slightly on a tilt. Several spears protruded from her back. Her sides were heaving. Blood was trickling down. She groaned and writhed distressfully. Iffleplum's heart went out to her. He choked and stumbled over to the Yäkkh-Ârbhû with blurry eyes. Tears came welling up for the fate of his friend, the wolf.

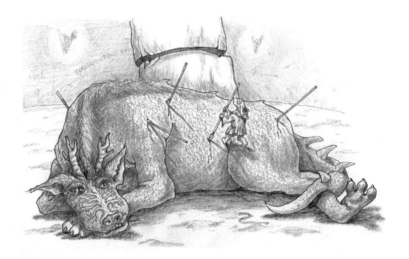

I couldn't save poor Fluff-Ruff, he thought, *but at least I can help her!* Gathering his courage, he scrambled up the Yäkkh-Ârbhû's stretched hind-leg. Tugging on a spear, he drew it out and flung it away. The Yäkkh-Ârbhû jerked back and brayed in pain. The leaning old stone pillar lurched a little as her huge bulk bumped against it. The cauldron sloshed on top of it. And a flaming rivulet of boiling oil went surging down the other side.

"Stay still!" cried Iffleplum "Or you'll spill the burning oil on us! Stay calm while I try to pull out the rest!" He clambered unsteadily from spear to spear. One by one he eased them out and flung them down. But as he wiggled the last spear out, her red blood spurted in the air. *Oh! Oh! What can I do? What can I do?* he panicked. *Ah, wait! I know!* he thought. *I can stem it with my dwemmer-coat. I don't need my disguise—if I'm to end up in a monster's gut!*

He dragged his dwemmer-coat over his head. As he did so, something clunked against his ear. His eyes went wide. A warm memory sprang into his mind!

Athanôr's Heal-All Elixir! He still had a bottle in his pocket! He had forgotten all about it.

Hurriedly he fumbled it out. His hands were shaking as he unstoppered it. On his knees, he wriggled his way from wound to wound. Carefully, he tipped a single precious drop into every bleeding gash. The droplets sizzled for a moment on her skin. Then, to his astonishment, almost on the instant, her wounds began to heal! The cuts closed over and the blood-flow stopped. The liquid sent a warming wave of wellness through all her limbs. She felt it flowing right to up to her nose and down to her toes and as far as the tip of her tail. A few moments more and she lifted her head. Her strength was slowly coming back!

There was still a drop left in the bottle. Iffleplum hastily thrust it into the pouch-pocket of his skin. He was suddenly aware of the restless noise and heckling of the ghòrish crowd.

All around the Gorghòrond a muttering growl of discontent was rising. The ghòr-clans were getting impatient. Ghòrs snarled in irritation at the long delay in their dose of scheduled violence for the day. "Get on with it!" they bawled. And with a slow and angry beat, the clan-folk began to slam their spear shafts and axe-handles on the stony ground. *Thump! Thump! Thump!* Taking up the rhythm, the crowd began to stamp and yell: *Gore! Gore! Gore!* The uproar thundered over the Gorghòrond roof. Startled bats came swirling down again like falling leaves, swooping about with piercing shrieks in annoyance.

"Open the flodding gates!" bellowed Khòrättanäkh the Black behind the giant grills, banging on the metal bars.

Minions hastened to drag away the blocking beam. As the rusty metal gates squealed open once again a stream of maddened squeaking bats flapped wildly away down the tunnel.

A bunch of well-armed Black-clan ghòrs from Gûdârkaçh-Âhn now came running out into the arena. Khòrättanäkh was in the lead. They carried spears and shields and strange thick-bladed swords with sharp and rounded bulbous ends. Behind them came a gang of Ghòrkol Greys, lugging a long wooden beam on ropes and chains. Three other Grey-clan ghòrs set about snaring the Yäkkh-Ârbhû. They ran about, whirling lassoes, trying to throw them over her head. She wildly threw her head about to avoid them. Shakily, she struggled to rise. Iffleplum slithered hastily down from her back.

Snatching up his trident, he turned to face the ghòrish warriors. His little legs were shaking like jelly. Quoting from his *Legends* book, he kept repeating to himself. *The bravest knight is he who fights the foe afraid! The bravest knight is he who fights the foe afraid!* And now he knew—only too well!—what being frightened was; just as he had wished to know so long ago. He recalled that fateful day in the Wossle Wood, when Ifflemother had warned: "Those who seek the sword shall suffer by it," she had said. How right she was! *Oh, why didn't I listen?* he wailed inside himself.

Then the Ârkühm flashed into his mind again. And he recalled his tremulous answer to the Master on the *Golden Heart*: "But—what if my heart's not in them any more?"

"Yea or nay, you wished your heart away," the Ârkühm had said. "And now you needs must do your deeds and see what comes of that... Accept whatever comes," he had advised, "but keep your heart and head in Ühm."

He sighed in resignation. Bravely he stood his ground, trying to control the trembling of his knees. But as the hulking great ghòrish warriors came thumping towards him, all thought of Ühm fled from his heart. Baring his teeth, he grimly thrust his trident up at them. But Black Khòrättanäkh clouted him contemptuously out of his way with a mighty *whack!*

His trident went flying. He fell sprawling in the sand against the Yäkkh-Ârbhû's heaving chest. Now his ears were ringing with a different sound.

On the leaning side of the pillar, a gaggle of Grey-clan ghòrs were attempting to heave up the heavyweight wooden beam against the column, in case the cauldron tumbled down.

Baron Bûl-Òrhkû now suddenly realized what they were about. He heaved his huge bulk out of his throne-like chair and roared, "That's right! That's right! Tie down the wounded beastly—*Yäkkha*-beast-thing! And—and then shore up the Fire Pillar before it falls down! *My idea*—that was! My idea! Just so as the Games can get quicker back on track!" With a self-satisfied smirk he beamed at the audience for their appreciation. He shook a triumphant fist. "That's right, lads! Follow my orders! Do as I say! Shore it up! Shore it up!"

There were some sniggers at his fatuousity, especially from the Red-clan ghòrs in the Nhârghòrmûhl stands, who thought themselves the topmost of all the clans: proud followers all—of the great ghòrish King Mûhl-Äddârh-Òrm in his Root Realm Beneath the Mountain. They hooted scornfully at the Grey-clan ghòrs, as they struggled to raise the huge heavy beam. And even more so, when it slipped from their grasp and tumbled down. The Grey-clan ghòrs scattered and leapt aside.

"Aah! Get on with it! You mousey-grey morons!" bawled a Nhârghòrmûhl Red. "We haven't come all this way to sleep in the stands! Come on now! Give us *gore*—or we want our money back!"

The Grey-clan ghòrs shook their fists and yelled back foul curses in defiance.

But the crowd around yelled and stomped in agreement with the Reds. Many shouted fouler phrases from the stands. Iffleplum covered his ears and closed his eyes. *I want to go home!* he thought again, plaintively. He screwed up his mind and wished himself back in Ælfÿlon with all his might! He opened his eyes. But no—he was still there in the arena.

By now, the other Greys had managed to snag the Yäkkh-Ârbhû. She writhed and thrashed about, with three lassoes caught tightly around her neck. The ghòrs leapt and danced on the end of their ropes, as she tossed her head and wrenched them back and forth. Digging in their heels, they pulled hard in three directions. Half-strangled, still she tried to stand. But ramming his spear-shaft into the sand, Khòrättanäkh leapt forward and smashed her head down with his heavy shield. She sank down with a groan.

Khòrättanäkh clasped his hands above his head and shook them triumphantly. The crowd roared its approval.

The ghòrish warriors now rushed in, shoving Iffleplum aside. Wrapping chains around each of the Yäkkh-Ârbhû's legs, they hooked them on to sharp iron stakes. These they hammered quickly into solid ground beneath the sand and then jumped away in case she would react.

Khòrättanäkh was still playing smugly to the crowd. Iffleplum seized his chance. He grabbed an iron stake and with all his might he wiggled it back and forth and then wrenched it from the ground.

"Behind you!" roared the crowd. "Kill the clown! Kill the clown!"

Khòrättanäkh spun about. With a snarl he leapt at Iffleplum. But a furious bellow from the Yäkkh-Ârbhû distracted him. By now the Heal-All Elixir had done its trick. And before her chain was hammered in again, she staggered up with a sudden jerk. Iffleplum flung himself down flat on his face.

Stomping and roaring, the Yäkkh-Ârbhû ripped out the stakes! And spinning round she swirled them in the air. The chains and sharp spikes slashed across the Black-clan ghòrs and sent them sprawling down. Their spears and shields went spinning in the air.

Khòrättanäkh danced swiftly out of range. He snatched up his spear, which stood upright in the sand. As the Yäkkh-Ârbhû spun about to face him, he drew his arm back and carefully aimed it at her throat.

Iffleplum felt helpless. *What can I do?* he cried inside. His trident had been kicked away far beyond his reach. He found his fist wrapped round his conker for support. He clutched it to his breast. Swifter than thought, he wrenched the cord from around his neck. And whirling the hardened horse-chestnut round his head, with a wild yell he let it fly! His precious one-hundred-and-eighter flew swift and straight. The conker hit the ghòr smack in his eye.

"Gaah!" yelled Khòrättanäkh, half-blinded with the painful sting. He turned on Iffleplum with a snarl. But the Yäkkh-Ârbhû was still spinning like a whirlwind. And so distracted by the ifflepinn, a swirling chain caught the Black-clan ghòr around the neck. It jerked him off his feet. He crashed down on his back in a spray of sand as the Yäkkh-Ârbhû swung him round in a circle.

The Marsh-clan ghòrs guffawed and hooted in derision. "Yaah! Pathetic performance!" they cried. "Flodding amateurs!" yelled another. The Marshlander Clan Chief cupped his hands and bawled "Get up, you stupid pile of boggshrike squat!"

That was the last straw for Khòrättanäkh! He'd had a bellyful of insults from the Marsh-clan ghòr. Humiliated in front of all, he swiftly untangled himself and sprang to his feet. "Shut your face, you stinking marsh-maggots!" he roared out in rage, "Or I'll come and shut it for you!"

"Get gutted!" yelled back the Marshlander Clan Chief. He thrust his fist up in a derisive gesture.

Khòrättanäkh exploded in fury. With a venomous look, he growled at Iffleplum, "I'll get *you* later!" Then at a lumbering run, he hurled himself across the arena. With an angry roar, in one mighty bound, he took a furious flying leap up the barrier wall. Grabbing hold of a flaming torch, he scrabbled up trying to reach the Marsh-clan stands. "I'll break your scraggy necks, with my bare hands!" he snarled. But with his armoured weight, the metal sconce holding the firebrand tore out of the wall. He crashed back heavily to the sand, with a violent curse. The Marsh-clan ghòrs roared with laughter.

Khòrättanäkh leapt up with a face like thunder. "Gûdârkaçh-Âhn ghòrs! To *me!*" he cried to his fellow ghòrs, who were still groggily picking themselves up. "Let's show the Boglings who we are!"

"Hah! You think Gûdârkaçh-Âhn ghòrs can take on Marshland boys, do you—you daisy-footed prancer?"

"With our flodding eyes shut, bog-slime!" bellowed Khòrättanäkh in fury. He snatched up the sputtering torch. With a quick flick he hurled it at the Marsh-Ghòr chief. "Take that for starters!" The Clan Chief wasn't quick enough to duck. The firebrand bounced off the side of his head and singed the hairs on his pointy ear.

"Right! That's it!" he cried. "Come on lads! Let's do the lot of 'em!" Swirling his great curved battle-axe, he leapt down into the arena. The swamplings of Dräkhkännòr-Âhn surged after him. Gleefully they piled over the wall, yelling their clan-cry: "Dräkhkännòr ghòrs! Dräkhkännòr ghòrs!" Swarming down into the arena like a tribe of apes, they charged headlong at the Black-clan ghòr.

Khòrättanäkh danced back to give himself more room. Out of his belt he snatched a spiked mace. Spinning around in a circle, he slammed it into his rivals as they came. The Marsh-clan chief never knew what hit him. His mighty axe tumbled from his fingers as he fell senseless to the sand. The Black-clan ghòr spun rapidly round and round and the Marshlanders went skittling down with bloodied heads, like corn before a scythe.

"Gûdârkaçh-Âhn! Gûdârkaçh-Âhn!" yelled Khòrättanäkh in triumph. He snatched up the Clan Chief's huge curved battle-axe and waved it in the air.

As one, the crowd roared with approval! This was more inspiring stuff!

Seizing the moment, all over the Gorghòrond, the fight-frenzied ghòrs jumped excitedly to their feet! Here was the chance of a free-for-all! Opposing gangs of ghòrish clans with old scores to settle went leaping over the barrier wall. Nhârghòrmûhl Reds, Ghòrkol Greys, Marshland Greens of Dräkhkännòr-Âhn, Dun-Ghòrs of the Desert, hairy Ice-Ghòrs from the Snow-peaks, Dark-clan ghòrs of Gûdârkaçh-Âhn, and many more, went piling into the arena.

Baron Bûl-Òrhkû's bellows for order were lost in the tumult. Yells and battle-cries filled the air. A wave of wild ghòrs came screaming over the sand from every side, hurling themselves into the fray.

The Yäkkh-Ârbhû reared up in alarm as a clashing sea of swords and spears surged all around her. She crashed back against the Fire Pillar with a mighty wallop. The old stone column buckled and burst at its seams. The flaming cauldron went spinning off the top into the air! As it tumbled round, a stream of flaming oil slewed out upon the fighting crowd. Fiery droplets splattered everywhere, even drenching down upon the stands and setting ghòrs all ablaze.

Oh! What a shrieking and gibbering then was heard! Dozens of oil-boiled burning ghòrs howled out in pain! Frantically they beat at each other's flaming heads and clothes. In their frenzied haste, many of them knocked each other out.

The column teetered for a moment and then came tumbling down. A falling block of shattered stone struck the Yäkkh-Ârbhû a glancing blow. She crumpled to her knees, half-stunned. And a huge chunk toppled down heavily across her neck. She brayed in pain and struggled to rise. But the broken half-pillar piece securely pinned her to the ground.

Iffleplum floundered shakily to his feet. All around him battle raged, as the ghòrs gleefully battered and hacked at rival clans. Swords and shields clashed and sparks flashed in the air. Hammers and axes clanged. Iffleplum swiftly ducked to avoid the backswing of a bulbous sword. By a hairsbreadth he missed having his head cut off! But any second a ghòrish spear might spike him through.

For a moment, he stood there lost and bewildered, unnoticed in the midst of battle. And oh, how fondly now he thought of long-gone "boring" Ælfÿlon! And the safety of his home— home he might never see again!

His head still rang from the clout he'd received. And all foolish thought of fighting like a knight had gone.

Now he clearly saw there was no honour or glory in war and gore.

Helplessly, he stood there, in a daze.

Suddenly hurtling out of the scrum, Khòrättanäkh bore down on Iffleplum! His battle-crazed eyes were blazing red. The Marsh-Chief's great curved battle-axe he swung above his head to bring it down furiously on the ifflepinn.

Iffleplum's nose went white with fright. About to be split in two, he stumbled backwards over the body of a ghòr behind him. Its fallen spear lay across its back. As Iffleplum tumbled down heavily on the haft, the spearhead shot up in the air. Unable to stop his violent charge, Khòrättanäkh ran straight into it. The point rammed deep into his chest. It drove in through a chink in his armoured breastplate. The mighty Gûdârkaçh-Âhn ghòr gave an anguished cry of despair. It sank to his knees as the spearhead spurted from its back.

"Aagh! No! What a way to go!" gasped the ghòr in great dismay. "I don't believe it! Killed by a flodding snow-troll clown! How flodding *pathetic*." With a last strangled cry of anger, blood spurted from its mouth. The great ghòrish warrior gurgled and toppled over, dead.

The other Gûdârkaçh-Âhn ghòrs stopped their battling. They gaped in astonishment. Then howled in rage: "It killed Khòrättanäkh!" they cried. "The Champ's down! The piddly little white-clown killed the Chief!"

As one, the Black-clan ghòrs swung about in blazing fury. A ring of swords and spears suddenly surrounded Iffleplum.

"I–I didn't do it!" cried Iffleplum. "It was an accident!"

But the Black-clanners advanced with mirthless grins. Raising their swords and spears for the kill, they closed in on the hapless ifflepinn. He saw his death reflected in their smouldering eyes.

Oh, Ühmkyn! Oh, Mumkin! his heart cried out within.

He closed his eyes to await his fate.

362

Just then, the whole Gorghòrond shook! There came a mighty booming crash and a thundering rumble. Clouds of skreeking bats flew off the cavern ceiling. All around the arena the supporting pillars shuddered and split. Fissures snaked across the dome with a crackle like lightning. The reflective metal mirror sheets came hurtling down, smashing many of the battling ghòrs to the ground. The crowd screamed and leapt to its feet.

Pandemonium reigned.

All over the arena the fighting ghòrs had stopped in mid-strike. They stared about in shock. Their mouths hung open. The very cavern walls were trembling violently. Hanging stalactites broke off and fell upon their heads. A scattering of ghòrish warriors fell senseless here and there.

"Earthquake! Earthquake!" screeched the ghòrs, running this way and that in panic, like a nest of ants stirred up with a stick.

The whole Gorghòrond was in an uproar! The spectators scrambled for the exits, fighting each other in their haste to get out.

Then down the main passage came a braying bellow and a mighty roar.

The Yäkkh-Ârbhû's head perked up.

"No—it's *not* an earthquake!" she croaked. Her eyes grew bright. "It's a *Gnumpf*quake!"

And so it was! The barred gates burst asunder. The great rock-like horn of the Gnumpf's snout came crashing through them. The mangled iron gates went flying in the air. The whole archway crumbled and shattered into smithereens. The Gnumpf's huge head appeared. Enormous as the giant gateway was, the hump of the Gnumpf was larger still.

Like a thundering mountain it battered its way into the arena. The rock terraces above the gate came crashing down as its huge bulk smashed its way in. An avalanche of falling ghòrs bounced down off its back. The Gnumpf shook off the ghòrs and rubble with a wriggle like a wet dog. Lumps of stone showered down, knocking the ghòrs left and right.

The Gnumpf stared about him through the clouds of dust. Suddenly he spied the Yäkkh-Ârbhû with half a pillar across her neck. A mighty roar of rage burst out from its cavernous throat. The ghòrish warriors went flying with the force of it.

Crashing against the barrier walls they fell limply to the ground.

The Gnumpf stormed over to the Yäkkh-Ârbhû, his bushy back scraping the ceiling dome. He stopped and kneeled before her, his great heart thumping with sudden shyness. Open-eyed with awe, he saw the markings of her face. And indeed, they *were* patterned like a tree!

Oh, I did! I SAW a Yakkaboo! he thought. *It's She!* He gazed upon her, love-struck and with wonder in his heart. Her soft brown shining eyes reflected something similar back at him.

The Gnumpf had finally found his mate.

Gently he nudged the broken pillar off her neck with his rock-like horn. But as he did so, a ghòrish spear flung hastily bounced off his hide and landed in her flank. She screamed in pain.

The Gnumpf then whirled about and went berserk!

Roaring and stamping, with mighty swings of his head, he hurled the ghòrs in every direction. The terrified warriors dropped their shields and swords and scrambled for the exits. Shrieking and yammering, they crammed into the tunnel towards the ghòrish bazaar. Spectators and skirmishers alike fought and clambered over each other in their haste to get out first.

A handful of hardier Nhârghòrmûhl Red warriors stayed on to fight. But a strange sound suddenly stopped them in their tracks. Behind the Gnumpf, a weird warbling hullabaloo came echoing down the passageway. Bursting through the cloud of dust and rubble a rampaging herd of mattocks came in sight! The yodelling mattockeer-boys were on their backs, wielding lances and flaming rock-fire brands. The ghòrish warriors staggered back in dismay. Outnumbered and overwhelmed, they flung their spears and tridents in a last gesture of defiance. Then they turned and fled. The mattockeers drove after them, chasing them down the tunnel. The mattocks trampled dozens down, gouging the ghòrs with their snout-horns, while the mattockeers with their lances finished them off.

Bursting out into the cavern of the ghòrish bazaar, the desperate clan warriors fought their way through the packed and panicking crowds. Stalls collapsed as they struggled out. Fleeing in all directions, hundreds of clamouring ghòrs escaped down the many tunnels that maggoted through the mountains. Once free of Ghòrkol-Âhn, they fled away over hill and dale, hurrying back to their homelands without a stop, fearful of the "Roaring Mountain" following after them.

And ever after, around the fire-pits at night, they would tell the thrilling tale of the "Terror of Ghòrkol-Âhn" to little ghòrlings before they went to bed. And the story of the "Roaring Mountain that Walked" became a favourite legend of ghòrish lore and haunted their dreams from that day on.

*

Back in Ghòrkol-Âhn, the mattockeers thoroughly trashed the grog and drug shops of the ghòrish bazaar. They smashed the stalls, tore down the awnings and cleared away the smelly market alleyways. Over several days, they hunted down or chased away the last few ghòrs hiding in their cave-holes. There were a few brief skirmishes here and there, but the rumour of the rampaging "Mountain Monster" and its "mattock army" sped quickly through the whole of Ghòrkol-Âhn. Therefore most cave-dwellers fled at the rumour of their coming. Finally all of the ghòrs living under the Ârkon-ârkü Pass were driven out. Then all the empty tunnel-ends were blocked.

Watch-Wardens were later recruited to patrol the bounds and sentries posted to make sure no ghòrs ever came there again.

*

Meanwhile, as the rest of the mattockeers were trashing the ghòrish bazaar, Berric had returned to the arena. He found Iffleplum hunched against the barrier-wall. The ifflepinn was in a state of shock. He was mumbling to himself while staring into space. "I didn't do it!" he whimpered, as Berric tenderly hoisted him up into the basket seat on Martha Mattock's back. "It was an accident. I didn't do it!"

366

The mattockeer glanced over at the Gnumpf and Yäkkh-Ârbhû, who now had only eyes for each other. The spear was no longer in her flank and the Gnumpf was lovingly licking her back to health.

Berric clicked his teeth at Martha. The mattock set off carefully down the tunnel, picking her way out of the shattered main entryway to Ghòrkol-Âhn. The once secret gates, disguised as a wall of rock, lay sprawled and twisted, having shattered when the Gnumpf barged into them. They came out of the wreckage into the fresh mountain air. The warming sunshine of a late afternoon beamed down upon them.

Not far from the tunnel entrance stood a single gnorfish gnurt. The mattockeers had hastily set up the tent as a sickbay, in case any of the lads should come back hurt.

But Iffleplum saw nothing: neither sun, nor gnurt, or mountainside.

His eyes were misted over. His senses numb.

The great mattock hunkered down upon the grass before the circular skin-covered tent. With Berric's help, Iffleplum dazedly slid down from her back.

But he could no longer stand. After all he had gone through; his shaky little legs gave way. He fell to his knees, stricken with the memory of Fluff-Ruff's cries as the scalykrake carried him away. A rush of sorrow welled up in his heart. And he wept, with relief and grief. He had finally escaped from Ghòrkol-Âhn. But he had no joy in victory.

Fluff-Ruff was no more.

And his elfin-heart was lost in the avalanche, gone—*forever!*

Part the Twenty-Fourth

The Woodwose Awakens

*In which Iffleplum gives up his most precious thing
and awakens new life in the Forest King.*

ffleplum stared forlornly at the ground. He had failed
his friend. He hadn't even *tried* to save him. *Stupidly
standing there rooted in shock*, he chided himself.
Berric laid his warm hands on the ifflepinn's shoulders. "Come
you now," he said kindly, to try and jolly him along "There's
no more cause to fret. You're safe and sound. It's all over
now—take *heart*."

Iffleplum looked at him downcast. And a sorry sight he
looked. The charcoal crosses over his eyes and the clownish
circles drawn around them were smudged all over. Black
streaks ran down his tear-stained face.

"I wish I could," he sniffed. "But I have no heart for anything any more—*Oh, Berric!* I lost mine in the avalanche!"

"Oh, *that*, is it? Well, hang on—half a tick!" Berric reached
up over Martha Mattock's back and pulled out something
from beneath the basket seat. "I reckon this is yours, isn't it?"

Iffleplum gaped in disbelief. "My shoulder-bag? My elfin-
heart! How did—?

Berric tried hard not to laugh. "I found it caught on
Martha's snout-horns, as soon as she jumped back. She was a
sight quicker than you in the avalanche."

Iffleplum quickly flipped the bag-flap open. Oh! It *only* was!
His *Legends* book was still there! And his elfin-heart within—
still wrapped up in the elven net! He could feel its warmth as

he hugged it to his breast. "Oh! Oh! Thank you! Thank you!" He laughed and cried and chuckled through his tears.

"Well now, all's well that end's well—isn't that right?" beamed Berric smilingly.

"Oh, yes, but—oh, Berric! I found my friend again—the wolf—his name was Fluff-Ruff." He gulped and a lump stuck in his throat as he spoke his name. "The ghòrs captured him. They wanted us to fight in the arena. But then—a horrid creature called a scalykrake snapped him up—and—and then ran off with him!"

"Is it?" said Berric, feigning surprise. "Bit like that one over there, was it?" With a delighted grin, he waved his arm. Beyond the gnurt was a huge dead reptile on its back. Its mouth was open, showing rows of scimitar-like teeth. Lances and arrows protruded from its sides and neck.

"But—that's the scalykrake!" exclaimed Iffleplum. "Then what—?"

"How do you suppose we knew where to find you? We were scouring the mountainsides—digging in the snow—in hopes to find your body, when we spied this stream of squeaking bats all twittering over the sky. Mighty peculiar that—we thought—in the light of day! So we climbed up to see where they were coming from. Then out of nowhere, bounds this scaly beast with what looked like a dead wolf in its mouth."

"A dead wolf?" wailed Iffleplum in dismay. "Oh, Fluff-Ruff!"

"Yes?" croaked a feeble voice from inside the gnurt. "Plumkins?"

With a hearty chuckle, Berric pulled the tent-flap back. There on a mat lay Fluff-Ruff wrapped in bandages. A young mattockeer medic with a pony-tail was tending him. Iffleplum flung himself down upon the wolf's neck and hugged him hard for joy.

"Ooh! Ouch! Be careful! Be softer with your hugs! I'm covered in scaly tooth-marks! And it hurts."

Iffleplum backed off to look at him. The wolf's once golden eyes were dim. "Are you all right?" he asked. "You don't look so well."

"To be honest, I'm not exactly feeling at my best. But good heavens, Iffleplum! You look a sorry sight yourself!"

Iffleplum felt his face and found his finger-tips were black. "I'll take care of that," said Berric. He signalled to the healer to fetch a bowl of water. The young man brought it quickly. Then with a cloth Berric wiped clean the clown's make-up from the ifflepinn's face.

"Feeling better now?" he asked.

Iffleplum nodded. "Yes, thanks. My heart is not so heavy now. But—" His eyes fell again on Fluff-Ruff. The wolf's head had flopped down feebly on the mat. His eyes were growing grey. And his tongue was lolling sideways from his mouth.

Berric glanced up at the healer standing by. The mattockeer opened his hands in a gesture of helplessness. "I can do no more," he apologized. "The reptile's teeth were sharp and sank in deep."

"Fluff-Ruff, how do you feel?" asked Iffleplum anxiously.

"I can't say I feel at all," answered Fluff-Ruff weakly. "And it's hard to move my limbs. My legs are growing cold. To be honest, Plumkins, I'm not so sure I'll last the night. But I'm so glad you are here with me to say my last goodbyes. It's nice to have friendly faces surrounding you—when you're about

370

to pass away. Farewell, Plumkins—I feel my elfin-heart is loosening."

Fluff-Ruff gazed about him with glazed and staring eyes. "I see the spirit-wolves surrounding me: the ghosts of wolves that were. They are coming to take me away to the *Great Wolf Den* under the world. I hope they will accept me now. I did my best. But I must now answer to their call—the banshee wolves are howling—"

His eyes closed and his head sank sideways to the mat, his mouth open.

"Oh no! Don't leave us Fluff-Ruff!" choked Iffleplum. "You can't die! You mustn't travel on—not yet! Oh! But wait!" he said, as an idea sprang into his head. "The Elixir! I still have a little left in the bottle." He hastily pulled it from the pouch-pocket in his skin. "There's not enough to sprinkle on all his wounds, but Athanôr told me you can drink it too!"

Lifting up Fluff-Ruff's floppy head, he pressed the bottle to the wolf's lips and tipped the last drops down his throat.

They waited and watched him worriedly awhile. But Fluff-Ruff never moved. Berric shook his head sadly. Tears sprang in Iffleplum's eyes. He fell to his knees and put his arms around Fluff-Ruff's neck.

The wolf's body suddenly twitched. An eye opened. "Mmm! Tastes nice!" he croaked. "Uff! Strong stuff!" he coughed as a warming wave went surging down his body. It even tingled right down to the pads and claw-tips of his feet. His eyes began to brighten once again. His head perked up, and then his tail. "Oh, yes!" he chuckled. "It's working! It really is! I feel so much better, instantly! I'll soon be on my legs again, I'm sure! Wuff!"

Iffleplum and the mattockeers gave a huge sigh of relief. The wolf's eyes were goldening once more. "But first, while my strength is coming back—please—tell me what happened with the Gnumpf? Was he in time to save the Yäkkh-Ârbhû?"

"Indeed he was!" said Berric. "The pair of 'em are mooning all over each other right now. But he gave the ghòrs a right thrashing! They were terrified. They ran off like they had

their bums alight! And as for those who stopped to fight—
well, me and the lads did for 'em."

"But how did you know where—?" began Iffleplum.

Berric's grin widened. "Well now, when this here dead wolf
in a scaly-beast's maw, cries out 'Help! Help! Please!' We
thought that a mite unusual. We don't get Ummals much in
Angarsland. But we do know what they are. So being
somewhat soft-hearted folk, we let loose everything we had.
And right-quick we brought the scaly-critter to the ground."

"Yes! Thank heavens! They rescued me from old toothy-
pegs! But then—"

"Right! But then—" interrupted Berric "—he wouldn't even
let us dress his wounds. 'No time!' says he. 'Save my friends!'
Because you and the Yäkkh-Ârbhû were about to be made
mincemeat of, is what he said! We were up and ready to dash
in right away. But 'No!' he barked. 'There's a thousand well-
armed ghòrs in there!' says he. He reckoned they'd make
mincemeat of us too if we barged in! So he insisted we had to
go and find his friend—some ginormous creature he called a
Gnumpf! Otherwise we wouldn't stand a chance!

"'Never heard of it,' I said. 'How is it?'

"'Looks like a bushy hill on legs,' he said. We couldn't make
head or tail of that! "

"Yes, it took some strong persuasion, I can say! But at last,
I said 'For Ummals' sake! Quick! Quick! Quick! Just sling me
in a basket-seat up on the mattock's back. And let's go find
the Gnumpf. The silly beast is fast asleep."

"And fast asleep he was! We tried right hard to bawl him
back awake. But how do you wake a mountain up? Fluff-Ruff
reckoned he might stay asleep a year or more! So we even
thumped him on the head with sticks. But we couldn't make
him stir bit."

"Yes, "said Fluff-Ruff, "but then I had a smart idea! I went
and whispered in his ear—Yäkkh-Ârbhû!—and he woke up like
a shot! I explained the situation as fast as I could. When I said
the ghòrs were skewering her to death with spears—the next
second he was up and gone! I've never seen him move so fast."

A sudden crack and rumble of splitting rock rent the air. "Oops! I think he's back!" said Fluff-Ruff chirpily. They whirled about. Flinging aside the tent flap, they saw the hulking great Gnumpf humping himself out of Ghòrkol-Âhn's main tunnel gate. More of the rock-arch tumbled down as he squeezed his great bulk through. Most of the bushes were now sheared off from his back. The Yäkkh-Ârbhû came out behind him, stepping daintily over the rocky rubble. She blinked in the light and sniffed with delight at smelling the heady sweet fresh mountain air.

Majestically, the two great creatures strolled over to the gnurt, as stately as kings and queens. The Yäkkh-Ârbhû kneeled before them and spoke softly: "May I offer heartfelt thanks upon you all? I bless you for your help in ridding that dreary cavern-world of ghòrs. Too long have I lain in that darksome den. And I yearn to return to my forest domain and smell the leaves again. I feel I've soaked up ghòr-filth like a sponge. If we abide where foul-mouthed ghòr-folk dwell, we are darkened by their thoughts. And the taint of them long lingers in our hearts. We must needs cleanse them now of all that has gone before.

"That way, the *Lûmentir*—or Lightstream, as some call it in the Common Ummal-tongue—may flow freely though our hearts once more. Therefore I would well lead you to my forest's secret Sacred Grove. For we will all find heart's-ease and healing there. Will you not come? For my woodland valley is not far."

Her plan was happily agreed upon. For all were weary and welcomed any way to wash the ghòr-grime from their minds. Meanwhile, a few of them set up camp while the rest of the lads were scouring the caverns of Ghòrkol-Âhn.

*

In a few days, when the last of the mattockeers returned from underground, Fluff-Ruff was standing firmly on his feet again. He was now feeling well enough to trot along beside the mattock train. The camp was struck and the cavalcade set off in procession for the Yäkkh-Ârbhû's forest sanctuary. Only those whose mattocks had been hurt by ghòrish spears stayed on behind to tend to their wounded beasts.

The sun was settling into evening light as they reached the valley floor. There they stopped stock still and stared aghast. The sunlight cast a golden glow across a shattered landscape where once a forest was. The Yäkkh-Ârbhû gripped hard the ground for fear of falling down. The trees were gone! Her forest home was now no longer there! She looked upon a hillside bare. On every side were jagged stumps or torn down trees, their roots up in the air. And the trash of trampled branches littered everywhere.

The companions stood awhile in silent shock.

"Ghòr-work!" growled Berric.

"Oh, my sorry forest!" wept the Yäkkh-Ârbhû, when she found her voice again. "While I was captive underground, they came and cut my forest down—to feed their furnaces for making weaponry! Ghòr-folk have massacred all my lovely living trees—that took years in hundreds for to grow! The sweet young saplings and the wise old Elder Trees are all no more—alas! For now their elfin-hearts have sped. All woods and forests have a Spirit of their own. Have you not felt it when you have wandered in the woods alone? I wonder now— has even the Spirit of the Forest flown? Oh!" She stopped and cocked an ear.

"Oh, listen! Can you hear?—the air is filled with weeping! The woodland deeves are grieving for the passing of the trees!"

They listened carefully. And even the mattockeers began to hear a faint keening song of sadness in the air. A doleful lament of desolation sounded all around, for the soul of a forest ripped open and laid bare. They could almost see its life-force rising up like heat-waves from a summer road and vanishing in the sky.

"They are mourning for the forest gone," Yäkkh-Ârbhû said softly, "and Oh! Aiee! Aiee! Even more so—I hear—they mourn for the ancient Spirit of the Woods, who now weakens unto death, I fear."

374

A great sigh sounded, rising from her heart. "Come, follow me," she breathed and led them on through the ragged devastation of the stumps. At length she stopped at what might have once been a clearing in the woods. A large crowded circle of creature-kind were creeping in from every side: stags and dappled deer and goats, bears and badgers, a pack of wolves, foxes, striped pigs, hares and rabbits, hedgehogs, squirrels, otters, weasels, stoats, pine-martens, voles and field-mice, even snakes, all coming to a standstill quietly: all seemingly unmindful of each other's ancient enemies. Birds perched on the antlers of the deer and goats. Some sat even on the heads of the upright standing sad-eyed bears.

The Yäkkh Ârbhû looked sadly down at all her friends. "It is here where the Sacred Grove once stood," she whispered. "And look!—there lies the Woodland King, our Guardian Spirit of the Trees. All creatures—ummals and dummals all— have come to pay respect. And all the treeless forest spirits too."

A shimmer of half-seen tree-deeves and bark-sprites thronged thickly in among the animals and many were drifting up to seat themselves upon their backs. A swirling cloud of multi-coloured butterflies turned above them in the air. And now the companions also became aware of the tree- like dreaming dævas of the forest, flowing in on every side. They gathered silently behind them all, like tall transparent glowing ghosts.

The Yäkkh-Ârbhû and her companions moved closer in and the parting animals moved soundlessly aside to let them near.

A large figure like a fallen tree lay propped up against a rock. It was half buried in a mound of fallen leaves. Translucent tree-deeves were slowly covering him with leaves of oak and ash, chestnut, rowan, aspen, beech, and willow. Late autumn flowers crowned its wild and straggly locks. And a leaf-pile laid upon the rock made up his pillow.

The peach-bloom hairs stood up on Iffleplum's neck.

375

He gaped in wonder, while his nose went wildly through a through a host of colours, not knowing what shade suited his flustered feelings best. He raced through stupefaction, terror, joy, awe, and disbelief.

Surely this was none other than Old Wossul of the Woods? How could it be?

"But—but I *know* him!" exclaimed Iffleplum in astonishment. "This is our Old Wossul of Wossle Wood—in Ælfÿlon! How comes he here?"

"Why—he is the Spirit of *all* woods and forests, wherever they may be," the Yäkkh-Ârbhû replied. "And when forests fail—good Wood-Wight Wossul, the source of life in every tree—feels it deeply in his heart. He feels it even in the world of Men, for there—just like the ghòrs—they burn and hack and plough up forests everywhere. And as each forest is destroyed, his Spirit fades a little more along with them. I fear for what might happen once the life has gone from every forest bare."

"Oh, but is there nothing to be done?" asked Iffleplum anxiously.

"Alas, he fades a little every year when winter comes, for then all woods and forests fall asleep. But when the new year comes around again, he awakens weakly from his woody winter dreams. He then needs the radiant heart's-warmth of someone's elfin-heart who loves the trees, to bring the life-force back into his limbs. Whenever someone wanders in the woods in spring and gives their heart's-love to the trees—the Spirit of the Forest King leaps back to life again! And then he sings! And all woodlands burst back into leaf!

"But now I fear his Spirit is near gone. And if so—"

But as she spoke, Old Wossul's bark-like breast split open with a sudden crack!

All those around him jumped and caught their breath—then gasped!

A wispy spiral like a twist of grey smoke was rising from his chest. His heart-wraith lit up goldenly, in the last light of the

376

redly setting sun. It rose and curled away up in the sky and slowly vanished with the fading of the day.

"Oh! Oh! His elfin-heart has dwemmed!" wailed the Yäkkh-Ârbhû. "I fear too many forests must have died! Will all woods wither now at the hands of ghòrs and loveless Men? Oh! Iffleplum! Imagine a world without the welcome of the woods! Without the heart-ease that they bring! How dreary it would be!"

Oh Ūhmkyn! What am I to do? thought Iffleplum.

But inside himself he already knew. But he wrestled with his thoughts. His throat grew tight. His hollow heart was thumping hard against his ribs in fright.

Oh, Wossul! I've not found out how to use mine for me anyway, he sniffed. *I only hope I'm not too late!*

In haste, he fumbled open the flap of his shoulder-bag. Pulling out his *Legends* book, he swiftly ripped off the elven-net wrappings from around it. Hesitating, he hung on a moment more. Clasping his long awaited prize, he struggled with himself. His hands began to shake. But then a thought came trickling into his head.

What was that Ælrik Athanôr had said? "The thing that you desire most'—*that* you should offer unto others," he had heard him say. It meant nothing to him then. "It's a way of *freeing* us from forever holding on to things," Ælrik had said, "things we cannot take with us when we leave and 'travel on'."

Oh, come on then, Iffleplum—be quick! he growled through gritted teeth.

Trembling, he tip-toed to Old Wossul's side. Before he could feel any pang of regret, he flipped the book-clasp back. Briskly turning the book upside down, he shook the pages over him.

A moment's golden glow was all it took. His elfin-heart tumbled from the book. In an instant it was gone! It vanished in the crack of Old Wossul's lifeless breast.

All those around him watched expectantly with bated breath.

Nothing happened.

Iffleplum looked anxiously up at the Yäkkh-Ârbhû. Only the corners of her eyes crinkled warmly.

Then something seemed to change in Old Wossul's bark-like body. It began to crumple. Caving in, it began to slowly shrivel and wither away, like a rotting log dissolving in the winds and weathers of many a day.

"Oh! What's happening!" cried Iffleplum falling to his knees "It isn't working! I've given it too late!"

"Nay—wait!" the Yäkkh-Ârbhû cautioned him. "Just wait, and watch!"

With a ripping sound the shrivelling log-like carcass split down the middle. The crack widened. A burst of greeny-golden light shone forth. Out of Old Wossul's collapsing woody chrysalis, a resplendent youthful form arose, like a butterfly from its cocoon. Sparkling *lûmenü* danced all around him. He was young and lithe and full of light. His clothes were leafy robes of all the colours of the spring. His face—a mass of tiny fresh green leaves. But his eyes! His eyes were the same old eyes of ancient Wossul—ages deep.

"Behold!" cried the Yäkkh-Ârbhû. "Wossul Woodwose the Younger—as he reawakens every spring!"

And the Ummals and dummals all cried out in joy. The mattockeers gazed on with mouths agape.

The tall creature danced out of the woody chrysalis of his old remains, his radiant robes aripple like shimmering sunlight flitting through breezy leaf-flickered boughs. Bending low in a courtly bow, he swept off his flowered hat to the astonished ifflepinn, releasing a flutter of butterflies in a cloud. And tiny fledglings chirruped hidden in his twiggy hair. Iffleplum fell to his knees in awe.

"You gave your heart to the Spirit of the Woods," said the young Wossul Woodwose warmly. "So rise up from your knees, Sir Iffleplum of Ælfÿlon, for in return, all nature now gives its loving heart to you."

The Woodwose touched him with his twiggy fingertips on the right side of his chest. And a sudden sun-like warmth welled up swelling deep within his breast.

His eyes grew wide in wonder. And golden grew his nose.
His heart was overflowing in its joy and tingled in his fingertips and toes.

Oh, yes! It was! It *only* was! For now he knew!

His elfin-heart was back at last!

And the *Song of Ühm* sang in his breast!

As one, in sudden happiness, the ummals and the dummals
gathered round all gave voice to Old Wossul's *Song of Spring:*
Haroom! Haroom! Then the joyous sound of tree-deeves now
filled the air, singing their strange springtime songs of growth
for lullawaking trees. And all around the shattered stumps
burst into life! Shoots sprang up on every side, growing fast
and bursting into leaf.

Iffleplum stared about him in astonishment.

It seemed as if the Sacred Grove was newly rising all around
him. Trees surged up from the ground, like a phantom forest
forming ghostly arches overhead.

Oh! Oh! What's happening? he thought. Was the forest moving all around him, or had his head begun to spin? *I haven't eaten any more of those spotty mushroom things. In fact, I haven't eaten anything for ages. Am I falling in a hunger faint?*

For everything began to turn as dizzily as he felt when riding on a merry-go-round upon the Froaksday Fair. The faces of his *harooming* friends went floating by and then began to blur. As they spun around they were slowly fading from his sight and disappearing in a mist. Now all his woozy eyes could see was a sea of whirling waving hands and smiling faces slipping backwards into pearly-pale and foggy gloom.

A moment more and they were gone!

Only he and the Woodwose now remained, suspended in a fog-white nowhere-land. He felt as if lost in the Lonely Realm once again.

"Oh, where are we?" whispered Iffleplum. "I want to go home."

"We aren't anywhere," the young Wossul Woodwose smiled. "Right now, we're *in between*. This is *Faery*—or the Doorway of Return to Life! A whirly way back to the fields we know. Look down Iffleplum, beyond your toes, and you will see whither now your heart would go. Are you not already homeward bound?"

With a puzzled frown, Iffleplum looked down upon the ground. His eyes widened then, his pupils growing large and round. And his ears began to sing!

He stared at the forest floor in shock—for he was standing inside a faery mushroom ring!

Part the Twenty-Fifth

Home Again, Home Again

*In which Iffleplum learns that all life may be but a dream.
And even storm-pogs are not what they seem.*

ffleplum's pulses raced. The blood was pounding in his head. A misty forest loomed around him. "But—but—is this—?" he began, confused.

"Yes, it is the very same," said Wossul Woodwose with a smile. "The very selfsame faery ring. Did you not call me here? For I heard the cry, 'Oh, Wossul come!' And here I am. And the selfsame day it is—the First of Spring in Ælfÿlon!"

"But how did I get back here again—here and now?"

"Hah!" replied the Woodwose. "It is always here and now. No other time exists! Have you ever been away from where you are?"

"Then—did I dream all this while simply standing here?"

"It was no more or less, a dream, than what you are dreaming now. As real as dreaming you have just awakened in a faery ring. Better you find out *who* is dreaming and forget about the dream."

"But—but all that seemed so *real*. And I woke up there each day, where I went to sleep the night before. It was always *there!* So I thought I was a year away! "

"Oh, yes—years may seem to pass while in a dream. And on awakening you know it was not so. Does how long something lasts determine its reality? Is a long old creeper more real than a fresh new shorter one? And now you think that that you're awake again and Ælfÿlon is more real than your dream of Ümmulon. Hah! When you wake up from *this* dream too—then you will see—then you will *know*."

"Know *what*?" asked Iffleplum in puzzlement.

"Aha!" said Wossul Woodwose knowingly, tapping the side of his nose. With a twinkle in his ancient eyes, he simply smiled and replaced his flowered hat. Hopping away over the mushroom ring he danced off between the ghostly half-seen trees.

Wide-eyed with wonder, Iffleplum watched him disappear. His heart was all aflutter with strange feelings of gratitude and regret as the wonderful Woodwose was swiftly swallowed in the mist.

Then suddenly he found his legs were free! With a joyful bound he tried to leap out over the faery-ring. But like a rubber ball he bounced back in again, as if flung off from an invisible and springy wall! Oh no! The force-field of the faery-ring still hemmed him in!

Oh, Ühm! I forgot to ask him to free me from the spell! he thought. *I'm stuck again!* He vainly gazed after the Wood-wose, but he had gone. Now a feeling like the Darkstream fell like a shadow on his heart. And an eerie prickle crept all along his spine. He turned around. Unpleasant things were creeping up behind. He had felt that feeling once before. And he knew just what they were. Two dark familiar shambling shapes came looming from the foggy gloom. They stopped and stood there outside the ring, their mothy eyes a-sparkling.

Yes, Nightshade and Baggyneck were back!

And with a leering grin, Baggyneck held out a mouth-like wheezing sack.

Iffleplum rolled his eyes and groaned. "Oh, no! Not again! For Ühmkyn's sake! After all that I've been through! You think I'm still afraid of shadow-folk like you? You don't even exist unless I think you do. You *only* don't! So shove off! Go on! Just go away!" He flicked his fingers in the air, dismissively.

The Grope's grins faded in dismay. Their mothy eyes grew dim and their mouths went slack. At Iffleplum's unafraid attitude, even Baggyneck's grabsack caught its breath. It seemed to choke with a gag in its throat. With a soft hiss, it fell limply dangling from the Grope's fist and piled up soggily on the ground. Baggyneck stared down at his lifeless sack in shock. He shook his head in disbelief. And his wobbling wattles trembled in agitation.

Like bullies everywhere, without feeding on their victim's fear, the shadow-folk had no strength of their own. Glumly they glanced between themselves. Their mouths turned down. Nightshade spread wide his arms and shrugged. Despondently, the Gropes began to back away from him. And as they went, they began deflating like balloons, dwindling down in size and slowly dwemming in the mist. A moment more and they vanished in the foggy brume.

Then Iffleplum felt a feeling like the Lightstream flowing through his breast. Oh yes, the *Lûmentir* was flowing freely through his world as the Khämmârkaï Kaïdar had said. Iffleplum began to shake with laughter. His twin-hearts, left and right, felt full of joy.

As he laughed in wonder, from afar the sudden trill of faery pipes came floating through the air.

The peach-bloom hairs stood up upon his arms and neck! Goose-flesh prickled over all his skin. He had heard that thrilling faery trill before!

At once, the moving music made the mists curl up and roll and fade away. Again the normal light of a waning day returned. And the last rays of the setting sun shone redly through the reappearing trees.

Iffleplum turned towards the flute-song and the light. And there, to his delight and unbelieving awe, he saw a shaft of red-gold dying sunlight strike the Piper's flowered head!

A tall and flowing figure, in fluttering leafy robes of all the colours of the spring, was wending its way down the hill between the trees and swaying as he played. The voice of his flute was a wondrous woody melody. And all of nature seemed to sway in harmony with his tune.

Iffleplum stood stunned.

Old Wossul is the Piper of the Spring! he thought, thunderstruck. *Or, Young Wossul, I should say!*

His mouth hung open. Holding out his hands in wonderment, he felt a light touch on his fingertips. He looked down. And there she stood! The half-seen tree-deeve damsel he had tried to rescue from the ring. She was still holding to his finger-ends, as lightly as a butterfly. The translucent moppet-fay beheld him with her now wide sparkling eyes.

Then *crack!* a branch snapped somewhere high above his head and startled him. He looked up into the misty trees.

Then *smack!* someone walked straight into him head down, colliding with his chest. He stumbled back, bowled over by the sudden unexpected thump. Shaking his head, he looked up. And there above him, stood the Mufflewump, dazedly rubbing his head.

Iffleplum scrambled to his feet again and jumped for joy!

384

"Oh! Grubbin!" he chortled in delight. "Grubbin Hawk-weed! It's *you!*" The downcast figure looked up in some sur-prise. Having wandered head-down in a gloomy daze, the Mufflewump had trampled right through the faery ring and squashed the mushrooms flat.

And with that, the holding spell was gone!

On the instant of release, the moppet-deeve sprang into the air. She planted a kiss upon Iffleplum's brow as she sailed by. And skipping smartly away she vanished through a crack in the nearest tree. Where he felt her kiss, a small white starry flower sprouted suddenly above his eye. For wherever tree-deeves blow kisses in the spring, white starry flowers known as *moppet-kiss* pop up in the grass.

"Oh, hello, it's you is it, Iffle-Plumkin?" said Grubbin Hawkweed dolefully, "Yes, of *course* it's *me*. Who else but a mufflewump, busy reminding himself how sad he is, would bump into a friend and knock him down? I wasn't expecting anyone in this part of the wood. Don't you know they say it's a bit enchanted hereabouts when the sun goes down?"

"I do have *some* idea," said Iffleplum. "I *only* do."

Still rubbing his head, Grubbin raised his eyes a little. "Oh, I see you're wearing moppet-kiss. Some kind of new fad is it? Takes all sorts, I s'pose. All very nice, but it's probably full of ticks, you know—*and* pollen, I shouldn't wonder."

Iffleplum looked up in surprise, to see the tiny white flower nodding above his eyebrow.

The Mufflewump stepped back alertly. "Eh! Don't nod it all over me, will you? I'm not over-keen to start my hay-fever off so early in the spring."

"Oh, Grubbin! Grubbin! You blessed Mufflewump! It doesn't matter, you doleful chump! You broke the spell! You broke the spell!"

"Oh, did I? Well, I'm sorry then. I'm always breaking something. It's my great ungainly feet, you see. Folks are always telling me, 'Get off out of it, you great cloggy farmer-footed chump'—so jolly, jolly, off I go—"

"Oh, never mind!" laughed Iffleplum joyously. "Come on! Come on! Let's go! The sun has nearly set!"

Tugging him by the arm, he hurried the Mufflewump down the hillside towards the Flowing Bowl. Long before they reached the rim-road, the sun sank behind the Mauven Mountains in the west.

As it vanished, the moppet-kiss fell from his forehead and left there not a mark.

"There he is! Good old Plumkin! Over here!" was the cheer that greeted him, as Iffleplum and the Mufflewump came down into the Flowing Bowl. "Come on, Grubbin, join the throng!" they cried. "Cuppicks' cart is waiting to take us all on down!"

The day was darkling, but the grassy hollow was ablaze with lights and still full of feasting folk. Granpaw, Ifflepaw, Erf, and Mumkin, and a crowd of friends were gathered round a horse and haywain, down before the Barrow-doors.

Ifflemother hoisted Iffleplum up into the driving seat. "I told you, be back before the sun went down!" she scolded. "Oh, my! What a mess you look."

Iffleplum nodded happily. He didn't care a bit.

He was home again!

But then, glancing back across the crowd he had a nasty shock. He gripped his mother's arm.

Over the rim of the Flowing Bowl he saw someone he'd rather not—Old Owleyes Astronomo! In his ragged cloak and leaning on his knaggy stick, Scragmire the Storm-pog came hobbling down among the revellers.

386

Ah! Now Iffleplum understood! In his visions in the ring, it was *him* he'd seen falling from the tree! His joy now once more turned to dread! The storm-pog purposely weaved his way through the crowd towards them, one foot clinging to his knaggy stick.

But there, astonishingly, above his head—a heart-shaped red balloon was bobbing on a string held in his hand. The storm-pog came swiftly limping up and stopped beside the cart.

"Harr!" cried he. "We thought we would arrive too late! We did betake our goodly self to climb a tree. For we would untangle this here heart-balloon for thee—but alas! a spindly branch did break under us! Forsooth, nigh did we fall swiftly to our doom—yet perchance grasped we a nether branch, whereon our goodly self did cling right mightily. Nay, be not affrighted! For no harm befalleth us; we did but bang and hurt our knee. And thus finally, dear boy, did we gladly clamber down. But thou hadst gone. Thus thereupon did we hobble here as hastily as we might, for to bring this gift for thee." He handed up the balloon string to an astonished Iffleplum, who took it gingerly.

"You—you climbed up—to get my red balloon for me?" he exclaimed.

"Harr! For very sooth, we did, thou beamish boy!" said Astronomo. "For when it upped and blew away, we marked thy deep distress. Therefore, precisely where it fell we did note well, forsooth. Us seemeth, nigh in Wossul Woodwose's Sacred Grove it did come down. Whereupon, our goodly self did hasten thither speedily. Thus were we there before thou wert. We had betook ourself but halfway up the tree, when thou didst fling thyself into the ring. An unwise trick, if we may say. Alas, before we could recall a counter-spell to set thee free, perchance, yon Mufflewump did trample o'er all and burst the fungal boundary. And alas, we do esteem, by such a folly, he did bring bothersome bad luck upon his head."

"Hner!" groaned Grubbin. "Might have known. Jolly, jolly, there I go. Anyways, what more bad luck could I have, than to be born a Mufflewump—with a name an ears like mine?"

Somewhat ashamedly, Iffleplum looked in the Soothsayer's kindly old owlish eyes.

"Oh, but I thought—I had thought—" he faltered "—that you were after my elfin-heart?"

"Oddsbods! What sayest thou? Our elfin-heart is hale and hearty. What would we with another?"

"Oh! I see—so—then you never came down to Ifflenook? And you never cursed me with the wanderlust? And then— then there *wasn't* any waterspout—oh! And so—no *Golden Heart*—or anything? Was it all my dreaming in the ring? Was it all in my imagining? But then—then why were you following me about all day?"

"Cusps and configurations, dear smoothly boy! Old Ifflepaw has saved our life! Perhaps 'twas worth far more than gifting him a prophecy. In gratitude, our elfin-heart beseecheth us to watch well over thee, and all thy family, should aught untoward befall! Oh, yea! This Froaksday, we do confess, we have closely spied on thee. 'Twas but to be on hand, should thou find thyself in need. Oh yes, indeedy!"

"Oh, I see. Then, I'm sorry, Mister Scragmire," said Iffleplum. "Forgive me, for I owe you an apology, I *only* do! I'd thought badly of you in my mind. For when I heard Old Iffy's tale, I imagined you were wild and greedy, like other storm-pogs that I've heard about."

"Ah, dear boy. Judge not someone by his *kin*. Not all of us of one kind is the same."

"Well now," mused Ifflepaw, "it seems all my watching out and worriting, was for nothing."

"Harr! Thou wert always looking outwards, thou old fruit," the storm-pog smiled. "There is nought occurs without, that doth not *first* arise within," said he, tapping the side of his head—which of course baffled Ifflepaw even more.

*

And so it was that the grateful ifflepinns invited Owleyes Astronomo Scragmire to the Froaksnight Celebration supper down at Ifflenook. A merry throng clambered into Cuppick's cart, Grubbin Hawkweed and Astronomo among them. The Umbelope lit a lantern, hanging over the horse's head on a jouncy pole. He clambered up into the driving seat. "Giddyup, Dapplenose!" cried Cuppicks heartily slapping the reins. And the rickety cart set off down the rocky road to Merryvale.

Beyond the ifflesnugs of Bumble-on-the-Hill, they rounded a bend on the hillside, emerging from the eaves of Bumble Wood. Twilight had deepened over the valley. Now all of Merryvale lay out before them, like a jewelled carpet, soft-coloured in the gloaming. Like fallen stars, tiny lights twinkled in the village of Merry May and in the ifflesnugs and faraway farms way down the vale beyond. Yellow lantern lights of the home-way wenders were bobbing on the hillsides and along the little lanes below. It was a magical sight. And Iffleplum's heart now warmed to his land, as he had never done before.

His eyes brimmed with happy tears at coming home.

He snuggled up to Ifflemother cosily. But then the words of the wall-eyed boatman now came floating through his head. "I grant you three witches," he had said.

That's strange, thought Iffleplum. *What happened then? The ferry Dogmother warned me of THREE witches, but I never saw more than two.* One hand was resting on his mother's knee, the string of the bobbing heart-shaped red balloon wound around his thumb. While the other snuggled in the pouch-pocket of his skin. His fingers suddenly felt something silky smooth and sandy at the bottom. He took a pinch of it and held it up before his face. Particles of light like *lûmenü* danced above his fingertips. Sparkles reflected in his eyes like stars.

Oh! Could it be? The dust of Dwêmòrìæ that so sparkled in the air?

The stardust turned and twisted itself into a tiny faerylike form that fluttered in his face—for his eyes only! For no one else seemed to be aware.

"Well, here I am—the Witch of Dwêmòriæ Sands," said she in a whisper with a smile.

"A Sand-Witch!" gasped Iffleplum.

"*Yea!* Verily a Sand-Witch am I—but eat me not, oh hungry one! Feast only on me with thine eyes. For I am but the Sandman's aid for dusting you to dreamless sleep."

On the instant, her faery form dissolved in sparkling dust as she plunged into his eyes, unseen by anyone but himself. He blinked and rubbed them hard in sleepy disbelief.

"Sandman's dust!" he chortled to himself. "So it *was* real! It *wasn't* all a dream in the faery-ring! I have *been!* And I *have* seen Ümmûârkon! And there *is* a way back there and home again!"

Then, loving-laughter bubbled from his heart. And his eyes welled up with tears of joy.

"Well now, Goldie-nose," said Ifflemother warmly, hearing his chuckle, "who's a happy little ifflepinn? Did you have a pleasant day?"

Iffleplum laughed uproariously at that. He tried to answer her, but a huge yawn got in the way. His eyelids of a sudden drooped. And before the cart was halfway home to Ifflenook, he had fallen fast asleep with his head on Ifflemother's lap.

And a huge smile of satisfaction on his face.

Glossary

Abbreviations.

Dæv. *Dævârkavâhl* (the ancient High speech of the High Elvene)

Dwv. *Dwæmavâhl* (the language of the Dwemmer-folk)

Ghv. *Ghòravâhl* (Ghòrish, the language of the Ghòrs)

Slv. *Sylvanavâhl* (the language of the Tree-deeves. (Dwv.)

Vâr. *Vâhl-Ârkamän* (the language of the Wizards and Men of the High Refuges)

Vüm. *Vâhl-Ümmulon* (the language of all Ümmulon, called "the Common Ummal-tongue" by ummals, and "the Common Tongue" by *Ühmenü* and Dwemmers)

Alphabetical order:
A, Æ, B, ÇH, D, DH, E, F, G, GH, H, I, K, KH, L, M, MH, N, NH, O, P, R, S, T, U, V, W, Y, Z

Âhn a title, meaning "first, foremost, highest or eminent." Used by Elves and Dwemmers to denote the *Âhn-Ühm*—the First Great Elfin-Heart of All. This title was usurped by the ghòrish clans in their arrogance, using it as a suffix adjoined to the name of their realms, each clan considering themselves the "foremost" or topmost clan. (Dwv., Ghv.)

Ämidhakhüm the Middleworld where Manlings dwell. See *khüm*. (Dwv.)

ârbhû tree. (Dæv.)

ârk refuge, protection (as Wise-Ârk Wizards); high, lofty, kingly. (Dwv.)

ârk mountain. (Vüm.)

Ârkon a high-wise saintly wizard-hermit, High King, or light-filled being. *ârkon* a peak, (or eminence) of light—as *Ümmû-ârkon*. See *kon*. (Vüm.)

Ârkü the Wise-Wizards or Seers of Ümmulon, who live in the High Refuges. Known otherwise as *Khäm-Ârkü*, q.v. (Dwv.)

Ârkühm the Arch-Mage or Master of the Ârkü the High Wizards of the Land and the Kingly-Servant Sage of Ühm the Spirit of the Land of Ümmulon and all creation. (Dwv.)

ärn there. See *när*. (Dwv.)

âyô! hey! hi! (Dwv.)

ælf an old spelling of *elf*. (Dwv.)

Ælfÿlon hidden land of the Elves. See *lon* and *ÿ*. (Dwv.)

ælfÿn elven. (Dwv.)

ælfÿnpinnü 'playmates of the Elves', the original name of *ifflepinns*. Singulars *ælfÿnpinna* (fem.), *ælfÿnpinnaï* (masc.). See *ælfÿn* and *pinnü*. (Dwv.)

ælfÿnühm elfin-heart. (Dwv.)

Ælvenü the Elven race; singulars *Ælvena* (fem.), *Ælvenaï* (masc.). (Dwv.)

dævakhäm 'the essence of dreams', or the misty haze which composes the "Sea of Dreams" around the keel of the *Golden Heart*. Used to keep the elfin-hearts within the aquarium and helps them sleep when bottled-up. (Dwv.)

Dævârkavâhl the ancient High speech of the High Elvene.

Dævârkü the High Elvene, the wisest of Elves.

Dräkhkännòr-Âhn the realm of the Marsh Ghòrs. (Ghv.)

dwa from. (Dwv.)

dwârn towards (from *dwa* + *ärn*). (Dwv.)

dwæm to go or be between. Original name of the *Dwæmahîn* or Dwemmer-folk. See *dwem*. (Dwv.)

Dwæmahîn, also *Dwæmü* pl. the Dwemmer-folk, a race of beings halfway between humans and Elves; singulars *Dwæma* (fem.), *Dwæmaï* (masc.). (Dwv.)

Dwæmavâhl the language of the Dwemmer-folk.

Dwæmòriæ see *Dwêmòriæ*. (Dwv.)

dwem to fade or dwindle. See *dwæm*. (Vüm.)

392

Dwemmers a silvery-skinned, flaxen-haired people, originally
called the *Dwæmahîn* 'the people in-between' being a blend
of the two races of Humans and Elves. But gradually the
name became confused with the Common Ummal-tongue
word '*dwem*' (to fade away), on account of their fashion of
leaving the world by slowly ascending the mountain of
Ümmûârkon until they faded into invisibility, never to be
seen again. Thus they became known as 'those who *dwem*'
the fading folk. (Vüm.)

Dwêmòriæ the Land of Dreams (originally the 'Land Between'
from *dwæm*). (Vüm.)

dhanüm indeed. (Dwv.)

dhâr fear. (Dwv.)

Dhârkästir the Darkstream of negativity that flows through
people's hearts. "It is a force that flows through all the
worlds: a channelling of all the lowest heavy thoughts of
people everywhere. It is made up of Greed and Anger,
Misery and Despair, Self-pity, Hate and Jealousy; Hopelessness, Unkindliness and wilful Negativity. And those who
forget their elfin-hearts and go astray, get sucked along in
such a stream becoming even worse and try to drag in others
with them all along the way." See *Lûmentir* (Dwv.)

Dhârkäsü the Shadowfolk, who feed on the fears of frightened
hearts; singulars *Dhârkäsa* (fem.), *Dhârkäsaï* (masc.). Fear
makes them grow and joy and happiness make them
dwindle. When they can't get fed on fear they feed on the
"essence" of blood and flesh from creatures that have died in
fear. This gradually densens them into material existence,
until they *can* eat blood and flesh. But their preference is to
feed on the *feeling* of fear with their hairy wormlike tongues.
See *dhar* and *käsaï*. (Dwv.)

dhûm to rest or reside. (Dwv.)

ekka 'fire' (Ghv.)

eterthalom to dig into the earth. (Slv.)

êyâ and, together with. (Dwv.)

êyl to be. (Dwv.)

flodh wet dung of gauhns and "grubbing mattocks". Often used as an oath or expletive. "Get out of the flodding way!" (Vüm.)

flôhdun 'flodding' from *flodh* 'dung', *-un* an adjectival ending. (Ghv.)

gauhn a large long-haired, long-horned browsing creature, standing higher than a bull, usually coloured in combinations of chestnut, purple, or green, with shaggy legs. (Vüm.)

gnurt circular hide-and-canvas tents made by the gnorfs. (Vüm.)

Gorghòrond a vast cavern-dwelling, as distinct from simple delvings or minings; the huge underground arena where the Ghòrkol ghòrs hold their competitions is such a gorghòrond. (Ghv.)

Gûdârkaçh-Âhn the realm of the tribes of Desert Ghòrs. (Ghv.)

ghòr a species that delights in blood and gore and battling. The plural in the Dwæmavâhl is *ghòrhîn*; in Ghòrish it is *ghòrhôn*. (Ghv.)

Ghòravâhl Ghòrish, the language of the Ghòrs. (Dwv.)

Ghòrkol-Âhn the realm under the Ârkon-ârkü Pass. (Ghv.)

hâe to approach. (Dwv.)

iggidagh 'downwards' (Ghv.)

iggun 'ugly' < *igg* 'foul', *-un* an adjectival ending (Ghv.)

iyl the; *iyl* ... *iyl* ... the ... of (the) .... (Dwv.)

käsaï a 'shining' shadow (a shade with its own inner light, that is, "a ghostly being or apparition"). (Dwv.)

kon peak, eminence. See *Ârkon*. (Dwv.)

kumbul 'chimney' (Ghv.)

kwa because, for; thus. (Dwv.)

kha with. (Dwv.)

khäm air or ether. (Dwv.)

Khäm-Ârk a Wise Wizard; *lit.* 'a worker with the Inner Airs'. (Dwv.)

Khäm-Elvenü a name sometimes given to Sky-Deeves, as 'Elves of the Air.' See *Khämmârkü*. (Dwv.)

Khämmârkäçh the inner airs or etheric realm. (Dwv.)

394

Khämmârkü Sky-Deeves; those who live within the 'Inner Airs' or *Khämmârkäçh;* singulars *Khämmârka* (fem.), *Khämmârkaï* (masc.). Those who harvest elfin-hearts in the *Only Sea* (the Sea of Dreams) are fish-tailed, as are the Mer-folk of the deeps, while those who shepherd Dreams in Dwêmòriæ are bronzed-folk with scarlet wings, or wingless runners ('Bounders') who can leap like antelopes. See *Khäm-Elvenü.* (Dwv.)

Khämmârkhond the capital city of Lün; the highest city in all of Ümmulon. (Dwv.)

Khämmü air-elementals; singulars *Khämma* (fem.), *Khämmaï* (masc.). (Dwv.)

khüm world, realm, or domain. See *Ämidhakhüm.* (Dwv.)

lämmen a ship; plural *lämnü.* (Dwv.)

lâr 'the' (Ghv.)

lon hidden land. See *Ælfÿlon.* (Dwv.)

Lûmentir the Lightstream that flows through people's hearts. See *Dhârkästir* (Dwv.)

lûmenü particles of living light. (Dwv.)

Lün, the land where Elves and the Dwemmers dwell. (Dwv.)

mahg 'much'; *mahg-mah* 'very much, completely' (Ghv.)

morri keeper, shepherd. (Vüm.)

mûhl root, world, realm. See *Nhârghòrmûhl.* (Ghv.)

Mhoggoth 'a Living Nightmare'; the *Khämmârkü* word for the creature that represents the collective Dream of War that passes often through the Land of Dreams. (Dwv.)

nâhl quick(ly), rapid(ly). (Dwv.)

när here. See *ärn.* (Dwv.)

nevâhl to be present. (Dwv.)

Nhârghòrmûhl-Âhn the Cavernworld of the Red-clan Ghòrs, called *Nhârghòrmûhlers* or *Nhâr-ghòrs.* They consider themselves the élite of all the ghòrish clans. Their livery is red, the colour of the *nhârga,* a snake from whom they take their name. (Ghv.)

ôah to come or arrive. (Dwv.)

ôhm home. (Dwv.)

òrôn gold. *òrôniæ* golden. (Dwv.)

pinnü playmates; singulars *pinna* (fem.), *pinnaï* (masc.). See *ælfÿnpinnü*. (Dwv.)

sligerith to slide aside. (Slv.)

snabbid from *s-nab-bid* 'he did come' (Ghv.)

snapfek from *s-nab-fek* 'he did extinguish' (Ghv.)

Sylvanavâhl the language of the Tree-deeves. (Dwv.)

tir river. (Dwv.)

ühm heart; plural also *ühm*. (Dwv.)

Ühm 'the Heart of All', also known as *Âhn-Ühm* (the Original or First Heart); fondly called Old Ühmkyn, the principle of the Awakening the Spirit of the Land. (Dwv.)

Ühmenü the Human kin of Ühm (pl.); singulars *Ühmena* (fem.), *Ühmenaï* (masc.). (Dwv.)

Ühmkynü the followers of Ühmkyn (pl.; see *Ühm*); singulars *ühmkyna* (fem.), *ühmkynaï* (masc.). (Dwv.)

Ümmûârkon The mightiest mountain in the centre of the mythical land of *Ümmulon*, reaching ever upwards to the sky. (Dwv.)

Ümmulon the secret hidden Land of Ühm. (Dwv. & Vüm.)

ürû old. (Dwv.)

Ürû-Ühm 'Old Heart' (an elder); a term of respect. (Dwv.)

vâhl language, tongue. (Dwv.)

Vâhl-Ârkamän the language of the Wizards and Men of the High Refuges.

Vâhl-Ümmulon the language of all Ümmulon, called "the Common Ummal-tongue" by ummals, and "the Common Tongue" by *Ühmenü* and Dwemmers. (Dwv.)

vîl in, at. (Dwv.)

ÿ of. See *Ælfÿlon*. (Dwv.)

yäkkh face. (Dæv.)

Yäkkh-Ârbhû a name meaning 'tree-faced beast'. (Dæv.)

zyutlyn 'bogey-thing' (Ghv.)

Lightning Source UK Ltd.
Milton Keynes UK
UKOW03f1429120614

233292UK00001B/17/P